THE TRUTH SEEKER

—⟨∞⟩—

"The name Dee Henderson is synonymous with authenticity. Her books shine with believable facts and descriptions while her characters think and act like the professionals they are. *The Truth Seeker* delivers another engrossing, enjoyable read."

ROMANTIC TIMES MAGAZINE

"Another fantastic, page-turning mystery by Dee Henderson! Heartwarming romance and exciting drama are her trademark, and they'll be sure to thrill you a third time!"

SUITE101.COM

"A phenomenal writer who blends the word of the Lord with romantic suspense that is truly exceptional."

THE BELLES AND BEAUX OF ROMANCE

THE GUARDIAN

—⟨∞⟩—

"An entertaining thriller-cum-romance-cum-conversion story is what readers get in this fast-paced novel.... Christian readers will relish this intriguing tale."

PUBLISHERS WEEKLY

"More than an investigative thriller, this is a great romance dealing with complex matters of faith."

ROMANTIC TIMES MAGAZINE

"Another exciting new thriller from an up-and-coming talent in Christian fiction."

LIBRARY JOURNAL

"Page-turning excitement...true spiritual conflict...romance. I can't wait to read her next one!"

HANNAH ALEXANDER, AUTHOR OF *SILENT PLEDGE*

┌─────────────────────────────────┐
│   │
│   THE NEGOTIATOR   │
│   │
│   ~∞~   │
│   │
│ Dorothy Parker Award of Excellence Winner │
│   │
└─────────────────────────────────┘

"Sterling romantic suspense."

ROMANTIC TIMES MAGAZINE TOP PICK

"Solid storytelling, compelling characters, and the promise of more O'Malleys make Henderson a name to watch. Highly recommended, with a cross-genre appeal."

LIBRARY JOURNAL

"Top-notch writing."

SCRIBES WORLD REVIEWS

┌─────────────────────────────────┐
│   │
│   DANGER IN THE SHADOWS   │
│   │
│   ~∞~   │
│   │
│ RITA Award Winner—the highest national award given │
│   for excellence in romantic fiction   │
│   National Reader's Choice Award Winner   │
│   Bookseller's Best Award Winner   │
│   │
└─────────────────────────────────┘

"Dee Henderson had me shivering as her stalker got closer and closer to his victim. The message that we have nothing to fear as long as God is in control was skillfully handled, but I got scared anyway! I highly recommend this book to anyone who likes suspense."

TERRI BLACKSTOCK, BESTSELLING AUTHOR OF TRIAL BY FIRE

"A masterstroke! ... Dee Henderson gives the reader not one but two irresistible heroes."

COMPUSERVE REVIEWS

THE TRUTH SEEKER

BOOK THREE—THE O'MALLEY SERIES

DEE HENDERSON

Multnomah® Publishers *Sisters, Oregon*

This is a work of fiction. The characters, incidents, and dialogues are products of the author's imagination and are not to be construed as real. Any resemblance to actual events or persons, living or dead, is entirely coincidental.

THE TRUTH SEEKER
published by Multnomah Publishers, Inc.

© 2001 by Dee Henderson
International Standard Book Number: 1-57673-753-5

Cover images by Tony Stone Images
Cover design by Chris Gilbert/Uttley DouPonce DesignWorks

Scripture quotations are from: *Revised Standard Version Bible*
© 1946, 1952 by the Division of Christian Education
of the National Council of the Churches of Christ
in the United States of America

Multnomah is a trademark of Multnomah Publishers, Inc., and is registered in the
U.S. Patent and Trademark Office.
The colophon is a trademark of Multnomah Publishers, Inc.

Printed in the United States of America

ALL RIGHTS RESERVED
No part of this publication may be reproduced, stored in a retrieval system, or transmitted, in any form or by any means—electronic, mechanical, photocopying, recording, or otherwise—without prior written permission.

For information:
MULTNOMAH PUBLISHERS, INC.
POST OFFICE BOX 1720
SISTERS, OREGON 97759

Library of Congress Cataloging-in-Publication Data:

Henderson, Dee.
 The Truth Seeker / by Dee Henderson.
   p.cm. -- (The O'Malley series; bk. 3)
 ISBN 1-57673-753-5
 1. United States marshals--Fiction. 2. Serial murders--Fiction. 1.
Title.
PS3558.E4829 T79 2001
813'.54--dc21

02 03 04 05 06—10 9 8 7 6 5

TITLES BY DEE HENDERSON

THE O'MALLEY SERIES:
Danger in the Shadows (prequel)
The Negotiator
The Guardian
The Truth Seeker
The Protector
The Healer
The Rescuer (May 2003)

UNCOMMON HEROES SERIES:
True Devotion
True Valor
True Honor
True Courage (March 2003)

"For this is the will of my Father, that every one who sees the Son

and believes in him should have eternal life;

and I will raise him up at the last day."

JOHN 6:40

One

The fire had been alive; it had left its signature in the coiled, twisted wood, the bent metal, the heavy ash. It was a tamed beast, but still here, ready to come back to life with a nudge. Lisa O'Malley walked with great respect up the stairs following her brother Jack into the heart of the fire damage. The heavy boots he had insisted she wear were welcome as she realized it was glass crunching beneath her feet. Lightbulbs and picture frames had shattered in the heat.

The fire coat was harder to get accustomed to. The Nomex cloth was rough and it felt like thirty pounds on her back as she struggled to keep her balance. When Jack worked a fire he ran stairs wearing the coat and an air tank, carrying another forty pounds of gear. She didn't know how he did it. The man rarely showed a serious side, but it was there when he was doing the job he excelled at.

Reaching the upstairs landing, she turned her flashlight to inspect the hallway ceiling and walls. The superheated gas created by the fire had reached down five feet from the ceiling, burning into the paint and wood, marking a suicide line. Two or three feet down indicated a severe fire; five was explosive. The firemen confronting this fire had been taking their lives in their hands in facing it head-on.

"Watch your step, I don't trust this hallway. Stay close to the north wall."

Lisa returned her flashlight to the floor to pick her next steps. Jack had hesitated before letting her come up. The house was safe for now, but with the weight of walls and joists shifting to beams not designed to handle the weight, every day brought the structure closer to collapse. It had rained yesterday, making the damaged wood swell and further stressing the structure.

She was careful not to get snagged by a nail or by exposed wiring. The fire crews had pulled down part of the hallway ceiling and torn portions of the walls back to the studs in order to locate dangerous pockets of lingering heat. Six days ago this had been a two-alarm fire. In the smoldering remains, still in his bed, the body of Egan Hampton had been recovered.

She reached the back bedroom and stopped.

"An accident—" She could only shake her head in disbelief. The furniture was charred, the mattress burned down to the springs; books on the shelf were now warped spines enfolding wrinkled pages of ash; the alarm clock was a chunk of deformed plastic adhered to the bedside table; the television tube had cracked and buckled in.

The only items not burned or blackened in the room were a portion of the bedding that had been protected by Egan's body and a section of the floor rug that had been under the bed frame. The bedroom door was still on its hinges but it had burned on both sides to a fraction of its normal width.

"Like I said, it was a hot fire."

She stepped with caution inside the room, instinctively looking up to make sure she wasn't going to get hit with something. The ceiling was open in sections, revealing part of the attic, and in one place she could see all the way through to the sky.

Through the destroyed window she could see the orchard and nursery, the buildings and commercial greenhouses that comprised Nakomi Nurseries, the business Egan had built up over the years and recently passed to his nephew Walter to manage.

Jack dealt with fire every day; he knew how it moved and breathed and burned. She'd learned enough from him to understand the patterns. This looked like a flashover—everything in the room heating up, reaching burn point, and suddenly bursting into flames *en masse*. "Did the room smolder and smoke before flashover or was it a steady fire? In the police report Walter said he saw the smoke and then a flash and called 911."

"It began as a smoldering fire." Jack knelt and picked up large shards of glass from the shattered window. "Look at the smoke stain that burned into the pane of window glass."

He used the crowbar to pull off the bottom piece of the window frame casing and turned it over to show her the details. "You can tell it started as a floor fire burning upward because the fire swept across this wood and out the window. Had it initially been flames at the ceiling coming down the wall and out the window, the burning would be pitting on the top of the wood, not this charring underneath."

Daniel had done the autopsy on Egan Hampton. While smoke had killed the man—carbon monoxide had been found in his lungs indicating he'd been alive when the fire started—there was also a puzzle. He had suffered a contusion on the left temple coincident to death. It wasn't severe; the bruising had just begun to seep into the deep tissue.

The explanation could be as simple as something falling on him when the fire began, but it needed to be explained. And there was the fact he had taken what had been determined to be two sleeping pills. Within the doctor's prescribed dosage, but still a factor to be looked at. For now the autopsy results were inconclusive.

As with all cases that could go either way, it had come back to the central staff at the state crime lab for another look at the autopsy results in light of the case circumstances. Her boss had dropped the case in her lap Friday afternoon.

As a forensic pathologist the question she asked was simple to state and often maddeningly hard to answer: Was the death suspicious, warranting a murder investigation, or accidental?

Lisa loved a good puzzle, but not one that arrived to ruin a weekend. She'd read the reports yesterday, concluded only that she needed more information. "It would help if you could tell me this was an arson fire."

"It was a hot fire, but then it's been a hot, dry summer. The house has no air-conditioning, and the furniture and flooring had absorbed the afternoon heat. We found a lot of dry rot in the roof, and with this being a small back bedroom the fire was able to flashover within minutes."

"The fire started at the base of this wall?"

"As best we can tell, he fell asleep and dropped his cigar. We found the remains of one there." Jack pointed. "It hit what appears to have been a burlap bag of laundry. The fire moved across the floor, you can see the distinct burn line—" he traced it with his hand—"and eventually reached into the closet where it had an unlimited fuel load. It built in intensity and then moved back into the bedroom along the ceiling— see the bubbling in the wood? By then it was moving hot and fast."

"How long before the smoke blanket dropped low enough to kill him?"

"The fire probably took four to six minutes to get a footing. From then to a killing blanket of toxic smoke, you're talking maybe two minutes at the outside. The window was open, and the door, an unfortunate reality for him. The airflow would cause a natural eddy of smoke into that corner of the room over the bed."

She looked at the damage, now more able to understand why Mr. Hampton had not awakened. The fire Jack described would not be loud enough to wake a man sleeping heavily under the influence of two sleeping pills and building carbon monoxide. By the time the fire surged from the closet back into the room, the smoke would have been thick enough to kill.

She looked again for what might have caused the bruise. "The heat weakened and collapsed the plaster?"

"The house is old construction, they used a plaster paste over wood, and you can tell that most of it broke away. Directly above this room in the attic were cardboard boxes storing his wife's things, including clothes."

"Another fuel load."

"Yes. Once in the attic, the fire was burning on both sides of these joists."

"So falling plaster could account for the blow." Lisa walked to the remains of the bed frame and started searching the area. "Is there any evidence of a picture on the wall? Something else that might have fallen on him?"

Jack started tugging back debris.

They searched for ten minutes and found the remains of two picture frames and a shelf. The shelf would have been heavy enough, or an item on it. She felt herself relax. "One of these items is probably what caused the bruise."

"Agreed. The cat was found there." Jack pointed to the far corner of the room.

"Cat? What cat?"

"It wasn't in the notes? There should be an addendum to the fire report. Craig found it during the fire mop-up. We figured the cat was on the bed, got a face full of the smoke, retreated to escape the fire, then got trapped."

"A cat losing all of its nine lives? I thought the door was open."

"It was open when we came up the stairs fighting the fire. I suppose it's possible the force of the water pushed it open, but that would be apparent in the burn patterns."

Jack crossed over to the door and carefully swung it to take a look. "The door was open during the fire. If it were closed, this door edge around the knob and the edge back by the hinges would have been protected by the door frame, but both show serious burning."

"Then why didn't the cat bolt from the room?"

"It's hard to tell a burned cat's age, but it looked young. And a cat is not going to jump through fire at the window or past fire in the doorway. It tried to hide and the smoke eventually overcame it. We've seen it before."

"Jack?"

"Up here, Ford."

Footsteps sounded on the stairs as the detective assigned to the case came upstairs. He had been talking with Egan's nephew Walter. The house was going to have to be demolished in the next few days. Walter was in the process of recovering what essential papers he could from the downstairs office.

"Ford, do you know what happened to the cat?" Lisa asked before she realized Walter had also come upstairs with the detective.

Walter was the one to answer. "I'm sorry, I buried the cat this morning. I didn't realize it would be a problem. The crows had been attracted by the death; I found them in here." He swallowed hard. "Listen, it's in a shoe box buried at the end of the garden. It will take only a minute to get it for you."

"No," Lisa replied, stopping his retreat. "It's okay. Jack just told me it had also been killed."

"Egan liked that cat. It was from a neighbor cat's spring litter. I guess the house was lonely at night since Patricia was taken to the nursing home. He never liked pets before."

Lisa saw Walter look again toward the bed and knew it was best that they leave. She could see how hard this was on him. He was in his forties, lean, a landscaper by profession with an appearance that fit it, his jeans and gray T-shirt sweaty in the heat. At close range, the ravages of the last six days—the healing burns, the stress, the grief, and the lack of sleep—were all there to be seen on his face. He'd tried to reach his uncle but had been unable to get past the flames.

"I've got everything I need to finish up my report. We were just coming down." She was comfortable with the assessment that this had been a tragic accident. The dead cat disturbed her, but Jack was right, pets died in fires. She'd think it through again tonight, look one last time at the autopsy results, and if she didn't see anything else, she'd recommend to her boss that they sign it off as an accidental death.

Lisa was relieved. The last thing she needed was another murder investigation.

U.S. Marshal Quinn Diamond walked through the concourse at O'Hare, carrying a briefcase he hated, his cowboy boots leaving an echo behind him. His face was weathered by the sun and wind, the lines around his eyes deep. He was not a man to enjoy the crush of people, but at least Chicago was better than New York or Washington.

He had planned to take a direct flight from Washington, D.C., to Montana, spend his month of vacation at his ranch, let the physical hard work wipe away the aftereffects of two months spent tracking down who had murdered a federal judge.

Instead, he was in Chicago on very short notice. The folded newsclip in his billfold was from yesterday's *Chicago Tribune*. There was a book signing Tuesday night for a Sierra Club book entitled *A Photographic Guide to Birds in the Midwest*. The author's name—Amy Ireland Nugan.

Quinn had been checking out of the hotel in Washington when the news alert service tracked him down. It had been so long since the last lead. Was it her? Was it the Amy Ireland he had sought for so long?

He'd been able to get a few answers. She was married to a Paul Nugan. She was the right age, thirty-seven. Amy had been seventeen when she disappeared from Justin, Montana, twenty years ago.

The same day Amy had disappeared, his father had been shot in the back out on the southern range of the ranch near the bluffs.

After twenty years of searching he had finally accepted that Amy must have also died that day, but if she had instead fled and appeared sometime later in Chicago—he didn't think she would have pulled the trigger, but she might have been with someone who had.

If he could solve what had happened to Amy Ireland, maybe he could get a lead on who had killed his father.

He had almost given up hope of ever finding a trace of her. He'd eliminated dozens of Amy Irelands over the years, but this one…the sense of hope was back. It fit. Amy had been a high-school photographer with a passion for what her camera could reveal. She'd had real talent even in her teens. Quinn could easily see her making it a future career.

He had to know if this was the right Amy Ireland. And if it was, he had to be very careful not to send her running again. Practicing patience was not going to be easy.

His partner, Marcus O'Malley, would have joined him if Quinn had alerted him to the hit on the name; he was that kind of friend. But Quinn hadn't wanted to interrupt Marcus's chance to spend time with his sister who was undergoing cancer treatment at Johns Hopkins and his new fiancée, Shari. Instead, Quinn had called an old friend.

Quinn found Lincoln Beaumont waiting in the United Airlines' business lounge. If he hadn't known better, on first impression he would have assumed lawyer or investment banker, not retired U.S. Marshal and now private investigator. "Thanks for coming, Lincoln." He tipped his cowboy hat to the lady with the retired marshal. "Ma'am."

"Emily Randall; I handle Lincoln's research." She was a nice-looking lady, businesslike in her handshake, feminine in her dress, and confident in her gaze. "It's nice to meet you, Mr. Diamond."

"The pleasure's mine," Quinn replied with a smile. Lincoln had been right; she'd be perfect if it became necessary to have someone approach Amy.

The smile directed at him showed curiosity. He was accustomed to it; he made no attempt to disguise the fact he was a misplaced man in the city. Why that should draw women was a phenomenon he accepted but didn't really understand.

It didn't attract the attention of the one lady he wanted to notice him. No, he changed that. Lisa O'Malley noticed; she just found his interest uncomfortable to deal with and more often than not scowled rather than smiled when she saw him.

He was determined to get Marcus's sister to accept a dinner invitation on this trip through Chicago. She'd been ducking him long enough. He wasn't after something profound; he just wanted to change her rather mixed reaction to him and replace it with a solid friendship. He visited Chicago on a regular basis; he wanted to be able to call Lisa when he was in town and have her actually be pleased to hear from him.

Eating alone was a waste of time, so was spending his downtime at a hotel watching TV. He spent enough time with strangers. Lisa he knew, and she was the kind of friend he wanted: loyal, fun, and smart, with a stubborn streak he liked to ruffle. It was a bit like rubbing a cat's fur the wrong way. She was cute when annoyed, and calling her ma'am always got a reaction. One thing was certain: Lisa's life was never boring.

He smiled as he thought of the excuses she was likely to throw up to the invitation to dinner and unfortunately misled Ms. Randall into assuming his smile was in response to hers. Before she could say something that would put them both in a fix, he calmly turned the conversation. "Tell me what you've found out about Amy Ireland."

Her hair smelled like smoke, her jeans were going to have to be bleached to remove the ground-in ash, and she'd managed to rub the back of her neck nearly raw with the sweat and heavy pressure of the fire coat. Miserable didn't define it. Lisa paused to let Sidney out of his cage before heading to the shower. The ferret was a recent pet and one of her favorites; he scampered up her arm to push into her flyaway hair, and she sneezed. "Sorry. I'm covered in ash." She lowered him to the floor and with her foot sent a small rubber ball rolling down the hallway. Sidney gave chase and leaped to stop it.

Lisa glanced into her office as she headed to the shower and saw the answering machine blinking. Work would have paged…Jennifer. She abruptly changed course, hoping it was her sister.

It was Jennifer, and the recorded message was three hours old. Regretting having not been home to take the call, Lisa picked up the cordless phone and punched in the hospital number, hoping she wouldn't have the bad timing of catching Jen when she was sleeping. Jennifer's fiancé Tom Peterson answered, reassured her that Jennifer was awake, and passed the phone over.

"Thanks for calling back." Jen's voice was soft and Lisa had to press the phone close to hear, but compared to some days when the pain and the fatigue slurred her words, Jen sounded good.

"Hey, it's my pleasure. I had to work this afternoon or I would have called earlier. Are you having a good day?"

"I'm running a fever."

"That's excellent!" Lisa sank into the nearby chair, overjoyed. Jennifer's immune system, overrun by the cancer, was finally getting a foothold to fight back.

"I'm going to lick this yet." The optimism in Jennifer's voice throughout the weeks of hospitalization hadn't wavered, even though it was there in spite of the facts.

"You better believe it." The cancer was around Jen's spine and had touched her liver. The odds were severely against her, everyone in the O'Malley family knew that, but they also knew Jennifer had to win this fight. It was incomprehensible to imagine life without her.

Lisa rubbed her eyes and winced as the smoke residue made them burn. Staying positive was mandatory; yet it came at a cost. There was so much fear inside—she had seen too many people die. It was her profession to deal with death, but this situation was going to crumble her defenses and shatter her heart. Jennifer had to get well, she just had to.

The cancer was doing permanent damage each day it progressed, and the toxic radiation and chemotherapy being used to battle the disease were inflicting their own lasting damage. Lisa wished she had chosen pediatrics as her medical specialty like Jennifer had instead of forensic pathology so she could be less aware of the painful truth—death was coming. Unless the process could be checked, she was going to lose her best friend.

It was a struggle to force her voice to stay light. "Tom's there, so I gather you're enjoying the evening."

"You better believe it. Mushy movie, good-looking date…"

Lisa had to laugh. "Being engaged suits you."

"The wedding won't come soon enough."

Jennifer had set her heart on getting married October 22; it was looming a short five weeks away. The family had already caucused with Tom: If the O'Malleys had to arrive en masse in Baltimore and have the wedding at the hospital, they would make it happen for her. "Have Marcus and Shari arrived?"

"They got in this afternoon. Shari is a sweetheart."

"Yes, she is."

"So what were you working on this afternoon?"

"Follow-up on a fire case from last week. I dragged Jack along with me out to the scene and spent two hours climbing around in a burned-out house. It was hot, heavy, dirty work. I haven't been this beat in ages."

The doorbell rang. Lisa turned; she wasn't expecting anyone. She was tempted to ignore the doorbell, but her car was in the drive making it obvious she was home. Which local kid had she not bought candy from for the junior high band trip? She'd seen Tony and Mandy yesterday. Chad.

She reached for the spare stash of cash she kept tucked inside the baby panda cookie jar on her desk along with an assortment of hard candy and slipped the money into her pocket. The problem was that she always said yes, and all the kids knew it. And to miss someone— She'd long ago determined not to let that happen. She moved through the house, taking the phone with her.

"Kate brought me the *Chicago Tribune* and the *Sun Times*. Was it the Paretti family fire? I saw the write-up in the metro section."

"No, thank goodness." The Paretti family had died in a house fire on Monday. "This one was an old farmhouse out in Villa Grove. It looks like a dropped cigar started it." Lisa looked through the front door's security hole and flinched. "Jen, I need to call you back. Quinn's here."

"Is he?"

"He's supposed to be in Montana," Lisa said darkly. "And I've got enough ash in my hair it looks gray," she muttered, releasing the chain and turning the dead bolt, "while he looks his normal, elegant self." Her brief glance had been enough to confirm that. In the habit of cops, he was standing three feet back from the door and off to the side while he waited for her to answer the summons, his thumbs resting comfortably at the pockets of his jeans, his hands halfway to his concealed weapon.

He was tall and lean and fit and would probably live to be a centurian. From the boots to the cowboy hat to the way he walked through a crowd, he was a man who knew where he came from and was comfortable with it. She distrusted the politeness and niceness. He was Marcus's partner, and the stories she had heard about what the two of them had pulled off over the years… Appearances were deceiving with this man.

His black hair was often smashed by the cowboy hat, and the deep lines around his blue eyes showed his habit of spending his days outdoors without sunglasses. It should have made him look ruffled; instead it just added a relaxed tone to the already strong sense of presence.

She didn't like the fact that at five foot four she had to tilt her head to look up at him. His presence intimidated witnesses he was interviewing, and he worked so hard to change that perception when he was off duty that it unfortunately just made her more aware of it.

Quinn worked all over the country with her brother, and while she warily tried to keep track of him, he still caught her off guard at the most inconvenient moments.

"He's gorgeous enough to make your toes curl, and he's one fine date."

"You should know." Jennifer had dated Quinn two years ago. Last year Quinn had dated her sister Kate. Lisa had no intention of being number three. Not that she minded losing out to her sisters, but it was the principle of the thing.

There was something humiliating at being thought of as third. And any guy who dared ask out three sisters in the same family either had a lot of guts or a lot of nerve—in Quinn's case, both. She thought her answer to his last dinner invitation had been creative, eloquent, and final. She'd sent him a petrified squid.

"Smile at him. And call me back."

"Maybe," Lisa replied to her sister's laugh. She hung up and forced herself to open the door.

"Hello, Lisa." She looked confused to see him; Quinn considered it an improvement over annoyed. A wave of cold air washed out from the house as she stood in the doorway, one hand gripping the door frame and the other resting on the screen door handle. "I was in town, I thought I'd say hi," he elaborated.

"Oh. Hi."

He tipped his hat, the brim rough against his fingers, and silently laughed as he scanned and enjoyed. Freckles. Baby blue eyes. Hair so fine and thick the sun set its color and the wind defined its form, much to her dismay and his pleasure. Cut short to try and tame it, her hair now curled and bobbed as she moved.

Her voice held a touch of the full world—Quebec French, South American Spanish—the blend and tone of her voice changed with each passing year as she added traces of the people she met. She'd been in Venezuela six months ago and some inaccessible part of Africa a few months before that, absorbing the local culture and fitting herself in. He loved listening to her voice. He wanted to add to it a touch of Montana drawl. "Can I come in?"

She flushed and stepped back. "Yes. Sorry. I just got home."

Bad timing on his part. Black ash streaked her left forearm, her faded yellow shirt was sweat stained, and her jeans were grimy at the knees. There was a marked tiredness to her polite smile, and something had scraped her right cheek.

As she turned his eyes narrowed at the blisters he saw on the back of her neck. A fire scene, and for Lisa that meant victims. He couldn't get a break even when he most needed one. She was obviously not in the mood for company tonight, even though she probably needed that distraction more on this evening than most others.

"I was just talking with Jen." She lifted the phone she carried, looking awkward. "Let me hang this up. I'll just be a minute."

"Of course," he said gently. He'd seen Lisa's sister last week; the reality of that call explained part of the droop to Lisa's shoulders. The situation was a source of stress to everyone, but for Lisa... Quinn knew how close the two of them were. And with Lisa being a doctor—the placating words others said in reassurance would not help her. She understood how much the hopeful language covered grim reality.

He'd do what he could to get that stress to drain away tonight, even if he had to resort to badgering her into getting angry and letting that tension loose against him. It was one of the odd times where ruffling her into reacting would be the right thing to do.

She turned toward the hallway, and he shot out a hand to grab her arm. "Hold it, you've got more company." The animal nearly tripped her as it darted between her socked feet. It scampered across his boots and returned, intrigued by the smell.

Quinn scooped him up in a worn, callous hand and held him at eye level, he and the animal showing equal curiosity. His smile was easy and amused. "One of your more interesting choices." He settled the animal on his shoulder and it reached up to explore his hat. "Take a shower, Lisa, clean that scrape, and I'll take you out somewhere nice to eat."

"I've got plans for tonight."

"I know. With me." He didn't ask her to extend the lie by trying to come up with what the plans were. She was a lousy liar. And since Marcus—the oldest and thus guardian of the O'Malley clan—was currently half a continent away, he was stepping in by proxy to make happen what was best for her. She needed a relaxing evening out. She started to protest and he interrupted. "Marcus and Shari have been talking about wedding plans; I thought you'd be interested."

She shot him a quelling look, annoyed that he knew details before she did, but reluctantly gave in. "Drinks are in the refrigerator; help yourself."

He turned that way, lowering the ferret to the floor, knowing better than to stay put and give Lisa a chance to get her bearings. When she dug in her heels she was a formidable opponent. "Has she fed you yet, buddy?"

Two

Lisa rested her head against the shower door and let the cold water take the sting out of the sunburn on the back of her neck. How did she get into situations like this?

She had been planning a quiet night at home with maybe a record on the stereo and her topographical maps of the Smoky Mountains spread out on the table to plot her next vacation trek. She'd just bought the vinyl thirty-three with "Rainy Night in Georgia," "Worried Man Blues," and "Kentucky Rain" for a quarter at a garage sale yesterday morning, and it was the type of music that suited her mood for tonight; she'd enjoy the vacation planning. Instead of those evening plans—she wasn't sure what she had ended up with, other than the frustrating realization that she was being nicely manipulated.

Quinn was comfortable enough to just drop by whenever he was in town, and she had no idea why he continued to do it. It wasn't like she had sparkling, interesting conversation to offer. She got positively tongue-tied around the man. He had a free evening, and he wasn't the type of guy to spend it alone. She knew better than to think of it as a date.

It fit Quinn's pattern. Even his dates with Jennifer and Kate had been more focused on having someone to spend his time with than anything serious, the mood more laughter and teasing than romantic. But Lisa didn't fit that same mold as her sisters, and she knew she'd disappoint Quinn if he expected the same thing from her.

It went with her miserable track record that Quinn had arrived while she looked like a charcoal block. She wasn't vain about her looks; she was the middle of the O'Malley sisters in that regard and comfortable there—classical beauty was Rachel's, sultry was Kate's, Jennifer didn't count as she'd be a petite size six for her wedding—but it would be nice if Quinn didn't have a knack for catching her at her worst.

She flinched under the spray as a blister broke. The sun had done a number on her today, and Jack's air-conditioning was out in his car; the ninety-two-degree heat had wilted her. If Quinn felt the heat of the day, it wasn't obvious. His body simply absorbed the sun and turned his skin a deeper, darker tan.

It wasn't that she didn't like Quinn. Her brother's partner was…an interesting man. Tenacious in a quiet way, he had to be in his midforties and it showed in his demeanor. She'd rarely seen him be anything but relaxed, calm, and professional. But he tracked down fugitives and worked cases with a single-minded focus she rarely saw even among the cops with whom she worked.

She didn't understand the man. He owned a prosperous ranch in Montana, was obviously more comfortable on the open land than in the city, and yet he worked as a U.S. Marshal traveling the country. Whatever his history was, it was tightly held.

She knew herself very well—she just didn't want to go out with a guy where getting her heart broken was inevitable. She didn't know how to play it casual. If Quinn hadn't settled down at forty, he wasn't going to. She could get hurt letting herself get close to him.

If Kate and Jennifer weren't good enough to get him thinking about settling down, there was no way she would be. And she didn't have the ability to let people come and go from her life and not record the scars—too many people had already left.

The water slowly began to ease the ache in her muscles. She shampooed her hair for the second time.

What were they going to talk about after the first ten minutes? She washed away the soap, then realized her hair still felt rough. She reached for the shampoo to do it a third time. She knew it would just be a tangle of flyaway strands when it dried.

She hated talking about herself, and he had to have already gotten his fill of the O'Malley family gossip just by being around Marcus. The case—it was the only thing she really was comfortable talking to Quinn about. And that would make great conversation.

It didn't make sense that the cat had died.

She frowned at the thought, but because it was easier to think about work than Quinn, she let herself follow the tangent, puzzled.

The cat would have awoken early, long before the fire blocked the doorway. Either the doorway was closed so the cat couldn't get out—and Jack had said it was open—or the cat hadn't been able to wake up.

What would a sleeping pill do to a cat?

It bothered her that Egan had taken two when his doctor's notes said he was reluctant to take even one and used them only sporadically. The fire had been early in the evening. It wasn't like he had taken one, still been awake hours later, and then taken the second one. He had taken two sleeping pills, gone to bed, turned on the TV, and smoked a cigar.

She dropped the shampoo bottle.

Smoked a cigar, but the ashtrays and cigarettes were in his office and on the kitchen table. He'd been having himself a treat, a last cigar.

She swore as soap ran into her eyes, hurriedly stuck her head under the water to rinse the shampoo out, grabbed for a towel, and made the mistake of hitting the hot water on instead of off, nearly scalding herself.

It hadn't been a tragic accident. Not if he had also given his cat a sleeping pill, not wanting to die alone.

It had been a suicide.

Quinn paused by the painting on the wall by the kitchen phone, captivated by the fourteen-inch watercolor. The wildflower garden was a vibrant explosion of color around a reflective pond, the scene alive and yet at the same time tranquil. He leaned down to read the signature. A Sinclair. In the kitchen. He laughed softly at the discovery.

Lisa was so casual and careless about the art she acquired. A collector himself for decades, his mother had been a professional artist; he envied Lisa's talent to spot something excellent. She bought something because she liked it and had no concept of how good she was at making that choice. He was going to have to convince her to come wander the downtown galleries with him. He needed something for the office back at the ranch. He had found a Calvin Price sculpture in New York and needed two paintings to make the arrangement complete.

With regret that the odds of getting her to part with the watercolor were nil, he moved on to dry his hands and got down two glasses from the cabinet.

Lincoln Beaumont and Emily Randall had promised some solid answers on Amy Ireland Nugan by noon tomorrow; there was only so much background information that could be dug up on a Sunday without it being obvious they were looking. What they had found so far was inconclusive, going back only as far as New York where Amy had lived before coming to Chicago.

His father was dead; Amy Ireland was going to be at the book signing Tuesday night. A link would last forty-eight hours. Quinn didn't think Lisa would understand the favor he was paying her by being here instead of investigating tonight. He didn't plan to tell her why he had come to Chicago; it was a quiet, private search. He'd rather have Lisa irritated at him than feeling sorry for him.

He heard the water stop then a door close. Lisa was not a woman who lingered over makeup and hair—with her looks and smile she already caught plenty of attention, and her attempts to tame her hair tended to frustrate her and make the problem worse. He picked up the tall glass of cold fruit juice he'd poured for her and walked back toward the living room. She'd looked not only parched and tired but stressed. He hoped to the depths of his heart that the victim had not been a child.

He should have found something better to say. She'd looked so defensive about being caught just back from a crime scene that it had made him want to wrap her in a hug. She usually showed so much intensely focused energy that he was caught off guard by the moments that showed the other Lisa—tiny in stature, drained of energy, showing the strain of her day.

He'd seen her slogging through marshes to reach a murder victim, dealing with the remains of a lady who had died at home and not been found for a week, coping with a stabbing victim. He'd spent the last two months watching her put together the forensic evidence they needed to identify who had murdered a federal judge. She was incredibly good at her job.

But she was defensive about it because others had made her that way. It wasn't something a woman was supposed to enjoy doing. Doctors were supposed to go into the profession to heal the living, not investigate deaths. Lisa didn't enjoy what she saw on the job, but she was wise enough to be good at it. He understood Lisa well enough to know she had never chosen the easy or the traditional. She'd been going her own way for a long time. She had the strength to deal with unpleasant facts, to face them head-on and do what needed to be done. He admired that enormously.

He didn't mind her job; he liked a maverick—he was a bit of one himself. And she wouldn't be Lisa without that fascinating contradiction. She was the only lady he'd met who intrigued him more the longer he knew her. And while he didn't want her to treat him like a brother, he did wish she would relax with him like she did with her brothers.

He heard her coming, her voice pitched low, letting him know a ferret had found her. For a lady who had lizards and snakes and mice for pets, the ferret was practically conventional.

Quinn looked at her casual blue cotton shirt and clean jeans and sighed. "You want a hamburger somewhere. I was going to suggest a nice restaurant."

"We're not going out to eat." She reached for the briefcase on the floor by the couch, opened it to retrieve her phone log and her cellular phone, closed it with her left foot, then juggled the items to one hand as she dug her keys out of her pocket.

The slight distance to her voice, her attention and concentration on her own thoughts, a precision to her movements—he'd seen it before, her shift-into-work mode.

Even when relaxed she tended to be restless, spinning something in her fingers, tapping her foot, unconsciously always having energy moving. But it changed when she locked into work and her concentration centered on a puzzle, her very stillness a mark of her intense focus.

She had no idea she could be read so easily, but then he'd been studying her for a long time. At least she hadn't reached for the small black canister rolling around at the back of the briefcase. To his relief she was a woman who didn't mind fighting dirty and wasn't above taking help along if she was going somewhere she thought might be trouble.

Unfortunately, her track record with getting into trouble was well established. She was nearly as bad as her sister Kate. For years Quinn had watched Marcus quietly try to keep close tabs on the two of them. Kate, a hostage negotiator for the Chicago police department, had been known to walk into situations where a guy had a bomb; Lisa just walked into murder scenes, determined to find a killer. "Where are we going?"

"To ask a man to exhume a cat."

Three

I'd ask you to clarify that, but I'm afraid you mean it literally."
Lisa glanced over and found Quinn watching her with that mildly amused look he got when he was humoring her. She had to force herself not to drop her gaze. She had been relishing the fact she was squashing his dinner plans for the evening, but he was turning the tables on her. The man knew exactly what she was thinking.

"I do." She scooped up Sidney, the animal's coarse warm fur, long body, and slight musky smell familiar and comforting, and walked back to the spare bedroom to put the animal back in his cage. Sidney clasped himself around her wrist and sniffed her fingers, with reluctance returned to his home when set down, then promptly chattered as he spotted the ping-pong ball in his cage and hurried to pounce. Lisa rubbed her finger down his spine, then closed his cage door. The animal was playing from the moment he woke until he dropped asleep from exhaustion.

When she returned, Quinn hadn't moved. "Please explain."

She didn't want to share case details with him, but if they were not talking about work, she didn't know what to say. "Bring my briefcase; the case folder is inside."

"Drink this first." He held out a tall glass, one of her good company glasses with its little red rose pattern around the rim. She favored the plastic thirty-two-ounce monsters that fit her car's cup holder.

The tone in his voice said it was nonnegotiable and she was impatient to leave. She gulped the juice down, then slowed to savor the last of it. It tasted like nectar. She set the glass down on the side table atop a book club newsletter. "Okay?"

"Better." He picked up her briefcase. "Keys." He held out his hand for them and she didn't argue the point, simply handed them to him. She'd let him wrestle with the slightly off-center dead bolt.

She waited at the edge of the walkway while he locked the house. In the drive his car was parked behind hers. "I'm driving," she insisted as he handed back her keys.

"Fine, but I'm riding with you. Your word, or I won't move my car."

It wasn't beneath her to try to give him the slip, but she hadn't been intending to; she'd only thought about it. "My word," she agreed grudgingly.

It was almost 7 P.M. The sun was low in the sky but the heat was still intense, and when she unlocked her car door it hit her like a wave. She should have risked the possibility of a late afternoon summer thunderstorm and left the windows open a few inches.

Her car was a mess.

Quinn was not known for being neat. He had a wonderful lady who kept his ranch house in order, but when he traveled—there was a reason he stayed in hotels. If he saw this mess in her car, all those times she had teased him would be wasted. She had thirty seconds while he moved his car to the street.

She rapidly grabbed what she could and shoved it into two plastic sacks she found tucked between the seats: her fast-food dinner sack from yesterday, a pair of jeans that needed to be returned to the store, three coffee cups, a thermos that now had floating green stuff growing in the liquid, overdue library books, and a birthday gift bought but not wrapped that was now three days late.

She was normally so neat and organized, so proud of how she kept her house and car that she got teased about it by her family; instead of that, Quinn was going to see her after a week in which her schedule had been one of a thousand interruptions. It wasn't fair.

She popped open the trunk and dumped the sacks there.

"You didn't need to clean up for me."

She slammed the trunk closed. "Shut up, Quinn."

"Yes, ma'am."

He opened the driver's door for her. She stopped, caught by surprise, looked at him, and then eased inside with a slight smile. She should have expected it; Quinn was consistent to a fault about politeness.

He held the door for ladies, let them step inside first, insisted on carrying things and getting the car when it rained, always picked up the check, made a point of waiting for a lady to speak first. But when he did those things for her, there was an extra twinkle in his eyes; he liked doing them because he knew it would fluster her.

She found that reality amusing but would never admit how much she enjoyed the unspoken dance. She kept hoping to catch him off guard, but in the years she'd known him he always managed to keep a step ahead of her.

She started the car and turned the air-conditioning on high while he circled around the car to the passenger seat.

"Is there a baseball game on tonight?"

She flipped on the radio and punched in WGN, relieved to find his guess was right. It was a town favorite, the Chicago Cubs playing the Chicago White Sox. The familiar voice calling the play-by-play was a welcome addition; it eliminated the need for conversation. She pulled out of the subdivision and considered traffic on a Sunday evening to choose the best route northwest.

Quinn settled his hat on one knee. "Tell me about the day. I can tell it's been bad."

Just when she wanted to be annoyed with him, his voice changed and he said exactly the right thing. No wonder both Jennifer and Kate had raved about the man when they dated him. He placed a high value on listening. She let herself relax a bit. "The file is on top in the briefcase."

He retrieved it.

She looked over when it had been silent for several minutes to find him studying the photos. There was nothing gentle about his expression. She looked away, not sure what she thought of that expression and the intensity in it. He looked like what he was: a cop.

"It doesn't look like arson."

"It's a suicide, Quinn, and I missed it. There's an addendum in there on a cat that died. The bedroom door was open, and yet the cat died in that bedroom. Egan fed his cat a sleeping pill, took two himself, smoked his last cigar, and lay down to die."

She felt annoyance. "I just didn't think suicide; that was stupid. It fits this case like a glove. His wife has been moved to a nursing home, he'd passed running his business to his nephew, friends admitted he was lonely, and his cat died in a room with an open door. He killed his cat."

"If you're right, be glad he didn't show up at the nursing home and kill his wife, then himself."

"I know."

She pushed her sunglasses up and rubbed eyes still gritty from the smoke. She was botching a case right in front of him. It couldn't get worse than this.

Walter Hampton had arrived at the farmhouse before them. He was waiting beside a white-and-blue truck advertising Nakomi Nurseries. "Quinn, he's a grieving man; I'd prefer not to have him think this was a suicide until I know something definite."

"Relax, Lisa. It's your case. I'll stay in the background."

She parked behind Walter's truck. "You couldn't stay in the background even if you tried."

"I'll admit, I rarely try." He opened his door, got out, and slipped on his hat.

She had considered calling Detective Ford Prescott or Jack, but it was now after seven on Sunday evening. She was here to retrieve a cat, have a brief look around. If she found something, she could always call them back to the site.

Lisa waited for Quinn to join her before walking forward to meet Walter. She struggled to find the right words. "Mr. Hampton, thank you for coming back over to the house."

He turned his baseball hat in his hand. "Your message said it was important."

"This is awkward, but I need a favor. Would you mind exhuming the cat?"

"Of course. Let me get a shovel; it will take me twenty minutes at most. The shoe box is buried at the edge of the garden."

The lingering suspicion that it had been foul play and Walter had been involved eased even further with his immediate agreement. "Thank you. If we could borrow the key again, we'll be in the house. I need to check one last item."

"Of course." He reached into his pocket for the key and looked from her to Quinn.

She stumbled over the error; Quinn was not in the background when he was standing right beside her. "I'm sorry. Mr. Hampton, this is U.S. Marshal Quinn Diamond."

Walter dropped the key as he handed it to her, then dug it from the dirt with an apology. He nodded briefly to Quinn. "Mr. Diamond. Let me get that shovel."

She watched him walk toward the detached garage. "I feel sorry for him," she said quietly to Quinn. "This is tough."

"The guy is nervous."

"Because he dropped the key?"

"He didn't look at me once we were introduced, but given the circumstances, I don't suppose I can blame him. He knows there's something you're not saying." Quinn turned toward the car. "Get the flashlight, let's go to work."

She walked back to the car and opened the trunk. She found the flashlight in the box with the roadside flares and the jug of extra windshield wiper fluid. The flashlight gave a weak beam. She should have changed the batteries before coming.

"What are you looking for in the house?"

"I just want to see the scene again from a different viewpoint."

He walked with her up to the house and wrestled the front door unlocked.

The house groaned around them as the evening breeze picked up. The charred smell of burned wood hung heavy in the humid air. "Let's check the office area; maybe he wrote a final note," she suggested to avoid facing the upstairs for a few more minutes. She'd be surprised if there was one; statistically most suicides didn't leave one, but it was possible.

Walter had boxed what papers were salvageable from the desk. If there had been something in the office, he would have likely found it, but Lisa thumbed through the box to double-check. They spent time searching through the downstairs rooms but came up with nothing specific. There was no diary, no letter, no note left in his Bible.

"I'm going to look upstairs again," Lisa said, accepting the inevitable. Quinn joined her. The flashlight flickered as they reached the steps.

"Wait," Quinn cautioned. "I saw another flashlight in one of the desk drawers."

He disappeared back into the office.

Striking the flashlight against her palm a couple times brought the beam back. Lisa shone her flashlight back up the stairwell. She needed to see if there was any other evidence of a last evening: a favorite book, a keepsake like a picture nearby. If this was a planned suicide, Egan had probably changed his normal nightly routine in more ways than just a cigar.

A flash of movement at the top of the stairs stopped her. Something was up there. Something fell, and she heard the unmistakable bark of a squirrel. The last thing she needed was an animal disturbing the scene.

She started up the stairs. "Quinn, there's a squirrel trapped up there."

She reached the landing, choosing her steps with care. The beam illuminated the animal at the end of the hall, its golden eyes gleaming back at her. She could sense the poor thing's terror and the panic it must feel with the burned smell all around. How was she going to get it out of this house? She couldn't leave it here.

It darted toward the bedroom, and she moved to close the other doors in the hallway, eliminating other places it could run. She was aware her foot was on something soft an instant before the world moved.

The wood gave an explosive break, and she was falling into darkness.

It was pitch black. Her flashlight was gone. She was lying on her back, and she had landed on something sharp.

Lisa struggled to breathe, could feel the shock swallowing her, couldn't stop the narrowing of her vision.

She was impaled on something; it was a horrific realization. It hadn't punctured a lung, but she could feel the agonizing pain ballooning through her chest.

"Lisa! Where are you?"

The voice was edged with panic. It echoed through the clouds of billowing, choking ash settling on the remains of the collapsed stairs and flooring, settling on her face and clogging her breath, smothering her. All the annoying things she had ever thought of him she silently apologized for.

"Quinn."

He had to have exquisite hearing to catch her faint whisper; as soon as she said his name, his light moved toward her. The beam pierced the cloudy ash and struck her face, and then he was scrambling over beams and through rubble toward her. He jammed the flashlight into a crevice and pushed aside the remains of shattered flooring and part of a stair step.

In the wavering light she saw him flinch, and she tried to offer a reassuring smile. He yanked off his shirt, the buttons flying. "Hold on."

She couldn't get enough air; she had to know. "What…land on?"

He didn't answer her.

It must be bad.

She shivered and felt a warm flood rush across her hand as her vision went black.

Four

Quinn, quit fussing."

"I'll fuss as long as I like. Get used to it," he retorted, his voice abrupt but not his hands. He was trying to figure out how to get Lisa out of the car without touching something that would cause her more pain, and it was proving to be an impossible problem to solve. Eight days in the hospital and about the only thing on this last Monday in October that hadn't changed was her irritation with him.

Finally accepting that there was no pain-free way to do this, he turned her legs toward the street and slid his hands under her arms. "Here we go." He eased her to her feet, holding his breath as her mouth went thin and taut. She was too stubborn to admit how bad it hurt, but her forearms rested against his chest and he braced to take her weight.

Her head bowed as she fought the pain off. He didn't catch the words she said, but he got the drift. He ran a soothing hand across her hair, silently giving her time.

"Don't you dare let the other O'Malleys see this."

"I won't."

They had a little conspiracy forming as they stood there and the other two cars pulled into her driveway behind them. A shift of his body shielded the distress she was in from her family. The ride to her home had been hard; there was no way around that. She had insisted the doctors release her today, and she was paying for it.

She wouldn't be walking anywhere very fast, anytime soon. The joist rebar had done more damage than a bullet. Two inches to the left and it would have paralyzed her, two inches higher, killed her outright. As it was she had suffered through four days in intensive care and four days on the general ward to deal with the trauma, surgery, and massive amount of blood loss. Displaced ribs were slow to heal.

The other O'Malleys saw, but they silently pretended not to.

"Okay. I can make it."

He kept a firm grip under her forearms as she straightened. Only after he was sure she was steady did he reach back into the car for her things. He handed her the cane she'd been ordered to use for the next few days.

"I am so glad to be home."

He set her suitcase on the drive. She was trying to close her left hand with its broken index finger around the cane. Watching her cautious movements made him hurt; he shifted the cane to her other hand and moved her injured hand to rest on his forearm. "Let's get you inside." One of the others would bring in the suitcase.

"Who's been taking care of my animals?"

"Kate or I have been by every day."

All of the O'Malleys with the exception of Jennifer were here, and it had taken a concerted effort from the others to get Jennifer to stay in Baltimore. She had been prepared to be on the first plane out, chemotherapy or not.

Quinn had never met a family more united than this one. The seven of them were related not by blood, but by choice. At the orphanage—Trevor House—they had made the decision to become their own family, had as adults legally changed their last names to O'Malley. Two decades later this group remained incredibly tight.

And they'd made him part of it.

He'd felt the change in the last week. They'd always made him feel welcome, but it was different now. When it came time to move Lisa home and get her settled, they had passed that assignment to him without even asking.

He was under no illusions of why. Lisa's accident and his part in it had hit this family hard. Their group reaction had come in stages. It would have been fascinating to watch if he hadn't been in the middle of it. As it was, he was simply trying to survive it.

Stage one had been direct. Jack had slugged him. A fast right cross had caught him on the jaw line and come close to rounding what had always been a rather square jaw. Quinn had found himself flat on his back in the hospital parking lot, looking up at the sky, feeling like a truck had hit him. He hadn't even seen it coming.

Quinn had shaken off the stars to find Stephen, the paramedic in the family, standing over him, yelling at Jack. Quinn had moved to touch his jaw, and Stephen had looked down and given him a blistering order not to move or he would finish what Jack had started. The dynamic duo of brothers had been mad at him for letting Lisa get hurt; they'd just differed on how to most effectively make their point.

Marcus had arrived in the middle of the exchange. The man had flown back from Baltimore and arrived to find his sister still in surgery. Quinn had stayed on the ground precisely because he was the man's partner. Marcus was the oldest O'Malley and guardian of the group, and he took Lisa's welfare personally. Marcus wouldn't just make his jaw ache, he'd break it. It wouldn't be the Christian thing for Marcus to do, but it would be the older brother thing to do. Quinn wasn't willing to find out which would win out.

They were worried; therefore, they were mad. And in the simple equation of guys looked after girls, he was responsible. They'd made their point.

Jack had cooled off first, had offered him a hand up. Quinn had warily accepted. Frankly, getting hit had helped. He'd deserved it for letting Lisa get hurt.

The brothers had accepted his apology, and the four of them had ended up pacing as a group while they struggled to wait for Lisa to get out of surgery.

Stage two had been the sisters. Jennifer, Kate, and Rachel had insisted on hearing the details of what had happened.

He'd spent over an hour on the phone with Jennifer. As a doctor she had wanted to know everything he could remember about Lisa's injuries. Kate had asked for details because as a cop she wanted to find something that would implicate someone as responsible.

Rachel had been the toughest to deal with. A trauma psychologist, she had worked her way under the 'I'm fine' cloak of words to the truth. She had pulled out what it had been like from the first sound of wood collapsing, through the realization of how bad Lisa was hurt, to the desperate realization Lisa might not make it to the hospital. By the time Rachel was through with him, he'd been taken apart and put back together. Effective, but incredibly draining.

Stage three was to give him a chance to make it up to Lisa. It was the hardest to accomplish because it was self-driven. Until Lisa was back on her feet and no longer dealing with the aftereffects of the injuries, he was going to feel responsible. She'd been hurt on his watch. He should have protected her. He'd failed. He didn't need her brothers to point that fact out, or conversely, her sisters to tell him it had been an accident.

He felt responsible.

Quinn hoped getting Lisa home would turn the corner. He wanted this behind them even more than the other O'Malleys did.

While the others began to unload the flowers that had packed Lisa's hospital room, Quinn walked her slowly to the front door. He and Lisa were passed several times as they walked, Jack and Stephen joking with her about what her ferret Sidney was likely to do with the florist shop she was bringing home. Lisa joked back, but her comebacks were at a fraction of their normal speed.

Rachel held the screen door for them.

"Couch or chair?" Quinn asked Lisa quietly.

"Couch."

The strain in Lisa's single word bit. The car ride had jarred the injury and this walk was capping it off. Her back muscles were going to spasm if she didn't relax.

He grasped her elbows and eased her down.

She sucked in a deep breath. "Thanks."

Afraid she'd started to cry, he brushed back her hair and raised her chin, knowing she was going to tense on him but more petrified of the possible tears. He read the pain clouding her eyes. "What do you need?"

He'd startled her. He waited for it to pass, not moving away, and was rewarded as her eyes softened with humor for the first time in days. "New ribs. But I'll settle for something to make me forget the ones I have."

"This will do it." Rachel joined them carrying a prescription bottle. "Jennifer said this muscle relaxant would take down an elephant."

Quinn reluctantly eased back, leaving her to the care of the family descending on her. Kate came into the room bringing Sidney. The guys turned toward the kitchen debating over what to fix for dinner.

"I want a steak," Lisa interjected into the conversation.

"Not for another week, doctor's orders," Stephen called back.

"Stephen."

"Live with it. We're having fish."

Lisa made a face even as she laughed.

Quinn got himself a soft drink, took a seat across from Lisa out of the way, and settled in to just watch her. Marcus had once described Lisa as the one they had simply chosen to envelop. Having watched her family interact long enough, he now understood it.

Abandoned at birth, in seven foster homes before Trevor House, Lisa had never felt like she fit in. She'd arrived at Trevor House independent to a fault, a lizard peeking out of her backpack. The group had simply enveloped her then and they were doing it again now.

This last week he'd watched them override what was her instinct for space with a smothering presence of love. Even if she tended not to reach for it, she drew her strength from it. He was gaining a rapid education in how to deal with her that he wasn't going to forget.

She'd never been alone; Marcus had tried to make himself comfortable in the hospital chair late at night, Jack and Kate through the days, Rachel and Stephen in the evenings. Quinn had taken the predawn hours when the dreams tended to haunt her, when he didn't have to hide what he felt from the others.

She'd been hurt while with him and the guilt was heavy.

He listened to Lisa laugh as she played with Sidney, saw the strain in her face ease as the muscle relaxant kicked in, and for the first time in a week his heart settled back into a normal rhythm. He never wanted to come so close to losing her again.

He had to go all the way back to the time surrounding his father's murder to find a week more draining than this one. Physically exhausted from lack of sleep. Emotionally drained by how long and hard the battle had gone on before Lisa was out of danger. Spiritually…turmoil was a good word.

Three of the seven O'Malleys were new Christians—Jennifer, Marcus, and Kate—and their expectations for what Jesus would do to heal Lisa…their expectations were so high.

At two in the morning he'd been sitting with Kate and Marcus in the hospital cafeteria privy to a strategy session on how to get Lisa to listen to the truth. It had been uncomfortable. Quinn agreed with their objective, and at the same time felt like he was betraying Lisa by talking about her behind her back.

Kate thought it would be better to push the subject of God while Lisa was still dealing with the turmoil of almost dying and there might be a window of opportunity available. Marcus had been a little more cautious but had agreed with Kate. Quinn had tried to urge Jennifer's approach that had been so effective in reaching the two of them: a steady one that didn't push to hard.

Now Quinn was praying for wisdom. Marcus and Kate...he wouldn't want the two of them focused on him, and he was afraid that would be Lisa's initial reaction.

"You look down," Kate said softly, settling on the arm of his chair.

Trust her to get to the point. "I'm okay."

Kate borrowed his soft drink. "Your heart's been on your sleeve for a week, you might want to tuck it inside again before she realizes it," she whispered.

Quinn leaned his head back to look up at her. The lady he had dated for a few months and come to consider one of his most important friends knew him very well. He would be lying to say his emotions weren't involved; eight long days focused on Lisa had intensified everything he felt. But Kate was seeing what she wanted to see. He laughed softly and didn't have the heart to break her bubble. She was happy; she wanted Lisa to be happy. "It's noticeable?"

"But very cute."

"She's on my case for fussing."

Kate grinned. "And you do it so well. You can fuss over me if you like."

"She's already talking about when she goes back to work."

"I know. It's crazy to be going back to work so soon, but she needs it. It's a distraction."

"She's going to be hurting for months."

"Yes." She squeezed the back of his neck. "She'll recover. Did you hear from Lincoln?"

The investigation into Amy Ireland Nugan had been forced to the sidelines by circumstances, and it took a moment for him to refocus. Kate knew the history. "Lincoln got word from his contact in Canada last night. They confirmed Amy was born in Quebec, eventually moved to New York, then here. It was a different Amy Ireland."

"I'm sorry."

"So am I." There was no way to put into words what it felt like to lose another promising thread. Giving up hope of finding the man who killed his father took something of his spirit with it, and it was happening as each promising lead failed.

"It won't stay unsolved forever, Quinn. Nothing does."

He appreciated the thought. It wasn't in him to give up, but eventually he was going to have to. He had sought the truth for so long, but the deadline he had set for himself long ago was approaching. He'd have to get on with his life without the justice he needed. It was a terrible thought. He nodded toward Lisa and changed the subject. "Are you staying here tonight?"

"Yes. Craig's covering my pager."

"Thanks."

"Dave's coming over when he gets off work. You want to stay around and keep Lisa company while Dave and I go for a walk?"

"You just want to go flirt with your boyfriend."

"You got it."

"I'm glad you found him." He felt more than a minor protective interest in who Kate had in her life. Their friendship had happened more by accident than planning. The first few meals had been informal and spur of the moment—sharing a sandwich while she sat through a day-long negotiation, buying her a hot dog at a ball game, helping her haul a new couch into her apartment and sitting on the living room floor sharing a pizza before they returned the moving truck.

Quinn had found Kate to be a great friend. He'd started worrying about her like her brother Marcus did, wondering what risks she was taking in her job. It had taken only a few months of spending time with her to know it mattered to him that she eventually find the right guy to share her life with.

He'd been relieved when Dave came on the scene. The FBI agent was a guy who had already proven he'd do what it took to protect her.

"He's a good man." She ruffled the back of his hair. "Something like you."

"I'll stick around."

She glanced at her sister. "Lisa could do worse."

He took back his glass, found Kate had left him the ice, and smiled. "Don't you start. She can make up her own mind." He wanted another chance with Lisa. He was determined to get past the last eight days and back on plan. He still owed her dinner and he was determined to get an opportunity to deliver on it.

Five

Quinn, you don't need to stay."

"Quit protesting; I'm not going anywhere." He turned on a table lamp and then reached back and killed the overhead light, having seen Lisa rub her forehead more than once, a telltale sign that she had a growing headache. The rest of the O'Malleys had left a short time ago; Kate and Dave were catching a private moment together watching the moon come up.

"Even if I said I was tired and I want you to go back to the hotel?"

"You've had two naps today, you're hurting because the painkiller is wearing off, and you're feeling sorry for yourself. So which do you want first? Something for the pain or a distraction?"

She frowned over at him. "I'm home; I'm fine. And you don't listen."

She wanted a fight; he smiled slightly and refused to give her one. "No, I don't."

"I wish you'd quit feeling sorry for me…or guilty."

He got to his feet. "Give me a break. You nearly got yourself killed a few feet away from me. I'm allowed." He stopped in front of her and held out both hands. "Come on. You've been sitting for an hour. If you don't get up and move, your back will lock up."

She frowned as she looked at his hands, thinking about it. He laughed and wiggled his fingers. "Come on."

Her hands slid into his and he felt how cold they were. He reassuringly grasped her hands, careful how he held her injured one, and pulled her up. As soon as she was steady, she removed her hands from his and pressed one against her left ribs.

"Aches?"

"Every time I breathe," she admitted. "Want to do me a favor?"

"If it's not going to get me into trouble with one of your brothers."

She tipped her head and smiled at him. He was a goner for that smile even if she didn't know it. "What do you need? Maybe we can just not tell them."

"I've been craving a milkshake. Kate won't tell."

Not exactly what her doctor had in mind. And she needed something hot.

"It's practically all milk," she offered.

"I don't suppose it will kill you."

"Fix it while I peek in on my pets?"

He laughed. "Sure. Go on."

"Thanks."

"You're welcome," he replied dryly. "Go."

He watched her walk slowly down the hall and enter the spare bedroom she had turned into a home for all the living things she collected. He shook his head. She was a walking contradiction—annoyed at him one minute, flashing that smile the next.

He went through the dining room to the kitchen and opened the freezer. Vanilla or chocolate? He thought about asking, then decided he might as well make his favorite. He opened the chocolate ice cream.

He fixed two milkshakes, cleaned up the counter, then dug around in the drawers for two straws. He carried the glasses with him to find Lisa. She already had a habit of forgetting to eat when she worked, and the last several days had been little more than IVs; the calories would do her good.

Quinn stopped at the doorway, watching her. She was in her element with things that crawled and swam.

The mice were awake, three adorable white and one sleek brown tumbling over the hollow climbing blocks she'd carved. Sliding aside the mesh top of the cage, Lisa took a moment to reach inside and greet them. They scampered across her palm and tickled her fingers. She refilled their water, then closed the cage lid.

"Where did you find the brown one?"

"A neighbor's pet; Scott was moving and couldn't take it with him."

She opened the jar of fish food flakes for the guppies she was raising. He had taken the time yesterday to clean the tank, change the filter, and replace the evaporated water. With close to two dozen baby guppies swimming among the upper leaves of the plants it had been an experience. He didn't think he'd accidentally killed more than a couple. As she closed the cover the fish began to grab the flakes, shaking off smaller pieces.

"Hi, Truebody." Lisa tapped on the glass of the second fish tank. The praying mantis moved up the twig it clung to toward the light. She lingered over the third large tank, talking to the iguana. Oscar was one of her favorites.

In the next cage a hamster pushed its way out of a burrow of shredded white paper. "Baby, what have they been feeding you?" The hamster had grown fat in the last ten days—very fat.

"Kate thinks she's pregnant."

"Really? Oh that will be so cool. I hope she has several." She tilted her head to look at him. "You know, you could do with a pet…"

He laughed. "On a ranch the size of mine, it has to be able to fend for itself."

"Nothing smaller than a breadbasket?"

"Not unless it can outrun a wolf."

The parrot whistled, stalking back and forth. "I haven't forgotten you, Iris," Lisa reassured. She opened the cage door and offered her hand. The bird stepped up gracefully and ducked its head as Lisa brought her out of the cage. "Did you miss me?"

The bird shook her head and fluffed her feathers.

"Yes, you did, I recognize that huff." She stroked the bird's chest and it preened and cooed back at her.

"A dangerous pet to have, given your others."

"I know. But we've got an understanding, don't we, girl? She got loose at the pet store and sort of chose me. Landed right on my shoulder."

He didn't miss the way her voice softened at that statement.

She put Iris back in her cage and folded down the cover to tuck the bird in for the night. "It looks like everyone lived through my absence."

"We tried, although I'm glad you said the grade school had taken the mole."

"Charlie was adorable."

"If you say so." He held out the second glass he carried. "One milkshake."

"Thanks." She took it, sampled it, and nodded her appreciation. "Good."

Sidney was awake and ringing the small bell attached to the top of his cage. Lisa knelt down, picked up one of the empty paper towel tubes stacked on the supply shelf, and offered it to him. The ferret stood on his back legs to grasp it and haul it back into his cage. He proceeded to push his head inside and wiggle his body through it, chattering in a high pitch as he rolled. He reappeared, grabbed it with his feet, and tumbled it around.

"He loves those things."

"Almost as much as he does things he can chase." She got to her feet. "I appreciate the time you and Kate took."

"We didn't mind. Although I'm pretty sure Kate drowned your plants."

She laughed, then groaned at the pain it caused. "It wouldn't be the first time. I need to sit down." She waved him back toward the living room. "You never did tell me what they discovered at the house."

He shortened his stride to match her slow walk, glad to see her balance was improving. "The major beam under the bedroom had cracked. When it gave way, the flooring and hallway folded and collapsed into the den. Unfortunately, you were in the hallway at the time."

"It wasn't somewhere I stepped?"

"No."

"Well at least that's nice to know." She gestured with her glass to the briefcase by the door. "Is the Hampton file Jack brought over in there?"

"Lisa."

"I want to see it, just for a minute."

He opened her briefcase and got the case file. They had autopsied the burned cat Walter Hampton had gone to retrieve. He waited until she had eased herself down on the couch. "You don't need to do this now."

"Quinn."

He reluctantly handed her the folder. She flipped through to read the lab results. He already knew them. He was prepared for the disquiet in her eyes when she finally looked over at him.

"The cat showed no signs of a sleeping pill."

"No."

"I got hurt for nothing," she said softly.

"The toxicology was run several days after the fact. It was a stretch to consider something would be found."

She shook her head. "The pill wouldn't have had time to entirely dissolve, and even crushed it would have been so concentrated it would have still been there in measurable doses, fire or not." She dropped the folder and rubbed her eyes. "I went out in the field on another of my hunches, determined to check the scene, and got myself hurt. It wouldn't be funny if this weren't what...the fifth time?"

He perched on the arm of the couch. "You wouldn't have been doing your job if you didn't pursue what was a logical question. And there's still an open question of why the cat didn't escape the room."

"As Jack says—pets die in fires. There's not enough to say it was a suicide. In a way I'm glad I was wrong; it's awful to put a family through that."

She rested her head back against the sofa, studying him. "I haven't told you thanks for what you did. I knew when I saw your face that it was pretty bad. I'm sorry; I should have told you thanks ages ago."

His hand tightened on the glass he held so he wouldn't reach out and rub her slight frown away. "You're welcome."

"I would wake up sometimes late at night and see you there beside the hospital bed praying."

He stilled. "Did you?" He'd been praying all right, scared to death the infection would spread, that the antibiotics wouldn't work, that he'd lose someone more precious to him than any lady he could remember.

"That was...nice of you."

"It's okay, Lisa. I know you don't believe." He'd watched her for years, putting together pieces and glimpses of her past, trying to understand why she appeared so indifferent when the topic of faith was mentioned. She was normally so curious about every subject under discussion. It frustrated him because he wanted to change it but couldn't figure out how.

"I think it helped."

She seemed bothered by that more than pleased, and his eyes sharpened as he searched her face, absorbing that impression, testing it. She shouldn't be reacting that way. "Well I had a vested interest," he said lightly. "Not having you around to bug me would have been a bummer."

"No, I mean it. The pain would be bad, I'd wake up and see you praying, then it would ease away before I could page a nurse for more pain medication."

"You're serious."

"Yes, I am. I nearly told Jennifer."

He reached over and wiped away a tear as it slipped from the corner of her eye and down her cheek. "Tell her. And I'll keep praying for her." It was killing him to have Jennifer sick; he could only imagine what facing that was doing to Lisa.

"Thanks." She wiped away the other threatening tears and gave a rueful smile.

He wished she believed. Jennifer did, Dave and Kate, Marcus. It brought a strength and a peace and certain knowledge of the Resurrection. Lisa didn't have that hope, and she so desperately needed it.

He'd survived the death of his father because of his faith. Without that hope… But the solution was not going to be as simple as he had thought, as simple as convincing her to come to church with them and hear the truth. There was ancient hurt there, buried deep in those blue eyes he had thought he understood.

"Did I hear you've got a scrapbook?" he asked to help her out.

"A few of them."

"Jen could use one for all the cards and gift notes she's receiving from friends and former patients. I thought of it when I saw her hospital room."

"That's a great idea."

"She'll be out of the hospital soon. She's headed toward a remission." He had to keep believing that, for Lisa's sake as much as his own. He didn't want her to have to bear the loss of Jennifer, would do anything to protect her from that if he could.

"Maybe," she said, but it was filled with doubt. She set aside her glass, and her expression lightened, became almost humorous, as she studied him. "You look exhausted."

"I always look tired," he replied, amused at the doctor's tone she reverted to on occasion with him. "Trying to sleep in the city is like sleeping in a bright noise factory."

She laughed, groaned, then frowned at him for causing it. "Do me one more favor. Go back to your hotel, dig out a bed, and sleep for twelve hours. You really do look like one of the walking dead."

"You're sure?"

"Yes."

"I'll call it a night if you promise me you won't even think about going anywhere tomorrow. If you won't give yourself a week at home, at least make it a few days before you go back to the office."

"I can sit there as well as here."

"I'm serious. It's too early. You'll just give yourself a relapse."

"I already promised Marcus I'd stay home tomorrow, make it a half day Wednesday."

"Good enough."

The patio door slid open and Dave and Kate rejoined them, Kate laughing as she tried to untangle herself from Dave's arms. "Lisa, one of your neighbors has a dog that's baying at the moon."

"That's Wilfred. He's English."

"Who, the neighbor or the dog?" Kate asked, dissolving into a fit of giggles as Dave scooped her up. "Would you put me down?"

"Not till you admit I was right."

"Lisa, tell him bats don't fly this far north. He swears one was going to land in my hair, and he had to protect me."

"Actually…" Lisa looked at Dave to get the right answer, "they do occasionally. The brown wedge-wing bat is native to Ohio and does come into Illinois."

Dave grinned over at her, then looked back at Kate. "See?"

"Oh, you—"

He stole a kiss and set her down. "I'd better get going. Lisa, it's a delight to have you home."

"Thanks, Dave."

"I'll walk out with you," Quinn decided, retrieving his hat. He didn't want to leave, but as much as he'd like to take advantage of Lisa's lowered guard and risk asking a few questions, a sense of fairness wouldn't let him do it. "Lisa—" what he would've liked to say she wasn't ready yet to hear—"take care. I'll see you later."

"Good night, Quinn."

He turned the lock on the front doorknob. "Kate?"

"I'll get the dead bolt."

He nodded his thanks and stepped out with Dave.

"A nice night," Dave commented, pulling out his keys.

"Beautiful," Quinn agreed, looking up at the full moon.

"Heading back to your hotel? Or do you want to join us down at the gym?"

The late night basketball games were a tradition when the O'Malleys were in the same city. It was a good way to deal with the stress. "Another time."

"If you change your mind, we've got the court till eleven."

Quinn unlocked the door to his rental car. What he would really like was a four-hour horseback ride checking fence line—a chance to think, let a week of stress bleed off, and figure out what to do next.

He'd pass on the basketball game; the O'Malleys were too perceptive. Marcus and Kate already knew where his interests lay, and the others would figure it out. The last thing he needed was Lisa feeling pressure from her family.

He started the car, turned on the lights, and waited for Dave to pull out. Quinn held up a hand in farewell as the car lights crossed his back window.

Dave turned left at the thoroughfare and Quinn turned right. He was staying at the Radisson Hotel downtown near the regional marshals' office. To break the absolute silence in the car, he turned on the radio, changed it to FM, and found a country station. As he glanced back up he saw headlights flash in his rearview mirror. Someone else was leaving the subdivision.

Traffic was light for a Monday evening, and out of habit he kept half his attention on the traffic behind him.

He needed gas and a newspaper. He turned off at Route 43 and pulled into a new gas and convenience store at the corner of Sherman and Waukegan. All the pumps were free and he pulled to a stop at the first. Ten minutes later, having paid for the gas and the newspaper, he walked back to his car.

As he pulled back onto the road, a dark green Plymouth pulled out from the graphics art printing business across the street. It pulled across to his lane, two cars behind.

Quinn adjusted the rearview mirror, his eyes narrowing. Once was something to note, twice unusual, three times—he reached for his cellular phone. He entered his partner's pager number, then punched in an added code unique to him. Interrupting a basketball game…

His phone rang back moments later. "Hey, Quinn, coming to the game?" Marcus was breathing hard. "Adam and I have got Stephen and Jack on the ropes. We could use your awesome defense in center."

"I've got a tail."

"Where are you?" Marcus asked, his voice instantly turning serious.

"Waukegan Road, just passing the railroad tracks. I'll be at Willow soon. I'm going to divert north on Sunset. See if you can pick him up."

"Same dark green Plymouth?"

"Hanging two back." Quinn removed his Glock and slid it under the newspaper on the seat beside him. There was a sense of cold anger settling inside. "I think he tagged me at Lisa's subdivision."

"We're moving. Stay on the phone."

When Quinn had left after a visit to the bookstore where Amy Ireland Nugan had held her signing, he had noticed the Plymouth behind him. It had been there again three days ago across from the hospital.

Lisa's subdivision.

He'd just put her in danger. "Marcus, get someone on a phone to Kate, tell her to be on her guard. Just don't let Lisa know."

"Dave just walked in, he's already calling."

Quinn turned north on Sunset and watched as the Plymouth also turned, now directly behind him. The front license plate was gone. Looking back into the car headlights there was no way to identify the driver; he couldn't tell if it was a man or woman, and he had learned the hard way not to assume.

The tail was making no attempt to keep back at a safe distance. "I'm coming up on Route 68."

"Don't risk the Edens, head east into Glencoe and come south on Green Bay Road. There'll be enough traffic we should be able to get near him. Dave and I will try to get beside and behind him."

"I'm heading for Green Bay."

Quinn wanted to slam on his brakes and catch the driver by surprise; he forced himself to be patient and wait on backup. Why a tail in Chicago? Why across from the hospital? There were always men being released from prison who would be more than happy to make trouble for him, but there had been no release bulletins mentioning cases from here.

Had something in Lincoln's investigation caught someone's attention? He didn't see what it could be. And if Lincoln had picked up a tail, he would have mentioned it.

"We're on Green Bay, coming up on Tower Road," Marcus said. "Where are you?"

"Turning on Green Bay…now," Quinn replied, using the brief moment in the turn under the streetlights to try and see the driver of the other car.

The Plymouth suddenly accelerated through the intersection and turned north.

"He broke off! He's heading north on Green Bay."

Quinn swiveled around to try and catch the license plate. "I've lost him." Traffic was too heavy to immediately U-turn.

"We're pushing to catch him."

"He'll likely be heading to the Edens."

"Dave's diverting now. I'll keep coming up Green Bay."

Quinn pulled into Tudor Court and turned back north.

They spent the next twenty minutes with the three cars crisscrossing the area looking for the Plymouth.

"Marcus, I'll meet you at the 7-Eleven on Route 68 and Pfingsten," Quinn finally called, ending the search.

"Two minutes."

Quinn parked and shut off the car but left the radio on. "Lord, what now?" he asked, seeking wisdom he didn't have. The tension was just beginning to drain away. It wasn't the danger of the threat so much as the unknown of what he was dealing with, the realization Lisa had been brought into its periphery.

He hated his job at times. It was rare to get so angry, but fatigue and frustration were combining. "Lord, I'm tired of dealing with tails and uncooperative witnesses and threats that come veiled and not so veiled. How long are You going to leave me chasing leads that go nowhere?"

His future should have been clear. Instead, he felt like he was having to live life one day at a time, constantly reacting. He had to figure out what had happened to Amy and his father. He desperately needed the closure.

"I want to go back to ranching full time, Lord." He rarely let himself admit how much internal pressure had developed. He had hoped getting back to the ranch for a month during his vacation would help ease that pressure and push off the decision for a few more months.

He returned the Glock to its holster with a sigh.

He really didn't need this happening tonight. A year ago getting tailed would have been just one more thing in life to roll with.

Tonight—Quinn picked up his hat and rolled the brim in callous hands. He was going home. He was letting go. Even if it meant leaving the man who had killed his father free.

The sadness of that was overwhelming. But it was time.

Lisa. Quinn's hand tightened around the rough fabric as he frowned. She was hurt. She was going to have Kate and Marcus—for all the right reasons—pushing her out of her comfort zone. She struck him as needing a friend. And he was lousy at walking away in those circumstances.

She wouldn't be thrilled if he stuck around; he would feel guilty if he left. "Lord, I didn't need this either," Quinn muttered, checking the mirror as car headlights swept across the window. The car turned in the opposite direction; it wasn't Marcus.

He'd been a Christian a long time, but some of his friends were not Christians. It was a dichotomy he had accepted over the years as the place God had put him. He couldn't be a light among a sea of candles. It wasn't a comfortable place to rest, constantly having to tug a dark world toward God while not getting sidetracked by it.

He was forty-four. The days he wanted to hang around entirely with guys were long gone. If he had to take extra care in how he was friends with a woman, then he would find and watch that line, make that extra effort. Having friends in L.A. he could call when he was in town, someone in Dallas, someone in Chicago—they made it possible to accept the other drawbacks that came with a profession that sent him around the country.

And if over the years he'd bought more than a few wedding gifts— well at least he had the good sense to choose wonderful ladies to be his friends.

Quinn wasn't going to get romantically involved with someone he couldn't marry—he'd already had a lifetime of dreams not coming true. He wasn't about to let himself head down a road that before he took the first step he knew would not lead anywhere. Life was about choices, the toughest ones involving where he put his time.

During the last year Jennifer had come to believe, then Kate and Marcus. There was hope for Lisa. Distant, but there. She would be his friend either way—

Car headlights reflected across the mirror and this time the car pulled into the parking lot.

Marcus pulled into the parking space beside him and got out of his car to circle to the passenger side, leaning against the side of it. Quinn rolled down his window. Marcus crossed his arms across his chest as he thought about the situation, then looked over at Quinn. "Someone looking for you? Three times—he's tracking your movements. Why?"

"Your guess is as good as mine. If he was looking for a chance to deliver a message, he's already had it. And if he's watching for someone else—well he's not a professional. Have you noticed someone following you?"

"No."

"Just me. Wonderful. I didn't exactly advertise I was coming to Chicago."

"Amy Ireland?"

"Maybe, but why? It was a dead end. She's Canadian, not even the person I was looking for."

"You made the newscast when the house collapsed and Lisa was airlifted to Mercy General. Someone saw you were in town."

"It makes about as much sense as anything."

"Watch your back in the morning, and check the car before you turn the key. We'll run the release sheets in the morning, see who's out there with a grudge."

"Sorry I interrupted the game."

Marcus smiled. "Don't be. Jack looked relieved. I'll shadow you back to the hotel."

"Lisa?"

"Dave was going to swing back by. Relax. If trouble did come calling, no one would get past Kate."

"True. Still—" Quinn started the car. If it weren't for the fact he'd possibly be bringing danger back to her subdivision, he'd go watch Lisa's house for the night.

Marcus pushed away from his car. "Next time, back up into him. A car accident would be appropriate in the circumstances."

"Believe me, I was tempted."

Quinn headed back to the hotel, Marcus driving a few cars behind. Quinn slowed to pull into the hotel parking garage and Marcus lifted a hand in farewell and pulled past him. Quinn hesitated, then started circling toward the top floor. He'd seen the results of more than one car bombing in his lifetime. If he missed something during the check in the morning, better to blow up the roof than the basement.

Six

What time is it out there?"

Lisa reluctantly admitted the truth. "Four A.M."

Jennifer chuckled softly. "I'll send you some of my dawn. It's gorgeous. My hospital room faces east. And you were prescribed sleeping pills for a reason. Take them next time."

Lisa had lain awake long enough the shadows in the bedroom had become furniture and clutter, the open sliding doors to her closet creating the only cave of blackness left undeciphered. This Wednesday, her second morning back home, was starting much as her first: The sleep she wanted refused to come. If she tried to get up she'd wake Kate, who was sleeping in the second spare room down the hall. So she had lain here letting one sister sleep, thinking about another, until the clock finally made it unseemly early only on the East Coast.

"The last guy I saw who took sleeping pills burned alive in a fire." She didn't mean to be morbid, but Jennifer was the one person in the family who not only understood but also expected to hear the truth about what was going on.

"Doozy of a nightmare?"

"In spades." Lisa shifted uncomfortably, the two bandages hurting and the pressure on her back reigniting the sensation of fire inside her chest. "The scars are a mess. I took a shower for the first time last night; the stitches look like they were done by a guy with a fishhook, and those are just the ones I can see in the front. I don't even want to think about my back. I do a better job on a cadaver after an autopsy than he did on me."

"He was in a bit of a hurry. You were bleeding to death on him."

"Well, I hate to think what he'd have done if he had to crack my chest and go after something vital. I've already got enough displaced ribs barking at me."

"Lizzy, I saw a faxed copy of the chart. That bar hit practically everything vital there is inside you. Go swallow another painkiller."

"I already did. They make me dopey."

"The scars will heal, the bright redness will fade."

"I'm complaining." She didn't complain, not normally. She hated feeling this way.

"You're allowed." The empathy traveled a thousand miles. Lisa knew Jen was hurting too; the radiation pellets they had inserted to deal with the cancer around her spine were being removed a few at a time this week, lest they so decay the vertebra in her spine it collapsed.

"How's Quinn?"

Lisa groaned. "Sticking like a shadow."

Jen laughed. "I really like that guy."

"He's okay."

"Uh-huh. If you like handsome, sweet, thoughtful, and tough."

"Try strong-willed, stubborn…" The normal list that came so easily to mind petered off; it was habit now more than meant.

"You like him," Jen said softly.

"Yeah. Some."

The silence stretched, that of old friends and open hearts.

"Lizzy, I promise the right guy won't mind the scars."

"Tell me again why we are up at the crack of dawn?"

"I want to go to work."

Kate paused in pulling on her tennis shoes. "That's what I thought you said. I think you need to see another doctor. One to look at your head."

"I'm not spending another day stuck here bored out of my mind," Lisa replied, not feeling up to facing another sister with the truth. Kate was just annoyed because she never liked mornings; she'd get over it.

Dave had come over again last night. She'd heard Kate and Dave whispering, then heard the TV in the living room come on as they found a late movie to watch. She hadn't heard Kate turn in until well after 1 A.M. "If you want me to drive myself—"

"No. I'll take you. But couldn't you wait for something like the actual sunrise?"

"Not if I'm going to talk to Greg. He gets off at eight, and he's working the triple homicide/suicide from Pilsen. I want in."

Kate pushed fingers through her hair to straighten it, reached for her pager, and clipped it onto her belt. "You could ease back into work, you know, take it slow. Marcus will read you the riot act if you dive back in and overdo it."

Kate was right, but she wasn't going to let it change her plans. "How would you feel if someone sidelined you for part of a month?"

"Okay. Valid point. But I'm not leaving without coffee."

Shifting the cane to her other hand, Lisa turned toward the bedroom door and glanced back to grin at Kate. "It's already made. You can carry mine to the car for me."

Her sister laughed. "Head toward the car. I'll catch up."

Lisa took her at her word and walked down the hall, stopping in the dining room to dump her purse on the table. She pushed her keys into her pocket along with her staff ID, a credit card, and twenty dollars. She'd do without something to carry today.

Walking down the sloped driveway with caution, she unlocked the passenger door and slid her cane in the back, then eased herself into the car. She gingerly turned, wishing she had thought to bring out a pillow for her back. As the muscles stretched, she gritted her teeth at the pain. She stopped moving and it eased off.

Kate joined her, carrying two blue thermal travel mugs, the bases of the cups designed for the car's cup holders.

Lisa accepted hers with a thanks and wisely stayed silent as Kate got settled and started the car. Lisa didn't think her sister would appreciate an observation on how pretty the sunrise was this morning. Its beauty was hiding the coming reality; the day was predicted to be unseasonably warm, in the nineties with high humidity. It meant there would be several heat deaths today.

Kate slowed at a stop sign in the subdivision.

"Stop, Kate. That's Walter Hampton." Lisa recognized the white-and-blue truck of Nakomi Nurseries. "I want to say thanks for the flowers and the visit."

"Lisa."

"Stop."

Kate pulled to the side of the road.

The house on the corner had sold recently to a young couple from San Diego; they had moved in last month. There were several trees on a flatbed truck along with several bushes and rolls of sod. Walter was working on digging out part of a prior rock garden along with three other workers. They were obviously trying to get the most physical part of the work done and the plants in the ground before the heat of the day arrived. Lisa wasn't that surprised to see Walter out working with one of his crews; he had struck her as more of a doer than an office manager.

Lisa unbuckled her seat belt and carefully reversed her movements to get out of the car.

Walter had seen her; he set down his shovel to walk down the yard. They met halfway. "Miss O'Malley." His smile was genuinely pleased.

"It's good to see you, Walter."

"You're looking much better on your feet."

"I'm recovering fine. How's your wrist?" Walter had been walking back to the house when the beam collapsed, had helped Quinn dig her out.

He flexed it. "Almost good as new."

"I wanted to say thanks for the flowers. They were lovely. And numerous." He had sent a bouquet every day.

"I had a greenhouse full just waiting to brighten your day."

"They were appreciated. How is your family?"

"My brother Christopher is having a rough time of it, and my aunt Laura is now complaining that Egan doesn't visit her anymore. Personally, it feels good to be back at work. We're coping in our unique ways."

"I'm returning to work myself."

"I'm glad for you."

She looked over the scope of what he was undertaking, impressed. "The yard will look wonderful when it's complete."

"I hope so. It's a vision in my head at the moment; we'll see if I can make it appear."

"It looks like you got an early start."

"In this business, 4 to 6 A.M. is best; you don't want to be stuck in traffic with a couple ten-foot white birch trees." He nodded toward the car. "Heading downtown? There's construction on the Edens south of Winnetka today."

"One of the reasons for my early start."

"You'd best be heading that way then." He wiped the dirt from his hands on his jeans. "Can I give you a hand back to the car? The ground's a bit unlevel."

"I wouldn't turn one down. The cane makes me feel a bit old before my time." She walked back with him.

Lisa settled back in the car and introduced her sister. Walter nodded a greeting across to her. A final good-bye, and they pulled back onto the road. "Has that case closed?" Kate asked.

"Yes."

"It looks like the nursery does a good job, though I'm surprised to see them in your neighborhood."

"You should have seen the size of the Nakomi Nursery grounds, they must do business around the entire Chicagoland area. Walter strikes me as a hard-working guy who loves the business he's in. Expanding it would be the natural thing to do."

"For someone you've met three times, you've got a definite opinion of him."

"The flowers he sent from his greenhouses were picked on the optimal day to last as long as possible in a vase, and did you notice the patch of yard they were getting ready to sod? Someone took the time and care to leave a twelve-inch patch of grass around a wild violet in an area otherwise stripped and prepped for the sod. I have a feeling that was the work of the boss." Lisa bet the flower would be taken home and potted at the end of the day. It showed the business was more than just a job.

She reached for her coffee and wondered if she had the endurance for a half day at work. She hoped she did. She was pushing it to return to work this early, but it was the one place she could lose herself and put the accident behind her. She needed her life back.

"Have you thought any more about what we were talking about last night?"

Kate was watching the road. There was nothing offhand about the question even though Kate's body language was trying to convey that impression.

Kate had been her usual direct self last night, wanting to talk about the Bible passage in John she had been reading. Half the family had become Christians in the last three months—Jennifer, Kate, Marcus—and it was making for some sincere, heartfelt, but awkward family conversations.

Kate was passionate about her new faith. Excited. Like most new Christians, she was trying to convince everyone around her to believe too. Lisa didn't have to wonder what motivated her actions. Kate cared. Lisa couldn't fault her for that. But she wasn't interested.

In another month the excitement would fade, the subject would get dropped.

In a family with few secrets, there were still some things about her life before Trevor House that Lisa had kept private.

During her years in various foster homes she had attended Lutheran, Catholic, Presbyterian, and Baptist churches. As a child she had been exposed to religion more than most of them. A typical Sunday school teacher did not expect to get grilled on the various points of theology by a fourth grader.

They had all tried to answer her, surprised by her questions and the depth of what she wanted to know. They had all given good answers based upon what their denominations taught. Lisa's problem had been that while the answers were similar, they weren't the same.

When she had probed to ask why, each said the other perspectives were well-meaning but wrong. Trying to end the confusion had only increased it. Even as a child she had hated feeling like she was being humored. And over the years, adults tended to dismiss the confusion as just a fact of life…she had never been able to accept that.

Kate, Jennifer, and Marcus becoming active in a church hadn't been that big a deal before the accident. Lisa had listened and watched the three of them, respecting the change yet keeping her distance from the topic.

Since nearly getting killed, there was a conspiracy ongoing among the three of them to get her to believe too, and she was getting tired of it. About the only one who hadn't been pushing the subject of religion recently was Quinn. He believed, but it was different when she was with him. The few times the subject of religion had come up it hadn't felt like she had to be defensive. She frowned slightly at that thought and forced her attention back to Kate. "No, I can't say I've thought about it."

"It's important."

"I know it's important to you. And I'm happy that you've found something you and Dave can share. But it doesn't mean I have to share it too."

"Why are you so absolute in not talking about what the Bible says?"

Lisa didn't want to have this conversation. She didn't want to pit herself against Kate, against Marcus…against Jennifer. A conversation with Quinn was one thing, but family…

She understood like no one else in the family what it meant to die, to return to dust. The process began when the last breath was taken, and while she had never said as much to Kate, she knew what the Gospels, the first four books in the New Testament, said. Mark and Luke both said Jesus breathed His last; Matthew and John said Jesus gave up His spirit.

Jesus had hung on a cross for hours and died. The Bible said that explicitly. And if that was true, she knew what had happened to Him five minutes later, an hour later, three hours later, a day later. She didn't know the exact entomology of which flies lived in Palestine, but they would be cousins of those she understood very well from here. She knew the basics of Jerusalem two thousand years ago at the time of Passover: crowds, dust, heat—and flies. There would be no body left to resurrect three days later, not a body recognizable as the man Jesus.

Maybe if the Bible tried to argue He died for a few minutes, even an hour…but days—

Lisa knew from bitter experience that life ended forever with that last breath.

The old memory returned, a sharp stab, coming back in color and texture and terror. Lisa raised a shaky hand to adjust her shirt neckline. She silently cursed as she tried to shove the memory back into the past and get that floating dead face out of her mind. She was normally so careful to skirt everything that might brush against the memory, and instead she'd walked herself right into it.

She took deep breaths, slowly calming down. She'd had enough of this conversation. Kate was not one who did subtle, not unless it was on the job where she would willingly make small talk for hours if it was necessary to negotiate a peaceful conclusion to a dangerous situation.

"People don't rise from the dead," Lisa replied bluntly, knowing it would end the conversation for now. And just to make sure it stayed ended, she reached down and turned on the radio.

"It's been abysmal without you around, Lisa."

Her boss rose to greet her with a welcoming smile. Lisa walked slowly into his office, returning the smile. Ben Wilcott was in his late fifties, had overseen the state crime lab for the last eleven years. "Thanks, Ben. I almost got caught up on my reading thanks to your contributions—though I think the doctors were a little startled to see copies of the NIJ Journals and FSA Bulletins on the bedside table."

"I know how hard it is to go cold turkey from work, and I'd like your opinion on those National Institute of Justice proposed protocols."

"I took notes," Lisa replied, having anticipated the request. "And the Forensic Science Academy has another seminar scheduled on fiber collection and analysis. I think it would be a good idea to send Kim."

"I'll get it arranged. Can I get you something? Coffee? A soft drink?"

She'd worked for him too long not to know when something was coming that she wasn't going to want to hear. "I'd love something cold."

He brought her back a cold soda and one for himself, then settled in the chair beside her rather than behind the desk. "Classic looking cane."

Lisa spun its white ivory handle and burnished mahogany wood. "Stephen's contribution."

"I was surprised the doctors okayed you coming back this soon, even for desk duty."

She smiled. "They were afraid I meant it when I said I'd go sailing if they insisted I take a vacation. Seriously, I'm looking forward to being back."

"Gloria was asking about you."

She sipped at the soda, wondering where this was heading. Ben was walking one of the wooden nickels his granddaughter had given him through his fingers, and he only did that when he was thinking about something during a meeting unrelated to the topic at hand or when he was waiting for the right time to mention some news. "Is Gloria here today? I was surprised not to see her at her desk outside your office."

"Funding came through to move the police file archives into the new cold storage warehouse. She's in her element cataloging and organizing the move; making it happen has been her personal crusade."

"That's wonderful news. That funding has been held up for, what? Two years? How'd you ever get it to happen?"

"Actually, that's what I want to talk to you about."

She lowered her drink, her smile flickering.

"The new police commissioner wants a reexamination of all unsolved murders over five years old in light of new forensic techniques. I told him I'd do it…"

"…if you got funding to combine the archives."

"Exactly."

She could see a rushing train coming her way. "Ben, one of the lab guys, Peter—"

"I need more than a good technician. You spend a good portion of your days out at the crime scenes, and you've worked directly with cops, you can interpret the case notes. You're on desk duty for the next several weeks anyway, and you know better than anyone what evidence is worth the time to analyze."

"Don't do this to me."

"Sorry, it's done." He gave her a sympathetic smile. "Don't worry, it's not Siberia. And I'll owe you one when it's done."

Bribery still worked. She considered him and wondered how hard she could push it. "A new mass spectrometer?"

"I'll see what I can work into next year's budget."

Whoa. She should have thought larger; that had been a fast yes. He was serious enough about this she might have been able to wrangle another technician slot.

"You'll do it?"

She rubbed her eyes, hating this proposition with a passion, remembering her last visit to the police archives. The files were in poor shape, only a fraction of the records had been computerized, most cases had to be located from incomplete and fading handwritten indexes. And the older the case, the more disorganized the evidence. She owed Ben more than one favor, but still… "You're asking for a miracle. Those cases are cold for a reason."

"Anything you need, ask."

"A vacation is sounding better all the time—"

He laughed and got to his feet. "Thank you, Lisa. I knew I could count on you." He offered his hand to help her up.

She accepted, already dreading the next few weeks. She was getting exiled, graciously, but exiled.

"I took the liberty…you'll need a place to work. There is a lot of material." Ben's executive assistant, Gloria Fraim, pushed open the door to the task force room. Basically, it was one large open room located one floor below the laboratories. It could be configured to suit the needs of the particular situation from a large disaster to a multiagency case.

A series of worktables, a whiteboard, and a light table had been moved in. Metal shelves on rollers lined the inner wall; they were stacked with black boxes two deep. The boxes were worn and sagging, the writing on the ends barely visible because the black ink had faded.

Lisa rubbed her finger in the dust on one of the box lids. This case hadn't been worked in years. She scanned the row of boxes. "These are all the cases?"

"Sorry, only about half. We've been setting aside the unsolved murder cases as we find them." Gloria walked over to the other side of the room and pulled the blinds up on the wall of windows, letting in the sunlight. "I asked for you."

"Did you?" Lisa smiled; she should have guessed. "I don't know if I should thank you."

"Before this is over you will," Gloria promised. "You've always enjoyed a challenge. Some of these cases that haven't been solved will break your heart."

"What shape are the files in?"

"Photograph film is brittle, paper yellowing. About what I would expect. Stop by the cold storage records room in the next few days and take a look at the entire project. It's quite impressive. We're bringing over the archive files in batches, transferring the most vulnerable of the records to CD-ROM, using charcoal to deal with the odor and moisture in the paper files, indexing and computerizing the cases records."

"Massive doesn't begin to describe that project."

"We'll get it done on time, although I'm afraid you'll have to deal with the murder cases in their original shape from the police archives. We'd need to hold them up several weeks to take them through the charcoal process."

"I'll talk to Henry about the ventilation and get some air filters in here before I start opening decades worth of history. It won't be a problem."

"Is there anything else I can arrange to be brought in for you?"

Lisa looked around the room that would be her home for the next few weeks. It had the essentials: quiet and space. She smiled. "You know me, Gloria. I'm sure I'll collect things as I need them. I've just got a larger office to fill up with my toys."

They shared a laugh, for they were both pack rats. Gloria a neat packrat who knew where everything could be found; Lisa was more one to pile and make it fit. "I could use a good assistant to help get these case files entered in the NIJ database."

"Diane Peller. She's already begun working on it."

Lisa nodded. Diane was good.

"We've changed the locks on the room; you'll hold the only key."

"Thanks." It would save her having to move the files and evidence she was working on to a vault every night. "Get the log and let's review the inventory here. I'll sign off and take over chain of evidence responsibility."

Janelle Nellis, dead at age forty-two, found murdered in her garage. The case was fourteen years old. Lisa held the X-ray film up to the sunlight coming in the windows. Shot in the back from close range, one bullet hitting her left lung, the other nicking her heart. The ballistics report said it had been a .22.

Lisa sneezed and gasped as pain tore through her chest. It eased slowly and she took a cautious breath, wiping her eyes with the back of her hand.

She moved the desktop air filter closer. She had chosen one case at random to look through while she waited for Kate to arrive. After barely half a day, she was exhausted and ready to go home. She had badly misjudged how much energy she would have.

Pushing away the sense of fatigue, she spread out the dozens of crime scene photos on the table. The struggle that had occurred was obvious—part of a storage shelf in the garage had been pulled away from the wall, cardboard boxes were crushed. Janelle had tried to get away from whoever had shot her.

Her body had been found at 7 A.M. by a neighbor. She had last been seen alive at 6 P.M. the evening before leaving work at a deli shop eight blocks from her house.

"Okay, Janelle. What can you tell me?" Lisa started reading the autopsy report. It was an old College of American Pathologists format, and she had to flip through the report and the attached documents to tug out information that on current forms had their own designations. It was strange to realize just how little toxicology had been available fourteen years ago, and the radiograms she had in the medical examiner's packet were faint and minimal in number. Even in a murder case film had been deemed too expensive to do more than the basic X-rays.

Establishing time of death would be the key to solving a murder case like this and it was annoyingly broad in the autopsy report. Sometime between 10 P.M. and 4 A.M.

She frowned at that finding. A death discovered less than twenty-four hours old in an open garage on a summer night: state-of-the-art technology today could pin down time of death to within two hours using entomology evidence, temperature of the body, a careful exam of rigor formation. She read the autopsy report with care, looking for clues she could tease out of the narrative. If the doctor had made detailed notes he may have given her the evidence she needed, not realizing how significant an observation would be years later.

This wouldn't be such a bad assignment if she had chosen it for herself. This lady deserved justice. The more she read, the more interesting the case became. The bullet slugs had been recovered; she had an old evidence tag number. If she were lucky she might still be able to find them in the ballistics vault.

"So this is where you are hiding."

Quinn startled her.

"Welcome to my new office," she replied dryly, closing the file. She had a comfortable chair. She was waffling on her opinion of the rest of the assignment. "You're my ride home?"

"Yes."

Lisa saw Kate's handiwork. "I should have guessed." She gathered up the case photos and autopsy report, then returned everything to the evidence box. "Could you put this box back on the shelves with the others?"

"Sure."

He looked curious as to what she was doing in here but didn't ask. Lisa got to her feet, leaning heavily on the cane until she could straighten.

"Do you need to get anything from your office?"

"No. I'm ready to go."

She locked the doors to the room and pocketed the key. They went down to the lobby and she signed out while Quinn returned his guest ID. He held the outer door open for her.

"So how was the first day back?" he asked as they stepped into the hot afternoon sun. The only relief was the hope of rain; the sky to the west had the heavy dark look of potential thunderstorms.

"An experience." Lisa grasped the handrail, determined to walk down the stairs rather than use the ramp.

"Plan to tell me about it?"

She reached the bottom of the stairs, and they began the slow walk to the parking lot. Quinn's stride was so checked he was barely moving so as not to outdistance her. "I'm stuck in the dust bowl of history. They've got me reviewing cold cases for at least the next month." He indicated his car and opened the passenger door for her. She lowered herself carefully inside. "Thanks."

She leaned her head back and closed her eyes, relaxing into the warmth of the seat. It felt wonderful against her aching back. "This was not the day I envisioned when I left for work this morning."

He pulled into traffic and broke the silence several minutes later. "You going to kick this depression?"

She opened one eye to confirm that smile she heard. He was gorgeous when he smiled. She closed her eyes again. "Eventually. Just let me enjoy the bad mood for a while."

His chuckle warmed her heart. She needed someone who would

accept with lightness what could at times be for her a slow transition away from work.

"Could I interest you in an early dinner?"

She was tempted but accepted reality. "Not today. Just home. I want a nap."

"Another time then."

She forced herself to stir. She'd be asleep if she left her eyes closed for long. "When are you heading back to Montana?"

"You don't want me to stick around?"

It had just been a question, but he had made it something more. Quinn was joking, he had to be, but she wasn't sure. "Quinn—"

"Relax. My flight is Sunday."

She grimaced; she was stumbling over her words again. "You've got a beautiful home, your ranch." She had enjoyed her one visit to his ranch even though it had been under stressful circumstances. That expanse of land gave Quinn roots, something she could admit privately that she envied. He could afford to leave the ranch for his job because he always had it there to return to.

"It's beautiful no matter what the season. Anytime you want to sell that Sinclair, let me know. I've got just the place for it."

It wasn't often she heard envy in his voice. "I picked it up by chance over lunch one day," she said with a slight smile and a small shrug.

"By chance."

"I liked it."

"Remind me to tag along when you window-shop someday."

Early dinner, stick around, tag along someday… He was definitely asking for something that she was hesitant to consider. He'd turn the force of his personality in her direction and she'd end up caring, try to please him, then manage to fail miserably at it.

"What else do you splurge on besides art? And travel? I noticed some interesting reading on your coffee table. Zimbabwe is next?"

"Only if the college anthropology team goes for a dig next year. Otherwise I'm planning to stay stateside for a while."

"Got anything planned?"

"Some serious backpack trekking. Fossil hunting. Caves. Everything I won't be doing for a while. I had tentative plans to go rock climbing next month."

"They're only postponed."

Postponed for months. Somehow she didn't think her back was going to tolerate hefting sixty pounds of tent and gear while she walked for ten days and fifty miles anytime soon.

The air conditioner ruffled her hair, sending tendrils across her face. She used both hands to push it back. She shouldn't have cut it so short; at least when it had been long she'd been able to secure it in a ponytail. Quinn adjusted the vents upward.

"Tell me about this new assignment."

Work—she could handle that topic. "Ben wants me to review the old murder cases to see what new forensic tests can do with the evidence. He's using it as a way to get funding to combine the archive files. I know it needs to be done, but…" She was whining. She shut up.

"You were hoping to get back into the field."

"Crazy, I know, but yes, I was." She bit her lip and looked at him, wondering if he would understand. "I need to. Does that make sense?"

"Sure it does. So does waiting a few weeks. Your job will still be there; it's not going to disappear while you take some time and heal." He grinned at her. "It takes longer than that to train your replacement. Consider the assignment the compliment it is. Take what they are expecting and give them back something better."

"This is your version of a pep talk?"

"Yeah."

"You need to work on it some more."

He burst out laughing.

Seven

L isa loved her house, but it was testing her patience tonight. She walked on carpet squishing with water out through the back door, carrying her cellular phone. "Jack, when are you getting off duty?" She'd caught him at the fire station, relieved to find he hadn't been out on a call. She circled to the back of her house, looking at the gutters.

"Eight. Need something?"

"My gutters must be clogged. That brief rainstorm was wonderful, but it had me finding towels. My swamp is back, and this time it came in under the back door."

"Your swamp monster returns? You mean it didn't just unlock the door and wander through the house? Face it, you've got a living thing in your yard. It never dies."

"Jack." Next she was going to hear about those stupid monsters from the swamp movies he loved.

He relented and turned serious. "I'll swing by and take a look."

"I appreciate it." She'd called him because no matter how badly she disrupted his schedule, she knew he would say yes.

She walked around to the garage to see what would have to be moved in order to get the ladder out. Jack would have to do it. She did carry in the box floor fan to help dry out the carpet.

At least the water had turned only about a foot and a half of carpet into a soggy mess before she'd realized the problem and stopped the flood. An evening of moving air should go a long way to drying the carpet out, although in this heat the pad underneath might mold in even that short time.

She'd have to ask Jack if he thought the carpet should be pulled up. The idea of handing him pliers to pull up the tackstrip for the carpet made her wince. On second thought, maybe she wouldn't ask. She carried the wet towels through to the laundry room and started another load.

The three-hour nap she had taken when she got home had been wonderful; she had awoken to the sounds of thunder and rain. She'd enjoyed listening to the rain until she got up and walked down the hall.

She was going to have to get a load of dirt dumped to raise that portion of the yard so water would flow away from, not back to the house. The downspouts were set to direct the water from the roof well out into the yard, but when they clogged, she had trouble.

Surprisingly hungry, Lisa wandered into the kitchen, wishing she had gone grocery shopping. She settled for pulling out a box of Velveeta cheese, cutting off the end that had dried to toss into the trash. She made herself a toasted cheese sandwich.

She was finishing the sandwich, feeding the crusts to Sidney, when the doorbell rang. She dumped the paper plate, returned Sidney to his cage, and went to meet Jack.

He wore a blue T-shirt with a small white fire department emblem stitched above the pocket. It was the same shirt some enterprising kid at the last fire department open house had decorated with fabric paints, adding a red fire engine that looked like it had a flat tire. Jack loved the shirt. It was now too small for him; it had shrunk when washed in hot water, and the paint had begun to crack and flake off. But getting Jack to let the shirt die was impossible.

"What's this?" Lisa accepted the drink he handed her.

"A slushy. Grape. It seemed to fit."

"Jack—you had to?" His sense of humor was impossible to tame.

He tore open the wrapper on a stick of beef jerky. "I had to." He waved his dinner at her. "Show me the damage. Your brother is here to save the day."

"You'll try," Lisa agreed. "Whether you succeed—" She got an ice-cream headache drinking the Kool-Aid in crushed ice. "Come with me."

Jack followed her into the house. "Where's Sidney?"

"You can play with him later."

"Lizzy."

"Later."

"I brought him a new toy."

"Does it make noise?" Lizzy said.

"Of course."

"They do make quiet ones, you know."

"They also make earplugs." Jack bumped into her when she abruptly stopped. "What a mess."

"Tell me about it."

He gingerly walked across the wet carpet to open the back door and look at the source of the problem. "If it rains any more, you'll have a river coming in."

"I need you to look at the gutters."

"Gutters, smutters. I need a shovel so I can dig you a swimming pool. You would never have a water bill to fill it."

"Jack, you've been asking me to put in a pool for the last three years. I'm not going to do it."

"You let me build the deck."

Lisa didn't bother to point out she'd let him build it under their brother Stephen's supervision. "Lumber is not the same as concrete."

"Concrete is more fun."

"You just want to plant your hands in it and be remembered for posterity."

"A guy has to have a goal in life."

She laughed as she pointed back toward the garage. "Outside."

Twenty minutes later, Jack was on a ladder at her roofline. "Got yourself a forest up here." He turned and playfully tossed a handful of storm-stripped leaves in her direction.

His grin was infectious. "You need gloves."

"I'd just get them wet."

He leaned over to look down the length of the gutter. "Got a broom?"

"Somewhere. Hang on."

She found it where it actually belonged, hanging on the garage wall. She took it back to Jack and held it up. "Here you go."

He climbed the rest of the way onto the roof and walked along the edge with a casualness that spoke of easy comfort with both the slope and the height. "Here's your problem. Your wire end cap was knocked loose, let the drain clog." He retrieved it and cleared the drain spout to replace it. "You want to try and work on the yard next weekend? I'll be glad to heft bags of dirt around for you."

"As much as I would love to be your boss for the day, I think it's going to take more dirt than we could get down at the yard department of the Home Depot store. I think I'll give Walter—Nakomi Nurseries— a call. Since he's got a job in this neighborhood, he might be able to just bring out a truckload of dirt one afternoon and dump it."

"That would certainly solve the problem." Jack strained to reach over and clean out the turn of the guttering. "So how's Quinn?"

"What?"

"I heard you two went out to dinner."

How had that started? "The grapevine was wrong." Which surprised her because the family grapevine rarely got facts wrong. "He picked me up from work is all."

"I thought…never mind."

Her eyes narrowed. "What did Kate say?"

"Nothing."

She leaned against the ladder and jiggled it enough to make the metal ring. "Jack…don't make me want to tip this over. It would be a pain to pick up."

"You would too." He sighed. "Quinn was asking about directions to Casa Rio."

She blinked. Next time she was going to have to be more selective before she said no to dinner.

Jack tossed down more leaves. "I could be talked into taking you if you'll please lose that sad puppy dog expression."

"I haven't been to Casa Rio since my birthday."

Balanced on his heels, Jack rested his arms across his knees. "Quinn remembered it was one of your favorites. The guy has a good memory for details."

"I'm noticing."

"Why didn't you say yes?"

"Jack—"

"This is your brother asking."

"I didn't want to give him the wrong idea."

He looked stunned. "Quinn? He's not like that lowlife Kevin."

"Speaking of which—you didn't have to bust Kevin's nose."

"Sure I did. He made you cry."

"Jennifer exaggerated." She scowled. "What did he call me?"

"Lisa—"

"I know you. Kevin said something and you hauled off and hit him."

"He had it coming. And you should have dumped the guy long before."

She shifted on her feet, uncomfortable. "Probably."

His face softened. "Someday you'll have to tell me why you didn't."

She hated having perceptive brothers. "Maybe."

"Quinn is a safe date."

"This is a crazy place to be having this conversation."

He grinned. "I like it. You have to look up at me."

"Would you finish and get down here?"

He stood. "I've got time for a walk in the park if you're interested."

The subdivision had a small pond and walk path a block away. It sounded like a nice way to end the evening. "I'm interested."

Quinn squeezed into a tight parking place one block west of Dearborn and Grand and reached for his suit jacket. Lincoln's message had been urgent. He checked that the jacket covered his weapon, secured the car, pocketed his keys, and kept an eye on the crowds around him as he walked toward the gallery where Lincoln had asked to meet him.

Downtown Chicago at 9 P.M. was a busy place to be as those who lived in the city came out to enjoy the fall evening and mingled with tourists looking for the nightlife. He found himself watching traffic, looking for a dark green Plymouth. He hated mysteries, and one that tailed him was not likely to just go away and remain gone.

Dara's was one of a number of small galleries that thrived in the art culture that dominated Chicago. It was much like dozens of others he had patronized over the years, although this one tried to maintain the prestige of its heritage with its rich burgundy canopy over the entrance and its address just four blocks off the magnificent mile, even as the art it carried had become more and more modern. The reason for the black tie became obvious as he approached the gallery and saw the sidewalk podium and the assembled valets. A new show was opening tonight.

Guessing Lincoln had arranged the invitation, he gave his name to the host at the podium. He noted the quiet advance word that passed between the host and doorman. The word *buyer* had an interesting impact no matter which gallery he visited.

The opening tonight had brought out the champagne, a few art critics he recognized on sight, and a crowd that would please the owner. People were lingering as they discussed the various paintings; movement around the gallery would be a challenge.

Quinn scanned for Lincoln while also doing a quick summary of the paintings. All those in sight were oils. The painter was…intense. It wasn't displeasing to the eye with dark colors dominating the works, but the subject matter—mostly scenes of the city at night—would be an acquired taste. He settled in to move around the gallery with the pace of the crowd.

Someone else might have painted the moonlit Chicago river as romantic; this artist had instead made the black shadows in the water dominate the work. He quirked his eyebrow at the violence it suggested. It took talent to create such a subtle impression.

"Thanks for coming."

He glanced to his left to find that Lincoln had joined him. "Interesting request. I didn't know you were into art."

"I'm not," Lincoln replied dryly, making Quinn chuckle. "To your far right, a couple in their fifties talking with a vivid lady in red who is toying with a glass of white wine."

Quinn set the back of his left boot heel and turned without appearing to move. He scanned the room, passing over the threesome Lincoln had described. The lady in red was probably also in her fifties, but she wore the age very well. She was photogenic, obviously involved in the discussion, animated, captivating.

"The lady in red—Valerie Beck."

"The artist of tonight's exhibit."

"Yes."

"Her name, her work, doesn't ring a bell."

"No reason it should," Lincoln replied. "Wander to the back; there's something you should see."

"You want to give me a hint?"

"I don't want my opinion to sway yours. Go have a look."

What Lincoln was not saying mattered as much as what he was. Quinn looked one more time at the lady in red and nodded.

What had Lincoln found?

It took him several minutes to reach the archway into the next room. It was merely the middle of the gallery, another archway indicating another room. His way was blocked by a large group of guests, the critic from the *Chicago Fine Arts and Sculpture* magazine commanding a good portion of the room so he could hold court on what he thought of a retrospective painting of the Chicago World's Fair.

Quinn slid past the crowd with some reluctance. The man needed a history lesson if not an art lesson, and he was half inclined to stop and give it to him. He actually hoped the man would write the drivel he was saying in his review so the rest of Chicago could see his lack of insight. The painting was an interesting piece, not as dark as some of the other pieces. Once the group drifted on he'd have to come back and do some serious consideration—it might fit the space he had available in the ranch's dining room.

He stepped through the second archway.

Photographs, not paintings. He stopped in the doorway, absorbing the change in mood and tone of the work. There was a photojournalist quality to the subjects chosen: people dominated, events. The photographs did not have the technical expertise he would have expected from an artist of Valerie Beck's caliber.

The room had only two other guests casually perusing the pictures; there was no crowd here.

This was the work of a different artist. He searched for a title and an artist's name to confirm his hunch.

"She called that one *Endurance*."

Valerie Beck had joined him, as vivid up close as at a distance. She was looking with great indulgence at the photo he had been examining. It captured the start of the Chicago marathon, although it was hard to place the year of the race.

"My daughter's work."

Quinn checked his discomfort and wondered where Lincoln was. He didn't know yet what he was supposed to be looking for, but it was apparently in this room. "The photographs show talent. You have reason to be proud of her, Mrs. Beck."

"This is the best she'll do, I'm afraid. My daughter was murdered a decade ago. She always wanted a showing of her work."

Violence, and something that had caught Lincoln's attention...Quinn could feel the threads crossing. "A tragedy. But this—" he looked around the room—"is an act of love."

His words brought a grateful smile in return. "I received more enjoyment out of putting together this showing than I did choosing works for my own."

He was playing this by ear, not sure what to ask. Quinn nodded to a photograph to his left. "I like this one."

"Horses. Rita did love them."

"She also had a great subject. He looks like he was a jumper."

"I believe he was. Do you collect art, Mr.   ?"

"Diamond. Quinn Diamond. And yes, I've been known to buy a piece I like."

"Diamond—a lady's best friend?" She smiled at him as she touched the sleeve of his jacket. "Indulge me, Mr. Diamond, and I'll tell you about some wonderful photographs by a promising young photographer."

He returned the smile, relaxing, liking her. "I would enjoy that."

And for the next twenty minutes he did, hearing about a daughter from a mother who loved her, obviously missed her, and remained very proud of her. The word *murdered* still resonated as a harsh, discordant ending to the story, but she seemed to have moved past it enough to recover the good memories.

They had almost circled the room when he stopped in his tracks.

"My daughter. She was sixteen when that was taken."

It was a five-by-seven-inch snapshot, a casual picture, hanging low on the wall among a display of awards. Rita looked very much like a younger version of her mom even at sixteen. Rita had her arm around the shoulders of another teen, both girls holding cameras. The other girl in the picture was the very girl he had sought for so long: a smiling Amy Ireland.

"I do love this man." Lisa curled up on the couch and reached for the remote to adjust the volume. Tom Hanks and Meg Ryan were about to kiss for the first time. She snuggled the phone closer to her shoulder. "Jennifer, does Tom kiss this good?"

"Better," Jennifer replied smugly.

It was a quarter to eleven; Jennifer had called shortly after 10 P.M. to pass along word that she'd found the movie playing on the romance classics channel. It wasn't the first time they had watched a movie together long distance. Lisa was feeling quite relaxed. A muscle relaxant had ended any pain and a canister of Cheetos lay open on the table.

"Who was the last guy you kissed?" Jennifer asked.

Lisa grinned at the intrusive question. "Jack. He cleaned out my leaf-clogged gutters tonight."

"Brothers don't count."

"Well it wasn't Kevin," Lisa replied, grateful that was true. For all the mistakes she had made with Kevin, that hadn't been one of them. She was choosy about whom she kissed.

"Good. I never liked that ER doctor." The movie went to commercial. "Quinn was a good kisser, but there was an awkward height difference."

"What? You admit he has a flaw?" Lisa teased.

"He'd be just about right for you."

Lisa squirmed against the cushions, remembering the couple times he had held her as he helped her move from the car. Jen was right…his chin had brushed her hair as he held her, sent a quiver direct to her gut. If he kissed her… "I don't intend to find out."

"Why not? He's interested."

Jennifer was reading what she wanted to see. Quinn might be interested in a friendship, but nothing more. "No he isn't."

"Want to bet?"

Having already walked into a family bet once tonight compliments of Jack and his latest dare, she wasn't touching this one. "No, I don't. Besides, even if he's interested, I'm not."

She was smart enough to know there would be nothing casual about a relationship with Quinn, not on her side. She had a habit of being overly cautious and then abruptly just handing her heart over and saying here. There wasn't a safe middle, and unfortunately she hadn't chosen well the few times she had risked it in the past. She still had the child's habit of making an all-or-nothing decision.

"Quinn's not that old," Jennifer said, puzzled.

Forty-four. There were nine years between them, but Lisa had never thought his age was the problem. He wore it well. It was what it said about him that was the problem. The guy should have settled down long ago. But it would be putting down the guy to make that point, and she found herself reluctant to be critical. Knowing Quinn, there was probably a decent reason behind his unwillingness to settle down. "I don't want to live in Montana," she replied, lying through her teeth as she let herself dream a little.

"You would love it and you know it."

"Can you see me being a stay-at-home wife?" Living miles from a decent-sized town, with only Quinn and the ranch hands for company…it actually sounded wonderful. She liked the city, but she got out of it every chance she could.

"You'd have your pilot's license within six months," Jen replied. "And it would take a couple years just to identify all the wildlife that stops by. I heard Quinn saw a cougar last winter."

Lisa perked up at that news. The closest she had ever come to seeing a cougar was finding pawprints in the snow as she hiked through the mountains. "Really?"

"It came all the way down to the main barn."

"I hope he didn't kill it."

"Knowing Quinn, he probably sweet-talked it into moving on. Besides, just think of all the land you could explore. Aren't there caves on his property?"

"Several back in the bluffs."

The movie came back from commercial. Lisa was relieved. It was only a matter of time before her sister worked the conversation around to the subject of religion. Jen was only marginally more subtle about it than Kate. Religion and Quinn had become favorite conversation topics for her sisters. Talking about a guy with any of her sisters was always done at her peril. They had long memories for what she said…and what she didn't say.

"Oh, I'm going to cry. This is so sad," Jennifer said as Tom and Meg said good-bye, possibly forever. Lisa moved aside the phone as Jen blew her nose. Personally she thought the movie was a little overblown. Nobody was this romantic in real life although Marcus and Shari came close. But it never hurt to dream.

"Lincoln, what is going on?" The Italian restaurant a block east of the gallery had partially emptied, due to the late hour. Quinn ordered coffee and a sample platter of appetizers to give them an excuse to linger while they talked.

"It's Amy Ireland?"

Quinn was still trying to take in the stunning realization of what Lincoln had found. "Yes. She attended a two-week camp sponsored by the Chicago Museum of Art when she was sixteen. She must have met Rita Beck then. And since I don't remember seeing Rita on the camp roster, it explains why I missed finding the connection."

"I thought it was Amy, but I'm not exactly in a position to ask Mrs. Beck."

"Why not?"

"I'm trying to prove that Grant Danford did not murder her daughter."

Quinn winced. "The case you've been working the last two months, the guy serving a life sentence."

"Rita was twenty-five when she disappeared. Her body turned up eight years later buried on Grant Danford's estate. A witness placed Grant and Rita together the last day she was known to be alive, contradicting his statements to the police. The jury came back with a murder conviction."

"You think he's innocent?"

"His sister does; she hired me. After two months of looking at the case— I think there's a whole lot more there than what came out at the trial. Not that Grant is helping me much. The man is being a royal pain to work with, asking questions in answer to my questions instead of giving me straight answers. I've been interviewing everyone involved in the case that I can find."

Quinn considered his friend, thought about it. Lincoln chose the cases he worked these days. He wouldn't have taken this one, stayed with it this long, if he didn't have a gut instinct there was something to find. The sister probably sincerely believed Grant was innocent—and Lincoln had never been able to turn down a plea from a lady. Quinn wished him luck. Clearing a guy already in prison was a tough challenge. "Why were you at the gallery tonight?"

"Filling in background, looking for people who knew Rita."

"Seeing who came to see her pictures." If Grant really was innocent—killers tended to return to their victims, even years later.

Lincoln nodded. "Footwork. I'm doing a lot more of it now that I'm retired."

And still liking the work, Quinn could hear it in his voice. "I'm going to need to talk with Mrs. Beck at length about her daughter's friendship with Amy. And as soon as Mrs. Beck learns Amy Ireland has been missing for twenty years, it's going to bring back a lot of painful memories; she may shut me out. And she's definitely not going to want to help me if she knows the two of us are old friends and that it was you who found the connection between the girls."

"The fact Rita was missing eight years before being found might actually help you—Mrs. Beck will identify with another mom needing closure." Lincoln considered him and slid the check over. "And I won't take our disassociation in public personally, as long as you're picking up the tab when we sit down to compare notes."

Quinn picked up the bill. "You drive a hard bargain."

Lincoln smiled. "I learned from the best. Emily should also be able to help you out with the background work. She hasn't wanted to touch the Grant Danford case with a ten-foot pole; she thinks he's guilty. She'll be able to do some research for you without people connecting her to what I've been working on."

"I appreciate it. I need to find out everything I can about that summer the girls met before I talk to Mrs. Beck."

"You'll be amazed at Emily's resourcefulness."

"Can I also see the Danford files? I'll need to be prepared before I step into the minefield of how Rita died."

"Come over tomorrow, I'll show you what I have." Lincoln spun the ice in his glass. "Lisa worked the case."

Quinn set down his coffee without tasting it. "She did?"

"She was the one who excavated the grave."

Eight

obin Johnson, age thirty-one, shot and killed during a convenience store robbery. The case was seven years old, unsolved. Lisa slid the first X-ray onto the light table over the special hotshot bulb that could get more light through the old film, then swung over the high intensity magnifying glass. She frowned at the fracture lines in the skull that radiated across the left parietal bone in an oblong starburst. Robin had been hit—a hard blow from something blunt, long, and heavy.

She scanned the other X-rays she had on the light table. The angle of the bullet went from the abdomen up into the chest. Robin had been knocked down and then shot? The cruelty was incredible. Lisa studied the films, absorbing everything they could tell her. There had to be something she could do with this case.

Two hundred and sixty cases. Arbitrarily, counting boxes and thumbing through the printout of unsolved murders, Lisa figured she could solve 10 percent of the open cases through a solid forensic review of the evidence. That gave her twenty-six cases going back thirty years.

She had decided to identify the most promising cases and then take them apart: send unidentified fingerprints and bullets back through the current databases; analyze the crime photos, scrutinize the autopsies; read through the police reports, case notes, and depositions looking for contradictions and assumptions; and try the latest tech-niques for fiber, blood, and fingerprint collection on the evidence.

It was the last Saturday in October, and while it wasn't atypical to spend part of her weekend at work, she was doing it today just so she wouldn't sit around the house and brood.

He hadn't called.

Lisa crumbled the page on her notepad when she realized she'd been doodling Quinn's name, annoyed to have him intruding again. She missed the trash can, and the page joined the half dozen other crumpled balls that had flown that way during the day. Quinn was leaving for Montana tomorrow, and he hadn't bothered to call to say good-bye.

She didn't want to admit she'd been lingering around the house the last two nights on the hopes he would drop by, making sure she had her cellular phone nearby when she was out on the hopes that he would call. She had told herself she wasn't going to care; it didn't mat-ter...but it did.

She'd put the things he'd said and done into the expectations col-umn, and then the days had passed and he didn't call. She rested her head in her hands. She needed to go home. Go back to bed. Admit she'd pushed way too hard on her first week back at work. The fatigue was a good part of this depression. Her body hurt. And she deserved this pity party.

She gave herself five minutes, then forced herself to detach her per-sonal life from work and accept reality. He would have called if he'd realized it was that important to her; he hadn't meant the slight.

Go home or stay?

Stay. At least she could try to do some good here.

Work had always been the best way to get back her perspective. At least she was alive. She pushed her chair away from the light table and returned to the desk. Robin Johnson. She picked up the police report. She needed to see how far the case had gotten during the initial investigation. If they didn't have DNA available to tell them who the killer was, then what forensic evidence could do was provide that last piece of the puzzle; the investigation had to provide the framework.

The first success was going to be the hardest.

"You're working late."

Lisa blanked her expression before she looked up. Quinn. Her heart skidded to a stop somewhere around chagrined at what she'd been thinking earlier.

"Going to forgive me?"

Now she was confused. "For what?"

"Dropping off the face of the earth for a few days."

It was either a good guess or she hadn't blanked her face fast enough. "Oh, is that what you did?" She pushed out a chair with her foot in silent invitation, feeling the joy taking over and turning her day bright again just because he was there. He looked so good—a man shouldn't be able to make a gray shirt and faded jeans a fashion statement.

He pulled a white sack from his pocket and offered it across the table. "You didn't even realize I was gone." White chocolate-covered raisins, somewhat smashed. He had a habit of bringing something.

She took a handful, considered them, considered him. She gave a slight smile. "I realized."

Seated across the table, she got a chance to look at him more closely and her amusement faded. He looked tired, no...exhausted. The humor that was normally around his eyes was gone; the energy that pulled people toward him dimmed. The man looked discouraged. "You want some coffee?" she asked, feeling out the situation.

"I could use some."

She got up and took two mugs from the collection Diane had assembled and reached for the half full coffeepot. She brought the sugar bowl and a spoon back with her, knowing his preference.

"Thanks." He was silent as he drank the coffee. She wondered what was wrong.

He turned one of the photos on the table toward him. "No one solved this case?"

"Cold seven years. Somehow I don't think I'll be finding a miracle."

"She deserves one."

"Agreed. I'm just not a miracle worker, despite rumors to the contrary."

They shared a smile. "I've got faith in you." He leaned back in his seat and sighed. "I need a case. It's closed, but they said it would be somewhere in the archives Gloria is working on."

He'd come to ask a favor. She didn't know why it made her feel so good, but it did. She leaned forward and touched the keyboard, taking her laptop out of sleep mode. "Not a problem; I can access the larger database Gloria is building. Which one?"

"Rita Beck. She disappeared eleven years ago; her remains were recovered three years ago on the Danford estate. Grant Danford was convicted of the murder."

The image of bones turned chocolate brown from rich, dark topsoil clicked back into her memory in vivid detail. All the emotions she had felt at the time were coming back with intensity; Lisa tried not to flinch. "I remember the case," she said softly. "Her body was discovered buried near the stables." She pulled up the search screen and gave the case particulars. "I've got to learn to type," she muttered, punching the delete key.

Quinn laughed; it sounded a bit rusty, but it was a laugh. "I notice you're pecking with two fingers."

"And the busted finger isn't helping. Why this case?"

He hesitated. "Lincoln is working for Grant Danford's sister. He thinks there may be something to Grant's claim of innocence. And there's a possible link to a missing person's case I've been working on for a number of years. I need to see the full file."

"The district attorney made his name on that case. If he convicted an innocent man—" She frowned as the laptop went dormant and the search paused; if it locked up again she was going to resort to hitting it. Ever since she had expanded the memory, the machine had been acting up.

"Okay, here we go. Rita Beck. Box 46C2." She read the index. "It's been processed and is in the charcoal stage to remove moisture. It will be down in storage room five."

Quinn wrote down the number. "Stay. I'll have the evidence clerk get it." He disappeared before she could get to her feet.

Lisa collected Robin Johnson's case file and stored it away, hoping that Quinn would rejoin her rather than find the file he was looking for, say thanks, and sign out a copy. She really did want to help.

He came back with a sealed blue crate. She pointed to an empty table. "Let me unseal it, deal with the charcoal."

While she worked, he circled the room. Most of the open murder cases had been located, brought in, and slid onto the metal shelves. Gloria was down to locating a handful of stragglers.

The rudiments of a decent crime lab, including one very expensive microscope, had taken over the east tables. She was getting into the chase. There was a bold red *twenty-six* written on the whiteboard, and she saw him smile as he noted it.

She set out the contents of the box. "Where do you want to start?"

"I'll copy and take it with me."

She wanted to protest but bit back her words. He didn't look like he had slept much in the seventy-two hours since she had seen him last. "There's a copier next door. Stamp the pages as confidential; the evidence clerk can authorize the release."

When he came back she was shutting down her computer for the night. "When did you last eat?" She reached for her briefcase.

"I'm fine, Lisa."

"Don't bother to argue. I'm buying."

"Quinn, you're supposed to take the Do Not Disturb sign off the door occasionally so the hotel maids will clean the room."

"I'll remember—eventually." He crossed over to the room safe to store the Rita Beck files inside.

He hadn't bothered to unpack his suitcase; it sat open on the dresser, stacks of clothes spilling out. There was at least a week's worth of newspapers cluttering the table and tossed in a stack on the floor. Two Chinese carry-out cartons were balanced on the top of the wastebasket and several cellophane wrappers from peanut butter cracker packs were heaped on the bedside table next to the TV remote. His Bible, the leather cover so worn it was beginning to separate, was on the bed next to a pad of paper filled with his precisely printed handwriting.

She picked up water glasses and stacked them on the tray, swirling a finger in the ice bucket now full of room temperature water. Quinn needed someone to look after him.

"You like to sleep in the ice age?" It was all of sixty-five degrees in the room he had the thermostat turned so low.

He glanced back as he locked the safe. "This is comfortable."

"If you're an Eskimo."

He tossed his hat on the side table. It landed with a thud, sending a yellow phone message fluttering to the floor. "Let's go eat."

"After you take something for that headache."

He paused and nearly scowled, making her want to laugh. He had a thing about aspirin; he really didn't like taking them. "Yes, ma'am."

She leaned against the door to the bathroom while he rummaged through his shaving kit for the aspirin bottle. He opened the childproof cap and shook one tablet out into his palm.

"Two tablets, Quinn. One isn't even going to remove that frown let alone the pain."

"Just how much medical school did you have?"

"Enough to make it an order."

He swallowed them with a grimace and shut off the bathroom light. "Let's go eat."

"Which restaurant?"

"Sinclair's, downstairs."

It wasn't the casual restaurant she had expected; this was upper tier elegance and they were both underdressed. The room lights were dim, the music subdued, the decor rich. A group of five businessmen were finishing a late meal; two couples had tables near the windows.

"Two, Michelle, nonsmoking."

"Right this way, Mr. Diamond," the hostess replied with a welcoming smile.

That answered Lisa's question as to which restaurant Quinn normally frequented. She would have placed him at the more sports-oriented restaurant one level down, not amid this elegance. Apparently she had been wrong.

The hostess led them to a white linen covered table, two large vases of long stem roses framing the nearby window; she laid down two menus for them. Quinn held Lisa's chair for her. The hostess took their drink order and left.

Lisa glanced around before opening the menu. "This is a gorgeous restaurant."

"Peaceful," Quinn agreed. "They've got great steaks here."

"Another time for me. Unlike you, I had dinner."

Their waitress joined them a few minutes later, bringing Quinn's coffee and her ice water.

"Good evening. Would you like more time, or are you ready to order?"

Lisa closed her menu. "I'd like a bowl of French onion soup and a side salad, blue cheese dressing."

Quinn held up two fingers. "The same, Sandy." He handed the waitress the menus.

"It will be right out."

Lisa watched Quinn watch the waitress walk away. "You know her?" He'd been around Chicago enough in the last year she wouldn't be surprised if he did.

"She used to work over at the Renaissance Hotel, breakfast shift, if I remember correctly."

"You remember the waitresses."

He glanced back at her, a distinct twinkle in his eyes. "Sure. You don't?"

"I don't live on eating out."

He buttered a piece of the hot bread and offered it to her.

She accepted. "Is this called breaking bread together?"

"The Arabs say you can't fight with someone you eat with."

"Do we need to sign a peace treaty?"

"Insurance never hurts." He leaned back in his chair, stirring sugar in his coffee. "What's this I hear about Jennifer possibly getting out of the hospital?"

Lisa felt her fatigue disappear as a relieved smile took its place. "The doctors brought up the possibility this morning when the latest blood work showed marked improvement. If she gets another positive panel, she could be out of the hospital in a couple weeks."

"That's fabulous news."

"If it happens, the original wedding plans will be back on. Jen and Tom will get married in Houston near her home, so some of her pediatric patients can come."

"October 22?"

"Yes." It was Jennifer's parents' anniversary date, her way of remembering them on her special day.

"Soon."

"Not if you listen to Jennifer. She wants it tomorrow."

"Understandable. Are you going to stand up as one of her bridesmaids?"

"Yes. She's asked Kate, Rachel, and me." She'd been ducking that last dress fitting, not wanting to admit they might have to loosen the fabric of the dress so she could handle wearing it for three hours. Anything tight brought a lot of pain. If Kate was there and heard about it, Lisa would have the entire family to deal with again. She was supposed to be telling them the truth when they asked how she was feeling, and she had been doing a decent job of lying this last week.

"The wedding pictures will be lovely. A bride and three princesses," Quinn commented, and she couldn't stop the blush at that speculative gaze. "Have you decided on a wedding gift yet?"

She'd been worrying about that for weeks; gifts were not her thing and were never easy to choose. "I don't have a clue."

"We'll go shopping."

"We?"

"A really nice painting from both of us." He smiled. "Your taste, my money."

Oh, that would go over just wonderful in her family. Even if it was an interesting offer. She weighed the need against the comments that would be inevitable. "I'll buy the painting, you can buy the frame." The two were often equally expensive, and she was out of time to figure out what to get.

"Fair enough."

She was glad to see the laugh lines back around his eyes, even if it was amusement at her expense.

"Who's making the wedding arrangements for Jennifer?"

"Rachel has been coordinating the details since July, Tom and Marcus are handling the logistics." Their soup and salads arrived. "I'm surprised you didn't order a steak."

"Wait until you taste this. You made an excellent choice."

He was right; the soup was delicious.

Lisa was pleasantly surprised as the meal progressed. He was good company. Maybe it was the fact they were both coming off a stressful day that made it easier to relax; whatever the reason, she stopped try-ing to think before she answered a question. And if some of her answers brought a smile, it was at least as much his fault for the ques-tion as hers for the answer.

She looked at her watch as they lingered over coffee at the end of the meal and was surprised to find it was almost eleven. "It's late. I'd better head home."

"I've enjoyed the evening," Quinn replied, refilling his coffee from the carafe Sandy had brought to the table, obviously not bothered by the time. "Finish telling me about Jack. Is he going to have to move fire districts with the station house consolidations?"

"His has become one of the new hub stations. They've transferred another engine and two crews."

"How much more territory are they covering?"

"A mile and a quarter out from the station. It's dangerous."

"Budget cuts always are."

"Well it's my brother being asked to assume the risks."

"Who have you complained to?"

"Besides the fire commissioner, the mayor, and Jack's city council-man?"

"Write the newspapers next. Give them a good human interest story—sister who knows the risks is worried about her brother."

"Jack would murder me."

"Blame me."

She thought about that…Jack and Quinn…it would be about even.

He chuckled at her expression. "Remind me never to suggest something I don't mean."

"I'll think about writing the newspaper." She looked at him and slowly smiled. "Do you play the harmonica?"

"What? Where did that come from?"

"Ranch…cowboy…riding the range…playing the harmonica. Do you play?"

"I'm supposed to find the logic between that question and talking about Jack?"

"Yes. But you probably wouldn't understand. Just answer the question."

He slowly tipped back in his chair and gradually grinned. "Well, ma'am, now that I think about it—"

"You do! Oh, this is perfect. Can you teach me to play?"

"Explain first."

"Jack. He dared me to learn to play a musical instrument."

"When was this?"

"We were taking a walk the other night around the park…"

"Mistake number one."

She grinned at him for realizing it. "And we got to talking about what we hadn't done as kids because we grew up at Trevor House. Jack never got a chance to be a Boy Scout and I never took piano lessons."

"And the bet became?" He winked at her surprise. "O'Malleys. That wasn't hard to see coming."

He did know them; Marcus had walked into a few family dares over the years. "I have to learn to play a musical instrument and Jack has to do a dozen good deeds. The bet is payable by his birthday. Lose, and you're paying the other person's bills for a month—with your own money. I don't intend to lose." She couldn't afford to.

"I'll teach you to play."

"What's it going to cost me?"

He shook his head. "Uh-uh, I'm saving this one."

"Quinn."

"I'll be nice. It's me or the local piano teacher."

It wasn't that hard of a decision to make. "I can afford a harmonica."

"I've got a story I need to tell you."

It was late. Quinn had insisted on giving her a lift home, that they'd get her car the next day. Lisa turned her head against the headrest, pulled out of her quiet reverie of a relaxing evening by his words.

Secrets. How well she knew them, how well she understood that slightly different tone that came into someone's voice when the territory of such a memory was invaded. "We can take a walk around the pond, if you like."

He parked in front of her house instead of pulling into her drive. "No. I think I'd just rather sit out here if you don't mind."

The passenger door was already locked; Lisa turned to rest against it. "If you'd like. I'm comfortable."

She saw his smile in the faint light of the streetlight. "I'll make it the Cliff's Notes."

He reached over and adjusted the side mirror, killing time rather than speaking, for the street was quiet as it passed midnight. "Did Marcus ever tell you about the reason I became a marshal?"

"I once heard a rumor that it was to cover his backside," she replied, grateful it was true. She didn't have to worry as much about Marcus knowing Quinn was with him.

"That's the reason I stay a marshal," Quinn replied with a chuckle.

"Then no, I don't think I heard. Why did you?"

He hesitated over his words. She knew this man; hesitation wasn't a normal part of his makeup. She settled deeper into the seat, ignoring the sharp twinge of pain that shot across her back and curled her toes inside her tennis shoes. "We keep secrets in this family very well. Despite the grapevine, there's another, quieter code of honor none of us would ever think to break. Marcus doesn't talk about you, not the confidences…neither do Kate or Jennifer."

"I know that, Lisa. It's just been private for a very long time."

She wasn't sure she wanted to hear it. A secret shared implied a two-way street. And she didn't want to be sharing hers.

"When I was twenty-four, back from college, working at the ranch, I found buzzards circling what I thought would be a heifer who had died giving birth. What I found was my father, shot in the back. His killer has never been found."

There were no words for the grief she felt at the news. It welled up inside; she could see the scene as he would have encountered it. "It was a hot day?" she whispered.

"June 18, not a cloud in the sky. Out in the south pastureland by the bluffs."

Sandy soil, limestone based, coarse grass—it would have helped slow the ravages of decay beginning at the moment of death, but only slowed not stopped the reality. "I am so sorry."

"I became a marshal when it became obvious the case had become cold. I've been working it in my spare time ever since."

"That's why you don't spend much time at the ranch."

"I love the land and ranching as a lifestyle. I'll go back to it full-time eventually, but for now it's a reminder that there is unfinished business." He sighed. "That's the start of my story. There's more."

"I'm listening."

"A girl named Amy Ireland disappeared the same day my father was shot. She didn't live close by, but for Montana distances, her family would be considered neighbors. She was seventeen at the time. The police considered the possibility of a runaway, foul play, an accident…they worked the case for years until having to accept it also was cold."

"You think they are linked. The disappearance of Amy and the murder of your father."

"I've been working both to try to find out."

For twenty years he had been working the two cases during his off hours. She needed a better word than tenacious. *Committed*. He wasn't going to ever give up. She admired him for that. And for all the years she had known him, he had never said anything. She was disappointed in that but had to accept that her attitude toward him over the years had probably been the reason; it hadn't encouraged confiding something this critical. And then it clicked. "This has something to do with the Rita Beck file you requested."

"It does. Lincoln found a connection between Amy and Rita. They were friends when they were sixteen." He thrust his fingers through his hair. "I've spent the last three days looking at everything I know about Amy and the two-week visit she made to Chicago for an art camp. I'm more convinced than ever that the break I need might be found in their friendship—a teenage confidence, something Amy told Rita, that from the perspective of today will mean something."

"I'd like to help."

"I've been trying to avoid asking you to get involved."

That hurt. He saw it and shook his head. "Lisa, it's not personal. There's a lot that's going on unrelated to this right now, and I'd rather be cautious and limit this to Marcus, Lincoln, and myself."

Something that had him worried—something dangerous. Kate acted the same way when her gut was telling her something wasn't right. She didn't want people around. "Then why tell me now?"

"Because I need to see where Rita died. And I need you to show me."

Nine

The former Grant Dunford estate was forty acres in Lake Forest, backing up into the Lake Bluff Forest Preserve and the Skokie River. Lisa was grateful she was finally able to handle a car ride without having to brace for every turn. Quinn was a safe driver, but his attention was elsewhere and he was ignoring the speed limit to instead flow with traffic. The fact he said nothing during the hour-long drive was also a good indication he had other things on his mind.

She understood the intensity that demanded a case be solved. She'd been there. She understood now what had made him the way he was: patient, steady, but tenacious. What had happened to his father was always there in the background, lingering as an unanswered question, eating at him because it remained unsolved. It had to have contributed to why he had never settled down; he'd been focused on the past, not his own future.

He had gone to church with Kate, Dave, and Marcus, then had come over to pick her up afterward. As graciously as she could she had declined his invitation last night to join them. He hadn't pushed the subject, but he'd been studying her as he asked the question, noting her reaction. And what he had seen must have bothered him for he started to ask something, then caught himself and changed the subject.

The last thing she needed was Quinn deciding to probe that subject too.

Lisa knew she'd made a tactical mistake. Kate was the heart and soul of the O'Malley family, and when she keyed in that there was something wrong, she didn't leave it. Their conversation four days ago had triggered a red flag, and Lisa knew it hadn't helped that she'd cut off a similar conversation with Jennifer; a fact that might have gotten back to Kate.

At times she hated the family dynamics. If she read them wrong, couldn't finesse a situation, more often than not it triggered an issue into a state of prominence rather than getting it buried as she hoped.

All the O'Malleys had pasts that were complex and areas of their lives before Trevor House they rarely talked about. But those zones of privacy were around things they didn't talk about easily, not around things that were hidden. And she was hiding. That had Kate worried, and it was only a matter of time before Marcus came by. He wasn't a casual guardian of the O'Malley family. He cared enormously, would want to do whatever he could to fix what was wrong.

It would hurt to push them away and hurt if she let them in. She just wanted the past to stay the past. It couldn't be fixed, she knew that, but they'd try anyway because they were O'Malleys. Because they loved her.

She'd been the focus of the family since the injury, now this…. She had to figure out a way to get their attention focused on someone else. The power of the group could be overwhelming.

What she needed was an excuse to be so busy she could honestly say she didn't have time. It had worked before; it would work again. She'd just have to figure out how to stay ahead of them for a while.

She looked at Quinn, considering the unthinkable. If she said yes to a few invitations, she wouldn't be using him exactly. It wasn't like he ever saw someone for more than a few months, and that would be enough time to get out of this family scrutiny. And if she did say yes to a couple church visits—at least it would deflect their concern and give her some space.

It was the coward's way out of the problem.

It was depressing to realize she was seriously considering it.

"Who owns the estate now?" she asked as Quinn turned into the long, winding private drive that led back to the house, grateful for the time being that she could focus on work.

"Richard and Ashley Yates. They're in Europe for a month. They weren't thrilled with the news the old murder case was being looked into again, but Lincoln convinced them that it would be best to let him do it rather than risk someone else eventually investigating who would not be as cautious about keeping it out of the press."

Quinn parked in the estate's driveway turnabout. "We're going to be meeting with the manager of the stables. When the Yates bought the estate, they also bought Grant's horses and they kept him on."

"Samuel Barber? Berry? Something like that…"

"Barberry. Good memory."

"I'm surprised he's still working. He had to have been in his seventies when I met him."

"I spoke with him briefly—Scottish?"

"Yes. He was the one who found Rita's body. They were rebuilding the stone terrace behind the stables; the land slopes to the river, and it was terraced to make room for a level exercise ring. They were replacing and leveling stones when they found her remains."

"I've read Lincoln's notes, scanned the full file early this morning." He shut off the car and removed his keys. "You excavated her grave?"

She nodded; some of the realities of her job were best left unstated. She'd been here the good part of three days, the age of the crime scene having her working with archaeologist's tools to brush away the layers of dirt from the bones.

"Good. I won't have to wonder about evidence having been missed."

Even as she absorbed that compliment, he nodded toward the briefcase in back. "Bring the file? I'll go locate Mr. Barberry."

The stables were located near the back of the estate grounds, providing easy access to riding trails that disappeared into the heavily wooded forest preserve. There was also a swimming pool, adjoining pool house, and a tennis court on the estate grounds. Lisa remembered the house as being traditional English inside—heavy fabrics, polished wood. There had been a full suit of armor guarding the hall, rather hard to miss with its invisible man holding a jousting spear and four-foot sword. Grant Danford had been a man who liked to make a statement with his surroundings.

The estate grounds had lost some of their elegance; they gave the sense of being subtly neglected. It wasn't obvious—the sculptured flowerbeds, evergreens, and white birch trees were still beautiful—but nothing had been added, everything had simply grown and it had thrown off the balance.

She carried the briefcase and delayed joining Quinn, in no hurry to step back into this case. It had been a hot summer afternoon, not unlike today, when she was called out to the scene. The police had cordoned off the area, and while they tried to maintain need-to-know on details during the early investigation, the press had already staked out the roads to the estate when she arrived. Grant Danford was a man with financial and political power and had the enemies that went with it. This case had created a firestorm of interest in the press.

For three days she had labored here at the scene, painstakingly recovering the remains. The subspecialty of forensic anthropology took years to learn all its nuances, to read everything bones could say, but her years hunting fossils and going on archaeological digs had helped hone her skills. She knew how to recover remains and read a burial site, and those were the most critical steps in the process. Burial sites were the most fragile of recovery sites for evidence even though they looked the most sturdy.

An expert from the Museum of Natural History had joined her to help with the three-dimensional grid work, the careful record of the dig. How long Rita had been dead before being buried, how and even where she had been killed—the potential evidence in the gravesite was enormous and this one had yielded all of those markers.

She had worked in focused concentration with a scribe, a photographer, and an evidence technician to document and preserve each clue uncovered. By the time the remains were lifted to the black vinyl body bag, Lisa knew Rita Beck better than most people had when she was alive.

She'd been proud of the work she had done.

And now Lincoln thought the man convicted of Rita's murder might be innocent.

She wasn't supposed to feel it was a personal slap.

It was her job to speak for the evidence. She was legally required to be impartial, to state the facts contained in the evidence, to remain silent when the evidence was silent, to be persuasive in explaining when the evidence spoke. It was not her job to speak to guilt or innocence of the person accused. Sometimes her testimony helped the prosecution, sometimes the defense.

In this case, with the media swarming around it, she had been true to that impartial mandate down to the very choice of adjectives she used. When she had given her expert opinion at trial, she had limited it carefully to what Rita's body and grave had revealed. But the defense lawyers had tried their best to shred not only her statements but her reputation. She could feel the anger building just remembering those grueling days in court.

She rubbed her forehead. She did not want to be back in this case. If Grant had been wrongly convicted, her testimony had been part of that injustice. What she had said played a large part in the conviction; the body of the victim always did. It wasn't much help to know that it had only been part of the case the jury had heard. The jury had heard a total case and rationale for the crime and convicted Grant Danford on that record. But had she missed anything? Anything that would have been exculpatory?

"Lisa."

She moved to join Quinn and Mr. Barberry; they were talking at the door to the stable. She shook hands with Mr. Barberry, not surprised that he remembered her.

"We'd like to simply look around if that's okay with you," Quinn said.

"Take your time. I'll just be puttering around here."

Quinn nodded his thanks.

They left Mr. Barberry and turned to the stone walkway that curved between the barn and the large exercise ring. The open pastureland was to the west.

Quinn paused her with a hand on her forearm. "You don't have to do this if you would prefer not to."

She wiped her expression of emotion, annoyed that she had let her disquiet with the situation show. "It's no problem."

His eyes could pierce someone's soul. "Lisa—" he hesitated, obviously choosing his words with care—"you worked this case. It was gruesome. You don't need to be involved again. I can follow Lincoln's notes on my own, ask questions if something is unclear."

"You need to understand Rita's life and death if you're going to get a handle on her friendship with Amy. Did they stay in touch after that summer camp? Did they have other common friends? Did Amy ever talk about coming back to Chicago? Is it anything more than a coincidence that two friends both disappeared years apart and one of them turned up murdered? No, Quinn. I'm staying."

She forced herself to smile. "The main reason this case is unpleasant is the memory of the publicity that surrounded it. As a crime…Quinn, working a scene this old is one of the easiest cases I can have. Time consuming, but not that hard. Bones don't have skin that feels cold and empty eyes that look back at you."

"To watch you work, it isn't obvious the victims bother you like that."

Did he think she didn't remember the faces and the crimes? They lived with her, gray, terrified ghosts, trapped in the moment of death.

"The children are the worst." She shifted the briefcase to her other hand, needing to change the subject. "It's my job, Quinn. Let me do it."

She couldn't interpret his expression, but she was very aware it had changed. She wanted to squirm under that intensity. She could feel herself being summed up, prior assumptions rethought. If this was what suspects felt… It was hard to remain quiet and not start babbling.

"You see the victims, don't you? See the struggle to stay alive through their eyes and relive with them their deaths. That's why you're so good at figuring out what happened."

"Something like that." She looked away. He was hitting too close to the truth for comfort.

She started when his hand closed over hers on the briefcase. "Who'd you see die?"

She jolted and tried to jerk away at the soft question, but he had hold of her hand and wasn't letting her move away. His expression was grim and she instinctively tensed.

"Lisa."

She wasn't going to say anything. She didn't lie…and she didn't talk about it.

"Have you told anyone? Kate, Marcus? Any of the O'Malleys?" His voice was steady, calm, but she heard beneath that the intensity and the disbelief with the realization she hadn't.

He was pushing into turf that was off limits, and she mentally recoiled, her expression turning stony and cold. She lived with that ghost and victim because she had to, but she wasn't sharing the secret…especially not with Quinn.

His hand over hers tightened and his free hand turned her face back toward him. He held her gaze with his and rubbed his thumb against her chin. There was compassion in that gaze, so deep she could drown in it if she let herself. "I'm sorry for that memory."

"Let me go," she insisted, hating him.

"When you need to talk, I'll listen."

"I won't."

He pushed back the hair blowing across her face. "You don't need to defend yourself against me. I won't use the truth against you."

"So you think."

The hot emotion in his gaze frightened her. "Don't fight me, Lisa. You'll lose."

"You want too much."

"Yes, I do. I want your trust." He released her chin and her hand, stepped back and paced away, then turned back, looking incredibly frustrated. "But you're too stubborn to realize what you need."

He was into her past, was verbally hitting her with an intensity she had always known was part of his personality. He had his bone to worry now, just like the O'Malleys had theirs, and he'd be at it ruthlessly until he had answers. He'd crush her if he invaded that concealed truth. She couldn't afford his interest but didn't know how to deflect it.

"Quit looking like that."

"How?"

"Like I stepped on some favorite pet of yours," he muttered.

"Quinn—"

"Forget it." He rejoined her and took the briefcase from her hand. "Let's get to work." He took off his hat and dropped it on her head. "And I could do without your getting a case of sunstroke."

She watched him walk away, relieved to be out of the quicksand subject but distressed at the fact he was mad at her, and worse, that he was deciding she wasn't worth the trouble.

She awkwardly adjusted the too large hat, finding that abrupt action of his disconcerting. Even when mad, he still paused to shove his hat on her head.

He opened the file and looked back at her. "Take me through what happened here."

She pushed her hands in her pockets and reluctantly walked forward to join him. It was hard to get focused on work, but he'd made the transition with a completeness that was almost ruthless. "She was found back here."

She felt nauseous. She'd been weighed and found wanting; it wasn't a new feeling, but it made her regret what she'd said. Kate wouldn't have responded that way to him, or Jennifer. He wanted her trust. She'd concede reality: She already trusted him. She just didn't want to give him what he was asking for. Her past was private, and for her sake best left alone.

The terrace was formed from a curving wall of rocks about four feet high. She walked down the five stairs to the lower level, walked north along the path, her steps slowing, and then she stopped. It was like walking back in time. She let herself remember and then realized she had been standing there silently for several moments; Quinn was patiently waiting, watching.

"They were excavating this turn in the stones, reinforcing it so they could enlarge the exercise ring in this direction. They uncovered her left foot, still wearing the remains of a blue tennis shoe. We were called out."

"What did you find?"

"She was lying face down, buried immediately behind the rocks at a depth of about two and a half feet. She would have been buried deeper than that originally; the ground along here had been washing away over the years with the heavy rains, being pulled down to the river."

She crouched down, ran her hands along the weathered, flat smooth stones, each one heavy and about ten inches deep. "When we began work, this wall of stones had a back and forth tilt, they had been undisturbed for years and had settled. It looks neat now, but then…you could see grooves where the rains had cut into the soil and torn away the packed dirt between the stones. Nothing had been disturbed since she was buried here."

She sighed, remembering. "Her hands were behind her back. There were remnants of the duct tape used to bind them still around the bones." She frowned.

"What?"

She stood, glanced back at him. "Her hands weren't just bound at the wrist. The backs of her hands were pressed together and tape also wrapped around her palms. She had two broken fingers, as if she'd been grabbed, bound in that fashion, and thrown to the ground on her back, her fingers breaking under her own body weight.

"She had a dislocated left shoulder and wrenched vertebrae in her lower back indicating a struggle, consistent with how she had been bound. No skull fractures recording a blow to the head, no nicks in bones recording a bullet. The hyoid bone in her neck had mostly decayed, but I found a pressure fracture in the left branch of the U-shape bone and a break at the forming fuseline."

"She was strangled." Quinn's voice was cold. He had a special hatred of men who used physical violence toward women; that was so clear it was painful to see.

"Or at least put in an injury-inducing choke hold," she replied quietly. "At twenty-five, the three bones in the horseshoe formation of the hyoid had just begun to fuse. The pressure fracture indicates it was serious, but was it the fatal act? She may have been suffocated or even drowned as the actual cause of death. What I do know is she was grabbed by the neck during the time of her death. But the vertebrae damage is inconclusive as to how she was held."

Quinn took a seat on the steps between the terrace levels, opened the file, and laid out the pictures, studying them again. "You have a hard job."

She didn't need his pity. "We die and we turn to dust. I just know a bit more than most people about how that actually happens."

But the pictures pulled at her. She took a seat beside him and picked up one of the gravesite photos recording the excavation. She'd been lying beside the body in the deeper side trough they had dug to create a pedestal for the skeletal remains. They had to record what they found by grid and depth, for below the body was often trapped a treasure trove of evidence.

This photo was typical: She had her gold pen clamped between her teeth and a frown of concentration on her face as she tried to retrieve a fragment of thread and a button from the dirt with a long pair of tweezers, apparently not bothered that she was stretched out inches from a skeleton. The gold pen was more than a fashion statement, blood and bacteria couldn't get into the casing; it could be wiped clean with one of the foil-wrapped medical swabs she carried by the handful in her pocket when she worked a scene.

"What other evidence did you find?"

"Her only jewelry was a ring on her right ring finger. She wore no watch. Her clothes had decayed, but there were remnants of threads from a white polyester shirt with a blue front pocket. Her jeans had decayed to the seam threads and a zipper—cotton always decays fast— and she wore blue Nike tennis shoes.

"That clothing is significant because it matched what she was last seen wearing the day she disappeared years before. The ground around her body was unusual; there was a much heavier concentration of black topsoil than was found at the same depth just a few feet away."

"Not uncommon around a stable and landscaped grounds."

"True, but it made her remains decay faster than say a clay-based shallow grave."

"She was buried here. No one would notice the turned-over dirt?"

"The month she went missing, this stone wall terrace was built. It's why the police think this spot was chosen for the grave instead of somewhere in the forest preserve—an animal might have dug up the body there. This apparently had sod laid down to the edge of the stones, making it relatively easy to conceal the site if he had the time to work and dig the grave. And back then Grant Danford did not have the full-time staff working this property."

Quinn looked around the area. "How far back does the Danford property extend?"

"Roughly to that line of trees. From there you are on forest preserve land."

"No one from the house could see here."

"And as you can see, the forest preserve trails are nearby but not in the line of sight. From evidence in the grave, the type of bug cocoons found, she had been dead for a few hours before being buried. Small bits of gravel and wood shavings found on her shoes and under her body suggest the murder occurred somewhere in the forest preserve."

"She was killed the day she went missing?"

"An assumption, but reasonable. She was wearing the same clothes."

"Statistically, killers who abduct and kill in the first hours are strangers to the victim."

"This is a case, not a statistic. Grant Danford knew Rita; they had been casually dating for six months when she disappeared. During the missing person's investigation, he told the police he hadn't seen her the day she disappeared; during the investigation of her murder, a witness was found who placed them together walking the forest preserve trails that very afternoon."

"Was he ever really a suspect when this was just a missing person's case?"

"Not really," she admitted. "He had put out a large reward for information, cooperated with the police, added his political pressure to keep the case alive. But the case eventually became cold from lack of evidence."

"The cynical interpretation being that he stayed so close to the investigation he made sure they never looked where evidence could be found."

"Yes."

"And when her body was discovered here on his property, Danford became the chief suspect if not the only one," Quinn speculated. "They never looked any further once they had a witness who contradicted his original statement to the police."

"They moved pretty fast on making the arrest."

"He was overseas when the stable manager found the body?"

"England."

"If he was guilty of the crime, why in the world did he risk leaving the body here all those years?"

"Arrogance? He thought he had gotten away with it. Fear? Why mess with something he had dodged once? The vast majority of buried murdered victims are never found. That's a statistic you know as well as I."

"A crime of passion?"

She got up, walked a few feet away before turning back to face him. She didn't like that question because of its answer. "That's what the police concluded and the DA proved to the jury's satisfaction."

His eyes narrowed. "But?"

"That never felt right, not with the bound hands. Those case notes—you'll find interviews with practically every woman Grant ever went out with. He didn't type as a guy with dark fantasies, and that's what the bound hands, the struggle suggest."

"So he was convicted because of association with the victim and location of the grave."

"And testimony of a witness. Christopher Hampton testified that he saw Grant and Rita together the afternoon she disappeared. And by the way—you met Christopher's brother the other day."

She'd caught him off guard with that observation. "Hampton? Christopher is a relation to the guy who just died in the fire?"

"Believe it or not, yes—a nephew. Christopher was actually working for Grant part-time that year at the stables, as well as working part-time for his uncle. He wanted the chance to ride regularly and this way he could afford it. Christopher said he was taking his afternoon break, walking the trail to head over and get a late lunch for the other stable hands when he saw the two of them together."

Why didn't he speak up during the original missing person's investigation?"

"During the trial he admitted he was getting lunch for the guys, but he was also meeting his bookie, paying off a gambling debt, and he didn't want his uncle to know. Blaming his boss, the guy offering the reward wouldn't be to his benefit, and the only thing he could testify to was that he saw the two of them walking on the forest preserve trail about 2 P.M. He chose to stay quiet."

"Did you believe him?"

She shrugged. "I suppose. It seemed credible."

"He bribed Grant Danford for his silence."

"What?"

"Lincoln uncovered it. Found out about the gambling problem; found out from the bookie that there was no way Christopher could pay his debt, and yet a few days later he had the whole amount in cash. And Grant as much admitted it when Lincoln pressed on the matter. Christopher demanded Grant pay up or he would go to the police. And he apparently paid him quite handsomely over the years Rita was missing."

"So Christopher told the truth at the trial—he did see them together the day she disappeared; Grant knew it and suppressed it."

"Yes."

This didn't make sense. "Why didn't Grant just say he had seen her if he's innocent like he claims?"

"His explanation—Rita had asked him not to mention she had been by; her parents wanted her focused on college, her photography, and her career, not dating a much older man. When the police first asked if he had seen her he said no, then felt like he couldn't risk changing his story later. And once he paid off Christopher—big mistake. Christopher just kept coming back for more."

"How does Grant explain her body being found on his property?"

"He blames an unknown killer," Quinn replied, his opinion of that in his voice.

"I'm surprised Lincoln took his claim of being innocent seriously. Grant was dating Rita; she was seen here the day she went missing; her body was found on his property. It doesn't leave much room to maneuver. Not to mention the fact this murder is eleven years old. New evidence is going to be hard to find."

"But why did he kill her? You said yourself a crime of passion doesn't easily fit the image of the remains. They had been going out six months, were apparently happy together even if her parents were against it. What triggers a man in a relationship to suddenly turn murderous, choke, and kill?"

She couldn't give him a good answer. "You said he's apparently hiding secrets, being uncooperative. Was there one that she found out? If not a crime of passion, then was it a crime of necessity? Does Lincoln have any ideas? Any other suspects?"

"No. Right now he's simply talking to everyone who testified at the trial." He set aside the file. "Do you think Grant Danford is guilty?"

Her answer would carry some weight with him; she didn't answer right away. She thought about that summer. So many had wanted Grant to be found guilty…but the evidence she'd testified to had been solid, and she remembered the victim. No matter how powerful the man, it was the victim she had focused on. "Yes."

Quinn thought about it, thrust his hand through his thick hair. "I tend to agree with you. The lie, the bribe—he really wanted to keep hidden that he saw her that day. That points to guilt. But Lincoln isn't so sure. I can't dismiss that. And if Grant is innocent—then someone else killed her. Someone who is still out there. What are the odds a murderer kills only once?"

What a tangled question. The only real answer was it depends. There were as many varieties of killers as there were reasons to kill. The gamut ran from domestic disturbances that got out of hand to killing someone picked out at random. She'd unfortunately seen examples of them all.

Quinn didn't wait for an answer. "I've seen enough to understand the basics of the case, what memories it's going to bring up when I talk to Mrs. Beck. It was headline news for the duration of the case, that's the biggest point I need to know. Let's call it a day."

Lisa was more than ready to agree.

He waited for her to join him on the steps, put a hand on her back to steady her. It was an impersonal gesture, done casually, but she found herself welcoming and relaxing against that touch.

He paused by the pasture fence. "Grant had a good eye for horses."

"Really?"

She leaned against the railing beside him. Quinn pointed. "The chestnut is exceptional. Not a racer, but he'd be a great saddle horse. Do you ride?"

"Enough not to fall out of the saddle."

"I'm surprised you've had a chance for even that. I've noticed in the city it takes money, access, and time."

"Right to all three."

"Maybe next time you come west there'll be time to help out your education."

"Maybe." She didn't expect to have a reason to go back to his ranch, but she wasn't going to say that, not when he was offering an olive branch back to the friendship of yesterday. She lifted off the hat and held it out to him. "Thanks for the loan."

He accepted it. "Something else we'll have to fix. You need your own."

"Yours smells like horse."

He curled the brim, his expression practically one of affection. "It's been kicked around for a few years." He slid it on, then whistled; the chestnut raised his head and came ambling over.

The horse nuzzled his shoulder, tried to knock off the hat. Quinn rubbed his muzzle. He glanced over at her and smiled. "You can pet him. He's just a big baby."

"Who's interested in knocking you over." She stroked the chestnut's shoulder, feeling the powerful muscles flex under her hand.

"But at least I can't step on him by mistake." The chestnut chose that moment to take a playful nip at Quinn's shoulder.

Lisa stepped back, laughing. "I'll stick to my pets, thanks."

"Rita loved horses."

"Did she?"

"Mrs. Beck had several of the photographs Rita took of horses on display at the gallery." Quinn's voice turned serious. "Amy loved horses too."

"That's pretty common when you're sixteen. And Amy lived on a ranch. It was probably one of the reasons the girls became friends."

He looked at her intently, telling her something with his eyes before he spoke. "I've been wondering if this was one of the places Rita took her pictures. If Rita had known about this stable when she was sixteen. If the two girls hung out here and got to know Grant Danford."

Lisa blanched. "You think there's another body here?"

"If he's guilty—kill one girl, why not two?"

"Quinn."

"There has to be a reason he killed Rita, a good solid one, not that flimsy one they sold at the trial. You said yourself it wasn't a good fit for the way the remains were found. Think about it. Assume Grant really is guilty.

"What if Amy came to Chicago again when she was seventeen? What if she had a fight with her mom, her boyfriend, just got on a bus or hitchhiked here to see the girlfriend she'd been sharing all her secrets with for a year? They returned to the old places they had enjoyed, this place being one of them.

"Amy's a runaway, needs a place to stay, and Grant's a man who is concerned about what is going on, knows them both from the year before, persuades Amy to let him help fix the mess she's gotten herself into. And when Amy disappears as suddenly as she came, Grant convinces Rita he helped Amy patch things up with her family and that she left to stay with her aunt out east for a while."

Quinn was spinning a story that was killing her with its specificity because it was only too plausible, and it was making her sick to see it.

"Only Amy never left. She's dead and her body is buried somewhere out there in the forest preserve. And years later Rita is seeing Grant, having never really lost her crush on this guy that was nice to her and helped her friend, and maybe on that fatal day they take a walk and she stumbles on something that was never supposed to see the light of day again: Amy's skeleton.

"Grant can't have that Jane Doe identified, Rita knows he was supposedly helping the runaway Amy, and he can't convince Rita to ignore it. He has to shut her permanently up. But he's also learned his lesson and he can't bury her in the forest preserve, not if he wants her to remain lost forever. So he buries her on his own estate at the one place he can dig without his staff being suspicious."

"Stop it. Okay? Just stop."

"It fits. I need to know."

She closed her eyes, then opened them to look at him with painful clarity. "We both do."

Ten

Lisa leaned against the railing on the back deck, letting the quiet of the Tuesday night settle inside and ease her tension headache. The problem with getting close to Quinn was that his burdens became her own. She wanted to be able to help him solve the mystery of who had killed his father, what had happened with Amy, but she didn't have the emotional energy to give him. Extending the job she did at work to her time off gave her no chance to unwind.

She should have taken that vacation after all. She would be so glad to have Jennifer's wedding to go to, have a four-day break, and a chance to get away from casework that was uniformly grim.

The patio door slid open; Kate stepped out and came to lean against the railing beside her.

Lisa glanced over. "Find your shoes?" Kate had moved home yesterday but as usual had left a trail of stuff behind.

Kate quirked a grin. "One of them. I must have tossed the other into that bag after all."

"I'll give you a call if I find it."

"They aren't my favorites; if they're gone I can't say I'll mind."

Kate had come over for more than just her shoes; Lisa knew that. She sipped at the glass of ice water she held, not in a hurry to break the silence. They'd been friends for over twenty years; she knew Kate. She'd get around to the point sooner or later. Beneath the calm appearance there was a fine layer of strain and tension; it showed in the small tells of the way Kate's hands gripped the railing, the way the Southern tone in her vowels had stretched out.

"You've been really down this last week since you got home. Is there anything I can do?" Kate finally asked.

"Trade jobs for a few days." Lisa's smile was tired. "I'll be okay, Kate. I'm just coming back slowly. The fatigue is hanging on with a persistence I didn't expect."

"You want to do a movie some evening? Share a laugh?"

The idea sounded like a wonderful break for both of them. "I'd enjoy that."

A shooting star descended within a ten-degree arc of the full moon. Lisa followed its trail down, wondering if the meteor had burned up in the atmosphere or would become an interesting find for some rock hound.

"I see you got the yard depression filled with dirt."

"Walter Hampton from Nakomi Nurseries brought out a load of dirt and leveled out my sinkhole. He's bringing sod tomorrow and talking about shrubs, flowers, trees—he can't stand to see a great house not landscaped properly."

Kate turned to look at her. "What?"

"I'm going to have to twist his arm to get him to give me a bill. He's kind of like Quinn, just smoothly rolls over your objections with a smile and does what he likes."

"Lizzy, Walter likes you."

"What?"

"I'm serious. The flowers on your dining table—he brought those over when he brought the load of dirt?"

She had thought it was simply a nice gesture. She'd been distracted at the time, had appreciated the gift because she loved beautiful things and it fit so easily with what she knew about him. "Yes." She rubbed her eyes, not needing this complication.

"Say a nice thank you for the flowers, chat with him while he improves your yard, and let him do what he likes. It never hurts to have a friend."

"I'm not going to bust his heart or anything?" she muttered, annoyed that Kate was right and she hadn't seen it.

"He just wants to do something nice for you. Let him. There's no obligation in that, and given how much this house means to you, spending time talking with a landscape expert would be enjoyable for both of you."

She trusted Kate's opinion. This house did mean a lot; she would love to have the yard looking really nice, and Walter did an exceptional job. Spending a couple hours talking plants and trees would be fun. "I'll do that," she agreed, glad to have the advice.

"Did you hear about Jack's first good deed?"

"Let me guess, you've been talking to Quinn."

"Guilty. He found it rather amusing that you asked him for music lessons."

Lisa wondered what else Quinn had told her and was painfully aware that if Quinn had talked out of turn, Kate was going to be chatting tonight about more than the family bet she had with Jack. Quinn wouldn't have broken her privacy; she knew him. Her voice was light when she answered; she was getting as good as Kate at masking her thoughts. "Well, it's not like any of the O'Malleys could help; none of you know how to play any instrument."

"I can whistle."

"It has to be something you use your hands to play. Jack insisted."

Kate thought for a moment. "I can hum a piece of grass held with my thumbs."

Lisa laughed. "I remember. You did get pretty good at that." Lisa relaxed. "I bought the harmonica. A good expensive plastic one. It cost me three dollars. I haven't opened the wrapper yet. So what was Jack's first good deed?"

"A roofing repair job for Tina Brown." Tina was in her sixties now, a friend of all the O'Malleys from the old neighborhood.

"Nice of him. I'm sure Tina appreciated it, and in this heat, that's a good deed he really earned."

The quiet between them returned.

"Anything else you want to talk about?" Kate asked, not probing hard, but probing nevertheless.

"Quinn's told you what's going on with Amy?"

"Yes."

"There's no way to search that forest preserve in a systematic way for remains over twenty years old without a few hundred volunteers. That's assuming, one, that Quinn's idea is right, and two, that Amy's remains are still there to be found. Grant would probably have reburied them somewhere else. And we can't get a warrant to search his former estate grounds without some solid evidence."

"So you're looking for that historical link?"

"Yes." Lisa sighed. "It's a mess, Kate. And I'm worried about Quinn, the way he's handling this turn in the case."

"He needs the case to finally break open. I'm glad you're helping him."

"Marcus is doing most of it, and Lincoln. I'm just helping sort out the information they find."

"It's costing you."

"Heavily. That gravesite excavation is still too current in my memory."

"Tell him."

"No. Quinn needs me in the loop." And even if it was in a grim way, she wanted a reason to be around him. "Quinn and Marcus are cops, not death investigators. I look for different things. Make different assumptions."

"He needs to be able to find justice."

"It's why he's never settled down."

"I think it's a major part of it."

Lisa sensed a change in the conversation leading toward a discussion of her relationship with Quinn and didn't want to deal with it tonight. "How are things going with Dave?"

Kate groaned. "He wants to go shopping for a ring."

Lisa straightened. "Really?"

"I'm not sure I do."

"Why ever not?"

"Every page I get I can see him tense up, and we're only dating. If we were married—"

"He's not going to ask you to give up your job."

"I know that. But I feel the pressure to find something less dangerous."

"His job is not exactly a cakewalk either," Lisa pointed out.

"I'm afraid I'm going to hesitate a fraction longer than I should during a crisis because I'm thinking about the ramifications of something going wrong."

Lisa shook her head. "The last thing you do is think about the consequences to yourself before you act. Trust me on that; I've seen you respond to too many situations." She smiled and slid a hand through her hair. "You're responsible for most of my gray hairs. Having Dave in the equation isn't going to change how you react. You'll just finally have someone always around when the crisis is over. Give Dave some credit, he wouldn't be asking if he hadn't resolved the question in his own mind. Besides, I'd be more concerned with him taking a bullet than you. You've got a SWAT team keeping you company. He's the guy on the front lines."

"You did have to remind me."

"You love him."

"So much it's kind of scary."

"Let him get you a ring. You don't have to set the date for the wedding. It's probably more insurance on his side that you're not going to do something stupid like act noble and say no for his own good. Admit it, you'd change jobs before you'd give up Dave."

"True." Kate held out her left hand. "I don't want anything fancy."

Lisa laughed. "I'm quite sure to get you to say yes, Dave will let you get what you prefer."

"I know him. He'll just overcompensate for my choice when he buys the wedding ring."

"One of the perks of going out with a guy who comes from very old, very deep money."

"True."

Lisa relaxed against the railing. She couldn't feel sad that Kate and Dave were making that next step. She liked Dave. He was exactly what her sister needed, someone who would stick forever.

But as happy as she was for them, she was sad too. The exclusive group of seven was going to become ten when Jennifer and Tom, Marcus and Shari, and Kate and Dave married. It was going to change, and while she knew there would always be a place for her, after they were married she knew she'd be thinking twice before she picked up the phone to call one of them in the middle of the night. It was those little changes she dreaded.

"I've got a favor to ask," Kate said.

"Sure."

"Would you consider coming to church with us next week?"

While she had known the subject would come up again, the question came out of the blue, and Lisa wasn't ready with a graceful answer. She simply shook her head. "I'll pass."

"I wish you'd come."

"Kate—" Causing friction in the family was the last thing she wanted to do, but Kate didn't know what she was asking. And Lisa was tired, didn't want to have to deal with this.

"You'd be welcome. They're a great bunch of people. And I'd like you to meet the rest of Dave's family, his friends."

"Have a barbecue; I'll come. Dave's place has room for a small crowd."

"You can't avoid the subject of church forever."

"Why not?"

"I've never known you to form an opinion without having the facts."

"I know what I need to know."

"Scripture is true, Lisa, even though you find it hard to accept. Jesus is the Son of God, and He did rise from the dead. He is alive."

"Leave it alone. Please."

"I always thought you were open-minded enough to at least listen."

"Insults aren't going to help."

Shock crossed Kate's face, then pain. "I'm sorry. I didn't mean it that way."

"And I'm a little sensitive about the subject right now. You, Jennifer, and Marcus have been laying it on pretty thick in the last few weeks."

Kate absorbed that. "We didn't mean to. I really am sorry, for all of us."

Now she'd made a mess of it. Lisa rubbed her face. "I'm sorry too. I didn't mean to bite, but I really would like you to just drop the subject. I'm tired. I'm not going to change my mind. And I'm really not interested."

It was so obvious Kate wanted to ask why, but she stopped the question and gave a reluctant nod. "All right, Lisa." Kate's pager went off. She glanced at the number, frustrated. "This job has lousy timing. I've got to take this one." She reached into her pocket for her cellular phone and punched in the numbers with her thumb. "Yes, Jim?"

Lisa saw the shift to an impassive expression, knew whatever was going on it was serious. "I'm on my way." Kate closed her phone and sighed. "I've got to go."

Lisa reached out and hugged her, not wanting her to depart with tension between them. "Be safe, Kate."

"Always." Kate kissed her cheek. "Get some sleep."

"Lisa, where do you find these records? That sax is wailing like somebody is in mourning," Quinn asked, wondering if he could convince her to change it without admitting it was getting on his nerves. It was Friday evening, and he and Marcus were camped out at her place, going through what evidence they had been able to gather, trying to formulate their plan of attack for the next day. Lisa had insisted she wanted to help and Quinn had finally conceded the point.

He was enjoying the chance to quietly invade her space. Her ferret was draped over his knee, half asleep. They had moved from the dining room to the living room after Lincoln got paged and had to leave. It was after 9 P.M., but Lisa showed no signs of wanting to call it a night.

Sitting on the couch, using the coffee table as a work area, she didn't bother to look up from the photographs she was sorting. "I like jazz."

"Your music taste is decades old."

"Really? I figured you would have heard it when it was new." She glanced over at him and smiled as his partner chuckled. Quinn made a face back at her. The last three weeks had done some good; at least she'd started to relax with him.

It was such slow progress.

The more he knew about her, the more he wanted to know. The attraction went deeper than like, but not as strong as love; it hovered there in the middle like a balance waiting to settle. It was an incredibly dangerous edge, one he worried about privately when he prayed. He'd always been able to control his emotions and how close he got. This time events were overtaking him and he felt like he was picking his way through a minefield.

The convergence of issues had created something he had never expected. Spending time with Lisa in the investigation had opened up a look at her professional life, just as helping her out as she got over the injury had opened a window into her private life.

She was intelligent, fair, independent, kind, and above everything else, curious. But when it came to being willing to talk about things of faith, that curiosity change to indifference. He had watched Kate try, then Marcus. Lisa had rebuffed them both.

Quinn frowned at that ugly reality, knowing something had turned off that curiosity, dreading both what it could be and how hard it was going to be to uncover. Lisa was formidable in keeping her secrets.

Of the three problems he'd faced—she wouldn't let him get close, she didn't trust him, and she didn't believe—he'd made progress on only one, and even that was fragile. She had let him closer than he expected, but she still wasn't ready to trust him, and he had gotten nowhere with the question of faith. He had the feeling getting her to trust him was going to be key to figuring out why her hackles rose so fast when Jesus was mentioned.

Lisa and her secrets—she wasn't going to give them up easily.

Neither was this case. Quinn forced himself to turn his attention from Lisa back to the work at hand. It was so frustrating. The search for information had bogged down. Grant was being uncooperative to the extreme, would answer nothing about Rita and when he had met her or if he had known Amy Ireland. It made Quinn more determined than ever to crack open what he was hiding.

Lincoln was trying to prove the man innocent; they were trying to prove him guilty of a second murder. Grant Danford was in a box squeezing so tight that it was going to eventually have to pop one way or the other. And it was actually easier to make progress on the case with all of them working together, looking at all the information gathered with different objectives.

From Amy's mother had come shoe boxes of photographs and slides Amy had taken during the two-week art camp. From Valerie Beck—told only of the search to locate Amy—had come old letters Rita had kept from friends, Rita's diaries—kept daily during her teens with sporadic entries into her twenties—and access to Rita's photographs. Rita had been intending to make photojournalism a full-time career and her film negatives were extensive going back to when she was fifteen. Lisa was trying to get them into some sort of chronological order.

Quinn watched Lisa work for a few minutes longer, then turned his attention back to Rita's diary. "What were you doing when you were sixteen?" he asked casually, curious if she'd answer.

She looked up. "What?"

"What were you doing when you were sixteen? Rita was boy and horse crazy by the sound of her diary."

"Lisa was into running track and pretending she didn't like Larry Rich," Marcus answered absently on her behalf. He was sitting on the floor using the couch as a backrest, leafing through old newspaper clippings from the initial missing person's investigation of Rita Beck.

"I was not," Lisa protested.

"Sure you were. I chaperoned that year's prom, remember?"

"I didn't go."

"You half did; you slipped out to meet Larry over at the high school gym so you could borrow his brother's motorcycle. You ended up going bowling if I remember correctly."

"Who told you that?"

"Larry. He was wise enough to ask permission before the two of you disappeared."

Quinn turned a chuckle into a cough as Lisa shoved Marcus's shoulder with her socked foot.

"Forget it, Sherlock; I'm still going to start vetting the guys in your life again."

"Kevin was a mistake, okay? I learned my lesson."

Marcus reached back and tweaked her foot. "Stephen stood there and watched Kevin's nose bleed after Jack slugged him. I was so proud of him. He asked about Jack's hand before he dealt with Kevin's broken nose."

"You should have read them both the riot act."

Marcus smiled. "I love you too. Where's that stack of letters Amy's mom sent out?"

Lisa shuffled through the box of material they had brought over to the house, found them, and handed the packet to him.

Quinn was grateful for their help, even if he did feel guilty that Marcus had chosen to stick around for the last days of his vacation to help out. It was clear just watching Marcus and Lisa together that his partner had decided to do some low-key meddling in her life.

He was relieved to see that the pain she'd been doing her best to hide appeared to be fading. She was not pausing to think before she moved as she had been; he'd only seen her reach to shield her ribs twice tonight. And that brace on her broken finger was going to be gone in another couple days if she kept fiddling with it. He wanted to reach over and still her hands as she worked at the tape holding it in place. Doctors had to be some of the worst patients there were.

Her parrot stalked along the back of the couch and stepped down onto her shoulder. Lisa absently stroked her feathers. "What's the matter, Iris? Peanuts gone?"

The parrot whistled. Lisa pulled another one from her pocket, still in its shell, and offered it. "Take it back to your perch."

Iris grasped it and flew with a rush of feathers to the perch by the patio door.

The ferret looked up, and then rolled over in Quinn's lap onto his back. Quinn obliged the silent invitation and rubbed Sidney's stomach. After a week of dropping into Lisa's home, it was obvious she'd be lost without the pets. They were part of her life. He'd remember that when her birthday rolled around.

"Who's this?" Lisa asked. "Amy took a lot of pictures of him."

Quinn accepted the photo she handed him. The teenage boy was throwing a bale of hay from the bed of a pickup truck to waiting cattle. "Amy's boyfriend at the time she disappeared. Fred Wilson. They had been going together for about two years."

"Nice-looking guy."

"Pretty devastated at her disappearance from what I remember."

"He was ruled out as a suspect?" Marcus asked, looking at the photo.

"He was rebuilding a fence with his dad the day Amy disappeared. No one was ever totally ruled out, but he's low on the list."

Marcus nodded and handed it back to Lisa.

"Did Amy have her camera with her when she disappeared?" Lisa asked.

"Good question. Yes, one of her Nikons was missing."

"Never found?"

"No."

"I wish we could find some kind of proof that she came to Chicago." She stretched carefully, taking the strain out of her back.

"If it exists, we'll find it," Quinn replied, certain of that.

The room became quiet as they worked.

"So what were you doing when you were sixteen?" Lisa casually tossed the question back at him. It caught him off guard; it was the first probe she'd made into his past. There was a wonderful irony to the fact she was asking while her brother was in the room.

"At sixteen I was doing my best to survive the rodeo circuit and seriously pursuing Ashley Blake, the soon-to-be-crowned Miss Montana."

"You didn't catch her."

"On the contrary. She made me the envy of every guy in the state for the next two years running. Then she married my best friend."

Lisa laughed. It was a good sound, with no hesitation part of it. "Why do I have a feeling you were part of that?"

"Jed's a quiet kind of guy. Ashley just needed an excuse to hang out with him."

"And it gave you cover from all the girls chasing you."

Quinn winked at her, then glanced at Marcus. "She's smart."

"No argument here."

Lisa didn't follow up on it, to his disappointment.

She looked back at her notepad and running list of issues. "How much money did Amy have access to when she disappeared?"

"Not much. Maybe thirty dollars according her mom."

"Unless she had been hoarding money for a while in preparation of leaving."

"Which is why we might be having such a hard time finding a record of her travel. If it wasn't a spur of the moment runaway, then she either got transportation arranged early or Rita made the reservations for her."

"Do we have access to Rita's accounts when she was sixteen?"

"Her mom sent over what she had, but there's not much there. No way to trace all the cash from her summer jobs. What she wasn't spending on film, she was spending on camera equipment. There's just too much money unaccounted for to tell."

Quinn turned the page in the diary. Rita's handwriting at age sixteen had been enthusiastic, the letters sweeping and the words expansive, the number of exclamation points and underlined words and sad or smiling faces making it very easy to formulate a good idea of who she was.

A happy kid.

Fights and secrets with friends, crushes, occasional comments about family, a lot of plans and dreams for her future.

She hadn't dated many of the entries and often had several that appeared to be written during the course of one day. He was in the section of the diary for the right year the girls had met. She'd spent five pages on her birthday party describing who had come and what they had said and what gifts she had received from whom, but he'd found no reference yet to the art camp or to Amy.

He turned the page and stopped at the first part of a new entry.

*Horses!! Sam took me to the forest preserve over by his house to ride
bikes and one of the trails goes by a big estate with its own stables.
It was so cool! There were like six horses and a foal out in the pasture. Mr. Danford told me I could come back and visit if I wanted,
bring my camera to take pictures of the horses. He was riding a big
sorrel that was just magnificent!*

"Gotcha," Quinn said quietly.

"What?"

He held out the diary to her. "Top of the left page."

She read the passage, then looked over at him. She didn't say anything for a long moment, and he understood that expression. There
was sadness there. "He knew Rita when she was sixteen."

"We'll prove he knew Amy too." Quinn was convinced of it now.

Eleven

Lisa twirled the plastic stem of a rubber-tipped dart between her thumb and first finger and considered the now slightly smudged, red *twenty-six* circled on the whiteboard. She sidearmed the dart toward the board and it stuck with a squishing sound just below the six. She scowled at the miss. Her eyes were blurry from the long days spent reading and the hours at the microscope. She ignored the darts on the floor that had not stuck and scored the four inside the circle. Four out of five was an improvement.

Two weeks working in the archive files and she had zilch.

She got up from the table, glanced one last time at the case she had spread out, and paced toward the far counter and the coffeepot. It was after eight on a Wednesday night, she was getting nowhere, and if she were smart she'd call it a night and go home. In the quiet night, the empty building, it wasn't just her imagination that had the victims haunting this room, that sat at the tables before their spread-out files, looking at her and silently shaming her for not seeing the truth.

She had to stop reading Stephen King before she went to sleep. The silence was accusing.

She dumped sugar into the coffee to help kill the headache and looked around the room at all the tables. There were seventeen cases presently set out, all ones that had shown promise. When one stopped yielding ideas, she had moved on to the next. And while results were still outstanding on most of the ballistic, fingerprint, and DNA tests she had requested, the first round had come back. She had added new evidence to several cases, but overall she had moved not a single case significantly forward.

There was a knifing death, a strangled assault case, two gunshot victims, a burned Jane Doe, three victims from an armed robbery gone bad…. The tables were weighed down under tragedies.

She had to find justice for somebody.

She'd even concede, cutting that goal of twenty-six successes to two if she could just get movement somewhere.

She could open another box and start a new case, but if she couldn't solve any from the first set she had already examined, it left little hope for the others she would open.

There had to be a better way to work this problem.

"What are the odds a murderer kills only once?" The question Quinn had asked lingered like an intriguing thread. In the unlikely event that Lincoln was right and Grant Danford was innocent, then there was a killer still out there. Or if Quinn was right and Grant had killed twice, what were the odds of a third time?

Two hundred and sixty cases—two hundred and sixty different killers?

No way.

Somewhere in this room there were cases that were similar. Find the common MO and she'd find cases she could link and leverage together.

It was a good enough idea to have her setting aside the coffee and reaching into the small refrigerator for a soda instead, knowing it would keep her awake unlike the coffee, a psychological difference if not a caffeine- and sugar-driven one.

Where did she start?

Group by age of the crime? type of crime? type of victim?

She was looking for a particular man, a particular killer. He would repeat himself.

The home invasions where robberies had resulted in a homeowner being killed—she'd already seen several of them. And the shootings—several were thought to be drug-related cases; those might be linked.

She went over to the shelves with the stacks of boxes she had yet to go through. Diane had done a first pass through the boxes, finding the original case numbers and figuring out which had some information already online, getting the basics entered for the remaining cases.

She brought up the database Diane was building and saw that all two hundred and sixty case numbers had been entered, and while the case subclassification had just begun, the date, location, and original detectives working on the case had been entered.

Lisa sorted the cases by date, called up the summary report, and printed a copy. She found a red pen, pushed the metal shelves around on their wheels to scan the boxes, and located the first case on the list.

The box was heavy and slid out to land with a thud on the tile floor. She sorted through the files until she found the crime scene photos. A shooting. She noted it on the printout and closed the box, then wrestled it back onto the shelf. The second case on the list was one she had already reviewed. An assault; the lady had died two days later from a fractured skull. She scrawled that in the margin.

The third case was on the top shelf. She eased the box down to the floor, holding her breath as it tried to shift before she was braced for the weight.

Lisa could feel an odd sense of relief building. This was a puzzle she now had a way to attack. She wanted a solution to at least some of these cases; it had become a very personal challenge. The victims were tugging at her, demanding justice.

❦

The buzzards were circling. Quinn reined in his horse at the sight, lifting his hat to shade his eyes as he looked to the south. He left his current job of moving cattle to veer off and investigate. In calving season they usually lost one or two heifers at birth and it was always a personal loss. He almost preferred losing one to the occasional wolf than losing one to birth.

He had been back from college only a few weeks and his back was sore, not yet accustomed to being back in the saddle for twelve hours a day. He rode toward the circling birds and found himself riding into darkness, the spacious landscape slowly disappearing from his peripheral view for the memories he was riding back into were black.

The bluffs were always dangerous places both to people and to cattle.

A man was on the ground, and even from a hundred yards away the red staining the back of the shirt was visible.

Dad!

Quinn choked as he woke in the hotel room to the strident sound of his beeper going off, sweating in the chilly room. The sheet was tangled in a knot around him. If he ever did marry, he'd run the risk of tossing his wife off the bed with his flailing around. The nightmare came more often now that he was actively working a lead for the case. He struggled out of the dream and back to the present, reaching for the pager that continued to sound.

He didn't recognize the number, but he couldn't ignore it. His hand reaching for the phone sent his watch and an empty water glass falling. He punched in the numbers. "What?" he growled at the intruder of his restless sleep.

"Quinn?"

"Lisa?" he queried, regretting the fact he'd barked. She'd hesitated to answer him. He turned around the alarm clock and the red lights glowed back at him. 1:42 A.M. He clicked on the bedside light. "What's wrong?" She had called him exactly once in all the years he had known her, and at this time of night…

"I can't see a clock and I'm not wearing a watch. What time is it?"

"Late. What's wrong? Where are you?"

"The office."

Some of his tension eased. Not at home with a problem, not in a car accident somewhere. But with that injury… "Are you okay?" Getting answers out of her was like pulling teeth.

"Quinn, I'm fine," she replied, her voice tinged with annoyance. "Now would you listen?"

He closed his eyes to stop his first reply. "I'm listening."

"I've found something you should see."

He waited and she didn't add anything. "Okay," he said cautiously.

"Well are you coming?"

"Now?"

"Quinn—"

"Hold it, before you get mad at me—you woke me up, Lisa. Give me a minute here. What's going on?"

There was dead silence that lingered. When she finally spoke her voice was edged with sarcasm. "Never mind. I'll call Marcus."

"Don't hang up," he ordered, half afraid she already had. He'd just blown it with her. And he deserved to. O'Malleys didn't ask questions. He'd seen Marcus catch a flight at a moment's notice when Lisa said she needed to see him, not asking why, the request itself sufficient. Lisa did not make unnecessary or trivial requests; none of the O'Malleys did. "I'll be there. Give me twenty minutes."

He held his breath until he got her terse reply. "I'll tell the security guard to expect you."

The bakery down the block from the state crime lab had its lights on, the staff beginning preparations for the dawn onslaught of customers. Quinn bought four still-warm blueberry muffins. It wasn't much of an apology, but it was something. Not hardly enough though. She'd actually called him before her family and he'd blown it. He had a headache and it was his own fault.

Quinn pulled open the door to the lab. He waited at the security desk while the downtown marshal's office confirmed his ID and the security guard cleared him, then clipped on the guest badge and headed upstairs.

The door to the task force room was closed, but light was visible beneath it. Quinn opened the door and was met with the assault of another wailing saxophone. He had to get her some better music.

Lisa was leaning over the light table, studying a set of X-rays. She had said she was okay, but it was a relief to see for himself. She had been here all day; she was still wearing the blue-and-white striped shirt he enjoyed because it set off her eyes fabulously, and her blue jeans were the well-washed pair speckled in white patches where bleach had washed out the color. He thought of them as her old comfortable favorites and knew when he saw her wearing them that she'd had something rough happen the previous day or night and had instinctively gone for comfort. "You're late," she commented, not looking up.

"Food."

She looked around, spotted the sack, and her smiled flashed immediately. "You're forgiven, and thank you. There's not even a vending machine on this floor and I'm famished." She nodded toward a desk. "There is safe."

He set down the sack and tossed his keys beside it.

"I've got four women found as skeletons across the Chicagoland area, just like Rita Beck. Only their four cases are still open."

He stopped in the act of ditching his hat. This was definitely worth being pulled out of bed in the middle of the night to hear. He dropped the hat on the desk. "Which cases?"

She gestured immediately to her right. "These four tables." The case boxes were open, the files laid out on the tables.

"Please tell me Grant Danford knew them all."

"Quinn...I just got started."

"Sorry. Tell me what you've got."

She sat down on the edge of the desk, picked up a marker, and began to add information to the rolling whiteboard she pulled over. "Martha Treemont, found in 1993, missing for six years. Heather Ashburn, found in 1995, missing for ten years. Vera Wane, found in 1998, missing two years. And Marla Sherrall, found last year, missing eight years."

"And if Grant Danford is responsible, add Rita Beck, found in 1997, missing eight years, and a suspicion of Amy Ireland, missing for twenty years."

"Yes."

"Five, possibly six cases, going back twenty years."

"That we know of."

He nodded, accepting the very valid qualification. If there was a pattern in these deaths, it was that the evidence of the murder was only uncovered years later. There would be more victims than just these five if they were linked.

He picked up one of the dropped darts from the floor, twirling it between his fingers as he looked at the dates she had written on the board. "A common MO in the victims?"

"A twenty-four-year-old architect student, a sixty-two-year-old retired widow, a forty-five-year-old former landscape nursery worker, and a thirty-two-year-old French bakery worker."

He was puzzled at that. "It doesn't fit Rita or Amy."

"Women, all single; different geographic areas, different economic statuses, a vast age range."

"Lisa, you've lost me. Having five open cases over fifteen years in this surrounding area where the female victim was buried is not surprising given the number of murders each year."

"You're right. And there are another twelve cases vaguely similar that I set aside as explainable to different factors—obvious gunshot wounds, known abusive situations, suspected family violence. But these—Quinn, I don't know how to better explain it than the fact the hair on the back of my neck stood on end when I scanned the reports. It's what isn't there. No obvious blows, gunshots, no apparent causes of death—just a skeleton appearing in the earth buried face down. Three of the four cases show hands behind the back, the other was moved before it could be noted; two of the cases show remains of duct tape."

Quinn winced. "An MO in the method but random victims."

"Exactly."

"Then let's hope it is Grant—or at least someone already behind bars." He read the names and dates, made an educated guess. "They weren't connected before because they come from different jurisdictions."

"Different jurisdictions over a long period of years, and several of the cases were not even in the computer databases until this review began."

"Where do you want me to start?"

"I need the who, what, where, and when summarized for each. I've got to get focused on the physical evidence and see how similar they really are. Quinn—"

"I know. If this is one killer, and it's not Grant, you just landed in one of the biggest, deepest messes of your life." Women were disappearing and turning up as bones years later.

She looked hesitant. "Thanks for helping. This may be a false alarm and there's nothing here. I was kind of rude about waking you up."

He reached over and slid his hand behind her neck, wanting the contact just to make his reassurance reach inside and go deeper than words. His thumb rubbed the back of her neck and she slowly relaxed under his touch.

He hated knowing he had contributed to her hesitation and wanted to ensure she didn't hesitate next time she considered calling him. "The ghosts in here are thick. If you're wrong, I'll buy you breakfast and enjoy the fact you asked for my company. If you're right—you'll be stuck with me and Lincoln like your own personal shadows. Please don't count my rather abysmal initial reaction against me. I appreciate that you called."

"Maybe next time you won't be so surprised when you hear it's me calling."

He smiled at that soft acceptance of his apology. "I found it a very nice surprise that I would like very much to have repeated."

She grasped his forearm and squeezed as she nodded.

He reluctantly lowered his hand. "Get started on the physical evidence and I'll start reviewing the files. We both know Rita Beck's case inside and out. If these have a similar feel, it will be obvious to both of us. Do you have what you need here, or do you want to go over to the cold storage evidence vaults?"

"I've got the basics here: the crime scene photographs, autopsy reports, and the X-ray slides."

"Then eat a muffin, and get to work."

She crossed over to the desk and opened the sack. "Do I have to share?"

He glanced over from the folder he had picked up and smiled at that subtle plea in her voice. "If that's dinner, then no, have all four."

"If I wasn't about to inhale this muffin I'd tell you thanks again."

"You're welcome. And you're easy to please."

She sat down holding the first muffin and spun her chair around toward the light board. "You have good taste in food, unlike Kate, who tends to get the banana nut ones."

"Good taste?"

"I'm not afraid to admit it when you're occasionally right."

"In that case, how about dinner some night and I'll show you what really good food is?"

"I like hot stuff."

"You would. I'll see what I can come up with."

"Thai is good."

"Plan to pick the restaurant too?"

She smiled. "Just broadening your palate a bit."

"You'll have to get more creative than that. I've eaten at the best ethnic neighborhood restaurants from New York to L.A."

"A challenge?"

"I can probably spring for two meals if you want to compare choices."

"Deal. I'm hungry. And I'm broke."

The admission made him laugh. "What did you buy now?"

"It's still on layaway at the gallery. I found a Krauthmerr portrait. It's fabulous. I needed a break Monday, so I took a late lunch and went browsing. The hike in my homeowner insurance payments is going to kill me but it's worth it."

She was so pleased with herself; he enjoyed enormously sharing that pleasure. "And I wonder why it is so hard to find something good when I'm at the galleries. You've been there first."

"Guilty."

He loved the fact they shared a passion for art. "Just to satisfy my curiosity, the last time I invited you to dinner—where in the world did you get that petrified squid you sent me in reply?"

Her eyes danced as she laughed. "Trade secret."

"I found it to be a very unique no."

"I'd hate to be thought of as less than original." She turned on the hotshot bulb to warm up. "If you can keep a secret, I'll show you my real treasures. They're in my office filing cabinet."

"You collect odd specimens."

"The more unusual the better. Would you hand me that red folder by your left elbow? It should be Heather Ashburn's dental records."

Quinn flipped it open, confirmed that it was, and handed the folder over.

She turned her attention back to work. Quinn watched her for a few minutes, then turned his attention to the first case and reached for the initial police report.

When he finished reading the details of the fourth case, dawn was less than an hour away. Lisa was taking measurements from a set of X-rays, jotting numbers on a pad of paper. "See anything there?"

She absently nodded as she moved the caliper. "Martha Treemont. There's a fracture in her radius as if her arm was first rotated behind her back and then struck a hard surface: The bone shattered up into the elbow joint. She put up a fight; that seems to be common to these cases."

Quinn saw her rub her eyes, and that frown was back. She had a tension headache and the way she was sitting her back was hurting too. He closed his file. "We need to visit the most recent scene. After you get some sleep."

She looked over at him and set aside what she was doing. "Marla Sherrall?"

"Yes. The way she was buried—it's Rita Beck all over again. Face down, hands behind her back, no apparent cause of death."

"Yes, it is," she admitted. "And you're right, it would be good to see the scene."

He leaned forward, rested his forearms on his knees, and studied her, something in her voice alerting him. "Lisa, what's wrong?" His voice gentled. "Did you work this case too? I didn't see your name on the reports, but I know you would have helped."

"No, I was out of the country when she was found. I did some of the lab work, helped during the analysis when the case got cold, but that's not it." She looked away from him as she got to her feet, but he could see the tension in her posture. "I once lived down the block from where she was found."

Twelve

Marla Sherrall's body had been found here, within sight of the hummingbirds. Lisa looked around the grove of white birch and weeping willow trees, the place peaceful but forever marked by the blight of what had occurred. The public park and small pond adjoined the zoo, the land an expansion area should they need to extend the exhibit space.

"I doubt she was killed here," she said quietly, pushing aside the low-hanging limbs of the weeping willow tree to get closer to where the grave had been discovered. It was an awkward place, isolated, but remote only in that the focus was on the adjoining exhibits in the zoo to the right side of the path, and not on this stand of trees to the left.

"Agreed. But he made an effort to bring her back here."

"Location is important to him. Maybe central." She studied the damage at the base of the willow tree. Decay had rotted the tree trunk, causing sap to run out. It was too near the zoo to use pesticides to kill the beetle infestation. Park personnel had been digging out the tree when their shovel had hit Marla's left arm, breaking the radius bone.

"It reads that way, given the chance he was taking to bury her here."

She nodded even as she tried to think like the man. Why here? There was a reason. Marla had been buried near water, sometimes a significant signature. She'd been buried in her own neighborhood. Was the proximity to the zoo significant?

Knolls Park was hidden in the north section of Chicago within an easy commute to downtown. The streets were narrow; the oak trees tall, old, and overhanging the streets; most homes brick two-storied, tall, and narrow with steep roofs. The upper-middle-class community was made unique by the small zoo. It was the community's pride and joy and thrived as the local alternative to the much larger downtown zoo.

This was a community that still had local businesses in its downtown—an ice-cream shop, an upscale clothing store, a bridal shop, a gift card shop, and two local restaurants along the main street. The French bakery where Marla had worked was between the library and the bank, a fourteen-minute walk away. They had timed it to figure out if someone could have stalked her from work, caught her alone on the path, and killed her here. But the location suggested it had been a much more deliberate act, planned long before it occurred.

Lisa stood up, studying the path. The grove of trees was only about twenty feet from the back of the zoo's aviary building. Behind the fine mesh of the nearest enclosure hung a row of odd-shaped, red-based water tubes filled with sugar water, nectar to the hummingbirds that were attracted by the color. Lisa knew the zoo, knew those birds, had watched them for hours as a child. They could dart and maneuver and hover with wings moving too fast to see.

She had enjoyed the zoo. It was one of the few good memories in a cluster so sharp and painful the explosive emotions were hard to contain even after all these years. Follow the dirt footpath and the next block over was St. James Street. She forced the thought away, even as she felt the tension grip her. She'd had enough of this place. "I've seen everything I need to."

"The bakery is still in business; let's see if it's the same owner. I want to know more about Marla's boyfriend."

"No." She said it too sharply and felt his attention change from the job to her in a fraction of a second. She moderated her voice. "I don't want to talk to him, not until we review his original statements when she disappeared and when she was found again. I want to be ready to spot any inconsistencies." And she'd be very sure to have a last-minute conflict so she wouldn't be available to go along with Quinn for the interview.

He studied her, then finally nodded. "All right. We'll wait."

Lisa turned back the way they had come, relieved to get out of here.

Quinn rested one booted foot on the bench in front of the Knolls Park Bank as he ate a turkey croissant sandwich. Lisa, seated at the other end of the bench, was so tightly wound up she started every time the outside book drop for the library was used. Whatever was wrong, the longer they stayed in this neighborhood, the worse it became.

He'd insisted that they stop at the bakery so he could at least look around inside. Lisa hadn't wanted a late lunch but hadn't been able to refuse since he knew the last things she'd eaten were the blueberry muffins over ten hours ago. She was nibbling her sandwich like it was plaster paste while he'd rate his as one of the best sandwiches he'd had in a long time.

He wished she would tell him what was wrong.

He considered deliberately stalling them longer to use the situation to probe for the reason. In another situation he would have done it, even though she was a friend. Kate had been that way; he'd had to crowd her to get her to open up. Jennifer had simply called and cried, and he'd had to wait out the tears before she could tell him what had happened.

With Lisa—the silence was different. She would never allow herself to break, it was a different weight she carried, and knowing that, he wasn't sure how to proceed. He had learned a long time ago that secrets, even those made to protect someone, always over the years came back to the fact they were lies to maintain and wore a person down. She had her secret buried deep, but this place was resurrecting it.

He hated the fact she was hurting and he wasn't sure how to help.

Quinn wadded the waxed paper wrapper into a small ball and lowered his foot back to the ground, straightening. "Ready to go?"

She didn't answer for a moment, then only glanced over at him. "Yes."

He didn't like the quiet of her voice. For the first time there was an edge of defeat to it. The fact she didn't protest when he dropped his arm around her shoulders and steered her back toward the car bothered him even more. "Let's go see a movie."

She glanced over, caught by surprise, and smiled. "Sure."

She could keep her secret; he'd just have to find out the answer another way.

Under the large lighted magnifying glass, the tweezers designed to pick up a single hair looked big and clumsy. Lisa held her breath to steady her hand as she separated another thread within the edge of the duct tape taken from Rita's wrists.

Two of the fours cases she had discovered had duct tape binding their hands. So had Rita's. It was improbable that the tape came from a common roll because the crimes had happened too many years apart, but if the tape matched to a common manufacturer—that would be useful knowledge. Certain brands were more common for consumer sales while others sold only through industrial channels.

Lisa carefully used the tweezers to count the threads. Forty-two threads in this tape weave. She groaned. She had hoped for fifty-four. She leaned back from the magnifying glass and closed her eyes to let them relax before she looked again at the tape.

Was it complete side to side, or had a strip of the tape been torn away? She focused again on the sides of the tape. It had been twisted around the wrist bones, and it took time to flatten it out far enough back to check the side edges. This strip of duct tape was intact. It did not match the tape from the other two cases.

Heather Ashburn and Vera Wane were linked. The duct tape in those cases had been fifty-four thread, seven millimeter, which typed it as the consumer brand of Triker Duct Tape. But Rita was forty-two thread, eight millimeter, and that made it a different brand she would have to track down.

If they couldn't find a pattern in the victims, then it became even more important to find a solid, consistent MO to the method of the crime. A difference in brand of tape was a problem.

She leaned back, rubbing the back of her neck. She did not need this.

What about Marla Sherrall? There wasn't duct tape available to help establish a common MO, but given where and how she had been found, how the excavation had been done—there had been no tape discovered but that didn't mean she hadn't been bound.

The cold storage warehouse was just that: cold. Lisa wished she had thought to grab a sweater from her office before signing through security to come over to this side of the state crime lab complex.

She walked down the tile hallway of the lower level, stopped at the third door, and unlocked it. While it had an official name nowhere near as descriptive, the room was called by those who entered here for what it was: the bone vault. The florescent lights overhead snapped on, bathing everything in sharp, bright light, intensifying the impact of the room. The skulls looked back at her, neatly lined up on foam circles along the shelf of the back wall—three men, two women, and two children.

It really felt like entering an open-air graveyard, one of the few places in the building where Lisa felt the silent stillness and foreverness of death. The morgue was not nearly so overpowering in its effect.

She reached for the evidence log clipboard hanging on the wall inside the doorway; glanced at the clock; wrote down the date, time, case number, the lab ID number next door where she would be working; then signed the log.

There was a long metal table in the middle of the room. She rolled it over to the storage case and started scanning for Marla Sherall's case number. Similar to an architect's storage case for blueprints, the long, flat skeleton drawers were eight inches deep, five feet long, and two feet wide. Finding the right drawer, she adjusted the metal table height and slid out the drawer onto the table.

Lisa covered the box with a lid, not for the protection of the remains but for the comfort of anyone she might pass in the hallways. She rolled the table from the room, locked the vault, and took the skeleton to the X-ray room.

"How long an exposure do you need?" Janice asked, holding the door for her to the lead-lined room.

"Let's start with ten minutes." Lisa didn't have to worry about the radiation exposure a hospital doctor would with a living patient. Ten minutes would give her any clues the bones hid deep inside.

It had been months since she had last held the bones; they were dry, and over the passage of years had lost their ivory smoothness. She carefully positioned the left hand for the first X-ray, then stepped into the adjoining room and gave Janice the all clear. The X-ray machine began to hum. Lisa watched the first X-ray film print roll from the developing machine fourteen minutes later. She had the clarity she needed. "Exposure time looks good," she confirmed.

Janice helped her set up for the left wrist picture.

An hour and forty minutes later Lisa had the images she needed. "Thanks, Janice."

"Anytime."

Lisa rolled the table with Marla's remains to the service elevator and took them to the task force room where she had set up an exam table.

She slid the X-rays onto the light table.

Was there a way to prove without the duct tape being recovered that Marla's hands had been bound the same way as Rita's? Duct tape around the wrists and also around the palms pressing the back of her hands together? It was a signature Lisa had never seen before. Finding it would be enough to link the cases.

Lisa started with the obvious break in Marla's left arm.

The radius bone had been broken by the shovel long after her death: The bone break was brittle, sharp-edged enough to leave splinters, grayish white in color after the dirt had been carefully removed.

In a living bone the edges of the break would have curls recorded in the bone layers as the pressure built and it finally snapped; the edges of the break would also have deepened in color over the years as the rest of the bones had to match the surrounding soil.

Marla's wrist bones were undamaged, but her palm—there were two breaks in the fourth and fifth metacarpal bones, the outer two bones of her palm. Even under the powerful microscope they showed no sign of healing; she'd died within hours of the breaks.

Lisa moved over to look at Marla's right hand and found a break in the outmost bone of the palm.

She leaned back in her chair, thought for a moment, then held her own hands out in front of her, considering the bones Marla had broken. When someone put her hands out to break a fall, normally one or two of the finger bones broke because they were bent back, or one or two of the wrist bones broke if she landed on the base of her palms. And if Marla had struck someone with her fist, she would have probably broken the long bones of her fingers.

To break the edge bones in her palms but not her fingers…

Lisa leaned forward and put her hands behind her back, pressing the backs of her hands together, and slowly leaned her weight back against the chair but found it impossible to shift her hands around with the backs of her hands pressed together. If Marla had been bound, thrown down to land on her back, she would have broken the small finger bones in her hands just as Rita had done.

This didn't make sense.

Lisa looked at her hands again, turning them palms up. Maybe someone had stepped on her hands? She turned to look at the X-rays only to stop midway in the turn, her thoughts taking a tangent.

She slowly nodded. Maybe.

She stood up, crossed over to the desk and put her hands behind her back as she suspected Marla's had been bound. She turned and let herself fall back against the desk, and felt the sharp sting of contact as her hands hit. It was the outer palm bones and not the finger bones, not even the wrist bones.

Rita had been pushed back and fallen to the ground. Marla had been pushed back and hit something but had been able to stay on her feet.

Lisa sighed, facing another dilemma. How did she prove that?

"Now that is a deep scowl."

Quinn turned away from the screen and the report he was trying to write, relieved to have the interruption. "Kate. Thanks for coming."

"I see you still hate paperwork."

"That's an understatement."

She entered the small room he had borrowed at the regional marshal's office and cleared a chair so she could sit down. "You called. Here I am."

He grinned; she was clearly having a good Friday off work. His call had woken her this morning, still curled up in bed at 9 A.M. While he'd been fighting paperwork all afternoon, she'd been out having fun.

He offered her the glass jar of jelly beans she was studying. "Orange still your favorites?"

She rolled the jar to keep stirring the mix as she selected a handful one at a time. "I never could figure out why they would make green. Who wants to eat green candy? They remind me of mold."

Quinn chuckled and took back the jar after she was finished; he had to agree.

"What are you working on?"

"Do you have any idea how many dark green Plymouths there are in this city, let alone the surrounding counties?"

"One at every used car lot at least. Do they still even make that color?"

"Unfortunately, yes. And checking out 826 Plymouths is impossible."

"It was probably stolen anyway," she replied cheerfully.

"Thanks for pointing that fact out." Quinn knew she was probably right even though there hadn't been a stolen car report. "I don't remember you being this perky back in the days we used to date."

"Dave took me shopping."

Quinn didn't react for a moment; he couldn't. "He took you shopping, and you liked it?"

His voice was so disbelieving she laughed. "We bought Jennifer's wedding present. She's going to love it."

"Did you?"

"It's this really great plush chair, at least a thousand colors, the most predominant one bright orange, very retro. It had to come straight out of the sixties."

"You didn't."

"She's wanted one for years. She always was a rebel under that perfect decorum."

"Kate—"

"Relax. After Dave about had a conniption fit we bought her a really nice and perfectly acceptable car. Well, we picked it out, at least.

It will be delivered from a dealer in Baltimore if she's still in the hospital, or a dealer in Houston if she's home."

"You bought her a car."

"A spitfire-red Corvette. She's always wanted one of those too."

"And you'll be paying on it for the next century."

"It's on plastic. And Dave owes my debts when we get married. He can afford it."

He broke out laughing. She was serious. "Kate, you're terrible."

"I know." She ate another two of the jellybeans. "Actually, everybody but Lisa is in on it. She can't keep a secret worth squat. So we'll tell her about it five minutes before we hand Jennifer the keys."

Quinn knew better than that about the secrets but kept his own counsel. "Let me guess, you're prowling for donations."

"Always accepted."

"In that case, Lisa's broke. Put me down for both of us."

"I knew I could count on you." She stretched out in the chair, her voice turning serious. "I know it's extravagant, and most people won't understand—"

"I do. Some people talk about a trip to Hawaii for their fiftieth birthday, a cruise when they retire. Jennifer has always talked about her someday-dream of having a red convertible."

"She doesn't have a lot of somedays left."

Six months, a year… It wasn't long if the cancer couldn't be stopped. "Kate—she'll love the car. Give her a chance to enjoy her dream. She'll understand."

"I hope so." Kate slouched in the chair and crossed her ankles. "So…back to the start of this conversation. You called. What's up?"

"Your shoelaces are untied."

"What?"

He snagged her left foot and lifted it to rest against his knee so he could take care of the problem. "You need new tennis shoes." These were so beat up this one about had a hole in the sole.

"Dave's already bought me at least half a dozen different styles and colors. He just doesn't get the fact these are my lucky pair. I haven't lost a handball match against him yet while wearing these shoes."

"The first sprained ankle is going to change that."

"Not likely. They're too loose. I'd just slip out of them." She looked at the very neat knot he had tied. "Perfectionist." She crossed her feet again, then looked back at him. "Now that you tried that subtle redirect that didn't do you any good—why did you call?"

He hated the way she could read people. He had been hoping against hope that he would hear back from someone with the details he was looking for before Kate got here, but his last outstanding query had come back an hour ago. He was out of options and he needed answers.

"Has Lisa ever mentioned much about when she lived in Knolls Park?" He got straight to the point, knowing that with Kate it was best to be direct.

Lisa was going to kill him. He had wrestled over what it meant to go to her family for help—to protect Lisa's right to privacy or to break her implied trust and share her secret. He didn't have a choice. What he needed to know, not many people could deliver; he'd found that out this afternoon. But Kate could.

If she knew something and was going to cover that truth, deny it, he'd see it as a slight distance entered her gaze and she shifted subtly into work mode, concealing her thoughts. But her expression stayed open and only turned puzzled.

"I didn't know she ever had. Her foster homes were all to the south and west of Trevor House." Her expression turned to a frown as she picked up on his shift in mood. "Why are you asking?"

He would have told Marcus first, but he knew the two of them. His partner would have absorbed the news and picked up the phone to call Kate; they were that tight on what was best to do for the family. In the end, he'd made the choice to go first to Kate. Marcus had the nationwide contacts, but when it came to Chicago, Kate knew the system, knew how to find facts buried deep.

"We were working a lead, a lady named Marla Sherrall who was found buried near the zoo at Knolls Park. Lisa said she once lived a block from where Marla was found." He pushed his hand through his hair, knowing what he was about to do would have consequences. "Lisa reacted," he hesitated over how much to say, "badly to the situation."

"Quinn…keep talking," Kate said softly.

"She couldn't wait to get out of the neighborhood, she didn't want to stop and talk to people who might have known the victim, made an excuse not to enter the bakery where Marla had worked."

"She shut down."

"Hard. It took me three hours after we left the neighborhood to get her out of that quiet…*despair*, for want of a better word. I don't like it."

"She never lived at Knolls Park."

Quinn looked at her.

And the silence stretched.

Kate's eyes darkened. "I'll check," she agreed quietly. In her voice was the firsthand experience of knowing what secrets in a childhood often meant.

Quinn could only nod. If Kate found what he feared… Quinn hoped Lisa would be in a forgiving spirit when she learned what he had done.

Thirteen

I t's a reach."

Lisa turned at his words, frustration written all over her face, and Quinn just waited it out. He was right, she knew it, but she didn't want to accept it. Her supposition over how Marla might have broken the bones in her hands was a very long reach. Even if true, it didn't prove her hands had been bound that way. It only was a hypothesis that fit what they hoped to find.

"It's not that far a reach." She dropped into the chair by the desk, winced at the jarring impact of the movement, and stared with frustration at the whiteboard. "And we need something to fit."

It was late Saturday, they had been debating the merits of the evidence in the four cases nonstop for the last few days. They were both tired enough it had come down to sniping at each other.

She was pushing herself too hard; he was pushing himself too hard. It wasn't worth it. For the first time Quinn was ready to admit solving something twenty years old wasn't worth what it was costing him in the present.

Lisa leaned her head against the back of her chair and looked at the map on the wall as she absently rolled her chair back and forth with her foot. "I can't believe all these dead ends. We can prove Grant knew Rita when she was sixteen—but he's already been convicted of killing her. We can't find any connection between Amy and Grant; we can't find any connection between Grant and these victims. I know all these cases are related, I can feel it, but I can prove only Heather and Vera are linked."

The map with red dots marking gravesites, blue dots marking victims' homes, and green dots where they had worked showed no discernible pattern. They were all over the Chicagoland area. Yesterday morning Lisa had proposed that maybe it was like the I-45 cases in Texas, a common interstate running within a short distance of all the sites, but there was nothing obvious on the map. No cluster of dots, no common thoroughfare.

"Go home. Get some sleep. We'll look at everything with a fresh perspective on Monday."

She turned in her chair at his words. "You want to give up."

There was accusation in her voice. She was a fierce little thing, and it pleased him, but at the same time one of them had to face reality. And in this case he appeared to be the one who had reached that conclusion first.

"I'm not saying these four cases might not be linked, I'm not even ready to rule out Grant as the guy who killed them. But I think we can rule out the idea of trying to match them to anything having to do with Amy."

He sighed when he saw her expression.

"Lisa, we may well be chasing something that is not there. Yes, Rita and Amy knew each other. But it's time to consider the reality that that may be the extent of it. They were friends when they were sixteen, kept in sporadic touch, and that is all that's there. We've found no trace that Amy ever came back to Chicago."

"Rita's diary for that period of time is missing."

"Lost, not missing," Quinn corrected. "It's frustrating because that is one thing that would rule in or out the hypothesis that Amy came here, but you have to admit, there would be other evidence too. Two weeks with four of us looking for that link and we haven't uncovered a thing. My idea is cold; I can feel it."

He had learned a long time ago how to be a pragmatist. If there was any more evidence to undercover regarding Amy, they would have found something by now. Lincoln had as much as indicated that was his conclusion over lunch but hadn't said it outright.

"You think Amy's buried somewhere out in Montana?"

"It's always been the most logical explanation for her disappearance, even if it is the most difficult to confirm."

"This is so frustrating."

"Go home. Forget about this for the rest of the weekend."

"I want to read through the Treemont case again."

"It wasn't a suggestion. I'll call Kate if you're going to be stubborn."

She scowled. "It's not nice to go behind my back."

The words stung, with an implication she wasn't aware of. "I only do it when it's necessary," he replied quietly.

Quinn walked through the front doors of the hotel into the near-empty lobby at eleven-thirty that night, tired—physically, emotionally, and spiritually. It had taken another hour to convince Lisa to go home. She would live in that lab if someone didn't take away her building keys.

Two more days, then he was going to call this search ended. Lisa needed her life back, she was working too many extra hours on a problem that was going nowhere. And he needed to release it rather than hold so tight he lost his perspective.

The day couldn't get worse than this.

Kate was sitting in a plush chair among the general seating across from the check-in counter, choosing the one chair that would put her back to the wall and watching those who entered the hotel. Tension coiled through his spine; he changed course to meet her. She got to her feet as he came over. He took one look at her expression, settled his hands gently on her forearms, and nodded toward the lounge. "You need a table or a walk?"

"Let's walk."

He wrapped his arm around her shoulders, reversed course, and pushed open the doors for them both. The night was warm but there was still a breeze. Kate shoved her hands in her pockets and they headed down the wide downtown sidewalk toward the river bridge.

"You got a page." He knew the signs. Kate could walk into tense situations and negotiate through them, apparently bored, transferring her lack of excitement to those emotionally charged scenes, calming them down, finding a resolution that was peaceful. Afterward though, all the emotions she suppressed discharged far away from work. He could see her burning through it.

"A drug warrant arrest went wrong. A cop got tangled in the middle of it, and two kids. It was a long afternoon."

He rubbed his thumb against the knot in her shoulder. "Everybody okay?"

"Yeah. I feel like punching something, but that's nothing new. The emotions will pass. I sat in the hall on the other side of a busted apartment door for six hours. Hot as blazes, I went through about a dozen water bottles, but not as bad as most cases lately."

"Keep drinking a lot of water tonight or your muscles will cramp."

"I will."

She would typically have called Marcus when she needed to unwind about a case, but she'd taken the time to track him down instead. She hadn't paged—because she knew he'd been with Lisa? The case she'd worked wasn't the reason she had come to find him.

"There was something waiting for me when I got back to the office tonight." She looked over at him. "You're not going to like this, Quinn."

They were at the river bridge. He turned her toward one of the benches where they could sit and watch the boats. Quinn braced his forearms against his knees, not looking at Kate because he had a feeling he knew what subject was coming and that his first reaction was not going to be worth seeing. "What did you find?"

"I had to call in nearly every IOU I had to find someone who could check Lisa's foster care files. If they had been court sealed like mine, I wouldn't have been able to get anywhere, but they were still available in the archives. I found a caseworker who had the clearance to look. Lisa was seven when she was placed with the Richards." Her tone of voice had reverted to fact mode, the cop was taking over, but he could feel the tension that she couldn't mask.

"They were a couple in their late thirties, had two children of their own, and cared for two foster kids. Their oldest boy Andy was two years older than Lisa. At that age Lizzy was a tomboy; she and Andy apparently got along great together, tagged around with each other from the start." Her voice went flat. "Preliminary adoption papers got filed."

Kate stopped talking. Quinn looked over and saw she was almost crying. He reached over to squeeze her hand. "What happened?"

"Andy drowned."

Quinn closed his eyes, absorbing that pain.

"A swimming pool. He hit his head doing a dive. Lisa couldn't swim. Almost drowned herself trying to help him." She scrubbed her hands down her face. "I followed up on a couple names I was given who knew what happened. I wish now I hadn't. She's going to hate me."

He rubbed her back. "No she won't. I started this. Lisa is above all else fair."

"Quinn, I found the minister of the church the family attended who did Andy's funeral, spent about an hour talking to him; he remembers them, remembers Lisa. Maybe I touched a guilty conscience, but he was pretty open once he knew who I was, why I was asking. The Richards were solid Christians; Lisa had been going with them to church, had even talked to the minister about salvation and being baptized. The Richards turned their grief over Andy toward Lisa, blamed her, sent her back into the system. She went through a couple more foster homes, then ended up at Trevor House."

He didn't say anything. It hurt too much.

"She never said anything to any of us about the Richards. I know something about the other foster families, but she never mentioned any of this. To yank preliminary adoption papers out from under a seven-year-old after she'd just watched her best friend die... I'm ready to be sick. The things I asked Lisa...I didn't know but still it's inexcusable. The comments must have cut like glass.

"The more Lisa expressed disinterest in church, the harder I pushed. Christians were the ones who had told her they loved her, gave her the most hope she'd ever had of having a family, and then tore her to shreds. She's got a right to want to have nothing to do with the subject."

"Have you told Marcus?" Quinn asked softly, hurting for Lisa, worried about Kate. She had obviously come to find him straight from learning the news. Kate's heart was to protect people, and when it was someone she cared about—this news was devastating to her.

"Not yet."

"Tell him. Lisa has lived with it for years. Let her have some room for now. And give yourself some space."

"No wonder Lisa is so convinced the Resurrection doesn't make sense, that people don't come back from the dead. She watched them do mouth-to-mouth and try to get Andy to breathe again and he never did." She pulled in a deep breath. "I'm so mad at what they did to her. As if it were her fault."

Kate wiped at tears now falling. Quinn turned her face into his shoulder, let her cry, absorbed her tears. He knew exactly what she meant.

Lisa had always longed for a place to belong, thought she'd finally found it, and tragedy had ripped it away. Even if he could understand the Richards' pain and grief, other Christians in the church had seen what was happening to Lisa, and no one had stepped forward to at least be another foster family and stop her from being sent back into the system. She'd had to deal with what happened on her own. He hated what it said. Adults should have known better.

Kate had had it no easier, but at least for her the system had been a relief, getting her out of a horrible situation. "You survived and got past the pain; Lisa will too. And this explains the independence, why she makes it so hard to get close."

"It used to hurt, at Trevor House, when Lisa would stand off to the side and decline when I'd invite her to do something. I thought she didn't like me, that it was something I had done. She'd spend her time instead with her pets, as if they were more important. And even now—she takes most of her vacations alone, trekking off into the world as if she doesn't need anybody."

"She probably tells herself that still," Quinn said quietly.

"It's not right."

"She trusts you, Kate. Even if you wonder about it, I've watched her, listened to her. She waits to see what you think before she makes major decisions. You really matter. You've stuck for twenty years. That's the best healing you could have given her. She loves you, even if she finds the words hard to say."

"I love her too." Kate looked at him. "What are we going to do?"

"Think. And do a lot of praying."

"She's gone to scientific reasons why the Bible isn't true, will argue the point from logic, rather than admit the emotional reason she's not interested. There are so many layers that would have to be stripped away just to get to this hurt."

"Jesus can heal it."

"Do you really believe she'll ever trust Him enough to risk getting close again? She started to believe once before and watched her life crumble."

"She's not a coward. And something that has to hurt this bad—she's thought about it, Kate. She's probably thought about it so much it's become a boulder in her past she can't move."

"There has to be a way to help."

"We'll find it. Go talk to Marcus. He needs to know."

Quinn paced his hotel room, picked up some of the clutter to avoid sitting down. He didn't know what to do. Yes, he did. He was just trying to talk himself out of it.

He tossed his hat on the bed, realized what he had done, and scowled. Wonderful; he'd just given himself three months of bad luck. He moved the hat to the table. The old rodeo superstition died hard. Throw a hat on a bed, the only way to get rid of the bad luck was to kick it out a door. The hat had been beat up enough as it was.

Quinn picked up the soda he'd sacrificed a dollar for at the vending machine down the hall, opened it with a snap, sat down on the edge of the bed, and pulled the pillows over to pile behind him against the headboard. He reached over and picked up the phone, punching in a number from memory. He needed to know.

It wasn't answered until the fifth ring. "H'llo."

"Lizzy, it's Quinn."

There was a momentary pause. "Hey. Hi. You told me to get some sleep. I was."

He leaned back against the headboard and smiled. "I can tell. Your words are wandering. Sorry I woke you up."

She yawned and her jaw cracked. "You're forgiven." He heard her shift the phone around. "What's up?"

She even used Kate's words. Quinn wondered if Kate realized that. Kate wondered about how close she and Lisa were, while someone else from the outside could see it so clearly. "No reason, I just wanted to hear your voice."

"Oh."

The silence lengthened. "Longer words, Lizzy. I didn't call to hear you breathe, as pleasant as that is."

"Quinn," she chided, even as she chuckled. "At least choose a topic. I seem to remember you were the one who started this conversation."

"I called to talk about the wedding," he temporized in place of what he really wanted to say.

"Did you?"

"It's next weekend."

"Please don't remind me. The last dress fitting is Monday."

She sounded worried. "What?"

"I can't wear the dress."

He thought for a moment, then winced when he understood. "Too tight?"

"Only if I want to breathe. It's not a dress that gives much leeway."

"I bet she's a brilliant seamstress."

"I hope so. But I'm not looking forward to it."

"If you need to pass on standing up at the wedding, Jennifer would be the first person to understand."

"If she can make it, I can."

"It's still on for her to get out of the hospital tomorrow afternoon?"

"If the doctors try to change their minds, she's going to leave anyway," Lisa replied, amused. "She's flying back to Houston on Monday."

"Marcus has our travel arrangements set for noon Friday."

"Good. Want to carry my luggage?"

"Do you pack like Kate or like Jennifer?" Marcus had just laughed the first time Quinn mentioned he was doing Jennifer a favor and taking her to the airport. He'd learned.

"No one travels with as much stuff as Jennifer. But I guarantee I'll have more than Kate."

"I'll handle it," Quinn promised.

"Thanks."

"I think I should wake you up more often. You're awfully polite tonight."

"I want a favor."

"Ask away."

"My first music lesson. Jack is already three good deeds up on me and I can't even get the scales to come out right."

"I forgot to warn you about one thing regarding choosing the harmonica as your instrument."

"What's that?"

"You have to be able to breathe." If she'd been able to strangle him through the phone she would have done it. "There will be time during the trip to Houston," he offered.

"Dave's flying us down?"

"Yes."

"Nice."

"It sure beats having your flight get delayed and then canceled."

"Very true."

The topic had worn down and a silence crept in. He wasn't accustomed to being the one keeping a conversation going. He turned serious. "I'm sorry I threw cold water on your idea about Marla."

"Don't be. You were right."

"If the cases are linked, something else will show up."

"Let's not talk about work. Even if that means we have to talk about the weather instead."

"The real reason I called."

"I didn't figure you woke me up to talk about the wedding."

Still he stalled but edged closer to what he wanted to ask. "When you joined the others at Trevor House, what was it like?"

She didn't answer for a long time. "Why do you want to know?"

"Something Kate once said. About hoping for a family."

"Kids who go to Trevor House are too old to find families."

"Why didn't you stay with the previous foster family? Why the transfer?"

"Mark Branton got a promotion. To take it, they had to move out of state."

"And they chose the job over you."

"It was a logical choice. Foster families are always temporary."

"Do you remember your first one?"

"Quinn, why are you asking all this?"

"I'm just trying to figure out what it might have been like growing up with so many different families."

"Do you really want to know?"

"Yes."

"I learned to make sure I cared about only what would fit in my backpack."

"I'm sorry about that."

She didn't say anything.

"Do you stay in touch with any of them?"

"No." She shifted the phone. "Most promised they would write. That would last maybe a year or until my address changed a couple times, then it would dwindle. And if you say you're sorry for me I'm going to hang up this phone."

"Can I think it?"

"Quinn, it was my life. At least it was better than Kate's."

"How did they make the decision to move you?"

"Change your line of questions already," she replied, frustrated. "I don't want to talk about this."

"It's important. How did you find out about the moves? Did you have much warning?"

"Well, I can't say I remember much about the first two," she replied with a sarcastic bite to her words. "I was a baby at the time."

"Lizzy."

"Sometimes they would tell me a few weeks before, okay? And

sometimes they would just come and get me."

"In the middle of the school year."

"Quinn…101 about being a kid in foster care. You don't get a say in what happens or asked what you would like. You go where they tell you, when they tell you, and hope there's a bed for you when you arrive and you're not on a cot somewhere in some office shelter because they messed up the paperwork."

"And that's the bright side?"

"In a word, yes."

"Trevor House was a relief."

"Of course it was a relief. The only people who got tossed out of Trevor House were those picking fights on a regular basis. Otherwise you got your walking papers the day after you turned eighteen. Can we change the subject now? Please?"

"I heard you went skydiving for your eighteenth birthday."

"About broke my neck," she replied instantly. "The chute didn't open, I had to go to the reserve chute, and I came down on a roadway instead of the field where we were supposed to hit. It was a blast."

"You're serious."

"Sure. I went up again the next day."

"What do you want for your birthday next year?"

"I can't say I've thought about it. It's not exactly soon."

"Well, start thinking about it."

"Does this mean I'm getting a birthday gift from you?"

"Depends what is on your list."

"Size or price?"

"Try ease of finding it."

"In that case, I really want a wooden yo-yo. I've been looking for one for years."

He laughed. "You're serious."

"Of course I'm serious. I can do a cat's cradle better than most, and walk the dog… It's just that these plastic ones are too high tech; I want a good old-fashioned, hand-carved, perfectly balanced wooden yo-yo."

He had a feeling this was going to be a very difficult gift to find. "Have a wood preference for it?"

"Mahogany would be excellent. Or a nice cherrywood, or even a white pine."

"A wooden yo-yo. At least you're unique."

"Always. Quinn, it's almost 1 A.M. Can I go back to sleep now? Or are you going to tell me why you really called?"

He got to the point. "I know what I'd like as a return favor for the music lessons."

"What's that?"

"A promise to listen."

"About what?"

"That's a subject for a future date. I just wanted to tell you what the favor would be."

"Just listen?"

"Yes. And don't throw whatever is nearby and handy at me at the time."

"I'm not going to like the subject."

"Maybe not. Call the favor insurance."

She thought for several moments. "Okay. Now I'm curious. You've got your insurance."

"Thank you."

"You're welcome, I think."

"You can go back to sleep now."

"With pleasure. Quinn?"

"Humm?"

The pause lasted long enough he wondered if she was going to say it. "Thanks for calling."

That'ta girl. He smiled. "Good night, Lizzy."

Fourteen

Lisa didn't believe in the Resurrection. Quinn closed the Sunday bulletin with its order of service and creased the edge of the paper with his thumbnail. It made sense, as soon as Kate had said it, that it would be the core doubt Lisa had to overcome. He wasn't sure how to even talk about the subject with her. He just believed it was true, and possible.

If he wasn't ready for the questions, she would take him to pieces with her way of probing a subject. So where was she going to hit the hardest—the impossibility of it? the evidence supporting it? the reason the Bible said it was necessary?

How did he convince someone who dealt with death every day to accept the Resurrection?

Where did he even start the conversation? He had to figure out a place to start, find the right words.

"Lord, what words of Scripture are going to cut like a two-edged sword to the heart of the problem?" He'd been wrestling with that question and he didn't have an answer. There was a verse, a series of verses, that would be able to make the difference.

He was considering using the passage in the book of John that described how Jesus spent the days after the Resurrection before He returned to heaven. But maybe he should go more directly to the underlying problem, set aside trying to answer her questions on the Resurrection and simply let her know again that Jesus loved her.

What he wanted to do was wrap her in a hug and get her to finally believe it hadn't been her fault that Andy died. Lisa might know it in her head, but he very much doubted she had accepted that fact in her heart. She had found with the Richards that love had been contingent on her actions, and if that fact had been absorbed into who she was…

How many people had he met through the years who rejected God's unconditional love because they judged themselves guilty and not worthy of that love? Lisa needed to know that God's love was so deep it would swallow that pain from the past. She might not feel worthy of being loved like that, but she needed to accept it. She needed that kind of love to surround her: unconditional, total love. But Quinn knew the reality: Lisa had survived by being reluctant to let someone get close… She would be taking a big step to trust God. He didn't need to deal with just the Resurrection, he needed to deal with Lisa's heart.

"Lord, I'm not cut out for this. I don't have the words." He couldn't afford to fail. If Lisa let him get close, trusted him, and he fumbled the discussion it would be a house of cards falling down. He couldn't afford to fail. "If someone is going to reach Lisa's heart, it will be You. Find a way under her reserve and help her hear. I can do my best to find words, but they are going to fall flat unless You help her understand. Draw her to You, woo her in. It matters, Lord. And it feels like the right time. Lisa needs to hear the truth and understand it."

Quinn took a deep breath, then let it slowly out along with the tension. Faith was about trust. God would give him the words he needed by the time he talked with Lisa.

As the choir finished the opening song, one of the elders of the church came to the podium to give the morning welcome.

Quinn turned his bulletin over, found a blank space, and wrote down a question.

Kate was sitting beside him. "Hand this to Marcus," he whispered.

She passed it down the aisle.

His partner read the note, leaned forward to look past Kate, then nodded to confirm Jennifer was expecting everyone to join her at church the morning of the wedding.

Quinn relaxed against the padded bench. That's what he had thought. There was no way Lisa would be able to decline that invitation. If there was going to be an opening for a conversation anytime in the near future, it would come next weekend.

There was no good way to predict how Lisa would react to the situation. Indifference was the most likely. And given how intense the emotions of her past were, he hoped the service next week and the people she met were the opposite of what she remembered from her childhood. It was the intangibles that would make the difference. Who came over to say hello, how much Lisa felt welcome versus put in the spotlight. The type of music, the choice of sermon topic. So many small things would make the difference.

Lisa had resisted talking to Kate, to Marcus. He had to try. "Lord, everything needs to come together next weekend." The prayer came from the bottom of his heart and it was followed by a quiet comfort. There was real relief knowing God cared even more about the outcome than he did.

The choir director came to the podium and asked that they stand for the opening hymn. There was a rustle of people and paper as hymnbooks were opened and people found page 212.

Quinn saw Kate reach for her pager, set to vibrate; seconds later Marcus reached for his. Both immediately reacted. "Move," Marcus whispered tersely.

"What?"

"Lisa's emergency tag. Move. Now!"

Kate threw open the passenger door before Quinn had the car stopped. Lisa's car was in the driveway but she wasn't answering the phone. An ambulance should have beaten them here; Quinn prayed Lisa hadn't collapsed before she got that call made. It would be like her to call family before medical help.

Kate was the first one to reach Lisa's front door only because Marcus was defensively scanning the area as he ran. Quinn closed the distance, getting there just as Kate, finding the door locked, hurried to use her key. She was sliding the key into the lock when the door opened from the inside.

Lisa was shaking. Kate grabbed her wrist, lifted Lisa's arm around her own shoulders, and took Lisa's weight before her sister hit the floor. "You should have stayed sitting down, I've got keys."

Marcus reached around Kate to get hold of Lisa's other arm until he could get through the doorway. "How bad is the pain?"

Lizzy looked confused, her pallor sharp. The phone in the house was still ringing because Kate had not closed hers when she tossed it on the front car seat to race inside when Lisa hadn't answered.

"Get her down. I'll get medical help," Quinn ordered, fear tearing through him at that look on Lizzy's face. Had a blood clot formed and broken free? She looked like she had had a small stroke.

"I–I'm okay." She blinked trying to focus and shivered. "H–he was here."

Definitely not okay. Quinn picked up the phone and hung it up to get back dial tone, then placed the call Lisa should have made first.

Marcus shoved aside the coffee table to get it out of their way.

"Who was here, Lisa?" Kate asked, easing her down on the couch.

Lisa tried to stop the shaking of her hands by gripping one in the other. "I shouldn't have touched it, we need to get prints."

Marcus's hands cupped both sides of her face, got her to focus on him. "Lisa, what are you talking about?" he asked, calm and clear.

She struggled to explain. "It was left on the deck."

Quinn turned his startled attention toward the sliding glass doors to the back deck. The lightweight white shears had ripped, caught in the lower sliding track of the closed door. He could see a plastic glass slowly rolling back and forth on the deck pushed by the breeze. He finally connected with what she was saying, quickly gave the last of the information to the dispatcher, dropped the phone, then headed toward the deck.

He rested his hand on his sidearm as he scanned the area, then eased open the door with his elbow to keep from leaving fingerprints. He stepped outside. Lisa had been working outside. Two sprinklers were watering the new sod and a hose was soaking the base of the new elm tree. Three geranium pots and a long cactus planter were on the table. The plastic glass rolling back and forth was disconcertingly out of place.

The breeze ruffled a square of white blown into the corner of the deck.

Instinctively knowing that was what Lisa was talking about, Quinn took out his pen, capped it, and used it and the edge of a matchbook to pick up the piece of paper.

"Quinn?"

"I've found it," he called back. "Hold on."

For something written to have resulted in Lisa's reaction…he stepped inside, knowing a hard reality. This house wasn't safe. "Marcus."

His partner was already moving to pass him, Kate having eased into his place beside Lisa. "I'll search the grounds," Marcus said grimly.

"Marc—be careful!"

"I will, Lizzy."

Quinn set the piece of paper down on the dining room table, already studying it even before he read what it said: white twenty-pound paper, folded over in fourths, a streak of dirt on the side from where it had fallen. He opened the folded page using his capped pen and the salt and pepper shakers to hold down the page corners.

The words were block printed in five neat lines.

DID YOU SEE
THE HUMMINGBIRDS?
MARLA LIKED TO
WATCH THEM WHILE
SHE ATE LUNCH.

Fifteen

Quinn felt a chill, felt his vision narrow, and then the fury swept over him. No wonder Lizzy was spooked. "Go cover Marcus's back," he ordered Kate immediately.

She looked over at him, startled.

"Do it, Kate. I'll take care of Lisa."

"Please," Lisa urged, trying to push her that way, "he may still be here."

Kate checked her weapon. "I'm going."

Quinn took one last look at the note and left it on the table. It had already done its damage. He eased himself down on the couch beside Lisa. There was a pasty grayness to her coloring. That note had struck terror—it was probably one reason it had been left. He let his hand brush across her hair, settle gently against her face.

"The guy who killed her," Lisa whispered, "he knew we were there."

"And he knows where you live," Quinn said simply, putting the situation fully into words. He briskly rubbed her arms. She was terribly cold.

"He called."

"What?"

"The phone rang. No one was there."

"After you saw the note?"

Lisa shakily nodded.

He had to have been watching when Lisa stepped out on the deck and found the note. No wonder she hadn't picked up the phone again. Quinn wanted to help Marcus and Kate search but had to trust they wouldn't miss anything.

"Where exactly was it left?"

"Tucked under the edge of the geranium pot."

"Did you see anyone? Anything else out of place?"

"No."

"When were you last out on the deck before this?" He wanted to simply comfort but had to know the details.

"Last night, no—" She frowned, then looked at him, confused. "I also went out this morning, early, after I fed the pets. I trapped a moth that had gotten inside and I went to release it. I don't know if I would have noticed the note or not, I was thinking about other things." She took a shaky breath. "I'm sorry, I didn't mean to panic like I did. I just...couldn't think."

The investigation could wait. He cradled her head against his chest and wrapped his arms carefully around her. "Let it go." For all the investigations and cases Lisa worked, she didn't deal with the personal threats that Kate did, and this was one of the worst by what it implied. He felt her shake. He closed his eyes and just rocked her.

The glass door slid open. Marcus and Kate came inside together. Quinn looked over, and Marcus silently shook his head.

"It's on the table," Quinn said quietly.

They went to see the note. Quinn heard the quiet discussion between them, heard the phone calls they made to Kate's boss to bring in the police, to their brothers Stephen and Jack.

Kate came to join them. "She's okay," he reassured softly, seeing Kate's intense worry. "Lizzy, are you up to going with Kate? One of your flannel shirts would be a good idea. You're cold." And he had to talk to Marcus, now.

Kate understood that silent message. "Come on, sis, let's get you something warm."

Lisa leaned back.

Quinn cupped her chin, holding her gaze. "It's going to be okay. I'm going to handle it." There would be no independent Lisa walking into this one on her own and getting into trouble.

"It's all yours," she whispered.

She'd change that once she was feeling more steady, but for now it was enough. "Go with Kate," he said again and helped her stand.

Lisa swayed as she stood and had to lock her knees; Kate reached to steady her. "This is embarrassing."

"No, it's not," Kate replied. "You were much more unsteady than this after that car crash two years ago."

Lisa tried to smile as she leaned heavily against Kate and took her first steps. "You were the one driving."

"You were the one that screamed dog."

"There really was a dog; he ran away."

"I still think you made it up. You just wanted to see me drive into a ditch."

The soft debate continued as they walked slowly down the hall. Quinn watched until they were out of sight before turning to Marcus. And all the emotion suppressed in the last thirty minutes showed on his face. "I'm going to pulverize him."

"After me."

"He stuck around to watch her pick up the note, called her just after she paged you and Kate, not saying anything but delivering the message just the same." Quinn could feel the fury at that additional twist of terror the man had caused. "What are we going to do?"

"The guy that killed Marla Sherrall was here. Are we confident that's the meaning of this message?"

"It's got to be a pretty vicious joke otherwise—someone would have had to have seen us Thursday in Knolls Park, known who Lisa was, and somehow figured out where she lived. It's not like she's in the phone book to be looked up."

"The killer lives in the neighborhood, he saw you two poking around, and he followed you when you left."

"A fact that gives you a real warm fuzzy feeling inside, doesn't it?" Quinn shook his head and hoped that was actually true so they would have a place to start looking. "Conversely, he's been following us for days. If Lisa's right and these cases are tied together, then who knows when or what question we asked that caught his attention. It may extend all the way back to the visit we made to Grant Danford's estate."

"What about before that? The guy in the Plymouth?"

"Someone after me using Lisa as a convenient way to get my attention?" Quinn let the idea roll around and gel. "Yes, it's possible. The hummingbird reference—it's the first thing someone would notice about that crime scene. And the fact I haven't seen the tail recently doesn't mean he hasn't been there, biding his time. Maybe we haven't stirred up a killer, we've stirred up a guy who wants revenge." He shook his head. "I don't know which is worse."

Quinn looked around, seeing now just how poor the security was at Lisa's home. Dead bolts and locked windows wouldn't stop someone determined to enter. If he'd come after her rather than just left a note— "She can't stay here."

"I'll take her over to Kate's for a few days, and we'll be able to get her out of town this weekend for Jennifer's wedding. It will buy us some time before we have to take more drastic measures."

"Marcus, if we put too much obvious police presence on this case, whoever this is will go underground as fast as he appeared and Lisa will never be safe. We've got to find him."

"Maybe we got lucky and he left a fingerprint. Maybe we'll be able to trace the phone call. We can quietly canvas the neighborhood, see if anyone noticed a car, someone they didn't recognize in the neighborhood."

"The landscaper. Walter Hampton."

"Do you think—"

It was too obvious and Quinn didn't think it fit the man's personality, but he knew better than to make assumptions. "He's got a crew
working at the house down at the corner. He's been around here to
dump dirt and lay sod. He may have seen something suspicious." The
sound of sirens noted the arrival of medical help and police officers.

"We get Lisa taken care of, then you and I are going to find some
answers."

Egan Hampton's burned-out house was gone; in its place was now only
a cleared-out empty lot. Quinn slowed as he drove past, wishing the
aftereffects of what had happened could be as easily erased.

"I'm surprised the fire didn't jump to that stand of oak trees,"
Marcus commented, also studying the site.

"No wind. Walter was fortunate. Had the wind been from the east,
the fire would have raced through the nursery."

The road turned and the now empty lot disappeared. They drove
along the east edge of the orchard. The manager at the greenhouse had
pointed them this direction to find Walter.

"There." Marcus saw them first.

Two men were wrestling a fifteen-foot elm tree onto a flatbed trailer
using a forklift to help with the massive ball of burlap-covered roots. Both
of them were straining to shift the weight toward the center of the flatbed.
From the language Quinn could hear through the open car window, the
man with Walter was cursing up a blue streak as the tree refused to move.

Quinn parked behind the Nakomi Nurseries' pickup truck. "It
would be impolite to stand and watch them work," he noted, even as
he prepared to do just that.

"Good. I'd rather be asking the questions before Walter has time to
think up the wrong answers," Marcus replied, a bite to his words.

"Lisa doesn't think he's involved."

"She likes people who are nice to her pets."

Quinn, who was normally the stand-back bad guy during interviews, found himself mentally reversing roles and wondering how hard Marcus was planning to push. His partner was rolling toward a boil. "He did help save Lisa's life," Quinn noted, more curious to get Marcus's reaction than to change his mind.

"And he's done a remarkable job at weaseling himself into her life since then."

This was an O'Malley family matter, and the skepticism level anyone would have to pass was stratospherically high. For Lisa's sake, Quinn was glad.

They walked toward where the men were working.

The tree finally slid to the center of the flatbed with the use of a two-by-four fulcrum. Walter reached around the tree for the first securing line. Only when it was in place did he acknowledge their presence with a nod of greeting. "Mr. Diamond."

"Walter."

The man working with Walter ignored them, pulled tight his gloves, and started threading the first rope through the metal tie-down ring. When the rope coiled the wrong way on him, a snap of his wrist straightened it. Quinn noted the neat coil and the precision of the man's movements in tying the knots, recognized his skill with the rope.

Walter grabbed the edge of the flatbed and swung himself to the ground. He left the other man to the job and walked over to meet them. As Walter approached, Quinn double-checked his original assessment. If there had been nervousness the first time they met, there was merely interest this afternoon. Walter met his gaze straight on. "What can I do for you?"

"We have a couple questions if you have a moment."

Walter rubbed the dirt from his hands. "Glad to have a reason to take one."

"I don't believe you've met Lisa's brother. This is my partner, Marcus O'Malley."

Walter was a little slow in offering his hand. "Marshal."

It was the job that made the man nervous. Quinn tucked that observation away for later.

"I saw you finished laying the sod at Lisa's," Marcus commented, introducing himself with the question.

"I also planted a tree and a couple bushes and flowers she picked out of the catalogs." Walter glanced between them. "Sidney didn't get into that honeysuckle, did he? I knew that was going to be a risk planting it so near the back deck."

"Sidney will dig it up long before he tries to eat it," Marcus noted. "He's already started with the snapdragons."

Walter winced. "At least he's got good taste."

"When were you last at Lisa's?" Quinn asked.

"Monday? No, Tuesday afternoon. Chris and I took the new elm tree over."

"You haven't been there since?"

Walter shook his head.

"Where were you last night?"

Walter frowned at the question, started to say something but was cut off. "He was bailing me out of jail," the man kneeling on the flatbed tying down the tree retorted. "Leave the guy alone. He didn't do whatever you're probing about."

Walter's expression flashed hot with anger. "Chris, shut up."

Chris—the brother who had testified at Grant's trial, the gambler willing to ask for a bribe. Quinn pivoted and did some poking of his own. "Where were you since you got out of jail?"

"Arrest me, and we'll have a staring contest over the answer."

Walter took off his baseball cap, ran his hand through his hair, then put the cap back on. The move was more to get control of his anger than to adjust his hat. "Ignore him. My brother is in an exceptionally bad mood today." Walter looked over his shoulder. "And it started with dumping a tree on a busy freeway!"

"If you'd used a less fancy knot that would actually tighten, your precious tree would still be in one piece."

"There was nothing wrong with my knot, the problem was your driving. If you dump this one too, I'm going to take it out of your inheritance."

"As if a chunk of dirt I can't sell would matter one whit to me either way," Chris retorted, pausing to loop the extra rope around the corner post of the flatbed truck before swinging himself to the ground. Quinn's eyes narrowed. Most people would have tossed it to the ground. "I'm leaving. If you want me to help plant this tree, you'd best catch up."

"Assuming you actually get the tree there."

"Walter, you might be older, but you're no more the boss than I am." Chris pulled open the driver's door of the truck pulling the flatbed. "I won't be waiting around for you if you're late." The truck pulled out, the tree rocking against its restraints.

Quinn seized the moment. "Walter?"

He looked over and scowled. "What?"

"Where was your brother last night after you bailed him out of jail?"

He didn't like the question but took heated pleasure in answering it. "He's living in the former nursery manager's house down at the south end of the orchard. You can see it from Egan's place. I dropped him off there; as far as I know that's where he stayed."

"And this morning?"

"I am hardly my brother's keeper. He dumped the tree at 4 A.M. He finally showed up back here around 1 P.M. Not only did he cost me a landscape job I worked two years to cultivate, he destroyed a good elm tree."

"And what about you?"

He bit back a retort. "Gentlemen, I spent last night cleaning up stupidity. Chris was driving a nursery truck last night, drunk, when he was arrested. He claims to have misplaced his car, which probably means he wrecked it. I spent this morning visiting my aunt Laura, who wanted to know how come my uncle Egan hadn't brought her coffee this morning, something he hadn't done in over a decade even before his death. And then I came back here to the office about noon to find I had a customer with a hole in the ground, no tree, and unexpected guests arriving. Now I really do need to go."

"Did you see anyone when you were at Lisa's house on Tuesday?"

"Is this really necessary?"

"Yes."

He checked his impatience and thought about it. "A kid on a bike—early teens? It was a blue mountain bike with red handlebars. And there was a mom, two kids, and a poodle. The dog barked so much I heard Lisa's parrot start to mimic it. That's all that I recall. The neighborhood is quiet. Anything else?" His tone of voice suggested there had better not be.

"One last question. Have you ever done any work in Knolls Park?"

"Not in the last five years since I've been doing the scheduling."

"Before that?"

"During the life of the business? Probably. But Egan kept business records as order carbons, and it's impossible to get the simplest question answered. If you're feeling adventurous, ask Terri at the office. She can point you to the file cabinets as well as I can."

"That's all we need."

With a terse nod, Walter headed to the Nakomi truck to go after his brother.

Quinn and Marcus walked back to their car.

Quinn started the car, then pulled onto the road. "What do you think? Walter?"

"It's obvious he could have left the note, but it doesn't type: too much the older brother, in control, forces life to fit his mold. He's getting Lisa's attention the direct way, finding reasons to see her."

"Christopher."

Marcus nodded. "He would have to have seen you in Knolls Park, but assume for now that somehow he did—"

Quinn thought about it and shook his head. "Christopher's not the type to leave a note," he decided. "He's too in-your-face. He wouldn't hide behind paper."

"So what did we learn?"

"Beyond the fact the brothers hate each other? Not much."

"Still—tell Lincoln to push a little harder. He's been wanting a reason to ask some questions about Christopher ever since he learned about the bribe Grant paid him."

"Have him look up any Knolls Park records?"

"Yes. Add it to the list for Emily to sort out."

Traffic had increased as the Sunday afternoon wore on. Quinn headed toward Kate's.

Marcus broke the silence. "I don't think the note was a cruel joke, I think the note really was left by Marla's killer."

"So do I," Quinn replied grimly.

Sixteen

We can rule out Grant having killed Marla."

At Lisa's voice Quinn looked up from the phone company log of calls to Lisa's home. She was tucked into one of the tall wingback chairs in Kate's apartment with a pink sweater around her shoulders, purple socks on her feet, and a quiet determination to ignore what her family suggested about lying down and trying to get some rest. He was relieved at the reappearance of that stubbornness, for it was a good indication that the shock of the morning was finally wearing off.

"Why?" he asked simply.

"He's in jail. It's obvious he couldn't have left the note or placed the call. So someone else killed Marla. Lincoln's right, and we're on the wrong trail."

"Lisa—" He didn't want to confuse the situation for her but had no choice. "It's not quite that simple. The note may simply have been a lucky guess by someone who saw us in the neighborhood." Even if he didn't think it likely, he had to make sure they didn't rule out anything.

His words caught her off guard. "A guess?"

"What was the first thing you noticed about the place where Marla was killed?"

She hesitated, then reluctantly nodded. "The hummingbirds," she whispered. She closed her eyes for a moment, then looked over at him, confused, angry, struggling not to cry from the intense frustration. "You really think this might have been a cruel joke?"

Her emotions were in such turmoil and there wasn't much he could do to help but promise it was going to go away. "We're going to figure out who it was; it just may not be a simple answer."

"What does the report show for the phone call?"

He set aside the printouts. "A cell phone."

"Nothing useful."

"What I expected," he clarified, hearing her disappointment.

Lisa tugged at the sweater, frowning at the thread she pulled by accident. "Why do you think it might have been an ugly joke?"

"Someone has been following me."

Frustration, annoyance, and fear all crossed her face. "So they go after me?"

"It got my attention," he replied dryly.

"That's why you didn't want me involved initially with the Rita Beck case."

"Yes."

"I want the details."

She had a right to them, needed to know them now. "The day you came home from the hospital I spotted him for the third time. He was tailing me as I drove back to the hotel." Quinn winced inside, realizing that if it was the guy also responsible for the note, he would have known her address for weeks. "Dave and Marcus almost got him that night. Since then—I haven't spotted him again, but a problem like that doesn't just go away. He's probably been watching me on and off ever since."

She frowned. "You were tailed long before we ever visited the Danford estate?"

"Yes."

"Quinn, which is it? Was the note left by the guy who killed Marla, who may have killed all the victims, or by someone who's been tailing you, watching where we go?"

"You're staying here until we can figure out that answer."

"You promise you'll take good care of my pets?"

"Guaranteed. I'll even give Iris her peanuts."

"I want to keep going to work."

"I'll take you, or Kate can. But until this is solved, you won't be doing any more unescorted window-shopping during your lunch hour."

She half smiled. "At least I'll save some money." The smile faded. "The note will tell us a lot. Andrew is good at the analysis. He won't miss anything. Prints, brand of paper, handwriting…"

"He's already promised to call you with updates as it's processed."

"So what are we going to do in the meantime? That's going to take days."

"Marcus had a good point. We may not know who this is, or what it is that we've done that has gotten his attention, but we've clearly succeeded. We've got his attention. So if we keep doing exactly what we have been, he'll likely come calling again. And this time there will be Lincoln, Marcus, Dave, and Kate around to help spot him."

"We keep investigating."

He nodded. "All the questions we were pursuing yesterday before this happened. Did Amy ever come to Chicago? Is Grant Danford innocent or actually guilty of killing not only Rita but others? I keep trying to track down the dark green Plymouth I saw. You keep working to connect the four cases you've found."

"I don't like the way this is escalating."

"Which is why we have to push harder and break it open. We are apparently a lot closer to the truth than we realize."

There was a rustle of sound as the front door was unlocked and opened. "Pizza's here!" Kate called.

"It's about time." Lisa set aside the book she had been paging through. "Even if a pizza from Carla's is worth the wait."

"You're hungry."

She gave a sheepish smile. "Fear does that."

Trust her to have the opposite reaction from most people. "I'm glad." He turned toward the hall. "Kate, you need a hand?"

"I've got it covered. Jack's coming, he was just parking his car." The front door opened again. "He can help."

"Sure I can. Help with what?" Jack asked.

"Drinks."

"I want one."

"Fix six. Marcus and Lincoln are joining us."

"Oh, okay. Got any fizzy water?"

"No, I don't have fizzy water. You can have lemonade."

"With pizza?" Jack asked in disbelief.

Quinn looked over at Lisa, saw her struggling to keep her laughter silent as they listened to Kate and Jack move into the kitchen.

"Jack, you're my guest. Quit complaining."

"I've got time to run to the corner store." There was the snap of a towel. "Missed," Jack said cheerfully. "Does Dave know you're practicing with that?"

There was a knock at the door. "I'll get it," Jack quickly volunteered.

The door was unlocked and pulled open. "Marcus, buddy! You stopped at the store?" There was the crinkle of paper bags.

"We did decide on pizza, yes?"

"Absolutely."

"Then Kate's cupboards need help. The jalapeño peppers are for Quinn and me. Save me a couple of those sodas."

"Marc—you're a lifesaver. Hi, Lincoln. Good to see you again."

"Jack."

There was the sound of the refrigerator freezer opening and ice being retrieved.

"Marcus—you're spoiling Jack," Kate complained.

Marcus burst out laughing. "And you're not? That pizza's got Italian sausage on it."

"Really?" Jack asked.

"It is almost your birthday," Kate conceded.

"As good an excuse as any," Jack agreed. "Hey, Lizzy, how are the music lessons coming?" he called down the hall.

She put her head in her hands.

"What else do you need, Kate?" Marcus asked.

"Plates and napkins. I think everything else is ready."

The group finally appeared in the doorway: Jack in front carrying four glasses, Kate behind him carrying three stacked pizza boxes, Marcus and Lincoln bringing up the rear with plates and towels. Quinn accepted drinks for himself and Lisa.

"Hey, kiddo." Jack sat down on the armrest of Lisa's chair.

"Jack."

He dug into his shirt pocket and handed her a small gift-wrapped package.

"What's this?"

"Open it."

She tugged at the wrapping paper. It was a small, thin, bright blue square with a grid at the top and a big red button.

"If you get another note that takes your breath away."

She pushed the button and a Halloween scream echoed through the apartment. Kate winced and Lisa laughed. "This is great."

"Jack, you've got to grow up someday," Kate noted, stopping beside him to ruffle his hair.

"Why?"

"Because you're acting like a fifth grader with your gag gifts?"

"Hey, this one was practically practical." Lisa giggled at her own pun.

"And her doctor would love me. Laughter's good medicine."

Lisa hugged him. "Thanks."

"You're very welcome."

Quinn caught Jack's gaze, prepared to be amused as Kate was but found himself instead looking at a very serious man behind the humor. He thoughtfully nodded and made a note not to get fooled again by the surface lightness. The humor was deliberate, a serious purpose behind the laughter.

"Lisa." Marcus held out a plate.

"Thanks." She accepted it and looked at the boxes being set out on the coffee table. "Kate, which one is just cheese?"

"I think I insulted Carla with your request. She gave me a lecture about the virtues of at least a vegetarian pizza."

"She'll forgive me when I call and rave about how good the pizza was."

Kate slid a thick piece from the box. "She put cheese in the crust for you."

"See? She's just protesting for the sake of it."

Quinn joined Marcus in starting on the supreme pizza.

"Kate, where's Dave?" Jack asked.

"He'll be here shortly. He was having dinner with his sister, then was going to pick up dessert on his way over."

"Cheesecake?"

"Knowing Dave, probably."

"Great."

"You just like to eat."

"Freely concede the point," Jack replied, taking his second slice of Italian sausage pizza.

"Lincoln, are you having any luck with dates I gave you?" Lisa asked.

"Where Grant Danford was on the dates the women disappeared?"

Lisa nodded.

"Emily is still working on it. He did some traveling, but proving where he was on a particular day a decade ago—not an easy proposition."

"Lisa, forget about work for a while," Marcus recommended.

"I've just got a couple questions."

Marcus tugged her purple sock. "They'll keep. Eat."

"Has anyone heard from Jennifer?" Jack asked.

Lisa perked up. "She was supposed to call after the doctor released her today."

"I talked to her this morning," Kate said. "She's going to call when she gets to the hotel."

"She should be there by now. Let's call and see."

Jack reached over and snagged Kate's phone. "What's the hotel number?"

"It's the Bismark Grand Hotel in Baltimore," Lisa replied.

Jack called information, was connected to the hotel, and asked for Tom or Jennifer. Nodding, he twisted his wrist to move the phone away to pass on the answer. "They've just checked in. He's ringing Jennifer's room."

He moved back the phone, smiling. "Jennifer? It's Jack. Want to marry me?"

Lisa giggled. Jack's opening was an old family joke.

"Oh, I don't know. We were sitting around debating if we should show up for this shindig of yours next weekend." Jack laughed. "Really? In that case I've got to be there."

"What?" Lisa whispered.

"She says I get to throw you in the hotel pool after the wedding," Jack whispered back, obviously improvising.

Lisa shoved him.

"You want to talk to Lizzy? She's acting pretty ditzy at the moment."

"Give me the phone."

"Hold on, here she is."

Jack passed the phone to Kate instead, who accepted it with a laugh. "Jen, Jack is being his normal jokester self tonight." Kate reached for another napkin. "Lisa's fine—although she had me order cheese pizza from Carla's again. How are you doing? Ready to fly home tomorrow?"

"Sure. Which ones? The true white or the cream?"

Kate turned to Marcus and mimicked writing a note. He reached behind him to the end table for her notepad. She nodded her thanks as she took it and the pen.

"What else?"

She started making a list. "Not a problem. If I don't have it, Stephen will." Kate looked over at Lisa. "Do you know if you kept one of Tina's lace handkerchiefs in your scrapbooks? Jen needs to borrow something old."

"I'm sure I did."

Kate added it to the list. "I'll bring everything," she confirmed to Jennifer. "Dave's flying us down at noon Friday. Have you tried on the dress again?" Kate smiled. "I can't wait to see it. I'd better hand you over to Lisa now." Kate passed over the phone.

"Jen? They're ganging up on me again," Lisa protested. She listened for a moment, laughed, then settled back in the chair. "Really? I don't know." Lisa glanced over, caught Quinn's gaze. "I suppose I could ask him."

He quirked an eyebrow at her, wishing he could hear both sides of that conversation. Jen said something and Lisa dropped her eyes, actually blushed, a fact that made Quinn sit up straighter and grin as he watched Lisa.

"No." Lisa snuggled deeper into the chair and turned her attention to pulling threads from the tear in the knee of her jeans as she listened to Jennifer. "Maybe." She shook her head. "No, it should be Rachel." She made a face at the phone. "Jen—"

"Oh, all right. Hold on." She held out the phone to Quinn. "She wants to talk to you."

Quinn accepted the phone with some surprise. "Hi, Jennifer."

"I need a favor."

He knew when it was time to be cautious. "Okay."

"Lizzy."

Quinn looked over, found her watching her. "Humm."

"She's being stubborn. I want her to be my maid of honor. But she wants it to be Rachel or Kate, and they both insist it has to be the others. My wedding is going to get here before it gets settled. So I've made an executive decision. It's going to be Lizzy. But I'm not there to convince her."

"Jen."

"Come on. After all this time, don't you have a little pull? Sweet-talk her into it or something."

"Or something." Still, Quinn smiled. "I'll see what I can do."

"Thanks. So have you asked her out yet?"

"Jenny."

She laughed. "I vote with Kate. It would be good to keep you in the family."

He couldn't think of a reply.

"Are you blushing?"

"Probably." His drawl had intensified, a good indication he was.

She laughed. "Then I'll be nice and let you go. But I want you at my wedding wearing your tux and your boots. And I'm putting you in charge of Lizzy while she's here."

"Impossible, but I'll do my best."

"Thank you. Pass me to Marcus. My brother and I need to chat about this bachelor party thing. I want Tom awake at our wedding."

Quinn laughed and complied.

Marcus accepted the phone. "Hi, precious."

"What did she want?" Lisa leaned over to ask softly.

"That would be telling."

"Quinn."

He loved watching her struggle with patience. "Later."

———— ◦◦◦◦ ————

Quinn watched Lisa stretch her hands over her head, her movements slow, then wince when she tried to straighten her arms. She hurriedly lowered her arms, taking a deep breath as she pressed her hand against her ribs. He saw it, Kate didn't. The family gathering had just broken up. Marcus, Lincoln, and Jack headed out together. Dave was still lingering. Quinn could understand that. He wasn't in a hurry to leave either.

"It's later. What did Jennifer want?"

Quinn looked at Lisa, then glanced over at Kate. "Kate, give us a minute."

Kate paused in picking up the clutter, looked at him, and stopped what she was doing. "I'll walk Dave to his car."

"Circle the block."

She grinned. "Did you hear that, Dave?"

He stepped back into the living room. "What?"

"You have to take me for a walk around the block."

Dave leaned against the doorjamb and grinned. "Really? I have to?"

Kate encircled his waist with her arm. "Yes." She glanced at Quinn. "We'll be back in half an hour?"

"Good enough."

The two of them left.

"You just tossed her out of her own apartment," Lisa remarked, stunned.

"She didn't mind," Quinn replied, amused, knowing it was true. He got up to finish the task Kate had been doing, replaced the candy dish and magazines that had been moved from the coffee table earlier, and carried the drinking glasses into the kitchen, using the time to decide what he wanted to say.

When he returned, he settled on the couch and studied her. "I'll get you out of being maid of honor if you're saying no because you can't wear the dress that long."

Lisa cringed. "That's what she asked you?"

"One of the things."

She leaned her head back against the tall wingback chair and closed her eyes. "Quinn, I don't want her to know. The last thing Jennifer needs to be doing is worrying about me."

"If you were to wear the dress for literally just the wedding ceremony?"

"Even if the seamstress could work magic tomorrow—" She shook her head. "The painkillers will help, but the maid of honor is the host of ceremonies for the reception. Even if I could change out of the dress, I'd be hurting and Jen's way too perceptive."

"Do you want to be able to say yes?"

She nodded.

"Then let me work out the logistics. I can make it happen without anyone realizing it's happening."

She looked doubtful.

"Trust me."

"Okay, I'll tell her yes."

"Let me tell her. I'll call in a few markers when I do it."

Lisa nodded. She awkwardly pushed herself out of the chair, then turned to look out the living room window. "Quinn, about the note?"

"What about it?"

"Do you think it was Marla's killer?"

"Yes." He left it simple and straightforward. It was always the better choice.

"I want to go back and look again at the scene where Marla was found."

"No."

She turned and looked at him. "It's not a light request. I need to see what I missed. It's time to ask a lot of questions."

"Lincoln and Marcus are on the case full-time now. There is no need for you to be in the mix."

"Quinn—"

"No. That's final. From both of us and your boss."

"You talked to Ben?"

"Yes. And the only way you keep working these cases is if you listen to what we're telling you. He has no desire to see you get hurt again, and Marcus and I don't want you in the way of the investigation."

"It's my job to investigate suspicious deaths."

She wasn't going back to Knolls Park until the person responsible for that note was stopped. "Whether you like it or not, you're a civilian and this is a job for a cop."

"Don't take away my ability to do my job."

"The limits are there for your own protection."

"I don't like it."

The mutiny of emotions on her face mixed together—relief not to have to face Knolls Park again, frustration that she was being ordered to stay away. Quinn kept his voice calm. "I know, but you'll keep within them anyway." He took a risk, invaded her space, settled his arms around her, and hugged her. "I don't want you thinking about any of this tonight. I want you to get some sleep."

He'd surprised her; she tensed but then he felt her relax. She moved her cheek against his chest. "Not going to call and wake me up to talk?"

She sounded disappointed. And he felt hope. "Another time."

Seventeen

They were all buried near water."

Quinn looked up from the police report on Mrs. Treemont. The whiteboard had become a grid: down the left side were the victims' names; across the top, common traits. *Buried face down* was marked for all of them. *Tape* was marked for Heather, Vera, and Rita. Lisa had added the word *water* at the top of the grid as a common trait.

"Rita, buried near a river. Marla, buried near a pond. Heather, buried under a fountain." She noted a *yes* in the grid boxes.

"Mrs. Treemont was found buried near her rosebushes, and Vera Wane was found next to her garage," he countered.

"We haven't visited the scenes." She put in question marks for those two names instead of a no. "The officer may not have realized the significance of location to this killer. Maybe there's water nearby and it simply isn't mentioned."

"Daylight," Quinn offered.

She wrote that as a common trait. "That has to be significant. It's not only the added risk he takes, it's the fact that it's true in all cases. He hasn't struck at night."

"What's that tell us? He works nights, so has to kill during the day?"

Lisa winced. "Or he's in a job where his boss doesn't realize he's gone."

"Lisa, we think he was watching the victims for some time before he struck, correct?"

"That would definitely appear to be the case with Marla."

"In order to take advantage of their routines, he'd have to snatch them about the same time of day he's been observing them."

She hurriedly found a piece of paper to jot down the idea.

"He watches them for several days if not weeks to learn their routine. He grabs and kills and then buries them, the location of the grave being a significant part of his MO," Quinn summarized.

"He can't be doing that with an occasional day off work. His job is taking him to his victims and putting him into their worlds."

"Exactly. A working man killer."

"But look at the geography pattern," Lisa noted. "Who would travel that kind of range? Be able to stay in one area for a week or weeks necessary to make the selection of a victim, establish her routine, and carry out the crime?"

"A salesman would be in and out. Even repairmen would be too temporary."

"A builder," Lisa offered.

Quinn slowly nodded. "Knolls Park has been undergoing a lot of restorations over the years turning it into an upper-middle-class neighborhood. And didn't Vera have a garage built recently?"

"Where's the master list of case names? All the people the police indicated they interviewed. If we take them for all the cases, sort them together—maybe there will be a common name across all the cases."

"Give it to Diane to work up. There are a lot of names in these files."

Lisa started marking pages with Post-it notes to photocopy for Diane.

Quinn set down his pen and rested back against the chair to look at the board. "We're making progress."

"Slowly. I wish we had some indication of who left the note."

"The odds of getting prints were small. I find it more interesting that he was so bothered by what we were doing, he risked telling us he was around in exchange for scaring you. That risk doesn't make sense."

"Maybe he saw it as an opportunity to tell someone what he did. It's a nine-year-old crime. He got away with it, but no one knows."

"A killer with an ego."

"The police didn't find anything when they canvassed my neighborhood?"

"No."

"Do you think whoever did it will leave another note?"

"Doubtful. It wouldn't take much to realize you're not home."

"I miss my pets."

"I know you do. I'll take you over to the house Thursday to pack for the weekend; you can see them then." He changed the subject. "How was the dress fitting?" She'd been gone about three hours this morning. Lisa made a face. "That good, huh?"

"She'll do her best. The dress just isn't styled to allow for a lot of addition in both the front and the back."

"Still feel like you can handle it for an hour? If so, I'll talk to Jennifer tonight."

"Even if I have to turn blue, I'll handle it."

"Let's go buy her wedding gift."

"Now?"

"Yes, now. I want to stretch my legs. And I've heard you can be a very efficient shopper when you choose to be."

"Who told you that?"

"Kate."

"Quinn, I prefer to crawl along like a snail and spend hours window-shopping. Kate is the one determined to get in and out in a few minutes. Anyone who shops with her is efficient; it's a matter of survival."

"Then let's go meander through a few galleries. With you, I don't think I'll mind dawdling along."

"Was that a compliment?"

"I see I'll have to be more blunt; let's try this again. Lisa, I want a couple hours of your company. Would you like to go shopping for Jennifer's wedding gift?"

"And I'll let you buy me dinner too."

He smiled. "Will you?"

"What's your absolutely favorite Chicago steak place?"

"No question there: Weber Grill."

"I always get hungry after I spend a lot of money."

Quinn laughed as she offered a hand to pull him to his feet. "Okay, Lizzy. We'll go out to dinner after we buy her gift."

"So are you going to walk me to the door or are we going to sit out here watching the stars until the sun comes up?"

Quinn reached over and picked up Lisa's hand and rubbed his thumb across her palm. He had parked on the street just past Kate's apartment, shut off the car and turned off the lights, but the radio was still on, adding a soft backdrop of country music. "I rather like late nights with you. You stop thinking through your answers after 10 P.M."

In the dim light from the streetlights, Quinn saw her smile. "That's because I'm falling asleep, but I'm too polite to do it in front of you."

He tugged her hand. "Why don't you come here for a minute?"

"What?"

"Now you're trying to think. Quit it and just slide over here."

"Oh." She was dense at times; he chuckled as she caught up with him and blushed. She slid over toward the center of the seat.

Quinn turned her slightly so she could rest against his shoulder, and then he wrapped his arms around her. "Better." He didn't try to make it more than a comforting hug. She was shy all of a sudden and he could feel the nervousness. He lifted her hand and placed it carefully against his. "Your broken finger has almost healed." The splint had been removed and the finger taped to the one next to it for some temporary support.

"Another two weeks," Lisa agreed, beginning to relax.

"How's the ribs?"

"You've broken a few in your lifetime?"

"A few," he agreed, lowering the number. It was more like ten.

"Multiply it by a few factors to account for the surgery."

He gently rested his hand against the injury, could feel the bandage under her shirt. "Still taking pain pills?"

"They ought to rename them knockout drugs. I'm sticking to over-the-counter painkillers to the extent I can."

"I'm glad there have been no complications."

"So am I."

The quiet stretched between them. He finally broke it, deciding to risk the subject. "I've been thinking."

"Have you? I've heard that can be a dangerous thing to do."

He leaned his chin against the top of her head and felt her chuckle. "Lisa?"

"Hmm?"

"Tell me about Kevin."

She stiffened, and he tightened his hold on her hands. "Please."

"You don't want much, do you?" All the laughter had left her voice.

"I watched Marcus pace with frustration over the situation. I know you got hurt. I'd like to know what happened."

He waited.

The song on the radio changed, then played to completion. Quinn didn't interrupt the silence between them; he knew Lisa was deciding if she was going to trust him.

"He wanted me to go back to practicing real medicine so he could introduce me to his family."

Quinn intertwined his fingers with those of her good hand and stopped himself from giving his opinion of that.

She squeezed his hand. "He surprised me. I lost my ability to be eloquent. I don't think he even understands what he did."

"He may have been going out with you, but he hadn't taken the time to know you."

"And you think you do?" she asked with some skepticism and lingering hurt.

Yes, he understood her, better than she realized, but this was definitely not the time to tell her he knew about Andy. "You're going to have to trust me enough to tell me about who you saw die. Then I'll really understand. But I know you chose understanding death as one way you would cope with that memory."

"I did," she finally agreed.

Relieved to be out of that quicksand, he rubbed his chin against the top of her head. "I also know you've treated with dignity those whose deaths you've investigated. I'm proud of you for being able to do that. I see too many cops and other law enforcement personnel who don't have that grace."

"That isn't hard to do, Quinn. They have relatives and spouses and children and friends. Everyone who dies still matters."

"Can I ask you something?"

"I don't know if I like your questions."

"Would you have married Kevin had he better understood you?"

He thought she wasn't going to answer she thought about it so long. "Yes."

"Why?"

"Quinn, I was proud of him and glad to be with him. He's a good man even if he has a bit of a big ego—ER docs have that failing. I admired the job he does, I liked the fact he was close to his family." She hesitated. "And he liked me," she added softly.

"I can understand why Jack broke his nose."

She tried to turn as she protested.

He stilled her. "No, hear me out. I said I can understand it, not that

I would have necessarily done the same thing. When he took that slap at your profession, he not only took a slap at part of you, he offended the family. He should have been proud of you, instead he dismissed what you did. It was a classic case of poke one O'Malley, poke them all."

"Jack shouldn't have been that touchy."

"He's your brother, he's allowed."

She turned her head to look up at him. "What about you?"

"What about me?"

"Have you ever been close to tying the knot, so to speak?"

"No."

"Why not?"

"Finding someone who loves Montana, likes art, adores me, shares my faith, and wants to settle down is not an easy proposition."

"Why not Jennifer? or Kate?"

"Lisa, get that tone out of your voice. I did not offend your sisters. And you think Jack gets defensive about family."

"They weren't good enough for you?"

"Sheath your claws," he remarked mildly. "Jennifer didn't want to think about leaving Houston and her patients, and I can totally understand that. They are her kids. And I already knew Tom was in the picture even if Jen hadn't yet figured that fact out. Kate—she's a good friend. Being more than that was never in the cards. So ease up a bit on me."

"You shouldn't have asked me out third."

Ouch. That one hit his gut. "True." He hugged her. "I didn't mean to hurt your feelings."

"It looks bad."

"You've got a right to be annoyed," he agreed cautiously.

"If you ask out Rachel, I'll murder you in your sleep."

"Cross my heart, I will not ask out Rachel." He hadn't been able to entirely hide the laughter that shook him.

Her elbow hit his ribs. "What?"

"I already did." She stiffened like a board. "I asked her first. Rach just laughed and said ask Jennifer."

Lisa slumped as if her bones had turned to liquid. "You didn't."

"Rachel's a bit of a matchmaker."

"This is humiliating. Fourth."

"I am sorry, Lizzy. I didn't intend it to happen this way."

"Let me up, I'm going inside now."

He tightened his arms. "No."

"I can make you regret that answer," she warned.

"Not till you accept my apology."

It became a silent battle of wills. "Okay, I accept your apology," she said grudgingly.

"Thank you. And I will make it up to you."

"I don't see how," she muttered, sliding back to her side of the car and searching for the shoes she had kicked off.

Quinn knew what it felt like to be in the doghouse; the worst part of it was he deserved it. He circled the car and held open the car door for her. "Lizzy?"

"What?"

"Don't stay mad forever."

It was after midnight in Houston. Quinn reluctantly set down the phone when he saw the time. A minute later he picked it up again and placed the call. It was answered on the third ring. "Yes?" Jennifer's voice was alert, focused, very much a doctor responding to a call from her answering service.

"Jen, it's Quinn. Sorry. It's not a patient."

"Quinn." He heard her smile in the warmth that flooded her voice. "I thought we still had a deal—you don't apologize for the time you call, and I don't get on your case about your lack of sleep."

"I'm not going to get much sleep tonight, I'm afraid."

"What happened?"

"I offended Lizzy."

"Quinn?" Her voice had gone cautious. She wasn't sure which side she should support.

He rubbed the back of his neck. "I asked her out fourth. She about handed my head to me on a platter."

"Oh boy. You did make a mess of it with her, didn't you?" She thought about it for a moment. "She'll get over it."

"You didn't see her expression. She deserves to be ticked at me. What do I do?"

"Apologize. And keep doing it until she tells you to stop, then apologize some more."

"Grovel, you mean."

"Good word."

"I didn't mean to hurt her."

"Good words to start with."

Quinn eased off his left boot. "I solved your maid of honor problem."

"Did you?"

"You can have a rolling maid of honor. Rachel gets before the wedding, Lisa gets the wedding, and Kate is master of ceremonies afterward."

She laughed. "And here I thought Marcus's fiancée, Shari, was the politician in the family."

"Deal?"

"Deal. And thank you."

"My pleasure. Now that I woke you up, tell me how you're doing."

"Don't you start. I just got off the phone with Marcus an hour ago."

"We don't want you to overdo it before the big day."

"Tom is hovering too."

"Good."

"Quinn?"

"Hmm?"

"The wedding's going to be hard on Lizzy."

"I know. She's happy for you but feels like the family is changing."

"Yes. I don't want her to be sad."

"Don't worry—I won't give her a chance to be. We'll see you Friday afternoon."

"Thanks. And she will forgive you."

"I hope so."

"Good night, Quinn."

"G'night, Jen." Quinn depressed the button to hang up the phone and get back dial tone. There were reasons to appreciate the size of the O'Malley family. He called Marcus. He didn't have to wonder if his partner was still up. Marcus answered and Quinn went straight to the point. "What did you find on the second note?"

They had intentionally not told Lisa about the second note he'd discovered when he went to take care of her pets this morning. Marcus had been working on it all day while Quinn did his best to keep Lisa otherwise distracted.

Marla liked the salted pretzels best.

The paper had been soggy, the ink beginning to run. It had likely been left with the first one but not discovered because it was tucked in the seam of the garage door, which they hadn't opened yesterday.

"No prints. Same handwriting. The reference does appear to be to the vendors inside the zoo."

"It's almost like he was toying with what to say. There was no evidence of another note?"

"Given where these two were found, I'd almost bet there was a third one that blew away."

"Does this change the game plan?"

"I'm trying to get confirmation that Marla really did like to watch the hummingbirds over lunch, if anyone remembers her buying pretzels, and prove these notes were more than just good guesses."

"Lisa was asking about seeing her pets. Do we tell her about the second note?"

"Not unless we absolutely have to. How was dinner out?"

Quinn squirmed. "Fine."

"Lizzy just gave me a call."

"Did she?"

"Yes, she did. Anything you want to tell me?"

Quinn thought about that for a moment, trying to decide what Lisa would have told Marcus. "No."

The silence stretched and Quinn refused to break it even though he understood his partner very, very well. It didn't matter how deep their friendship was, Marcus was going to take Lisa's side. "You're lucky she said the same thing."

Quinn felt a distinct sense of relief. "Why did she call?"

"No reason. Which tells me there was a reason and she chickened out. Is it something I need to know about?"

"She got annoyed that I asked her out fourth."

There was an appreciable pause. "You asked out Rachel too?"

Quinn winced at the underlying tone. "There are a few things I didn't tell you."

"This situation is causing Lisa enough stress and the last thing I need is you complicating it further."

"Marcus—"

"Fix it."

"I'm trying to," he retorted, frustrated because although his partner was right, there wasn't much he could do about it at the moment.

Marcus relented a bit. "Basic lesson for dealing with Lisa? Time does not make it better."

"I'll remember that."

"And tell her we know about Andy sooner versus later. If something gets said by accident and she finds out that way—"

"I hear you." Quinn picked up his belt buckle and fingered the letters marking the third place finish in a rodeo he could only vaguely remember.

"Kate and I have been talking. Next Sunday—start with 1 Corinthians 15:35."

"I wish you'd have the conversation with Lisa."

"Sorry, buddy; Kate and I have both been striking out. This attempt is all yours. Knock down Lisa's doubts about the Resurrection, and then we can start dealing with Andy. And that had better happen soon. I do not like her hurting and hiding it."

"I dislike it more than you do."

"Loving them is tough, isn't it?"

He had been trying to avoid that word. "And here I thought I was just trying to get Lizzy to accept dinner out."

"When did she get under your skin?"

"Besides when she smiled at me while she was bleeding to death?"

"Good point."

"I think it was the purple socks. When she looks beautiful in purple socks, there's a problem." He'd given up fighting the inevitable. His emotions were involved. What could he do about it? He'd already apologized to God for letting the situation get so turned around.

He should have understood much earlier that getting to know Lisa was not going to be like getting to know Kate. With Kate it had been a good solid friendship and no draw toward something more. He'd set out to have that same friendship with Lisa and instead got caught by the undertow of emotions that came with being with her. He hadn't been ready for it.

He should have ended the evening out with her tonight long before ten o'clock. He knew it. As enjoyable as tonight had been, it put them on rocky ground. Tangling up her emotions and his when they couldn't be more than just friends was foolishness.

He was about to learn a large dose of patience.

Lisa had been resisting Kate and Marcus's attempts to talk about faith because it had come with too much pressure. He was in danger of pressuring her because he needed her to believe. It wasn't a good position to be in. Lisa would be making up her mind on her own schedule, not his.

It was probably just as well. He had to pull back because she didn't believe. It was likely saving him from a more embarrassing reality. If she already believed and he asked her out on a real date, Lisa would likely turn him down flat. He gave a rueful smile. She'd probably say no with something even more creative than a petrified squid.

"Quinn, when you talk to her, don't push her to believe because you need her to. She'll spot that motivation a mile away. This isn't about Lisa and you; it's about Lisa and God."

Quinn got the message. Hurt Lisa and a hammer was going to come down. "I won't do that to her." Those who said chivalry was dead in the modern age hadn't met Marcus.

"Thank you. Get some sleep. You're going to need it."

"Very true. Page me if you get anything on those notes."

"Deal."

Quinn hung up the phone and ran his hand through his hair. He was too old for this kind of emotional mess. He didn't mind a long wait if there was hope at the end of it. But life didn't always give him what he hoped for; he knew that more than anyone. "It would help if Lisa believed. It would help if I didn't," he said quietly to his God. He was staring at an impasse.

The yard looked gorgeous. Lisa leaned against the back deck railing, feeling relieved to be back home, if only for a short time while she packed.

"Lisa, are these two suitcases it? You've got everything else you need?"

She turned as Quinn stepped out onto the deck. "Those two cases and the garment bag. Would you read my instructions on the animals' care, see if they make sense?"

"Already scanned it. Other than warning Todd that Iris considers your finger something interesting to taste, I think you covered everything."

"Iris and Todd get along just fine. I think the problem is you're a guy who doesn't have pets, and Iris was smart enough to know that. She was just joshing you about it."

"I just think she thought my thumb was another peanut."

Lisa picked up Sidney who had come wandering over the threshold to the deck. "Can we stop by the gallery next and pick up the picture?"

"If you like."

"Might as well get all the errands done at once. Come on, Sidney, time to go back to your home. Quinn, I promised Kate a call when we were done here. I want to see this chair she bought as a wedding gift."

"Lizzy, you can't even imagine it. Any bow she uses is going to disappear."

"White?"

"Probably the only color that isn't in that chair."

Eighteen

No. Hold it like this." Quinn reached over and corrected Lisa's hold on the harmonica. "Use your left hand to move it and your right to change the air flow."

They were somewhere over the state of Missouri, flying south to Houston. It was a gorgeous day, the plane now above a bank of clouds so the sun lit a bright white blanket beneath them. Kate had just moved forward to join Dave in the cockpit. Stephen and Marcus were deep into a game of chess while Jack had settled back in his chair to take a nap.

"I can't figure out how you remember the right distance."

"Think eights. Divide the harmonica in half, divide those two pieces in half as well. That gives you the four major sections. Then think left side of a section or right, and that gives you eighths. Every sound you make is a combination of which of those sections you cover and how you breathe."

She lowered the harmonica and looked at it with frustration. "Something this simple should not be this hard to play."

"Actually, it was a good choice. It will help your lung capacity come back." He laughed at her look. "Try again. You'll get it."

She leaned back in her seat and raised the harmonica. "Maybe I should just admit defeat and tell Jack he won."

"Before your first lesson is over?"

"I didn't say I was going to, only that I should." She tried a simple scale again.

Quinn settled back in his seat, did his best to keep a straight face.

"Quit looking like that," she muttered.

"Like what?"

"Like you swallowed a lemon."

"Would you murder me if I bought earplugs?"

"Slowly," she promised.

"Breathe."

She tried again. He couldn't cover the wince. "A deeper breath and you'll get musical notes instead of a screech."

"After the wedding, we're not going to do the traditional walk down the aisle," Jennifer explained from her chair in the center aisle, where she had been orchestrating this walk-through of her wedding. "Tom and I are going to stay at the front of the chapel and greet our wheelchair-bound guests so those who need to return to the clinic can leave first and those able to stay for the reception can have some extra time to make it over to the hotel."

Quinn listened with half his attention while he watched the more interesting byplay going on between Lisa and Kate. There was an animated, whispered conversation going on between the two of them as they sat on the top step of the stage. He knew trouble when he saw it. They'd only been in Houston twenty-four hours and the two of them were conspiring to drive him crazy.

One of them, and he wasn't quite sure which, had snuck into his hotel room and unpacked for him, then stolen his hat and returned it with a garland of flowers around the brim, alternating white and yellow daisies of all things. He was sure the choice of flowers had been Kate's, but swiping his hotel room key—that had to be Lisa.

Lisa giggled.

"Lizzy, what did I just say?" Jennifer asked.

She looked over at her sister, trying to look chagrined at being caught. "The reception starts at 3 P.M. sharp. And will Stephen please stay away from the cashews until after the guests have left."

Jennifer set aside her notebook. "What are you two deciding now?"

"You don't want to know," Lisa replied cheerfully.

"What if there's a fire alarm? How do you want to manage clearing the room?"

"Jack, thank you for that delightful thought; it was farther down on my list, but we can talk about it now. There are two handicap-accessible entrances, the doors by the choir loft and those at the front of the building. Jack, can you and Stephen manage thirty special-needs guests should the need arise?"

"Quinn, Marcus, Dave, you're recruited to keep the front aisle cleared," Jack decided.

"What about the lights going out?" Marcus asked from his seat on the front pew, his arm wrapped around Shari.

"I think the more relevant question is, what if the air-conditioning goes out?" Stephen asked.

"Guys, please don't give me worst case here. Nothing bad is allowed to happen at my wedding."

"Can I light the candles?"

"No, Jack. I have responsible people to do that. And no, you are not carrying the ring either."

Quinn coughed. He had to love this family.

"Everybody know their cues?"

"We're ready, Jen," Marcus replied. "And you've still got to decide if you want to throw your bouquet here before you go to change or later over at the reception."

"Reception. And I'll stay in my wedding dress too through the end of the reception."

"No you won't." A chorus of voices all vetoed that idea.

Jen's fiancé leaned over her chair to kiss her nose. "Pictures only. Then you change and watch the happenings from a comfortable seat."

"I'm feeling fine."

"Good. This way you'll stay that way."

"I want to stand for the ceremony."

"If you cut it to twenty minutes. Move the second song up to the prelude before you come down the aisle."

"Tom."

"Live with it."

"Then you owe me another kiss." Tom complied, drawing long wolf whistles from the family. He rested his hands on her shoulders, gently tugged her wig, and studied her blush. "You look good as a blonde."

"I was thinking about wearing a purple wig for the reception. That was my patients' vote."

"Knowing you, you'd do it too."

"I still might. Rachel, did I forget anything?"

"Rice."

"Oh—very important. Jack, if you cook the rice so I get hit with white soggy stuff I'm going to make you eat it."

Jack burst out laughing. "Jen, I hadn't even thought of that one. And why are you always picking on me? You know Kate dreams most of this stuff up."

"Whitewashing my car windows this morning—are you telling me that wasn't you?"

"I claim the fifth."

"I thought you would."

"And Dave helped."

Jen looked over at Dave. "Let me guess, you were trying to keep Kate out of trouble."

"Hey, he can get into plenty of trouble on his own," Kate protested.

"I just want you all to remember I have a long memory. This might be the first O'Malley wedding, but I doubt it will be the last." Her amused threat was met with laughter.

"Marcus and Shari are next," Jack agreed.

"Only if I can't talk Kate into walking the aisle first," Dave countered.

"We're eloping," Kate replied immediately.

She was greeted with a chorus of boos. "Sorry, you get the full wedding deal," Marcus insisted on everyone's behalf. "Jen, what else?"

"Rachel has managed a minor miracle getting the reception ready at the hotel. Kate's already volunteered to do the face painting for my young guests. I need someone to blow up the balloons for the animals Shari is making."

"Dave," Kate volunteered.

"Sure, I'll do it."

"Friends from church are going to handle the cake and punch tables. Anything else I forgot?"

"Where are you going for your honeymoon?"

"You think I'd tell you guys?"

"Home."

There was a burst of laughter from the family as Jennifer and Tom contradicted each other.

"Okay, we're done here. I'll see everybody tomorrow morning for church."

Marcus got to his feet and crossed over to kiss Jen's cheek, officially breaking up the walk-through. "Take her home, Tom."

There were numerous hugs and the group began to disband.

"So where do we want to go for dinner?" Jack asked the group, turning his attention to the upcoming evening.

Quinn settled his arm around Lisa's waist, stepping in to take over. "Lisa and I are going back over to the hotel."

"We are?"

"Yes."

She was puzzled but nodded, looking over at Kate. "I guess I'll catch up with you later."

Kate looked at him, then back at Lisa. "I'll wait up for you."

Quinn winked at Kate. "We'll be late." He looked over at Marcus, got a slight nod. Earlier this afternoon the two of them had planned out the next few minutes. "Come on, Lizzy." Quinn turned her toward the side door.

"Is there a reason we're not going with the others for dinner?"

"Yes."

Lisa laughed. "Going to tell me what it is?"

"I thought I'd show you." He held the door for her.

"Where are you parked?"

Quinn nodded to the right and jiggled his keys. "Over there."

He led Lisa over to a fire-red convertible.

"Wow. Nice car." She slid into the seat as he held the door.

He walked around to the driver's side, started the car. "The keys are getting handed to Jennifer tomorrow. Tonight we're just getting her to admit she wants one so that tomorrow she won't be able to refuse the gift."

Lisa's reaction was everything he could have hoped for. He wished he had a camera. He reached over, put a finger below her chin, and gently closed her mouth.

"The family bought her a car."

"You did too. We can debate who picks up your portion of the bill later. I may take it in kind for that Sinclair watercolor."

"Quinn."

"Honey, they wanted to surprise you too. Personally, I think it worked."

"They didn't think I could keep it a secret."

"Maybe one percent of it. Hold on a minute." Quinn backed up to the canopy entrance where Jennifer and Tom had just appeared.

"Jen, what time is the service in the morning?"

"Nine o'clock." She was studying the car. "Want to give me a lift tomorrow to the reception? I can arrive in style. And I don't think Stephen and Jack could fill a convertible with balloons."

"I thought you might like it."

"Anything red is hard not to like."

"I'll give you a ride tomorrow," he agreed. "You'd best get off your feet so you'll be up to walking down the aisle tomorrow. We'll see you in the morning."

"Till tomorrow," Jennifer agreed.

Lisa waited until he pulled onto the interstate. "She's going to be so surprised."

"I already told Marcus I'd bring a Kleenex box. Knowing Jen, she'll need it."

"She's good at happy tears. She's never going to make it through the service."

"Probably not. Tom will be ready."

Lisa ran her hand over the dash. "I'm glad they chose this. She needs her dream while there is still time to enjoy it."

Quinn looked over at Lizzy, concerned.

"The remission is just that, a remission. It's going to get worse."

"Don't borrow trouble," he said gently.

"I'm trying to be realistic. I just hope she gets a decent couple months with Tom before she's back in the hospital."

"Lizzy—"

"Ignore me. I just hate the reality. She is so happy—it's not fair that she's the one who is sick."

"She's at peace with the situation even if the worst happens. So is Tom."

"Because they believe."

"Yes."

"I think that makes it worse. It's false hope."

"You're wrong."

Lisa shoved back hair that was blowing in her eyes. "You really want to debate the question of whether life after death is possible with a forensic pathologist?"

"You don't have a monopoly on the truth, you know."

"About this subject I do."

"Kate's right. You're close minded."

"Quinn."

"I'll grant you that now is not the right moment to have this discussion, but we will have it, Lizzy."

"You're as stubborn as Kate."

"Tenacious. Especially when I'm right."

Lisa changed the subject. "Where are the speakers in the car?" She turned on the radio and turned up the volume. Quinn reached over and showed her which button changed the woofers. "Try that."

He pulled into the hotel parking lot as Lisa rummaged through the glove box. "Sunglasses, sunscreen, lip balm, hairbrush—let me guess, Rachel stocked it."

"Shari, actually."

"Did we get Jen any CDs?"

"Tom did."

Quinn circled the car to open her door. She didn't move. He chuckled. "Yes, you have to leave the car. It's not yours."

"I bought a piece of it, didn't I?"

"You just used it up on the drive here."

"Shoot. I was hoping we could go for a long drive tonight."

"You like convertibles?"

"Are you kidding? Look at this car. It's like a dream on wheels." She reluctantly got out of the car. "I want to know when I can get a matching one, only in blue. How much did this cost?"

"Honey, if you have to ask, you can't afford one."

"Well, I have to admit, the artwork will probably appreciate better."

Quinn walked with her toward the hotel lobby. "I want to talk to you about this mysterious invisible roommate I seem to have acquired."

"What now?"

"It seems someone replaced my jeans with several pairs several sizes too big."

Lisa giggled. "Did they?"

"You really are pushing it."

"I know. But you're so much fun to get."

"I was thinking you might want to turn some attention to Marcus."

"What did you have in mind?"

"If he sees me, I'm going to be toast."

"Then don't get caught," Quinn replied, amused. "Ready?"

"If you double-cross me…"

"Have a little faith. Go."

Lisa took the room key and disappeared down the hall.

Quinn stepped into the vending machine area and dug out change for a soda, killing time while he listened for the elevator. They all had rooms on the same hotel floor although they were spread out. As it had worked out, the guys were at one end of the floor, the girls at the other.

His soda was half gone when he heard the elevator doors open. He heard Shari and Marcus talking about dinner plans. Quinn glanced at his watch, then tamped down the amusement in his expression and went to intercept them. He needed to delay Marcus for two minutes.

"Hi, Shari, Marcus. Did either of you see Lisa downstairs?"

"No."

"I've lost her—again. I'm going to have to put a bell on her. Marcus, did you talk to Tom about Kate's gift? And note, I'm using that word loosely."

"Tom's going to help us smuggle the chair into the reception while Jennifer is changing. When she comes to the reception, it will be her throne for the afternoon. I've even got the photographer in on it. He's bringing a Polaroid camera so he can take pictures of the kids sitting on her lap and hand them out on the spot."

"Great plan. Let me know how I can help. If you see Lisa, tell her I'm looking for her."

"Will do."

Quinn headed toward his room, knowing Marcus would be a couple steps behind him once Shari turned the other direction toward her room. Lisa had had six minutes. She'd requested he make sure she had five.

He paused as though he were unlocking his hotel room door, then pushed open the door, catching the piece of paper Lisa had slipped into the door frame to prevent it from locking. He stepped inside to see Lisa rush into his room from the connecting room, her hands full.

"I thought you were going to intercept him for me!"

"I did. I got you the five minutes you asked for."

"I should have asked you for ten." She collapsed into the chair by the window, out of breath and giggling.

"Did you leave him anything?"

"From his razor on down the list, he's going to have to find everything again. I never realized how many places there were to hide things in a hotel room." She twirled the toothbrush between her fingers. "Who do you think we should give his toothbrush to?"

"Shari."

"Oh, that's conniving."

"He won't suspect it."

"I wish I were going to be here when he reads the note."

"You'll have your chance. He's coming down the hall."

"Quinn! Why didn't you say so? Let's get out of here." She shoved the items she held into the dry-cleaning bag and slid it under the bed. "So where are we going?"

"First, to take a walk."

"Let me go change to comfortable shoes."

"Two minutes. I'll meet you at the elevator."

They heard the door open next door. "Bye," she whispered and cautiously opened the room door, checked the hall, and slipped out.

Quinn waited until the door closed, then tapped on the connecting door. "Marcus?"

His partner opened the door and rested his shoulder against the door frame. "She fell for it?"

"Hook, line, and sinker."

"I wonder how long it will take her to realize she just raided Dave's room, not mine."

Quinn smiled and leaned in to check the room. "She even managed to short sheet his bed? She must have been flying."

"Never let it be said Lisa didn't enjoy setting up a good joke. Go on out for the evening, just stop by my actual room when you get back. I want to see Lisa's face when she realizes her mistake."

"Glad to. Can you slip Dave's key back before he realizes they were swapped?"

"Piece of cake."

"I ate too much, laughed too hard—I can't believe how exhausted I am."

"Admit it, you had fun."

Lisa twirled her new sombrero around her fingers. "I had a wonderful time," she agreed, "and my ribs ache."

Quinn rubbed her nose. "You've acquired a sunburn in the last day."

"My freckles are going to stand out in the wedding pictures tomorrow." She dropped the hat back on her head. "What time is it?"

He checked. "Shortly after 9 P.M."

"Suppose Jen will notice if I sleep in tomorrow instead of attending the church service?"

"Lisa."

"I was just checking."

"Ready for the wedding?"

"Not really." Lisa shrugged one shoulder, her expression defensive. "It's not just me. The entire family has been trying to cram a couple years' worth of practical jokes into the last weekend the family exists as the original O'Malleys. None of us likes the idea of change. We're reverting to our childhood."

"I've noticed. You're looking at the guy who's been on the receiving end of a lot of them." He held open the hotel door for her.

"Do you think Jen's mad at us?"

"Jennifer is so happy right now she would only be offended if she didn't think you all were having fun." Quinn tugged her hand. "Come on. The reception ballroom should be all set up by now. Let's go look at the decorations."

"I want to go crash."

"Half an hour."

"If I fall asleep on my feet, I'm told I snore."

He winced. "Did I really want to know that?"

"Just telling you, in the interest of full disclosure."

The hallway to the banquet rooms and the ballroom being used for the reception was empty and quiet. Quinn opened the door and turned on the lights.

"It's beautiful," Lisa breathed. There were balloons and streamers and white tablecloths and flowers of every kind. There were tables for the cake, the punch, and the gifts. "I want Rachel to plan my wedding. She's thought of everything."

"Her wedding present to Jennifer," Quinn agreed, impressed by what he saw. Jennifer would have a good wedding. It was comforting not only to know that, but to see it.

"So much love in this room." Lisa ran her finger along the lace pattern in the tablecloth. "I think I may cry."

"You'd have to borrow a napkin, I'm afraid. Jen already used my last handkerchief."

Lisa wandered to the bay of windows. "I hope it's a sunny day tomorrow, doesn't rain."

Quinn slowly followed, watching her. "If it rains, maybe she'll get a rainbow."

"Do you think she'll like our gift?"

"The painting? She'll love it."

"What Jen would really like is for me to believe."

She said it with such sadness…her ambivalence had been hiding an internal war over what was happening. He should have realized it. "You've been thinking about it, haven't you?"

She shrugged one shoulder, traced her finger along the windowsill.

"You want to talk about it?" he asked gently.

She sat down in one of the chairs and rested her forearms against her knees as she creased the brim of the hat. "Quinn, it hurts. I don't like disagreeing with the family. They're all I've got that matter to me, and I'm in a disintegrating situation with Kate and Marcus. Now Jennifer wants to talk with me." She looked up at him, and he could see the fatigue that had reached her eyes. "Can you please get me out of church tomorrow morning?"

He had no choice but to shake his head. "I wouldn't try. It matters too much to Jennifer that you be there." It mattered too much to him.

"You know, when Kate talks about believing, she gets so excited about it. Her eyes sparkle and her voice lightens, and she looks…happy. Marcus—" she quirked a sad smile—"he wants to pray about everything now. Jennifer says everything is going to be okay, even though she's dying. It's confusing. I just want my family back the way it was."

"Lisa, look at the truth. Believing in Jesus has changed their lives for the better."

"That doesn't mean what they believe in is true." She looked up at him. "I know you believe too. I'm not trying to be insulting, but knowing their lives are happier doesn't mean much. A doctor can give a patient a placebo and have the symptoms improve. It was the patient who believed that brought the improvement, not what he believed in." She sighed. "Can you prove it to me?"

"Prove what?"

"That Jesus rose from the dead?"

He pushed his hands into his pockets and leaned against the table across from her. "Why ask me? You're convinced you already know the answer."

"Do you have to rub it in?"

"Lisa." It wasn't the right time for this. She was too tired to have a complete conversation, was asking the question for reasons that made the situation even more difficult.

He pulled over one of the chairs, spun it around, and straddled it, folding his arms across the back of the chair. He studied her face, trying to decide how to convince her that the God he served was not only alive but loved her too. "Do you really want to talk about this? I'd be happy too, for as long as you like, for as many questions as you have, but only if you really want to have the conversation. I know the pressure you're feeling. You'd rather just have it go away."

"That's not going to happen. They're family. I'm tired. If I'm wrong, convince me. If you can't…" She shook her head. "I don't want what's coming. We've always been one family, solid, together, and it feels like we're in the process of splitting in two in so many ways—the wedding, Marcus and Shari's engagement, the deep division over faith."

"You have to be willing to trust me and listen." To talk about the Resurrection and not to talk about Andy was to ignore the elephant in the room; yet he could not bring himself to try and approach that subject. "What are your questions, Lizzy?"

"I know what happens when someone dies. It isn't that easy to set aside what I know for something you are asking me to believe. The two contradict each other. How can Jesus rise from the dead? And please don't give that 'because He's God' answer I've gotten all my life. If something so profound is true, then it should have more substance beneath it than simply someone's word that it occurred. There should be something on which faith could be based rather than a 'believe because I told you to' answer. That's blind faith, and I need a rational faith."

Quinn tried to make it as concrete an answer as he could. "When a child is born, he has features of both his mother and father. The genetics of both combine to form the child, correct?"

"Yes."

"In the Bible, Jesus is called both the Son of God and the Son of Man. He has traits of both God and man. Jesus, as God, existed forever. Jesus of Nazareth, the man, had a day He came into existence…and He also had a day He died. That's the death you understand, Lisa. When He was resurrected on the third day, He was still Jesus the Son of God, He was still fully divine, but He was also what the Bible called the first resurrected human, a look at who we will also be someday in the future." She started to interrupt and he lifted a hand. "Let me finish. You asked for a rational reason. I'm giving you one. People saw Jesus after the Resurrection. He appeared to the twelve apostles, then to five hundred of his disciples."

"That's supposed to be conclusive?"

"Lisa, if someone who looked like Kate and acted like Kate tried to take Kate's place, how long do you think they could fool you? An hour? A day? How long could they fool you if you had reason to doubt it was really her?"

She conceded his point with a nod.

"Jesus still bore the wounds in His hands and side. His friends could recognize Him, so He looked the same. His voice must have sounded the same. He could eat. But His body was clearly different— He could move through a closed door, He could vanish. Men and women saw Him after the Resurrection for over a month before He ascended to heaven. They recognized the man they called Jesus. They recognized His words, His actions, His appearance. An impostor could not have fooled so many people for so many days."

"You would argue that the historical record within the Bible is sufficient proof the impossible did happen."

"Look at what the men and women who saw the resurrected Jesus went out and did. They took the Gospel to the entire Roman world. Thousands of them were killed because they chose to continue to insist what they saw was true rather than recant to the authorities. You tell me, is mass hysteria over a common event going to last for a couple thousand years? And not only last, but stay consistent across all those years as to what actually happened? Fifty years after the event, people were still standing as eyewitnesses to the fact they had seen Jesus alive and resurrected three days after He had been crucified."

"It's only recorded in the Bible."

"On the contrary, what the apostles and early Christians did is recorded by secular historians of the day. Christianity did not have an isolated, obscure beginning. It happened in the open and was recorded as people who followed Jesus literally disrupted cities with their radical message."

"You would argue that Jesus is alive now, but in a different body, not one made of dust as ours are?"

"Lisa—"

"What?"

"Please don't get upset, but Marcus wanted you to see one passage from the Bible. I wrote it down." He slid the folded page from his shirt pocket.

"You were talking about me."

"Marcus loves you. He wants to answer your questions as much if not more than I do. Please, if you're my friend, read it."

She reluctantly reached for the note.

"Your question is not unique. This comes from 1 Corinthians 15:35 on."

"Your handwriting needs work."

"So does yours. Read."

He knew what it said, understood why Marcus had felt so certain Lisa should see it. *"But some one will ask, 'How are the dead raised? With what kind of body do they come?'.... "So is it with the resurrection of the dead. What is sown is perishable, what is raised is imperishable.... It is sown a physical body, it is raised a spiritual body....The first man was from the earth, a man of dust; the second man is from heaven. As was the man of dust, so are those who are of the dust; and as is the man of heaven, so are those who are of heaven. Just as we have borne the image of the man of dust, we shall also bear the image of the man of heaven.... For the trumpet will sound, and the dead will be raised imperishable, and we shall be changed. For this perishable nature must put on the imperishable, and this mortal nature must put on immortality."*

"You believe this."

"Yes, Lizzy, I do. This world was not designed to die; sin did that. But Jesus has beaten sin, and it gave Him the right to put on the imperishable as those verses describe. I believe the Resurrection is true. Jesus is alive. That's what Kate has been trying to convince you of, Marcus and Jennifer also."

She folded the note but didn't hand it back. "I'll think about it."

"Please—think hard." He hesitated, then said what his heart demanded. "Lizzy, even if you don't believe, I will still be your friend. Nothing is going to change that. I'm loyal to my friends for a lifetime. There are no qualifications."

She just looked at him for a long time, and then the smile that could make his heart roll over appeared. She got to her feet and lightly tapped his arm with the sombrero. "You're forgiven for asking me out fourth."

She would have passed him but he snagged her hand. "Lizzy."

She stopped.

"I saved the best for last."

Nineteen

She was going to have to tell him about Andy. Lisa rolled over on her bed with a groan, stared at the ceiling. It was 1:14 A.M. She was so tired it was making her punchy. She'd slept an hour only to have a horrible nightmare and wake shivering.

She turned on the bedside light, admitting sleep wasn't going to return soon. Quinn's Bible was on the side table. He'd handed it to her tonight and suggested she borrow it for a few days. She picked it up.

It showed its age. Quinn had carried it with him for years and it was falling apart. There were notes in the margins and verses underlined, some of them dated with cryptic notes beside them. In the front of the book were tucked a couple letters, a faded newspaper clipping—it was like glancing through a guy's version of a diary.

She was familiar with the book. She turned to the passage Marcus had noted and read it again.

She had prayed that Andy would breathe again and he hadn't. It had convinced her that Jesus could not work a miracle and bring back the dead as the Bible claimed. She'd dismissed the Resurrection.

And over the years she found it easier to ignore the subject entirely than rethink it. She'd learned at Trevor House that the only way to deal with the turmoil of the past—religion being just one issue of many—was to draw a line in time and leave the past behind.

It helped to know the Bible did try to argue that the body of dust returned to life. Not much, but it helped.

"They recognized His words, His actions, His appearance."

If Jesus was alive as Quinn and her family claimed, then His actions now should still be consistent with His behavior recorded in the Bible. He'd been a hands-on man, teaching, healing the sick.

Again she felt the same disquieting realization as when the pain had eased during her hospital stay because of Quinn's prayer. It had not been a case of her belief changing the situation for the better; it had been a case of Quinn's belief changing the situation. That required there to be someone else acting. And Quinn said it was Jesus.

Ignoring the time, she picked up the phone and punched in a room number.

"Quinn?"

"Lizzy? Hi."

"Can you meet me for a walk or something?"

"Sure." She heard the concern, and he didn't even comment on the time. "Five minutes? I'll tap on your door."

"Thanks."

She staggered to her feet, moved across the room to her suitcase, and unzipped it. She pulled on a white shirt and jeans, not really caring what it was her hand found first in her suitcase; she just wanted to get out of the room for a while. She was tying her shoelaces when he tapped on her door. She slipped her room key in her pocket and went to slide open the lock. His gaze swept across her, concerned. "Bad dream?"

She nodded.

"I'm sorry about that."

"I need a walk."

"We can take care of that," he assured. She pulled her room door closed. He wrapped his arm around her shoulders and turned her toward the elevators. Lisa reached up to grasp his wrist, appreciating the company. She would have normally gone for a walk alone. This was so much better.

They walked through the lobby and outside to the gardens that landscaped the open area between the hotel and the conference center complex.

"You're going to need a jacket. I should have thought of it upstairs."

It was kind of chilly out, but she shook her head. "I'll be fine for now."

She'd never been good about sharing secrets. She didn't want to talk about Andy. She needed to, but she didn't want to see the pity that would come into Quinn's eyes. It was better all around that she not say anything.

"Has Dave forgiven me yet?"

"He thinks it was Kate. She's denying it, of course, but she doesn't have much credibility on the subject and Dave doesn't believe her."

"I think I'm relieved."

"You should be. You really did a pretty good job for five minutes."

"I can't believe you had me raid the wrong room."

"Me?"

"I think this means we're even."

He smiled. "Just about."

She leaned her head back to look at the moon. "It's not full."

"You sound disappointed."

"I am."

"It's only full one day this month." He tightened his hand. "What was the nightmare about?"

She hesitated about answering him. "Do you dream about when you found your father?"

He stopped walking. "Yes."

"I dream about Andy."

He turned her to face him, his hands settling on her shoulders. "Do you?"

She looked up, wondering why he hadn't asked the more obvious question: who was Andy? He was looking at her with that expression she'd seen once before, compassion so deep she could drown in his gaze. "I don't like the dream," she answered awkwardly, pulling back from telling him the truth.

His thumb rubbed against her jaw line. "I'm glad you asked me to join you for your walk," he answered simply. "It will make it easier to get back to sleep." He tucked her back under his arm and resumed their walk.

"How'd we end up like this for the weekend? Friends? Paired off?"

"Does there have to be a reason? I can't just enjoy your company?"

"I don't understand why."

"Are you asking something I'm too dense to figure out? It is kind of late, you know. Why do I like you?"

She shrugged.

"What's not to like?"

"I work with dead people."

He laughed. "Your job? Lizzy, I don't mind it. Although I think you do at times. That's why you didn't protest to Kevin; you just walked away hurt. Part of you thinks he's right."

"I'm getting analyzed at 2 A.M."

"I've been thinking about it a while."

"Really?"

"Don't sound so insulted. Figuring you out has been a many years puzzle."

"Am I harder to figure out than Jennifer or Kate?"

"I don't compare."

"The mark of a wise man."

"You're an O'Malley. I've learned the basics." He tipped up her chin. "I'm glad you phoned me, although I admit I'm a little surprised."

"Why?"

"Kate's next door to you. I figured you would have woken her up instead."

"Kate? You've got to be kidding. I'd rather wake up a grizzly bear."

"She's that bad?"

"Dave doesn't know what he's getting into."

"What about you? Are you a bear of a morning?"

"Why do you want to know?"

"Curiosity."

"You'll have to come up with a better reason than that."

"Prickly. It must be bad."

"I've been accused of talking in my sleep."

"Really?"

"Don't sound so amused."

"Well, Lizzy, it all depends on what you say."

"You'll forget I said that."

"I think it's kind of cute."

"It's embarrassing."

"Tell me about the dream."

He caught her off guard. "No."

"Why not?"

"None of your business."

"Lizzy, your hair's damp. I don't think that was a shower."

"I keep my room warm versus icy like yours."

"Try again," he said gently.

"So it's a bad dream. Talking about it just makes it worse."

"You're sure?"

"Very."

"You're not exactly relaxing."

"Sometimes it takes a long walk. You don't have to stay."

He ignored that suggestion. "So what do you want to talk about?"

"We don't have to talk, you know. Silence is pretty nice."

"I know. But I like to hear your voice. You're starting to get just a touch of Montana drawl in your speech."

"You're serious?"

He laughed at her alarm. "It sounds good, Lizzy."

"No offense, but everyone who meets you will remember your drawl for years. It's kind of nice on a guy, but a lady…"

"You mimic people you listen to. Don't be so bothered by something that's very unique to you."

"I wish you wouldn't have told me."

He tightened his arm around her. "Actually, your voice is one of the things I like the most about you. I wish you'd call me more often just so we could talk."

She blinked. "You do?"

"Yes."

This was embarrassing. "I don't have anything to say."

"So call me and tell me to come up with questions. I can probably keep us talking for a few hours."

"Maybe someday." When she had a lot more courage than she did tonight. They walked around the garden in silence for a time. "I would have called you even if the other O'Malleys were still awake."

His thumb slipped into the belt loop of her jeans. "Would you?" She saw his smile. She'd pleased him with that answer.

"I'm ready to go back."

"We have to?"

"We've got to be up again in a few hours," she pointed out.

"Want to share breakfast?"

"I was planning to inhale a cup of coffee on the way to church. Besides, it wouldn't be fair to get you up before the last minute. You need the sleep even worse than I do."

"Be kind. I'm not that old."

"Your bones are creaking in the night air."

"Now you're pushing it, Lizzy."

She laughed softly; it felt good to tease him.

He turned them back toward the hotel.

The lobby and hallways were empty of guests.

"Thanks for the walk," she said when Quinn stopped at the door to her room.

"It was my pleasure." He smiled. "I'm tapping on your door in exactly five hours. I want breakfast."

She pushed him toward his room. "Good night again, Quinn."

The maid of honor was not supposed to cry. Lisa tried to blink back the tears, feeling her smile quiver. Jennifer, walking down the aisle on Marcus's arm toward the front of the church, looked absolutely beautiful.

Lisa accepted the wedding bouquet from Jennifer so her sister could turn and hold hands with Tom; Lisa passed the bouquet over to Rachel.

It had been an emotional day, church had been…uncomfortable, and now this—Lisa tried to sneak her hand up to wipe her eyes and caught a smile from Jack across from her. The day couldn't be more perfect.

They had timed the wedding to be twenty minutes. Jennifer was radiant, all the fatigue of the last week's activities pushed aside for this moment. Lisa listened to the song and then the minister begin to speak while she watched Jennifer for any sign of a sway, ready to steady her if needed. It was harder for Jennifer simply to stand than it was to walk, for nerves around her spine would pinch and suddenly flare as shooting pain.

Lisa had Tom's wedding ring slipped onto her middle finger so it wouldn't slide off until it was time to hand it to Jennifer. It felt heavy on her hand. Jennifer had bought Tom a beautiful, thick gold band. Marcus was holding Jennifer's wedding ring for Tom. He'd simply slipped the ring box in his pocket, being practical about it.

When it came time to get the ring off, Lisa found her hands had swelled under the tight grip she'd had on her own bouquet. She had to twist the ring free, feeling like every person in the packed church was looking at her. One of the children giggled and Lisa had to smile. Of course it would get stuck. The ring finally slid free and she very carefully passed it to Jennifer, glad to have her one critical point in the service completed. Quinn was to her right standing behind one of the ushers, helping the guests who needed an extra hand. If she turned slightly she'd be looking at him. She was careful not to turn in that direction, afraid to catch his gaze and find him smiling at her.

The wedding ended with a song and a long kiss that had Kate and then Rachel starting to softly laugh when Tom didn't release Jennifer. Seeing the real reason and knowing Jennifer would hate to have it common knowledge, Lisa dropped her bouquet, and the children, who were close enough to the front to see Jennifer's hand now clenched white, turned instead to look at her as Lisa tried to get her dress to turn so she could bend over and pick up the bouquet. It took clenching her teeth to move that way; she intentionally managed to roll the bouquet over to one of the girls Jennifer privately called her sweetheart. With a giggle Amy leaned over in her wheelchair to help. "You drop things like I do."

She said it loud enough some of the adults in the front row had to laugh. Lisa kissed the little girl and set the bouquet in her lap. "Hold it for me, please?" she whispered.

"Sure." Amy was missing one of her front teeth, making her s's whistle.

Jennifer slowly turned with her hand tucked under Tom's hand. Lisa shared a smile with her sister as the minister formally introduced the couple to the congregation.

The music began, and Lisa stepped aside as Jennifer and Tom moved to greet their special guests, starting with Amy.

Lisa watched Jennifer and found herself wanting what her sister had. Tom loved her so much. She finally felt it safe to try and wipe her eyes.

"Lizzy," Quinn's hand settled firm and warm against her shoulder, "come with me. It's safe to slip away and change."

Quinn thought it was the dress causing the threatened tears. She didn't try to correct the assumption. The pain was an ache that flared with each breath.

"This way."

He didn't try to take them through the crowds now filling the aisles, but instead moved back through the choir doors and into a hallway. "Watch your head." He ducked under the hanging streamers to slip back into the hallway where classrooms had become dressing rooms. "You want me to get Rachel or Kate?"

She eased off the wrist corsage. "Rachel."

"Two minutes."

Rachel joined her a few minutes later, laughing. "Didn't it turn out wonderful?"

"Excellent."

"Quinn said you're part of the reception surprise."

Lisa smiled. "He's keeping the plans to himself. I'm just following directions."

Rachel helped her out of the dress. Lisa breathed easier for the first time in over an hour.

"Okay?"

She nodded at Rachel rather than try to answer. She'd brought over a blue cotton blouse and jeans for the reception. Very casual, but they were doing it intentionally so Jennifer could also be talked into truly relaxing during the reception. If the fatigue she felt was anything like Jennifer's, her sister had to be exhausted. "Thanks, Rachel. Would you let Quinn know I'll meet him after I get my shoes on?"

"Sure."

Rachel slipped away. Relieved, Lisa pressed a hand against her ribs. It was definitely time for another painkiller. She swallowed it dry, making a face at the chalky taste.

"Ready to go over to the reception?" She turned too swiftly and hit the edge of the table with her hip. Quinn steadied her. "Lizzy?"

"I'm ready."

His hands settled on either side of her face and he tipped her head back, frowning. "When we get down to the reception you are sitting down." He slid his hands down to hold hers. "Between lack of sleep and painkillers, you're going to give me a headache here."

"You?" She rested her head against his chest, feeling the day catching up with her. "I'm really feeling it."

"How bad are the ribs?"

She laughed, then groaned. "Please don't make me laugh."

He carefully folded his arms around her, took her weight. "You did good today, covering for Jennifer."

"How many saw?"

"Marcus, Jack."

"Good."

"You were as beautiful up there as Jennifer was. The pictures will look lovely."

"You're being kind."

"Get me one?"

"What?"

"A picture."

"You really want one?"

"Yes. And you're fishing for more compliments." He eased back half a step. "Come on, I'll get you a seat at the reception and some punch and you can orchestrate things from the sidelines."

"My favorite job."

"Now why did I figure that might be the case?" He laughed at the face she made. "Come on, Lizzy. And you have to behave at the reception or I'm going to disown you."

Twenty

I wish we had long weekends away like that more often."
Lisa dropped her garment bag beside Kate's couch. "I need a week's vacation to recover from it. Weddings are exhausting." She collapsed on the couch, letting the cushions absorb her weight and support her back. Lisa watched the strands of a new cobweb sway by the overhead light and idly thought about getting up to knock it down.

"It was fun."

"I laughed more than I thought possible," Lisa agreed. "Did you see Jen's face when she realized the car keys were for her? I never knew someone could cry that much."

Kate reappeared crunching on a carrot. "I noticed she gave the keys to Tom."

"Best act of love I've ever seen. I don't think I would have given them to my husband. He might get dust on it."

"I noticed you and Quinn had a pretty good time together."

Lisa was too relaxed to mind the question. "We did."

Kate settled on the arm of the couch. "He's a nice guy."

"We haven't exactly been dating," Lisa qualified.

"Who said anything about dating?"

Lisa tucked her arm behind her head and smiled at her sister. "I know that tone of voice."

"Want some advice?"

"Not really, but I think I'm going to hear it anyway."

Kate smiled. "Don't let him get away. He makes you happy, Lizzy. That's special."

"Yes, it is." Her smile faded and she pulled over the throw pillow to cover her face, wrapped her arm around it. "Kate, what if we can't solve what happened to Quinn's dad? Will he ever want to settle down?"

"Yes, he will. And work can wait until tomorrow."

"Tomorrow is coming too soon."

"You're meeting with Lincoln in the morning?"

Lisa lowered the pillow. "Quinn was going to meet him for dinner tonight." She made a face. "I want my own bed."

"Maybe the analysis of the notes has revealed something."

"Notes? There was only one."

Kate bit her lip.

"There was more than one."

"Sorry, Lizzy. So much for keeping my mouth shut. They found it tucked in the garage door, apparently left at the same time as the note you found."

"What did it say?"

"Pretty innocuous. Something about pretzels."

"So who decided to keep me in the dark?"

"Lizzy—"

"Don't even try to weasel out of answering."

"Marcus and Quinn. They would have told you had it changed either how much was known or what should be done."

"Sure they would have."

"Please don't get mad at them."

"I'm too tired and in too good a mood to get mad." A beeper started to chirp. Lisa lifted her head. "Is that yours or mine?"

Kate went to check. "Mine. How did they know I just walked in the door?"

Lisa smiled. "Spies."

Kate called in to the dispatcher. "Where?" She scrawled down an address. "Lizzy, I've got to go. You've got apartment keys if I end up being gone a while?"

"I'm set. Want me to call Dave for you?"

"He'd just worry. But I'll call him if it looks like it will be a long deal."

"Be careful."

"Always." Kate grabbed her phone and the bottle of water she'd just opened. "See you later."

Lisa heard the door swing shut and Kate turn the dead bolt. Lisa debated whether to take a nap on the couch before she thought about dinner. She needed to unpack, and she had laundry to do if she was going to be here another week.

The wedding was over; Quinn's vacation was up in another week. The thought was depressing. She didn't want a life that simply revolved around work again.

She set aside the pillow with a sigh. It was an impossible situation.

She didn't want to do laundry. She could fix that by getting more clothes. Her new sod patch in the yard needed drenching. And she desperately wanted to see her pets.

She looked at her watch.

She'd go feed her pets. Twenty minutes at the house, she'd be back before it was dark.

She'd even leave a note for Kate.

Quinn rang the doorbell as he juggled the restaurant carryout sack. Knowing Lisa and Kate, they had found the most convenient thing for dinner, even if that turned out to be ice cream.

"Lisa, what—" Kate pulled open the door and stopped short. "Quinn."

"What's wrong?"

"She's gone out," Kate bit out. "She's late. And I'm going to kill her."

"Where?"

"I just got back from a page. She left me a note."

"Dump this on the counter." He handed over the sack and read the crumpled piece of paper. "Come on. I'll drive."

"She wanted more clothes. She could have raided my closet." Kate slammed the door behind them.

Quinn tried to lighten her tension. "Only if she's grown several inches in height since I saw her last." He held the car door for Kate.

"I can't believe she left behind my back."

"She wanted to see her pets. I should have taken her by earlier."

"Was it quiet here while we were gone?"

"Yes." He pulled into traffic. "This is not your fault, Kate."

She didn't answer him.

"How'd the page go?"

"The guy shot himself before I got there."

"I'm sorry, Kate."

"Not your fault."

"It's one reason you're angry."

"Drive faster. She said she'd be home no later than six-thirty. It's already seven."

"There could be simple explanations."

"And there could be bad ones."

He was already breaking the speed limit. He maneuvered through traffic and broke it further.

They were pulling into Lisa's subdivision twenty minutes later. "Quinn."

"I see it." There was smoke rising in the air. He could hear the fire engines rolling somewhere ahead of him in the subdivision.

"No. Oh no!"

It was Lisa's house, and there were two fire engines rolling to a stop in front of the house, men pouring off of them.

Lisa's car was in the drive. The house was fully engulfed.

"Lisa's inside!"

Jack swung the ax with every ounce of energy in his body, the muscles in his legs through his back propelling the blow. He didn't waste time on words. It was an accelerant fire unlike any he had ever seen; even the ground seemed to burn.

The shouts of men who fought the dragon were a noble chorus around him.

The second blow splintered the door at the lock; it swung open—and a wall of fire slammed out with ferocious intent. For a horrifying instant Jack was inside the fire, his face mask taking the brunt of the beast's breath; he was trapped by heat and light and angry flames.

Eighty pounds of water pressure per minute hit back; scalding steam roiled, and the flames slowly began to retreat.

One second.

Two.

Three.

They weren't getting through it fast enough.

At seven Jack surged through the doorway, not caring anymore what it was going to be like inside, stealing through the opening in the wall of flames to the left and toward the hall.

There was no way to shout, to hear Lisa against the roaring noise. She'd be down low to the floor trying to escape the smoke while trying to get toward a window…if she were able to still move. The smoke was too low, hugging near his knees. Her lungs would have already seared with the smoke, which made for an agonizing death. And the windows were the last place he wanted her moving toward—they had been laced and marked to burn. She'd reach safety only to have it denied her. And Jack knew from horrifying experience that once clothes caught fire…

He wasn't leaving her in this house.

A hand clamped down hard on his shoulder, squeezing twice, Cole signaling he'd search clockwise around the room while Jack moved counterclockwise. Jack reached up and tapped Cole's hand in agreement.

Only another firefighter would understand why they were inside an inferno when hope was so slim. The fact it was his best friend and the head of the arson group at his side—Jack was grateful. Cole was the most experienced man in the company. If there was a chance, Cole would help create it.

Which room?

Kitchen? Living room? Bedroom?

Pets.

Jack knew exactly where Lizzy would have tried to go.

And knowing that, it might just save her life.

He moved forward with Cole down the hall, judging distance by the number of steps he took, and felt for the door frame of the guest bedroom, committing himself and Cole to searching this room first, and possibly last, if the fire had its way. It was terrifying, the knowledge Lizzy could literally be lying one foot farther down the hall, and in this smoke he couldn't see her.

He was blind, and his sister was dying.

"Take out the window in the guest bedroom next!" Stephen shouted over the roaring flames. Quinn turned the long pike pole with its metal hook to break out the glass and latch around the burning windowsill. He could feel the heat blistering his face as he strained to tear out the wood, grimly ignoring the pain.

Marcus latched his fire hook around the wood to help. "Pull!"

Stephen had wisely given them a job, for neither of them could handle standing by to watch. Jack and Cole had risked their lives going inside to get Lisa. They needed a way to get her out. Quinn refused to accept the reality that he could feel, see, smell, and taste. The fire had already won. Water hissed around him as the flames roared and ate the water thrown against it.

"Lisa!" It was a shout from Kate behind him and to the right. Quinn risked seconds to look away and checked his movement midstroke. Lisa, running hard across the sidewalk from the direction of the nearby park into the street without looking, falling forward and catching herself as her feet moved from sidewalk to asphalt. Quinn dropped the fire hook and swerved sharply to cut her off.

Her eyes were wide, bright, and focused past him. "No!"

Quinn caught her, steel arms wrapping around to stop her. The force of the contact drove a bruise deep into his side.

"Jack, get out of there! Lisa's safe. She's outside!" Kate screamed over the roaring fire.

The top of Lisa's head caught Quinn under the chin sending sharp splinters of pain into his jaw and face. She was hard to hold. She'd learned to fight dirty and she wanted past him; in the adrenaline rush to reach her pets she wasn't thinking, just reacting. Those were her pets dying.

He forced her to turn away from the fire, not to watch, and felt her chest heave as she tried at the same time to breathe and speak. "Don't, Lizzy, please don't. It's already over."

He could feel it rush over her, could feel the shock break and the truth hit. Her body shuddered. She'd lost everything that mattered to her: the scrapbooks, the records, the art...and the pets. The pets she had loved were dead.

He held on because it was all he could do to help.

He could hear Jack coughing, Kate angry in her relief, and Cole ordering people back. The fire viciously roared as the roof collapsed.

It took Lisa minutes but Quinn felt the change. She stiffened as she took a deep breath. She braced and pushed herself a few inches back

THE TRUTH SEEKER 249

from his chest, stumbled, and found her footing again. She was reeling and fighting it and her eyes— His hands tightened and she tried to shake him off. "I'm okay. Go help Jack. Someone needs to help Jack."

Marcus read the situation in a glance, slid his arm around her waist, and took over. "Lizzy, you scared us, honey."

Marcus met his gaze, and Quinn understood the silent message. Quinn let his hand tighten on Lisa's shoulder. "I'll get Jack so you can see for yourself he's okay."

Lisa was sitting on the side step of the fire engine, silent, one tennis shoe off because she'd stepped on a hot ember and burned the sole. She was moving her socked foot slowly back and forth in the soot-blackened water rushing down the street toward the nearest storm drain, her gaze never leaving the dying fire. Her brother Stephen had wrapped a fire coat around her and she gripped it with both hands, pulled tight.

Quinn kept a close watch on her as he leaned against the driver's door of a squad car, waiting for a callback from the dispatcher. She was alone in her grief, her emotions hidden, her eyes dry. She'd lost what she valued, and he hated to realize how much it had to resonate with her past.

Kate sat down beside her.

Quinn watched as the two sisters sat in silence, and he prayed for Kate, that she would have the right words to say.

Instead, Kate remained silent.

And Lisa leaned her head over against Kate's shoulder and continued to watch the fire burn, the silence unbroken.

Friends. Deep, lifelong friends.

Quinn had to turn away from the sight, so much emotion inside it was going to rupture out in tears or fury.

He found himself facing a grim Marcus.

"Quinn, get her out of here."

"Stephen has already tried; she won't budge."

"No. I mean out of here. Out of town," Marcus replied tersely. "He goes from notes and phone calls to fire. He's not going to stop there."

Marcus was right. Lisa had to come first. "The ranch. She's going to need the space."

"Thank you."

"I'll keep her safe; now that it's too late."

"Quinn—we'll find him."

That wasn't even a question. He was going to hunt the guy down and rip out his heart.

"Lizzy." She was awake but looked unseeing out the plane window, her face still bearing the streaks of soot and her clothes the strong smell of smoke. Quinn tucked the blanket around her lap, then eased her head forward and replaced the jacket she'd bundled up with a pillow. He reached for her hand and closed it around a cold water bottle. "Ice water. It will help."

He loosened the cap when she tried and couldn't turn it.

He wished she'd say something, wished she'd at least cry, but instead she had pulled back into silence, turning her face away from him, watching the black night sky. Dave had chartered the flight for them so she'd have no one else to have to deal with.

Rachel had wanted to come along, and Kate, but Lisa had just shaken her head. It had hurt the others to see her pulling away from them, but Lisa hadn't seen that. She'd simply wanted to retreat on her own. And because he understood, he'd quietly suggested to her family that they give her a couple days.

He wanted so badly to reach out and pull her against him, take the pain away, but she wasn't seeking him out either, and that hurt, deep in his soul it hurt. She wasn't turning to him.

He reached over and held her hand. For the duration of the flight it remained lax within his.

Twenty-one

Quinn walked down the long hardwood floor hallway in the ranch house, past the sculptures and the art, the mail on the side table and suitcases still unpacked by the door. He accepted the phone from his housekeeper. "Jack?"

"How's she doing?"

Quinn didn't have a good description. "Still in shock. Too quiet." He worried about how long it would take her to come out of it. This Lisa, so passive she followed directions without comment, was a mystery to him. He hoped that if she couldn't sleep she'd at least seek him out, rather than slip from the house to walk alone. "How are you doing? Honestly?"

Jack's voice had deepened an octave and still sounded rough, an after-effect of all the smoke he'd inhaled. "I would not recommend running air tanks down until they start to chime. I'm thankful Cole was with me."

"It's painful, knowing the risk you took when she wasn't even inside."

"Quinn—" Jack's voice became grim—"if she had been inside, she'd have been dead. The flames were coalescing to the center of the house, the toxic smoke was as low as my knees. Every room was filled with the smoke; it was pouring through the air-conditioning vents like small chimneys."

"Arson?"

"The place was soaked in fuel oil. Poured into the ground and soaked into the wood of the patio. It went with the same ferociousness as a natural gas line break would burn."

"He wanted to kill her, not just scare her."

"He set the fire while she was out of the house; I don't think that was an accident. Marcus found a note tucked under the windshield wiper of her car. *Go away.*"

"The fire was a threat." Quinn felt sick. There was no more room to escalate but to murder. They had to find this guy. "How'd he start it?"

"Preliminary—a lighter tossed into the flower bed at the back of the house."

"No one in the neighborhood saw anything?"

"I'm sorry, Quinn. Her immediate neighbors were gone for the weekend, and the patrols that have been watching the neighborhood didn't see anything out of place. But my gut tells me he stayed. I don't think he set the fire and left the area. We're reviewing the news reporter's tape of the fire to see if there was anyone in the crowd that stands out."

"She didn't tell many people she was going to be gone or when she would return."

"He's close enough to her to know the details, either directly or second hand."

He had nowhere to direct the anger he felt. "Why didn't Lisa smell the fuel oil?"

"It's like motor oil: once it's soaked in, it's not going to be that obvious. And they were asphalting the driveway three houses down. Even I would have had a hard time separating the smell of fresh asphalt from the faint, lingering smell of fuel oil." Jack's voice turned rough. "Quinn, that note. Why does he want her gone? It has to tie to the murders you two have been investigating. Just how close are you to the truth that he would risk such a public action to slow you down?"

"I don't know. If we're staring at it already, I don't know what it is."

"Find out. Until you do, I don't know how we'll stop him."

"Was there anything salvageable?"

"Kate and I will find out tomorrow once the ruins have cooled down."

"Don't tell Lisa what you've told me."

"Not until she's ready to hear it," Jack agreed. "I'll call in the morning."

"Please do."

After he said good-bye and hung up the phone, Quinn just stood in the hall, looking unseeing at the floor, weary to the bone. It was almost dawn.

Lisa had had to start over so many times in her life. He didn't know if she had the reserves to do it again. She'd loved having roots, a place that was hers.

She'd loved that house. She'd needed that house. And now someone had taken it away. She struggled to let herself attach to people, would now add a struggle to let herself attach to another place knowing it could also get ripped away. There were only so many losses a person could take.

"Lord, I want to find whoever did this and rip away what he values most, make him feel the same hurt he inflicted." Quinn felt the ache settle back in his stomach, like a wound that wouldn't heal. He'd nearly lost her for a second time. "I'd give my right arm to know how to help her right now."

There was nothing he could do, that was the harsh part. He wished from the depths of his heart that he could share this ranch with her for more than a few days, he wished he could make her part of it and the roots of this house and land that went back not one generation but four.

"What's going to help, Lord? She's hurting. And it's breaking my heart."

Montana was doing its best to show itself at its finest. The sunset was painting the sky, the temperature was cool but comfortable, the evening breeze faint.

Lisa took a seat on the steps of the porch rather than take a chair. Quinn gave her the space, leaning against the post of the porch, watching the sunlight fade. The sounds of the night were beginning to rise: the faint sounds of cattle and horses moving around settling for the night, the quiet rising sound of insects.

As peaceful as the night was, Quinn doubted Lisa felt it. Five days. It was Saturday and she had yet to come out of the silent place where she grieved. Pets like people were mourned. Her face was drawn from lack of sleep. He couldn't get under that reserve, hadn't tried. He understood the patience of time.

His mongrel dog with the odd name of Old Blue—cattle smart, loyal to a fault—angled from coming to him to veer toward her, his tail moving slowly back and forth as he stopped near where she sat. Lisa didn't respond. The dog moved forward, nudged her hand, and rested his muzzle on her knee.

It was a silent standoff between the two of them and Quinn tensed.

Lisa finally reached forward and rubbed the dog's head.

And Quinn saw the first tear fall.

"Someone burned down my house and killed my pets."

Sitting on the porch step beside Lisa, Quinn just nodded. "I know."

She wiped her eyes with one hand, the other continuing to stroke Old Blue's head. Quinn was relieved that there was life back in her eyes, even if the emotion was primarily anger.

"Someone who had to be following us that day we visited Marla's grave. And he likes fire. We know that about him now."

"I had copies of the case files sent out." He knew the work would help, would give her a safe place to function while she dealt with the emotions.

"I want to see them."

"Let me get you something to eat first." She desperately needed some sleep too, but he knew he would get nowhere encouraging that at the moment.

"The files are in the study?"

"The white boxes stacked by the bookcases."

"I'll eat as I read."

He wrapped his hand around hers. "Please, go call the family first. It will help them—Kate, Rachel, especially Jennifer. And Marcus can fill you in on what he and Jack and Stephen have been able to find out." She'd talked to them when they called, but she'd been holding herself so far back from everyone it had made her words seem merely polite. It had been so hard on them to wait, not to fly out as the days slipped by, to give her the space she wanted.

"I'll call them."

Afraid he'd say too much if he stayed, he kissed her forehead, then got up from the porch step beside her.

"Jen, I'm sorry."

"Please quit apologizing. It's not necessary. I was absolutely sick when Marcus called to tell me the news."

Stretched out on the couch in Quinn's study, her head resting against the armrest, Lisa idly wrapped the phone cord around her finger. Her family loved her enough to forgive her for being rude. She'd pushed them away for five days and they were still there waiting for her when she came back to her senses. "Someone wanted to kill me, Jen."

"I know."

"I'm scared."

"I know that too."

Lisa reached down toward Old Blue and got her hand licked for her trouble. The dog rolled onto his side and she buried her hand in his warm fur. She had a feeling Old Blue wasn't a house dog, but Quinn had shown up with sandwiches and the dog at his heels. Lisa was pretty sure the dog was hanging out with her because of the food she'd been sharing but felt relieved to have him with her regardless.

"I miss Sidney so much. He was so special. And Iris—" She was crying again and wiped at the tears, furious with herself for having so little control, glad Quinn had given her privacy for this call.

"They'll find whoever did it."

She reached over for another Kleenex.

"You never told me why you left the house to go walk around the pond."

Lisa hesitated.

"Lizzy? You want to talk about it?"

"Quinn." She tried not to put all the confusion she felt over the man into the word, but it was there.

"I wondered," Jen said softly. "You two were pretty tight over the weekend."

"I went for a walk to try and clear my head. A lot of good that did me. If I'd been at the house, I might have been able to save my pets."

"I wish someone had been able to. I know Jack tried."

"They would have been terrified in those minutes before they died."

"I know."

Lisa forced herself away from the image that had haunted her dreams for days. "Quinn's being nice. He's hovering, kind of lost as to what he should do."

"I gathered that from the conversations I've had with him. Do you know what you want him to do?"

She wanted a hug but didn't know how to ask for one. He was

kind, and there, and wanted so badly for her not to be hurting any-more. It no longer surprised her that it mattered so much to him. Under the watchfulness he showed the world, he was a man who was as protective of her as her family. "He loaned me his dog."

"Did he?"

Lisa rubbed Old Blue's ears and heard a dog's version of a sigh of pleasure. "I think he's going to want him back," she remarked regret-fully.

Jen laughed.

Reality was settling in, and it left an enormous ache in her heart. "The house is gone, the art. All the scrapbooks. It shouldn't matter so much, it was just stuff." But it did. She could remember painting the rooms while Jack painted the ceilings, wallpapering the bathroom, rearranging furniture so many times Marcus wanted to strangle her when she said, "No, I like it better where it was, move it back."

All the firsts in that house—first dinner party for family, first mort-gage payment, first winter snow and shoveling the drive, first flowers in the spring. It was gone, and she was going to have to start over again.

"It was home."

"It was home," Lisa agreed. The first one she'd ever really had.

"Marcus said he was dealing with the insurance guy for you?"

"I faxed him power of attorney. Stephen said he'd help me find and fix up another place."

"What's wrong with Montana?"

"Jen—"

"I know Quinn's heart. He's the right guy for you."

"You're reading too much into the situation."

"I'm not saying marry the guy tomorrow."

"Thank you for that. Would you tell me something?"

"Sure."

"Did you decide to believe because it mattered to Tom?"

"Honestly?"

"Yeah."

"It was the only reason I went to church initially because it was important to him. But I started listening, and after a while I found something there that I wanted for myself."

"What was that?"

"Forgiveness."

"The drunk driver who killed your parents."

"Living with the bitterness for so long…I just wanted to be able to forgive and let it go so I could get on with my life. But I couldn't do it for myself. I found out that Jesus could do it for me, He could help me forgive."

"You believed in Him because you needed Him."

"I trust Marcus because I need to, but also because I know he's trustworthy. Which came first?" Jen asked. "There's no easy answer, Lizzy. Jesus loves me. He's helped me forgive a man I hate, helped me into remission with the cancer, worked out things with Tom to make me the happiest I've ever been in my life. I believe in and love Jesus because He is who He is. He's worth loving. Which came first? I don't know. He's just perfect. And I know Him. That's the most peaceful reality I've ever had in my life."

"I prayed for a family and He let adoption papers get ripped away," Lisa whispered. She'd never told that to Jennifer before.

"You ended up with the O'Malleys," Jen finally said, tears choking her voice. "And you make our family complete. Maybe He knew that."

Lisa closed her eyes. She wouldn't trade the O'Malleys for anything.

"Lizzy? Risk asking Jesus for your deepest need. You'll find out He's sufficient."

"That's assuming He's alive."

"You're not even protesting anymore that the Resurrection's not possible. You already know He's alive."

Her hand stole across her ribs to touch the scar. "Maybe."

"Let's go back to talking about Quinn."

Lisa heard the smile in Jen's voice. "Are you matchmaking?"

"I'm married. You wouldn't believe how great it is. Tom is—"

"What?"

"I look into his eyes and he lets me see all the way to his heart. He trusts me to love him."

"I always knew he was special," Lisa replied, having to talk past the emotion that welled up at Jen's description.

"He's going to take me over to the clinic tomorrow and let me be a doctor again for half a day."

"Enjoy it, Jen."

"I'm going to beat this, the cancer. I know it."

"I believe you."

"No you don't, not yet, but that's okay. I understand why. I've seen the lab work too. I'm just telling you now so I can say I told you so later on."

Lisa had to laugh, and then she turned serious. "Jen, if there's anything at all that I can do to help—I don't want anything to happen to you."

"I've got too much life to enjoy before I'm ready to think about heaven. Would you be willing though to do me a favor?"

"If I can."

"I want you to be able to believe. So whatever your doubts, face them, talk to Quinn if you need to, just don't push them aside for another day."

"Why don't you ask me to do something easy?"

"Sometimes the best things are never easy, or simple."

Thinking about Quinn, Lisa had to agree. "It's late your time. I'd better let you go."

"Will you call me tomorrow?"

"Sure. I want to hear how your patients like your new doctor's chair."

"My partners cringed when I moved it into the kids' waiting room. It's fabulous. Tom bought me a Polaroid camera so I can take pictures of kids in the chair to take with them."

"Have Tom take one of you in the chair and send it to me. I can start a scrapbook with it."

Jen tried to keep her voice light but failed. "Deal."

"Jen—" Lisa found it hard to put the emotions into words. "I love you."

"I love you too. And you're making me bawl here."

Lisa wiped her eyes as they laughed together. "Do you really think he won't mind the scars?"

"Does my husband seem to care that I don't have hair?"

"Point taken. Thank you."

"I want to be your matron of honor."

"Well shoot," Lisa joked. "I kind of liked Kate's idea of eloping."

"Be really glad you're half a continent away at the moment."

"He looks really good in a tux and boots."

Old Blue rolled over under her hand. She turned to glance down at him and froze. Quinn was leaning against the study doorjamb watching her—comfortable, boots crossed, smiling. He hadn't just arrived.

"Jen, I'll call you tomorrow." She abruptly ended the conversation, hung up the phone, feeling heat rise across her face.

Quinn crossed the room and set the extra mug he carried down onto the end table. "Your style of coffee." She started to sit up only to get sidetracked when he slid his hands under her ankles and sat down at the other end of the couch, her feet in his lap. "Tux, huh?"

She pulled a pillow over to cover her hot face.

"Eavesdropping doesn't normally reveal such nice compliments." He was laughing at her. "Quit tickling my foot."

"Honey?"

"That's not my name."

"We'll change it for a while."

"As long as I don't have to answer to it."

"I'm going to have to kiss you before long."

"That is something you had to tell me."

"Anticipation is half the enjoyment."

She lowered the pillow slightly because she just had to see his face. He was smiling at her, he was gorgeous, and… "I'd prefer it if you didn't."

His amusement turned serious and his hand rubbed her ankle. "Why not?"

"I don't kiss all that great," she muttered. He was going to anticipate it and she would just disappoint him.

His expression turned tender…and just a bit too delighted for her comfort. "Practice helps."

"You really should have let me know you were there."

"I know." He squeezed her ankle. "Lizzy?"

"What?"

"She was right, you know, about the scars. I won't mind."

"You should. They're ugly."

"I've got my own, unfortunately at about the same place too. I got gored by a bull back in my rodeo days."

She didn't say anything, couldn't.

"I got hung up and came down in front of him. He caught me between the seventh and eighth ribs, tossed me across the ring, and then nearly hooked the rodeo clowns who risked their lives to distract him."

"How bad?"

"I recovered. So will you."

She turned her foot in toward his ribs. "About there?" She'd guessed correctly. He was ticklish.

She was at a distinct disadvantage in the ensuing minutes. "Uncle! I give!" She was going to split open from laughing so hard. He finally relented and stopped tickling her feet.

She curled her toes. "Where's my sock?" She'd lost it sometime during the preceding minutes.

He closed his hand around her toes, his hand warm and solid, leaned over to pick up the sock from the floor, then paused. "Sorry, it looks like I'll have to buy you another pair."

She found the energy to raise her head from the arm of the couch. "That has got to taste horrible." Old Blue was having a good time taking the sock apart.

Quinn eased her feet aside so he could get up and rescue what was left of the sock before the dog made himself sick.

Lisa pushed herself to sit up, reached for the coffee mug he had brought her, and found it had cooled off. "Warm up the coffee, and let's get to work."

"You need some sleep first."

"Later."

He accepted the mug. "It was good to hear you laugh, Lizzy."

She smiled back at him. "It felt good. Go."

"I still think the water is significant."

"Part of his signature?"

Lisa absently nodded. She turned the page of the notepad, started thinking through another idea.

Amy. She drew a circle around the name, drew a link from that circle to Quinn's dad, and marked it with a question mark. They still didn't know for certain if Amy's disappearance the same day Quinn's father was killed were connected.

Amy had known Rita.

Lisa wrote down Rita's name and circled it, then linked Amy and Rita. She could see them now in her mind. Two teens, sixteen—camera; boy; and horse-crazy. Happy.

Amy missing; Rita dead.

The picture on the pad of paper was grim.

Grant had been convicted of killing Rita.

She added him to the page, hesitated, then dotted a line from Grant to Amy. "We have to find some way to place Amy back in Chicago."

"It's not there, Lizzy."

"I think it is. We just don't know the right question to ask." She drew a circle around the name Marla. Connected it to the circle of her house fire because of the hummingbird note—and felt the focus click in.

Egan.

She wrote the name down and just stared at the page.

It fit, but why?

That fire had been an accident; Jack didn't miss arson.

No more glimmers of an idea appeared. She shifted her attention back to Grant. Christopher had worked part-time for Grant at the stable, had blackmailed payment from him to keep quiet about Grant and Rita being together that last day, had later testified at the trial. It was enough information for her to add Christopher's name to the page and circle it.

She drew a line from Christopher to Grant, then drew another from Christopher to Rita. It was a moment of epiphany. Christopher had known Rita. It was obvious. He'd known who she was when he saw Grant and Rita together.

When had Christopher started to work for Grant? She scrambled to find the right file.

"What?"

"Just a minute."

She finally found the answer on a note Lincoln had made during his background investigation. Christopher had started to work for Grant when he was seventeen, in 1978. She was startled at that answer. He'd been working for Grant at the stables when Rita had first begun to come around at the age of sixteen.

She looked at the date, then back at her picture. Her hand shaking slightly, she drew a line from Christopher to Amy. If the girls had been hanging out at the stables, they would have certainly met a guy their own age working there.

Two teens, sixteen—camera; boy; and horse-crazy. They would have been flirting with Christopher.

The picture spoke for itself. From Grant, lines to Rita and Amy. From Christopher, lines to Rita and Amy. And Rita's body had been buried at the stable.

She felt a chill. "Quinn, what if it was Christopher who killed Rita, not Grant?" she whispered.

It fit.

Christopher had been there the day Rita went missing.

He had known Rita when she was sixteen and he was eighteen. Rita had chosen to date Grant, not him. Christopher had a temper. How many murders had she investigated over the years motivated precisely by that fact?

"Talk to me." Quinn had set aside his notes, was watching her.

"Christopher knew Rita. He was working at Grant's stables part-time when he was eighteen. He was there when Rita started coming around at age sixteen. He was there the day Rita disappeared. He had access to the site where she was buried. He had a temper. If he was jealous Rita had chosen Grant instead of him…"

"The blackmail?"

"Why not frame Grant? Extort money to keep quiet about the fact Grant and Rita had been together that day. Bury Rita somewhere that would point to Grant. Testify at the trial and put Grant at the scene. Christopher set him up."

She looked at Quinn as he thought it through. "Lincoln poking into the trial past would have spooked Christopher," Quinn said quietly.

"You said someone started following you while I was still in the hospital. This could explain that too. When you started asking about Amy and Rita…Christopher is safe as long as no one comes forward to say he and Rita knew each other for years. If Lincoln or you discovered that Christopher had as much a motive for killing Rita as Grant did…"

"Christopher knows where you live; he helped Walter plant the tree."

"Would he be the type of guy that would set a fire?"

"I think so," Quinn replied grimly. "The note. *Go away.* Someone is very desperate to see you stop probing into Rita's death…and the others'."

"We were thinking it would take a career like a builder for someone to cover the geographic area of the murders, be around long enough to learn their routines. Working for his uncle at Nakomi Nurseries, doing landscaping—Christopher would have had that flexibility."

"Lincoln has the records for the customers Nakomi Nurseries worked with in the Knolls Park area. If Christopher was in the area at the time Marla disappeared, we should be able to prove it."

"Emily has been working to figure out Grant's whereabouts on the days the women disappeared. Ask her to do the same for Christopher."

Quinn reached for the phone. "Is there any way to connect Christopher to Amy?" he asked as he dialed.

Lisa looked back at her page of circles. That two-week visit to Chicago.

She shifted around the boxes to find the pictures Amy had taken. "I need a picture of Christopher as a young man." She had met him in his late thirties at the trial, but she wasn't sure she would recognize him at age eighteen. Amy had liked to take pictures of friends, and there were several dozen people they had yet to identify in the pictures.

Quinn passed on the idea to Lincoln and they talked for a few minutes. Quinn reached over and hung up the phone. "Lincoln will find out where Christopher has been, check the Nakomi Nurseries' records."

"Let's hope he finds something."

"Lisa, it's a good idea."

"There's not enough evidence to prove anything."

"It fits. We haven't had that before. If the evidence is there, we'll find it."

"Someone burned down my house. At least this way it's one person who committed all the crimes."

"Walter said he and Christopher were working on a job a good two hours away when your house burned."

"You said yourself Walter protected Christopher over the gambling. Protecting him over a suspicious fire…"

"Walter knows more than he is saying."

"Let's find something conclusive that suggests Christopher is guilty before we accuse Walter of lying."

"Pass me Lincoln's notes."

She found them and complied.

Lisa looked at her sketch of circles. They needed to prove the motive that Christopher had not only known Rita but had possibly even dated her. "Was there anything in Rita's diary about a Chris or a Christopher?"

"I don't know that I would have recognized it as significant. You'd better review those that we have to make sure."

Lisa found the first diary.

She heard a soft rumble. She looked up and grinned. "That is your stomach growling."

"It's Old Blue's."

"Sure it is."

Quinn got to his feet. "I'll prove it to you. I'll go get a sandwich, and you can listen to Old Blue."

She chuckled. "Do that."

"You want something?"

"No. I'm fine."

∞

She was asleep on the couch. Quinn paused in the doorway, late coming back, having been sidetracked by a conversation with his ranch manager. He moved quietly into the room. The diary was cradled against Lisa's chest with one hand, a stack of old pictures resting in her lap. Her other hand rested on Old Blue's side. His dog was sleeping too. Quinn had a feeling he'd lost his dog's loyalty forever.

He thought about moving her. Thought about it and instead just settled into the chair opposite her, resting his chin on his fist. She was gorgeous as she slept.

Twenty-two

T ry this one." Lisa offered the long stick and the toasted marshmallow.

Quinn leaned forward and carefully slipped it from the stick. "It's
a good thing I don't mind the taste of burned marshmallows."

"This one came out better."

"You get too impatient. Hold the stick higher and turn it more."

He licked his fingers of the sticky marshmallow.

Lisa finished eating hers. It was only a bit charred. "Want another one?"

"Sure."

She reached for the plastic bag of marshmallows, watching Quinn
while she did so. Firelight flickered across his face. He was totally
relaxed, resting his head back against his saddle, using it for a headrest.
She liked that about him, his ability to set aside everything else going
on and totally relax. They were having a campout dinner although they
were only a half-hour ride from the house. Lisa had insisted that she
wanted a real bed for the night so the tour he'd been giving her of the
ranch had been cut short to four hours.

She rubbed the small of her back. It had been about three hours
too long. Quinn had said he would show her the south part of the
ranch tomorrow, but if this didn't ease off she was going to have to pass
on the invitation.

"Sore?"

"You weren't supposed to notice. My tailbone hurts," she admitted.

"You need to ride more often."

"I thought you said Annie was docile. I spent the afternoon convincing the mare I did not want to canter."

"I said she wouldn't try to knock you over or toss you off. I didn't say she was dead. There's a difference."

Lisa tossed her hat at him.

He grinned as he caught it with one hand, rolled the brim with the other. "A lady should never toss her cowboy hat to a guy."

"You're kidding. Why not?"

She reached down and tugged at the laces of her left tennis shoe. She swore her feet had swollen while riding during the day. She finally just slipped the shoes off to give herself some relief.

"It's kind of like a lady giving a knight of old her colors to wear."

"Really?"

"The hard part is the guy doesn't get a choice about whether he wants to accept it or not."

She slapped his leg. "Give me back my hat."

"Nope."

He leaned his head back and used her hat to block out the moon. "You got your full moon tonight. It's bright."

"It's beautiful. Get out of the city and you can actually see the stars." She skewered two marshmallows and held them out over the fire. "Thanks for giving me an excuse to take an afternoon off."

"Even if I had to practically drag you away from the files?"

"Even if." She leaned back against her saddle and braced the long stick against her knee to keep it slowly turning over the fire. It was a beautiful expanse of open sky. A quiet Tuesday night. Still. She'd loved the day spent with Quinn. He was so comfortable here on the open land. She loved it too. She could breathe here.

The fire popped, sending sparks into the air.

"Lizzy, we need to talk."

His voice had become serious. She turned her head to look at him. "About what?"

"Andy."

She wasn't expecting it, and the memory triggered by the name stole her breath. Every muscle in her back tensed. "No."

"You have to trust me at some point."

"I don't want to talk about it," she muttered, looking back at the fire. She didn't want to share her secrets. He didn't have to know.

He sighed, set her hat on the ground beside him, and interlaced his fingers behind his head as he watched her. "I know what happened."

She turned startled eyes toward him. "What?"

"Kate found out for me."

She shoved aside the stick, dropping it into the dust, not caring, as she surged to her feet and strode away. He'd invaded her privacy, gone behind her back, told her family…he'd broken her trust.

"Don't go far," he called quietly. The fact that he made no attempt to follow drew her slowly to a halt as she reached the spot where the horses were tethered. She stopped by Annie, resting her hand on the powerful shoulder of the horse. Annie shifted and turned her head, sniffed Lisa's shirt, and butted her arm to get attention.

Quinn knew. Kate knew. Kate would have told Marcus.

Lisa closed her eyes. "How long?"

She knew he heard her. Sounds carried in this quiet, open land.

"Since before you got the hummingbird note," Quinn finally replied.

Even before she had been staying with Kate. All the late night talks they'd had—Kate had known. Her sister had been pitying her. The anger that swelled inside was incredible.

She glanced at the horizon, decided the faint area of light on the horizon had to be the ranch house, and started walking.

The coarse grass, the ground rocky in places, hurt her socked feet, but she kept walking. If she didn't see Quinn for a month she'd be happy.

She heard him coming after her and ignored him.

He held out her shoes and she took them and flung them at him.

"Would you listen?"

She kept walking.

He went back to get her shoes and brought them back again. She considered throwing them at him again, but she was beginning to limp, and it was going to be a long walk. "You can't just walk away and leave a fire burning. You told me so yourself."

He caught her arm, brought her to a stop. "True. Stay right here while I go put it out. Besides, you're going the wrong way. That light is the town, about ten miles from here, not the ranch house."

She didn't get that confused about directions.

He took her shoulders and turned her farther to the west. "Over there."

He left her there, and she turned to see him walking back to the flickering fire. She took a moment to pull on her shoes and then started walking again.

He caught up with her fifteen minutes later, leading the two horses, both now saddled.

"I don't want to ride."

"Fine. We'll walk."

He'd known something had happened at Knolls Park and he'd had to go find out. "I trusted you," she said bitterly.

"I apologize."

She nearly told him what he could do with his apology.

"You're mad because it's a painful memory."

"Painful?" She turned away, swearing, wanting to hit him. "I see him underwater, dead, floating there, his face distorted and unseeing eyes open. I was seven. And I didn't need you to know!"

"Lizzy, I'm sorry."

She stumbled on a depression in the ground and slapped his hand away when he tried to help her.

She wished he'd go away.

He walked in silence beside her for several minutes. Quinn caught her hand. "Annie knows the way home, she won't let you get lost." He handed her the reins.

She took them because he surprised her. Quinn turned away and swung up on his own horse. He held out her hat to her. "We do need to talk about it." She took the hat and didn't bother to say anything. He held something else out to her, and she silently took it as well. His handkerchief. "I'll see you back at the house." She grudgingly nodded her head.

He nudged his horse to a walk and gave her the space she wanted. And Lisa finally felt free to let the pain wash away in tears as she walked.

She needed the walk. It didn't matter that her legs burned or that her tears gave her a headache. The walk was time to think.

She missed Andy. He'd been her best friend. He had a problem with dyslexia. Since her schooling had been choppy at best, she'd been struggling to learn how to read and he understood the frustration. It had been such a happy summer. They spent it working with a tutor the Richards had hired to help them both.

Andy—glasses, lisp, and more courage than sense. They'd climbed trees, hunted frogs, dug up worms, snuck flashlights and late-night snacks, had been against the same things and for the same things. He'd been her brother in heart and spirit.

And in a blink, he was gone.

She hadn't cared when she was sent to another foster home. She'd let no one else close for years. Until Kate…she'd been the most persistent of the O'Malleys, refusing to go away; Jennifer the kindest; and Rachel…as her roommate, Rachel had just ignored that a wall existed and assumed Lisa wanted to know all the details of her day whether she asked or not.

Lisa had thought about running away from Trevor House to get away from them, had in fact tried to do it one night only to have Marcus catch her in the act and sit her down on the back step. With the conviction of a future big brother he convinced her to change her mind.

The nightmares about Andy had haunted her during those years. Rachel, sitting cross-legged on her own bed, had always been the one who would sit and talk in the middle of the night when Lisa woke shivering and angry, hating the dream and needing the light on. Rachel had covered for her so many times when the floor mom wanted to know why the light was on. It was always Rachel who said she wanted it on.

Lisa picked up a clod of dirt and crushed it in her hand. She still woke occasionally, shaken from the nightmare.

Andy should never have died.

If Jesus didn't hear a prayer said in terror, it made no sense to trust Him when times were calm. It was when the chips were down that help mattered the most.

They'd said it was her fault.

Maybe it was. She could have talked Andy out of showing off. She knew that. And she hadn't tried.

The bitterness was an old memory, deadened by time and tears. She missed Andy; it hurt to talk about him, but it was the past.

The betrayal was new.

The last thing she wanted to deal with was her family and the entire subject of Andy. She'd kept it private for years, and now, in one action, Quinn had destroyed what she had protected for so long. She closed her eyes, feeling the fatigue wash over her. There was no way to undo what he had done.

"Come here, Annie." She swung up into the saddle, let Annie take her back to the ranch house. What she would say to Quinn…she didn't know.

———◦◦◦◦◦———

Quinn heard the horse coming before he saw it. He didn't move from his position by the stable door as she appeared from the darkness and came into the light. No matter what she said about her skills, Lisa rode well, was comfortable in the saddle. She came to a stop a few feet away and dismounted. The tears had flowed, then been dried. And that sight hurt.

"I'll take her," he offered quietly, holding out his hand for Annie's reins. His own horse had already been brushed down and stabled for the night.

She handed them to him. "We need to talk."

"Give me five minutes. I'll find you."

She nodded and walked toward the house.

He stabled Annie.

He found Lisa in the study, curled up in the recliner, her shoes kicked off, the late news turned on, but she wasn't paying attention to it. Her head was lying against the headrest, her eyes were closed.

Quinn sat down on the couch. "I did what I thought was best. But I never intended to hurt you."

"Of everything you could have done, going behind my back was the worst."

"I was wrong. I'm sorry."

She wearily opened her eyes. "Apology accepted. But you can't undo the results. I've got to live with them. Did you ever consider there might be a reason I didn't want the family to know?"

"I saw what the memory did to you. Burying it was not the right answer."

"Stephen's sister drowned."

The news shocked him.

"It was my choice to decide if the family knew about Andy, not yours."

The reality of good intentions…it didn't fix a serious mistake. She'd cleaned his clock, and he deserved it. "I truly am sorry, Lizzy."

"I dream about Andy. I can never remember what he looked like alive; he's always dead."

"Do you have a picture of him?"

She didn't answer right away. "In one of the scrapbooks that burned."

Quinn rested his head in his hands. "I'm going to shut my mouth now; I've done enough damage for one night."

"Quinn?"

He looked over at her.

"You did it because you cared. We're okay. I just don't want to talk about Andy. There's nothing more that needs to be said."

"There's one thing. What the Richards did was wrong."

"No it wasn't. They lost their son. Had I stayed, I would have tried to replace him…and that would have destroyed me."

There was wisdom in her quiet words.

She pushed herself to her feet and walked over to where he sat. Her fingers brushed his shoulder. "At least there are no more big secrets. Good night, Quinn."

"'Night, Lisa," he said quietly, squeezing her hand. She was wrong; there was one big secret remaining. He was falling in love with her. And it was going to be his secret for a lifetime the way things were going. She was never going to accept the Resurrection with this in her past.

Just friends. He wanted a freedom he didn't have to make it something more.

"Show me where your father was killed."

Quinn turned in the saddle to look at Lisa. After asking her to face Andy last night, he couldn't deny her right to the tough memories of his own. "Are you sure?"

"I need to see the scene. If it is somehow related to Amy…"

He nodded, accepting that it was necessary. "It's farther south."

"Quinn—"

"It's okay. I've been back here many times."

"Actually, I was going to ask if we could walk for a while."

He reined in his horse and laughed. "Sure."

She slid from the horse with a sigh of relief and rested her head against Annie's neck. Quinn frowned at the realization that this was more than just too much time in the saddle and quickly swung off his mount to join her. "Lizzy?"

"I think I'm getting motion sickness," she muttered, frustrated.

He rubbed her back. "You're serious."

"Oh yeah."

He wrapped her in his arms, hugging her, trying not to laugh because it was obvious she was feeling awful. "I am so sorry."

With her head buried against his shirt, her words were muffled. "Sure you are."

"I really am."

"Good, because you're about to get a blister in those boots."

"You don't want to head back to the house?"

She shook her head and took a step back. "I want to see the area. Marcus said it was near the bluffs?"

"Let me call my foreman, have him come out with a truck. There's no need for us to walk."

"Quinn—I'm fine. And if you're going to fuss, I'm going to get annoyed."

He moved over to his horse, opened the saddlebag, and retrieved two bottles of juice. "Okay. We'll walk." He uncapped one and handed it to her. "Let's head over to that crest. It will be downhill from there."

It was a quiet twenty-minute walk. November had arrived and the land was changing to reflect the coming winter, grass becoming dormant.

The bluffs were visible once they reached the rise in the land. Lisa stopped to look over the area. "It's an awesome vista. Water cut out the bluffs and the ravines?"

"See the streambed? This tributary runs down to the Ledds River. When the flash floods come, they tear through this land and reshape it."

"There are caves in the bluffs?"

"Dozens."

"I would love to explore them someday."

"Someday," Quinn agreed quietly. "We can walk down to the streambed. We'll have to ride from there, but it's not far."

The stream had dried to a trickle during the hot summer. They remounted the horses, crossed the stream, and Quinn led the way toward the bluffs.

"I found him here."

Lisa got down from Annie and retrieved the juice bottle. "You came from there?" She pointed back to the crest they had walked over.

"Yes."

She slowly turned in a full circle.

"He was shot in the back. From close range?"

"The sheriff figured about ten feet."

"So he knew the man who killed him, or at least had no reason to be uncomfortable at the idea of turning his back."

"Agreed."

"We're closer to the bluffs than I had assumed. Could a truck come back this far?"

"When my father was killed, the ravine we crossed had water flowing through it from a flash flood the week before. A vehicle would have had to come up from the south to reach here."

"What's out that way?"

"Besides rough terrain? About five miles of pasture, woods, and deep ravines."

She pulled out a piece of paper from her pocket and unfolded it. It was her sketch of the circled names and links they had suspected and proven. Lisa sat down on the ground and reached for her pen.

He recognized the slightly unfocused look on her face. "Have an idea?"

She nodded. "Come here."

Curious, he dismounted to join her.

"Why did someone kill your father?"

"We have no idea. Possibly because he stumbled across something he shouldn't have."

He stood at her shoulder, watched her darken the circle around Rita. "We also think she was really killed because she stumbled on proof of Amy's death."

Lisa leaned her head back against his knee, squinting against the sun as she looked up at him. "Stumbled on something." She looked down and darkened the circle around his father. And then she darkened the two lines that flowed into it. One beginning with Grant that ran through Rita to Amy to his father, and the other that began from Christopher and flowed to Rita to Amy and ended at his father. "See it?"

She looked back up at him. "If we can't prove Amy returned to Chicago, can we prove Chicago came to Amy?"

He blinked. "One of them came to Montana."

"Time for a break."

"Not yet," Lisa commented absently, reading the transcript from Grant's trial.

Quinn could have predicted that answer. He crossed over to where she sat on the couch and slid the report from her hand. "Yes, now. You said you wanted to see my old rodeo tapes." It was after 11 P.M. They'd been going through the files ever since they got back from the bluffs, and he knew she still wasn't feeling that great. She'd been sipping 7-Up all evening.

"What did Emily find out about where Grant bought his horses?"

"We just asked the question this afternoon. Give her time to find an answer."

"I know something is there."

"I think so too. And it can wait a couple hours. Come on." He pulled her to her feet and directed her toward the living room.

"So what are we watching?"

"The high school national rodeo championships."

"How'd you do?"

"Let's just say Montana sent the Lone Star State home without the trophy they dominated for a decade."

"Do I hear a bit of pride in that outcome?"

"Well deserved. I wore the bruises of victory for weeks."

She settled down at one end of the couch. "You fixed popcorn?"

"Ask nicely, and I might even share."

She picked up the bowl. "Ask nicely, and I might give the bowl back," she replied, eating her first handful.

He slid in the tape, adjusted the volume, and reached for the remote.

"So what did you compete in?"

"Bull riding, calf roping, steer wrestling. I stayed away from goat tying."

"Goat tying? They have such a thing?"

"Yep. They even give Horse of the Year awards."

Bull riding was up first. He watched her wince as the first rider appeared, survived six seconds, and was thrown off. Two rodeo clowns worked in tandem to distract the bull while the rider got out of the ring.

"Quinn. You did this for sport?"

"You spend a lot of time training before you ride one of these guys. Most injuries come from inexperienced riders making basic mistakes in balance and timing. It's a sport where errors compound quickly. In my case I simply drew a more experienced bull."

"What do you mean?"

"The bulls they use at the high school national championships are the same as the ones in the professional circuit. When you draw a new bull to the circuit, you've got a better chance of completing the ride than if you draw one with experience. I had the misfortune of drawing Taggert II. He'd been on the circuit for seven years, seen every move, learned a few of his own."

"Please don't tell me this tape has you getting hurt."

"No one gets hurt."

She watched, fascinated. "You get points for yourself and your team when you compete?"

"Yes."

Quinn didn't have to watch the tape to remember the competition. He settled back on the couch, crossed his ankles, reached over and tugged at the popcorn bowl that Lisa shared but didn't release.

Love was a bit like a wonderful piece of art. The best pieces were those that grew on him, were interesting for deeper reasons than the surface, became more beautiful the more he looked at them. Lisa was like that.

She glanced at him for a moment and blushed. "You're watching me again."

"Guilty." He loved watching her.

"It's disconcerting." She raised her hand to brush down her hair. "It makes me think I'm looking like a dust mop or something."

He laughed at the image and reached over to still her hand. "You look just fine. The sun gives you a tan and turns your hair blond."

"Streaky flyaway blond is not pretty," she muttered.

"It is if I say so."

"Flattery only works if it has an element of truth to it."

His dog came to join her.

"Why do I get the feeling I've lost my dog?"

She laughed as she offered Old Blue popcorn. "He knows a better thing when he finds it."

He took a handful of the popcorn.

"What's this?" she asked, indicating the new event on the tape.

"Calf roping. The calf breaks into the corral, the rider comes through seconds later. Lasso him, get off your horse, toss him onto his side, loop rope around his feet, then throw up your hands."

"Is it hard to do?"

"Much harder than it looks. Holding flailing legs to get the rope around fast is tough. And getting kicked in the face is more common than you'd expect."

"I don't know that I wanted to know that."

They watched the first several riders try their luck.

He saw the change in her expression, the look of distance appear. She'd just drifted away to thinking about work.

"Excuse me, Quinn." She pushed away from him, got to her feet, headed back to the office.

He thought for a moment about joining her but stayed seated. He knew how fragile ideas were until they crystallized.

He reached around for the phone. Despite his words to Lisa to be patient, he was anything but. "Marcus, how's it going?"

"The same as it was thirty minutes ago." He partner was not nearly so willing to change the focus from Grant to Christopher. "Give me another couple hours, Quinn. I'll call as soon as I find anything useful. Hold on. Lincoln just got here." His partner muffled the phone for a moment. "He's got news. Let me pass you to him."

"Quinn?"

"Hi, Lincoln."

"Does the name McLinton mean anything to you?"

Quinn's hand rubbing Old Blue went still. "Yes, it does. They own a ranch to the southeast of here."

"Grant bought three horses from a Frank McLinton over the lifetime of the stable."

"Can you get me the dates of those sales, or when he might have been out here to see the horses?"

"Emily's working on it."

Until a few days ago this was exactly the news he had hoped to hear. Now it just raised more questions. It put Grant back at the top of the list. "Any word on Christopher?"

"Not yet."

"Thanks for this. Call whenever you hear anything else."

"I will," Lincoln reassured.

Grant had come to Montana.

Quinn hung up the phone and went to find Lisa.

"Lisa."

She held up one finger, motioning for a moment of time. He crossed over to join her and see what she was studying that was causing the frown.

The excavation of Rita's grave.

She finally shook her head slightly and looked up at him. "What?"

"Grant has been to Montana. Emily found out that he bought three horses from Frank McLinton, the owner of a ranch southeast of here."

"When?"

"She's still getting dates."

Lisa leaned back against the couch, thinking about it. "Grant was out here to buy horses. That fits." She looked up at him. "How did he get the horses back to Chicago? He wouldn't have flown them back, so did McLinton deliver them or what?"

"Great question. Do you have the phone number of the stable manager? The Scotsman?"

"Samuel Barberry. It would be in Lincoln's notes."

Quinn found it and picked up the phone. It was late, something he would apologize for, but he needed the answer. It took a few minutes to describe what he needed to know.

"Normally I'd take one of the horse trailers from here and go pick up the new horse," Mr. Barberry explained. "Or if it was a horse coming from a distance, a couple of the stable hands would fly out, rent a horse trailer, and drive the animal back."

"Do you remember the horses Grant bought from Frank McLinton?"

"Sure. A nice chestnut and two bays. Greg and Danny flew out and brought two of them back, Chris went out to pick up the other."

"Christopher Hampton?"

"His brother Walter helped him drive it back. They've got distant family out that way."

"Do you remember when that was?"

"1980, '81? Somewhere around then."

"I appreciate the help, Mr. Barberry."

"Anytime."

Quinn hung up the phone.

"What?"

He looked over at Lisa and took a seat on the chair across from her. "One of the horses was driven back to Chicago by Christopher and Walter Hampton."

Her surprise at the news matched his. "Both brothers?"

"Two drivers, they must have driven straight through to Chicago. And the time is right. Grant bought the horse in either 1980 or '81."

"Amy disappeared in 1980."

He nodded. "Grant and Christopher were both here. Chicago did come to Amy."

She started tapping her pen on the table, and Quinn waited. "That tells us more than I thought we would find." She reached for one of the photographs on the table from the excavation of Rita's grave and held it out to him. "What do you see?"

It was a photograph taken looking down into the grave site. The skeleton beginning to appear was lying face down, the dirt had been brushed away so that Rita's arms and hands were uncovered. He looked back at Lisa. "What?"

"It matches what they were doing during the calf roping."

He looked back at the picture, stunned.

"It's a calf roping loop. Look at her hands. The tape first figure-eights around the wrists, then goes around the palms fast and then loops between the hands."

The silver reflection of the duct tape suddenly became the focus of what he was seeing. "Rita was killed by someone who knew how to calf rope."

"It's bigger than that. Someone who roped like that probably killed Rita, Marla, Vera, and Heather."

"Christopher."

She rubbed her arms. "I think so. And if that's true, it suggests Amy is buried somewhere around here, bound in a similar fashion," she whispered.

He absorbed that.

Lisa got to her feet and came over, closing her hands around his. "We need to go back to Chicago."

He slowly nodded. It meant Christopher had probably shot his father.

"Quinn? We'll find out the truth."

Twenty-three

"C hristopher did it."

"Convince me," Marcus said quietly.

Lisa scowled at her brother. She was so tired she could barely keep her eyes open, and he wanted to sit and review what she and Quinn had spent the day proving.

"Lizzy, I trust your conclusions. I just want to see how you reached them. You and Quinn are both very close to this."

She pushed back her chair and got up to walk over to the whiteboard. Marcus was right. And if she'd missed something in this list…it mattered. She'd already helped convict Grant Danford of a crime she was now arguing he did not do.

"The Plymouth clinched it."

"What? It was found?"

She nodded. "Lincoln found it this morning at a junkyard, crushed. Christopher had hauled it in. He said he'd hit a tree. It got him fifty dollars. He was the one following Quinn. As soon as we had that, the other threads started falling into place."

Marcus absorbed that, then nodded. "Go on."

She wiped the whiteboard clear to draw the circles she now knew by heart. "It's the number of links that point to Christopher, rather than any one piece."

She started with Montana. "It wasn't just Rita and Amy who were horse-crazy. So was Christopher. Quinn was the one who pointed out that to ride in the city, it takes money, access, and time. Christopher started to work for Grant Danford at the stable so he would have the ability to ride. Christopher met Rita Beck and Amy Ireland when they were at the stables taking pictures of the horses. Amy returned to Montana. A year later, Christopher went out to Montana to drive back a horse for Grant. During the time he was there, Amy disappeared and Quinn's dad was shot."

She started the list for Chicago. "Rita Beck. Christopher knew her. His testimony puts himself at the scene when she disappeared. He had access to where she was buried.

"Marla Sherrall. She was buried in the same way as Rita. Again, Christopher has put himself at the scene. He's driving the Plymouth, following us, he's the one leaving the notes about the murder, telling me to go away. He's nervous because we're investigating Rita and Amy and finding out we're investigating Marla is enough to push him into trying to stop me. He's running scared now as he feels the noose tightening."

"Why kill Marla?"

"Why he chose her? We don't know. It's the MO of the killing that makes them connected. But with Vera—the type of duct tape positively linked Vera and Heather. And we've placed Christopher knowing Vera. She worked for his uncle before she retired, knew his aunt. If she knew about the gambling—well we know Christopher had been trying to cover up that fact from his uncle."

"Martha Treemont?"

"A similar burial to the other victims, but we don't have a direct connection to Christopher. We're hoping to find it in the Nakomi Nurseries' records, that he worked a job near where she disappeared."

"Christopher burned down your house."

She nodded, hating him for that. "We think so. It's the fact Egan's house burned down. I don't think that was an accident," she said quietly. "We didn't find it, but he may have gotten away with murder. Egan didn't have to be the one who dropped the cigar. The only other person besides Christopher who might benefit from Egan's death is Walter—and that doesn't type. Walter wouldn't have risked a fire that near the nursery when a turn of the wind in the wrong direction would have sent the flames racing through the nursery grounds. The nursery is his life."

"Agreed. But Walter had to have known or at least suspected something about his brother. Lizzy, he gave Christopher an alibi for the day your house burned down."

"He's protecting the nursery, trying to be big brother. Christopher is named as a passive owner. If Christopher is proven to be the arsonist, the insurance company will come after him for the damages, and thus go after the nursery."

Marcus looked from her to Quinn.

"It's Christopher," Quinn stated. "And I want him."

Marcus nodded. "I'll get the search warrant."

"Christopher's home, vehicles, and the nursery grounds," Quinn added. "Jack thinks he can match the fuel oil if we can find him a sample of where it came from."

Twenty-four

The nursery grounds were busy on Saturday afternoon. Customer cars filled all the parking slots in front of the two long greenhouses; drivers were now parking in the grass on both sides of the road.

Quinn pushed open the nursery office door and felt a wave of slightly cooler air rush out to meet him. The front room with its open service counter, large scheduling board, and time clock was noisy with phones ringing and a fax machine active, but it was empty of customers at the moment. "Walter."

"Back again?" He tore off the fax, scanned it, and passed it to the office manager. "Write up the work order for this and check the inventory. I'll figure out which crews to assign later." Terri nodded, cast a curious glance at them, and turned toward the back office.

Walter picked up his gloves and walked around the counter. "What can I do for you?" He sounded willing to help but also looked ready to leave.

"We've got a problem."

Walter looked out the window, saw the squad cars pulling in, and stiffened. "Okay…"

"We're going to have to talk with your brother. Do you happen to know where we can find him?"

"I wish I knew. He was supposed to be working on a job at the new First Union Bank in Naperville, but he never showed. I had to send another site manager, putting the job three hours behind schedule. Why?" He groaned. "He's been gambling again, hasn't he? I knew it. What kind of trouble has he gotten into this time?"

"We'd like your permission to look around the nursery grounds while we wait on a warrant to his home."

Walter looked stunned. "What do you think he did?" He looked from one of them to the other, but they didn't answer him. "Listen, Christopher's got some problems, not the least of which is his temper, but he's an okay guy." He took a deep breath. "I own the house he's been staying in. The only thing Christopher has is a passive interest in the nursery business. As far as I'm concerned, you can look anywhere you like. I'm sure this can get resolved without going as far as a warrant."

Quinn looked at Marcus, got a slight nod. "I appreciate it. And I hope it can be resolved with a few questions. You'll be here for the next couple hours?"

"Here or up at the toolshed. I've been working on the sod baler."

"There's going to be an officer staying here at the office. Please don't move any records."

"Of course not."

"We'll be in touch."

Walter's business and home were landscaped and carefully maintained for a beautiful image. The house where Christopher was staying was the exact opposite. The yard needed mowing; weeds were growing in the cracks of the walkway from the driveway to the house.

A motorcycle was being taken apart in the front yard, a few feet off the driveway.

Despite Walter's offer, they had waited for the warrant to search the nursery grounds and Christopher's home before coming over. Quinn found the front door unlocked, knocked, and received no answer. He opened the door and stepped inside. Dumped in the hallway were two hockey sticks, a bike helmet, and a set of golf clubs. There was the faint odor of bacon grease in the air.

"Christopher? Police."

Quinn walked through the silent house.

Christopher needed a housekeeper. The place hadn't been dusted in months. The kitchen would take a few hours to clean; the dishes were piled in the sink and the counters were littered with coffee grounds and spots of jelly.

"Where do you want to start?" Marcus asked.

"I'll take the desk in the den. Why don't you take the bedroom and closets. If he's our guy, I think he'd have kept something as a memento. And if he's Lisa's firebug…well most arsonists like the paraphernalia of firemen."

Marcus headed toward the back of the house.

Quinn found the overhead light in the den had burned out and the lightbulb had not been replaced. He turned on the side table lamp.

The desk was a clutter of mail, open magazines, and jumbled newspapers; two of the drawers had caught on crumpled pages and not closed all the way.

Quinn tugged out the vinyl black cover he spotted under what appeared to be an insurance policy and found it was a month-at-a-glance calendar. It fell open at the current month. Quinn was relieved to see that Christopher apparently used it. The squares were filled with scrawled notes and times. He turned back several pages looking through the months. They'd be able to get a good idea from this who they needed to talk with to establish Christopher's whereabouts. He checked January and found it similarly marked up. Odds were good there would be a calendar from the previous year around here somewhere.

He pulled out the chair and tugged open the first drawer on the left. He found a thick brown book with its cover falling apart, held together by three rubber bands. Holding it together, he slipped off the rubber bands. It was a disorganized address book, stuffed with business cards and torn off scraps of paper with jotted phone numbers.

"Quinn."

Quinn slipped the rubber bands back in place and set the address book and calendar to one side to take with him later. He headed back through the house to join Marcus. "Find something already?"

Marcus nodded to the dresser on the far side of the room.

Quinn saw the pictures and walked forward as his jaw tightened, shocked.

Lisa paged through the printouts the office manger had run for her, looking for jobs Christopher had worked near where Vera had lived.

Walter tapped on the door. "Lisa, I've got a lead on where Christopher is, but he may not be there for long. Bring the printouts and let's drive over and get the marshals. I'd like this situation cleared up and settled. Customers are finding it rather disconcerting to see all the cop cars around."

She was surprised at Walter's suggestion but also relieved. They needed to find Christopher. She closed the printout and picked it and her notebook up. "I know it's troubling Walter, but it's necessary."

"I wish you'd just tell me what you think he did. I know Christopher. He doesn't always think before he acts, but that makes him a pain to have around, not a criminal."

Being left in the dark had to be frustrating. "It may not be that serious once we talk to him. You really think you have an idea where he is?"

"I tracked down one of his more questionable friends. Apparently there's a poker game going on this afternoon." Walter held the office door for her, and they stepped out into the bright sunlight. "We'll take the truck. Your brother said they were going over to Christopher's house."

She grabbed the door frame and pulled herself up into the truck, relieved that her back no longer barked with every move she made. The dust stirred behind them as Walter drove around the office building to the back road.

"Walter, have you ever been to Montana?" She knew the answer but wanted to hear it from him.

If he was surprised by the question, he still answered it. "A couple times over the years. We've got distant relatives out there."

"You and Christopher once drove a horse back for Grant Danford."

"Grant tell you that? We made a couple trips like that, for Grant and for his neighbor Bob Nelson. Must be twenty years ago now. What's that got to do with all this?"

Lisa took a chance and dug out the picture from her portfolio. "Do you remember ever having met this girl?"

He reached over and took the wallet-sized photo. His face went tight. "Where'd you get this?"

"You know her?"

"Sure. Christopher's got her picture on his dresser mirror."

Quinn reminded himself to breathe. There were several pictures of Amy, a couple of them taken of Christopher and Amy together. The pictures were in a small cluster near the corner of the dresser mirror, held in place by yellowing tape. "He kept the pictures of his victim."

"Quinn."

"Why else do you have twenty-year-old pictures taped to your dresser?" Quinn stepped back, clenching his fists to stop from touching the pictures. "He was involved in Amy's disappearance. He shot my father in the back."

"Maybe," Marcus said quietly.

Twenty years of looking had come down to a small collection of pictures in a run-down house in a suburb of Chicago. Rather than relief, there was intense sadness. This wasn't the vindication and justice he had sought; it was just the truth. "Where's Lisa? She needs to see this."

"At the nursery office. She was going to ask Walter about getting the customer records for the jobs Christopher worked, to see if he can be placed in the area where the women disappeared."

"It's why my brother drinks."

Walter's hands had tightened on the steering wheel. Lisa slid the photo back into her portfolio. "What do you mean?"

His expression was grim. "He was in love with her. He never got over the fact she dumped him."

"When did they meet?"

"I don't know all the details. She was here on vacation or something like that. I remember Christopher talking about her all the time. He made a big deal about getting a chance to see her when we went out to Montana to pick up a horse for Grant."

"Walter, she disappeared."

"What?"

"Twenty years ago, from her parents' ranch outside Justice, Montana."

"You're kidding."

"No."

"Christopher saw Amy that last day when we were out in Montana. We drove back home, and he never heard from her again. He started drinking heavily after that trip." Walter looked over at her, accusingly. "You're looking at Christopher, you think he's involved."

"There are some questions that need answers."

"He had nothing to do with it."

Lisa set her portfolio on the seat beside her, then turned to glance back at the Y in the road they had passed. "Walter, doesn't that lead around to Christopher's house?"

"Yes. But that road is blocked with sod pallets waiting to be picked up. We'll have to go around the other way."

The screen door banged shut as Marcus stepped out of the office. "Quinn, she's not here."

Quinn had pulled up outside the office, stayed in the car, his arm resting out the open driver's window, expecting Lisa to join them. "What do you mean?"

"Terri, the office manager, says Walter and Lisa were heading over to see us; they took one of the nursery pickup trucks."

That puzzled Quinn. "We should have passed them."

"Lisa may have wanted to see the cleared lot of Egan's home. They would have come around the orchard from the other direction."

"Let's go find them."

Marcus got back into the car.

Quinn drove around the greenhouses and the front of the orchard to where Egan's house had stood.

There was no sign of a Nakomi Nurseries' truck at the cleared lot. Quinn pulled in behind one of the squad cars to see if Lisa and Walter had been by.

The officer leading the group of men searching the site came over to greet them. "I was just getting ready to call you. We've found something."

Quinn got out of the car, waited for Marcus to join him, and they walked with the officer around the remaining foundation of the house. A small group of officers had assembled near the east end of what had been the garden. Someone had recently tilled under the plants and weeds, leaving the dirt evenly broken.

THE TRUTH SEEKER 295

"There was a patch of the garden you could see had been circled around rather than tilled over. We wondered why."

It was a four-by-three-foot square of packed ground one of the officers had dug into with a shovel. He now stood a few feet away with the other officers.

Quinn accepted the collapsible shovel, carried as part of the standard equipment in the squad car trunks, and walked over to the hole.

It was the end of a cardboard box, half collapsed under the force of the shovel, less than a foot beneath the surface of the ground. Quinn pushed back more of the dirt. He used the shovel to lift back the lid, then turned his head away at the rush of an awful smell. His eyes watering, he looked at what had been found: small bits of fur still present, scorched.

A cat. Or what was left of one.

There had been a second cat caught in the fire? Why hadn't Walter said as much? He had obviously buried this one too. Quinn looked closer at the cat and frowned. This one obviously had a broken back, the front and back feet were twisted in the wrong directions.

Was this the one that had been in the bedroom, the one possibly given a sleeping pill? Sleeping under the sedation, still managing to wake to the fire, heading toward the door scared…and getting viciously kicked so it wouldn't get away.

Even if there had been no sleeping pill, this cat had obviously met a more serious fate a few minutes before the fire burned it to death.

Someone had been in the house when the fire got underway. It hadn't been an accident, a suicide…it had indeed been a murder.

"Get a small black body bag, take this in."

"You're serious?"

He gave the officer a sympathetic look; the cardboard box was not exactly in any condition to be picked up. "You'll understand why later. Just do it."

—⚬⚬⚬—

"You've got it wrong."

Lisa braced one hand on the dashboard. The truck was beginning to bounce around; Walter was going too fast for the dirt road. Seeing the tension in his face, hearing it in his voice, she chose not to comment on his driving. "How do we have it wrong?"

"Christopher didn't have anything to do with Amy's disappearance. Grant did."

Lisa felt a shiver of warning inside at the way the conversation was changing. "What do you mean?"

Walter's gaze didn't leave the road. "Grant killed Amy."

"You know this for sure?"

He nodded.

"How do you know?" Lisa whispered, watching him.

"I buried her. Or more accurately, hid her." The truck rocked as he abruptly changed roads. "Grant accused Christopher of the crime, I stupidly believed him, and I hid her body; it was the last day before we left Montana."

"Why didn't you tell someone?"

"I had disbelieved my brother. If I had bothered to check out Christopher's story before I believed Grant's accusation, I would have known Christopher couldn't have done it. Instead I assumed…and I didn't ask those questions until it was too late."

And then she understood and felt incredible dread. "Did you have reason to believe Christopher could have done it?" She hesitated but had to ask. "Had he done it before?"

Quinn turned the ignition key. "Marcus, Walter had to suspect the fire was intentionally set when he found that cat."

"He knows his brother is guilty, is trying to protect him."

"He has to know about Amy too—those pictures."

"You'd think so."

Quinn pulled back onto the road, speeding. "Lisa's with Walter."

Marcus was already reaching for the radio to check in with the officer watching Christopher's home. Lisa had not been there.

Quinn frowned. "I don't like this. She was at the office with him, left to join us, but she didn't arrive at Christopher's home or here at Egan's. Where would they go?"

"Let's check the orchard."

Quinn took that turn in the road while Marcus put out word for the other officers to systematically search the nursery grounds.

"Walter, take me back." He had just pulled out of the nursery back road onto the interstate. "We need to talk to Marcus and Quinn. It won't do you any good to warn Christopher. They'll still track him down and find him."

"I was sorry about your house, the pets. I liked the animals, especially the parrot."

"Walter." She put steel into her voice. "Stop this truck."

"You know, I should have believed him. It wasn't like the situation I walked into wasn't suspicious. Christopher and Amy had been seeing each other practically every day during our five-day visit, although she made Chris keep it quiet. She had another boyfriend from school, you know, and we were leaving as soon as Grant settled on which horse he would buy."

Walter pulled around traffic into the fast lane, heading south.

"When I walked into the bunkhouse, saw her, then found Grant suddenly behind me in the doorway… Grant laughed. I should have known then not to believe him. He was laughing about what was going to happen to Christopher."

"So you protected your brother?"

"Nothing new there. I'd been doing it for years. He was always sneaking away—gambling, partying. If my uncle had realized that…" Walter shook his head. "Christopher would have been disinherited eventually. Egan was always talking about doing it, these last few years it was a fairly constant refrain. I'm relieved that he died before he could do it."

"Walter, where are we going?"

"She's not answering her pager."

"Do we know for sure she's with Walter?"

"She's not on the nursery grounds."

"She wouldn't leave on her own without telling us."

"I know. Let's get the truck license plate. We need an APB out." Quinn slammed the car door. "She's got a habit of getting into trouble…but this time we let her walk right into it."

Twenty-five

Walter, put that down. This is crazy." Christopher had been drinking, he was showing his temper, and he was honestly confused by what was happening. So was Lisa. *Petrified* was the right word. The gun Walter held was ancient, a fact that worried her more than comforted. A gun not well-maintained had a habit of exploding when fired. She'd not only end up shot, she'd also probably get blinded by the flash burns.

"They know you started the fires," Walter said.

"What? I didn't set any fires."

"You left the note on Lisa's patio."

Christopher flushed. "Fine. Guilty. But what has that got to do with this?"

"You've got to leave town now, before they catch up with you."

Kate would have known what to do, would have already defused this situation. Lisa tried to intervene. "Walter—"

"Shut up. Christopher deserves a chance to get out of town. And you're going to help ensure he gets it."

"A chance because of what?" Christopher protested.

"You were following them."

"Because you told me to! You said they knew about the cash Grant paid me."

"They know you killed Egan."

"Oh, come on, Walter. You know I didn't. I had no reason to."

"He was going to disinherit you."

"Well, he was effectively going to disinherit you too by selling the nursery to pay for Aunt Laura's long-term care. And I'm not the one who considers the nursery his life."

"He wasn't going to sell the business."

"I'm not arguing with you, Walter. You just might want to rethink your assumptions," he placated. "You've been wrong about me before. You're wrong this time."

"Why did you leave the note about the hummingbirds? And the pretzels?" Lisa risked asking.

Christopher shot her a glance, looking relieved. "I was bored, okay? You and that marshal spent half the day in Knolls Park while I killed time trailing you, then sitting in my hot car watching you eat lunch. It didn't take more than a couple questions at the local bar to figure out why you were poking around that area by the pond. The note I left was one of the tamer ones I invented that afternoon. I was just twisting your tail, poking fun at your job, nothing more."

"And the phone call?"

"What phone call?"

"You called that Sunday morning when I found the note."

"Honey, thank you for the compliment, but I was drunk that morning. I dumped the tree, then I went to curse up a blue streak at the local bar before I dealt with the mess. I never called you."

Lisa understood the frustration that spoke of honesty. She believed him, but it left a quandary. Who had called? It surely hadn't been a wrong number? "Did you ever date Rita Beck?"

His startled look told her more than he realized. "What is this, memory lane?" Christopher had reason to kill Rita. He'd been dating her before she started going out with Grant.

"They're looking for you, Christopher. Come on, we're leaving," Walter insisted.

"And go where? I've done nothing wrong."

Walter raised the gun. "Get out the keys to your car. You're driving."

They had set up a command post in the nursery office, taking over the building to leverage the phones and the fax. Jack and Stephen were helping with their invaluable knowledge of the area roads, the fire department districts not just familiar to them but memorized. As Quinn argued on the phone with the state tollway officer, Marcus opened the door. "They found the truck."

Quinn hung up the phone midsentence. "Where?"

"Outside a bar in Waukegan. Cops are canvassing the area now. Let's go."

Quinn circled the counter. "Jerry, call the regional office and get us those additional resources. I don't care if you have to threaten murder, I need every available marshal out here now. Jack, Stephen—come with us." He followed Marcus outside. "Christopher?"

Marcus nodded as he opened the passenger door. "They're showing a picture around now. He was there."

"Did anyone see Lisa?"

"Not that they've found."

"The truck was left behind. Does anyone know what Christopher was driving?"

"A blue '97 Ford."

"Can the DMV find tags?"

"Already called in."

Quinn was relieved there was no sign of blood or a struggle in the cab of the truck. Lisa was keeping her wits about her.

The sun had heated the cab. The crime scene technician had just opened the door of the vehicle and the heat rolled out. Careful not to touch anything that might disturb prints, Quinn lifted out the printout from the mat on the passenger side floorboard, saw Lisa's clutch purse, and picked it up as well. Lisa couldn't have realized there was trouble when she initially got into the truck. When had that changed? She wouldn't have come here of her own free will. And she certainly would not have left here by choice.

He leaned his head against the metal door frame, sick to his stomach when he found the small black canister still in her purse. He knew she would have moved the pepper spray to her pocket had there been any way she could do so without attracting attention. "Lord, don't let her get hurt. Please don't let her take chances that are going to get her hurt." He was more worried than he knew how to put into words.

Lisa was now with Christopher.

He handed the printout to Marcus. "She was looking for evidence that Christopher had been working jobs near where the other women were killed."

"Walter knows he can no longer protect his brother."

Quinn forced himself to start thinking like the men he was after. Christopher would need to run. And Walter wanted to help him. "They're three hours ahead of us. Where are they going to go?"

"Odds would say they're trying to leave the state," Marcus agreed, "but which direction? Indiana? Wisconsin? Across to Missouri?"

Lisa was good at directions, but she was now totally lost. After the sun went down, Christopher had been taking so many turns on so many winding roads that she could no longer even figure out which direction they were going. Somewhere in the heartland of Wisconsin, far enough north that they had not passed by a town in over an hour.

The shadows of the trees they passed became orderly and evenly

THE TRUTH SEEKER 303

spaced. "Don't miss the turnoff, Christopher."

"Would you let me drive?" Christopher snarled back at Walter. He had a hangover and the two brothers had been sniping at each other during the entire drive. Christopher turned left onto a dirt road, and the jarring made Lisa clench her teeth. Wedged between the two brothers, she was getting by far the worst of the ride.

Christmas trees. Through the pounding headache she finally understood what it was she was seeing. The Wisconsin land was a Christmas tree farm.

The building that finally appeared in the light was a large equipment barn, metal sided and plain. Christopher pulled around to the side of the building. She could run, disappear into the trees. It was the first time such a moment had appeared, and she wondered if her legs would support her for the effort.

"Come on, lady." Christopher hauled her out the driver's side door, and she yelped at the surprise and the pain as she hit the steering wheel.

Walter shoved open the side door of the building. It must have been closed up for months—the air was musty, the equipment covered in a fine sheen of dust. The light Walter had turned on was a single bulb by the door. He left the overhead lights off, and the light did not penetrate past all the equipment. Did they own this place?

"Sit down."

Christopher pushed her toward a bale of straw beside what looked like a baler. She was relieved to comply. She was doing her best to read the situation and figure out what was going on with the two brothers. It was obvious Walter was trying to protect his brother, but she wasn't sure what Grant had done, what Christopher had done, and what Walter had known about.

"See if there's gas."

Christopher picked up a flashlight from the supply shelf and disappeared toward the rear of the building.

Walter paced toward the tractor and back, shifting the gun from one hand to the other. He had grown more nervous as the hours passed.

She wanted to ask him why he was doing this, what he expected to have happen, but decided silence was the best course of valor.

Christopher had admitted to being the one who was following Quinn, admitted to being the one who left the notes, but his reasons in both cases made sense: He had been bribing Grant and was worried about the investigation. She could see him getting bored watching them and doing something stupid like writing the note just to tweak her tail.

Walter believed Christopher had been responsible for the fires that had killed Egan and destroyed her home. He was trying to protect his brother but was also trying to protect his own role in Amy's disappearance.

Christopher denied setting the fires.

If Grant had been the one who killed not only Rita but also Amy, then who had killed Marla and the other ladies? She had thought it was Christopher, but if he'd left the hummingbird note not out of knowledge but as a guess…now she wasn't sure anymore. Who had really killed Marla? She had been buried in the same way as Rita; it had to be a common killer. Lisa was too confused to figure out the answers.

"There's gas," Christopher said. "Now what are we going to do?"

"We need to change vehicles."

"I am not driving all night just so we can run out of gas again in the middle of nowhere. You didn't even think to get cash before you got us into this mess."

"It's not like you gave me much of a choice. They will arrest you on sight."

"Yeah, and the three of us traveling together makes us real inconspicuous," Christopher replied. "Did you really think adding kidnapping to flight would help things out?"

She was going to have to run. These two men were on a course to implode, and she would be an albatross to be discarded along the way. The fear was making her shake.

It was late. Quinn, Marcus, Kate, Dave—they would all be looking for her and they wouldn't stop until they found her. She tried to find comfort in that, but it was hollow comfort. Had they found the truck yet? If they had, would they even be able to get a handle on where to look next?

And if they did find her while Walter was in this mood... The odds of all of them walking away unhurt weren't good. She had been sure Walter wasn't the type given to violence, but now... She had been so horribly wrong. If only she could get him to calm down and start thinking again. If the brothers did split up, the last thing she wanted was to be leaving with Christopher.

"They had to go to ground somewhere."

"Walter owns the nursery. What else does he own?" Quinn asked, staring at the maps and the dots representing reported sightings, none of them having yet panned out. There was no pattern to them, which might at least suggest a direction of travel.

"The nursery is it," Lincoln replied.

"What about Christopher? Or his uncle? Is there anything still owned by the estate while the will is in probate?" Marcus asked.

"I'll get on it," Emily replied immediately.

Quinn broke yet another pencil under the pressure of his fingers. "They haven't used credit cards, they can't go forever on the cash they had in their pockets, they had to at least buy gas even if they are avoiding a hotel room."

"It's 1 A.M. With two drivers, they could still be on the road somewhere."

"But in which direction? We're at five hundred miles now and it's enlarging with every passing hour." Quinn was scared to death at what it meant. If Lisa wasn't found within the first twenty-four hours, the odds were she would be found dead somewhere.

"Quinn, look at this." Kate nearly knocked over Jack as she hurriedly squeezed around him at the table with the maps. "Sorry." She shoved aside items on the desk to set down the crumbled printout in front of him. It was the printout Lisa had been studying. "Marla, Vera, Heather," she said grimly, flipping between pages marked in red. "Nakomi Nurseries worked jobs near them all."

"Christopher."

Kate shook her head. "Walter."

"What?"

"Not only that, there's enough evidence in here to prove Christopher was elsewhere."

Quinn felt a sense of dread. "Walter."

He inwardly shook as the implications of so many threads he had connected incorrectly registered. Multiple murders…it was all about control. Christopher didn't have the personality to try and control his surroundings. He was hot tempered, irresponsible, a drinker. Everything about Walter was about control, about shaping and ordering the world to his vision of it, driving the nursery to his vision of the business, fitting his brother into a mold. The motive didn't make sense, but the probabilities did. The problem of every investigation was the question of motive, which was answered last, if at all.

"How did we miss it?" Kate asked, her voice edged with fear.

"Worse, does Lisa realize it?" Not knowing the truth, Walter was the brother Lisa would most likely trust.

Twenty-six

Marcus passed over the night binoculars. "Off to the east of the building about twenty feet."

Quinn took them and adjusted the focus. "Thank you, God," he breathed out the prayer and for the first time felt hope. They'd found the car. "Are they still there?"

"No windows, but there is a sliver of light under that side door."

The property had been in Egan's wife's name. The only good thing about the layout of the large stands of trees and expanse of the property was that they could block all exits from the property without giving away their presence. But flushing the brothers from the building without getting Lisa hurt—in a standoff the advantage would clearly lie with those inside the building.

"Let me try and talk them out, end this peacefully," Kate whispered.

Dawn was two hours away. It had been a long night searching. A confrontation after the men left the building—for all its advantages of getting them out into the open—it would also mean they were awake, looking for problems, and tightly controlling Lisa, putting her into the equation. She'd be their protection for getting out, and they would use her as their trump card. It was critical that they take her out of the equation. "No. We have to go in while we have surprise on our side." They didn't have time to wait it out.

"If that fails…"

"We won't fail," Quinn replied.

"Down on the floor! Now!"

Lisa jerked awake to a deafening concussion of noise and light so bright it blinded her. Her left wrist twisted painfully as she was yanked backward toward the bathroom door, her right ankle catching on the edge of the mower and the back of her head striking the door frame. She felt the desperation in the man holding her wrist, recognized Walter, and had no way to get traction to pull away from him.

Christopher had been near the front of the building for the night and Walter the back, neither able to stand being near the other. Men in ghostly black streaming through the blown-open doors had hit a jumble of equipment. If Walter got that door closed to the small cinder block bathroom that smelled of sour water and that spiders called home….

Her bound hands had lost their circulation. She couldn't get a grip on the now twisted duct tape that also formed a tether between her and Walter. He hadn't wanted her to be able to run while he slept, and the loop in the tape scared her to death. It wasn't neat, her hands were in front of her, but the mere fact Walter had reached for the tape told its own story. The gun Walter held caught the side of her face as he yanked her up and his arm encircled her neck. The move jerked her left arm around at a painful angle, twisted backwards so she couldn't even grasp his arm to try and get leverage to ease the stranglehold, and nearly broke her right wrist.

"Freeze!"

"Back off!"

Lisa gritted her teeth against the pain, tried to blink against the bright light in her face blinding her, had to go from memory for what was around her, stumbling back as Walter forced her to move. She felt her arm go numb as the nerves screamed.

"Let her go!"

Walter was edging around equipment moving backward toward the storage shelves. Was there an exit from the building back here? The pain was screaming and it was hard to think. If only she could fall or trip or somehow get out of the way, then they could stop Walter and this would be over.

The hold around her neck tightened.

Glass jars fell to the concrete and shattered around her feet as Walter backed into a shelf. She panicked as the overpowering smell of turpentine swallowed her senses; she tried to twist around but could feel her neck being crushed.

They shot him.

She heard it, felt the bullet hit him, and was yanked backward as he fell, his arm locked around her neck. She hit hard at an awkward angle, Walter's knee in the middle of her back. She heard her neck pop.

Around her there was a flurry of motion, voices, and hands. She couldn't respond. She couldn't breathe.

The last of her air was escaping and she couldn't draw another breath. The panic was overwhelming.

Desperate.

Panic.

She couldn't breathe.

It was no longer Walter's arm around her neck blocking her airway.

"Watch her neck."

They didn't understand, and she was desperate to make them understand, couldn't seem to move. "Lisa, hold on."

Her mouth was open, but her throat was closing. *Please, help me!*

"She's not breathing."

"Hold on, Lisa, Stephen's here. Hold on."

"She's not breathing!" *Quinn. Thank you, Quinn. Speak for me.*

Her brother Stephen appeared in her line of vision.

She could feel the calm descending, taking over the panic. The color was fading from her vision, becoming shades of gray, as her mind starved of oxygen. *Andy, oh Andy… I'm so sorry you died this way.*

"Get me an airbag and a knife. Move!"

She was going to die on her brothers. She wasn't going to be able to tell Quinn she loved him.

Her dying breath was past, her dying thought…she held tight to that final thought. There had to be a Resurrection. *Jesus, Son of God, help me.*

Twenty-seven

"Don't try to talk."

Quinn's hand was shaking as it brushed down her flyaway hair. She had no voice even if she wanted to whisper. She could hear the whistle of air. Stephen had done a tracheotomy. Was her neck broken?

She could feel her legs and the tightening of restraints as men worked around her. It was the most blessed feeling she had ever experienced. They had removed her from the warehouse.

Quinn had never looked so good. The grayness was fading to be replaced with light, with color. The numbness in her hands was giving way to strength.

Jesus, life is so precious.

"Shh…" Quinn wiped at her tears, his distress obvious, and she had no way to tell him they were happy tears. She'd learned well from Jennifer; they were flowing. For the first time in her life, they were flowing happy tears.

She was so relieved to be alive.

Had Jesus felt like this the first time He had walked from the grave? Life was more powerful than death. She could feel it, the wonder of it, as she curled her toes just to enjoy the sensation of moving. Eternal life. The promise had an incredible meaning having now come so close as to touch it.

She'd made a mistake, drawing a line in time and dealing with her past by pushing it all away. Faith was a choice. It was a decision. It had taken years to make, but in the end it was simple. Jesus was alive. She knew more about death than anyone should. Now it was time to learn about life—the abundant life Jesus had promised. Her curiosity was full blown. And Quinn was showing her the steady way it could flourish.

She wanted to be able to hug the man and convince him to give her a kissing lesson, to swat his arm for being late to find her, to replace his intense worry with a smile. She'd risk the words now, when she could say them. She'd risk *I love you* and not worry about his reaction. He wouldn't let her down.

She blinked as the sky changed colors and realized with surprise that the dawn was grabbing the sky in a moment of time, turning it alive. She had seen it before but had never lain on her back and watched it happen. She'd missed something.

Jennifer said she liked waking early to watch the sunrise because dawn was the new day Jesus promised. A new day. A new life.

She understood now why Jennifer was so confident in spite of the circumstances. She was holding on to Jesus. And He was still healing today, bringing life, restoring hope. Jennifer needed a breath of new life and she'd sought the One who could give it. Jennifer had brought a miracle to the O'Malleys by stepping out to believe.

Sadness suddenly flooded through Lisa as her heart broke. So many years had been lost. *I'm sorry, Lord. I got so angry at Kate for bugging me about You when she was just trying to love me. Is she going to forgive me?*

It was getting hard to breathe.

Lisa tried to rein back the emotions. Now wasn't the time to give way to the emotions. Not yet. The swamping sensation across her chest was more than just emotional, it was physical. She was losing her ability to breathe.

Quinn's face reappeared, swimming across her vision. "Enough." It was a curt order, and she could hear the fear underneath it. He wiped at her tears. "Calm down, Lisa."

Lisa locked her gaze on his. *Jesus, he prayed for me in the hospital and the pain eased. I'm the one asking this time.*

Quinn suddenly leaned across her and the world filled with noise and wind. It was a sound she had heard many times in the past. At least she would be awake for this helicopter ride. Quinn leaned back and she got her first glimpse of the red and white markings on the helicopter—they'd called in one of the Chicago trauma teams.

Marcus appeared in her line of sight. His hand gripped hers. She wished she had the strength to return the grip. "Ten minutes, Lizzy, and you'll be fussed over by the experts. Stephen and Quinn are coming with you. Kate and I will meet you there. I've got to deal with Christopher first. He's got a hangover that is making getting straight answers out of him impossible."

At least Christopher was still alive. She was incredibly relieved at that. She blinked slowly to let him know she understood.

"Good girl." He looked at the paramedic. "Get her out of here."

Quinn was praying.

Lisa angled her hand on the hospital bed toward his, nudging his first finger up with hers. It was about the extent of her energy. It was such a blessing to know the man was consistent through thick and thin.

He looked up. The relief that crossed his face was incredible. "Welcome back."

She blinked slowly in reply. She was in the ICU on a trachea respirator. That fact registered slowly. She was relieved to have the help to breathe. Her stressed body hurt.

He looked so tired.

Quinn reached across her for the buzzer. She wished he hadn't done that.

He gently brushed the back of his hand against her cheek. "Everything is going to be fine, Lizzy. I promise." She held his gaze, searching to see if the reassurance was forced but found only calm confidence.

She smiled with her eyes and carefully, just a glimmer, with her mouth, for any movement that caused the trachea respirator to shift would hurt. Stephen had done a good job, but he'd been forced to work in the field, and it had been fast surgery.

Quinn smiled back. "I've been praying for you to wake up. Sorry. I know you need the sleep, but it's so good to see your pretty eyes."

That Montana drawl over tenderness…she loved listening to it.

"Lisa, I'm Dr. Paulson." She shifted just her eyes. The man was smiling at her. "You've slept away about twenty-two hours now. How are you feeling?" She decided she liked the patient voice.

She closed her eyes, then opened them. All things considered, she wasn't feeling too bad.

"The swelling has been going down since you arrived. Did you know you were allergic to turpentine?"

She wrinkled her forehead.

"That choke hold started the swelling, but the turpentine aggravated things."

No wonder she'd panicked when she smelled it. Her subconscious would have been screaming a warning as the smell enveloped her.

"Everything is going to heal just fine. You won't have more than a faint scar when this is over." He checked the monitor behind her. "You're reading at 92 percent oxygen in the blood. Would you like to try breathing on your own for a moment, get a feel for how you're doing?"

She blinked several times, and his smile widened. "I thought you might." He squeezed her hand. "I hear you make a lousy patient, wanting to play at being your own doctor, so listen carefully to the real doctor—that's me." She wanted to laugh but couldn't.

"This might make you a little dizzy," he said gently. "That's normal. The swelling is down, but it will go down a lot more in another twelve hours. It's still going to feel like you're struggling to get air. I'm going to keep you on the trach respirator until the morning regardless, so don't try to prove you're fine. I know better. Still want to try this?"

She blinked more slowly.

With a smooth movement, the doctor disconnected the respirator and covered her trachea. "Breathe for me."

It burned, her airways were so swollen, but she was able to get her first natural breath. She took another breath, as deep as she could, and felt the relief.

"Very good." He let her stay off a minute, watching the equipment behind her. "Okay, just relax." Moments later the respirator was breathing for her again.

The doctor wiped her eyes. "You held at 84 percent oxygen. By tomorrow, you'll be left with a sore throat, a headache, and my bill."

She had a comedian for a doctor. Quinn chuckled for her.

She squeezed one finger of the doctor's hand in thanks.

"Get some sleep," Dr. Paulson advised.

She had more important things to do at the moment. She turned her gaze back toward Quinn. Two minutes ago he'd looked tired, every one of his years; now…his relaxed, comfortable smile was back as he lifted her left hand and slowly entwined their fingers. "I brought you candy corn and sweet water taffy, but I had to use them to bribe the nurses so I could stay."

He was staying. She'd been afraid he would take the doctor's word as gospel and leave her to sleep.

"The family is out in the waiting room." He looked at her, his expression turning serious. "I hope you don't mind. I asked to be the one to stay."

She loved him for it. She wanted so badly to be able to talk, to share the decision she had made. It would matter to him, and she didn't want to wait until tomorrow. *Jesus, just a couple words. Please. It matters.* She struggled to form the words.

With a frown, Quinn got up and leaned over to try and hear.

"I'm sorry, Lizzy. I don't understand."

The worry in his voice… It hurt too much to try and say the words again. She closed her eyes, trying to think of something else, and felt him brush the back of his fingers across her cheek. She couldn't even turn her head to press against his hand in appreciation. It was frustrating.

She opened her eyes, locked her gaze with his, and used most of the energy she had to lift her hand. She pointed. He'd left his Bible on the table beside his chair.

"The water?"

She kept pointing.

"The card? The Bible?"

She blinked fast.

"The Bible. Okay." He reached for it and she closed her eyes, relieved. She heard him sit back down. He moved the chair closer. Now what? She opened her eyes. He solved her problem by lifting her hand and setting the Bible on the bed. The item she sought she found by touch. The folded piece of paper was still inside the front cover where she had placed it when he let her borrow the Bible. She put it in his hand and rolled his fingers around it, the paper crumbling. She smiled at him.

It was a simple message. And he'd always been a smart man. She wasn't expecting to see him blink away sudden moisture in his eyes. "It makes sense?"

She let her smile bloom not caring that it hurt. Quinn's hand had a fine tremor in it as he intertwined his fingers with hers. This time when she managed to say a couple words they were clear enough to understand. "I believe."

He laughed, squeezed her hand, leaned close, and just smiled at her. She could drown in those fascinating eyes. "I'm glad."

She had so much to say and no way to say it. About faith. Andy. What she had thought during the darkness as she waited for him to come.

He turned their joined hands and kissed the back of her hand. "Who cares if it's hardly the appropriate place," he said abruptly. "I love you. And if you walk into trouble like that again…"

Only Quinn. She looked at him and silently formed the words *I love you too.*

"You're turning into a Jennifer on me." He wiped the tears, looked frustrated when the Kleenex turned soggy before her eyes were dry, then reached over to retrieve the box. "Did you really have to spoil my big speech? I've been practicing it for weeks."

She caught his wrist, the power and strength in it impressive, wanting to laugh, yet having to settle for a gentle tug to bring him down to her.

The kiss was a brush when she wanted a real one. "Tomorrow." It was a promise. He wrapped his fingers through hers. "Be good, and I'll stay here to see the dawn with you."

She closed her eyes. This was what it felt like to be treasured. And it felt good.

"I think I kind of like you being forced to whisper for a while."

In the last three days she'd learned to be quite expressive with her body language. Lisa caught Quinn's shirt collar with her fingers and tugged him down toward her. "Hear this whispered shout. You're heading toward trouble."

He laughed softly and kissed her. She leaned into it, loving it, then she regretfully pulled back. "Don't take away my breath."

"You take away mine."

It was a lovely compliment. She had napped on the flight back to the ranch. Quinn had invited all the O'Malleys to come out for a long weekend at the ranch. Jennifer and Tom had arrived the day before. She couldn't wait to see them. She wanted to hug Jennifer.

Jesus was so good. She'd found her verse, the one she remembered from her childhood, in Psalm 18:19. It was her verse, claimed and held tight. *"He brought me forth into a broad place; he delivered me, because he delighted in me."*

She hated to memorize, and the three-by-five card had been plastered to her bathroom mirror to help her out. It was the delighted part that had thrilled her as a child, and as an adult she appreciated it even more. *Delight* was a powerful word, and yet it could barely do justice in describing the depth of emotions she felt toward God. To know He felt the same about her was priceless.

Lisa slid her hand comfortably around Quinn's forearm. "Where's my dog?"

"Your dog, huh? I thought we were going to share."

Marcus had driven down from the ranch house to meet the plane. He opened the back door of the jeep and Old Blue jumped down and shook himself. Quinn whistled, and the dog came trotting over, ignored him, and nearly knocked her over. She knelt down to return the affection.

"Traitor."

She tilted her head to look up at Quinn and laughed at his amused disgust.

She straightened and slid her arm around his waist. "We'll get you your own dog."

He tugged at a lock of her hair. "I have a feeling every animal on the ranch is going to become a pet. Just don't make a pet of my horse."

"Now that's impossible. He blows on me and I fall over."

"Lizzy, before we get up to the house: You do realize Dave is carrying an engagement ring for Kate."

She leaned against him to whisper the truth. "I talked her into saying yes."

"Did you?"

She nodded. She was proud of herself. Payback. She had owed her sister a big one, and she'd been able to deliver. Kate nervous…she hadn't known her sister had it in her to get cold feet. But she had.

It had taken just a few carefully chosen whispered words. "You were right about Jesus. I'm right about Dave. Get off the fence." Lisa was still doing a little private dancing that she'd been able to push Kate so smoothly back on track. Although it had probably helped that Kate wanted an excuse to be pushed.

"Let's go to the house." Lizzy snapped her fingers and Old Blue fell in beside her as she walked to the jeep. She wanted to see Jack.

There were now two groups within the O'Malleys—those who believed and those who didn't. It was time to close the deal with Jack, Stephen, and Rachel. It was Lisa's new mission in life. She now understood the passion that drove Kate, Marcus, and Jennifer, that burning desire to share the Good News. Lisa wanted to grab Jack's arm and drag him to church. Kate had laughed at that pronouncement and turned the tables, pulled her back, and reminded her rather bluntly how Lisa had reacted when pushed too hard. Lisa knew Jack. It would just take some creativity. Jack was a challenge. She was ready for a challenge.

Quinn paused her. "Not with Marcus. Over here." He held out keys.

"What?"

He pointed toward the hangar.

And she stopped. "You didn't have to do this," she whispered, overwhelmed.

"I know."

"Why did you?"

"It gives me pleasure."

She could barely breathe as his words settled inside. "Quinn—"

The convertible was even blue.

"It's time someone spoiled you a little." He smiled at her. "Besides, you need an excuse to visit often in the next few months." He linked his hands around her and drew her back against his chest. "Like it?"

Her thoughts couldn't keep up with her heart. A tremulous smile was the best she could manage as the emotions overwhelmed her. "Thanks."

"You're welcome." He rested his chin against her hair. "I like doing things that bring out that smile of yours. It makes my old heart feel good."

She laughed and relaxed against him, comfortable suddenly with a man who had so often confused her. "You're not that old."

"I'm ancient," he countered.

She squeezed his arm around her waist. "Lay off that malarkey. Come on, I'll let you drive me to the house." He didn't move, and she glanced back. "What?"

He smiled. "Nothing."

"Uh-huh, something. What?"

"Kate said if you let me drive it I'd know that you really loved me."

"It takes Kate to convince you I meant it?"

He kissed away her frown. "I love you, Lizzy."

"I know that. I'm holding the car keys to prove it."

He laughed. "Let's go up to the house."

Twenty-eight

Quinn, is there a cave with water?"

The mood had become solemn the farther they rode. Finding where Amy had been buried—or as Walter had claimed, *hidden*—remained a mystery they had not been able to crack. The only thing that made sense was that Quinn's father had stumbled upon Walter and been shot in the back. Lisa had been back to look at the area with her family, but on this occasion she had asked only Quinn to come.

"Not that I know of."

"You said the day your father was killed that this tributary running down to the Ledds River was still filled from a flash flood the week before."

"Yes."

"Does it cut close to a cave?"

Quinn stood up in the saddle and looked around. "Farther down...see where the streambed bends? If the water had topped its banks, it would flow into the bluffs. That's how some of the deepest ravines have been cut. It's possible the water would cut into a channel near some of the caves."

"Have they been searched?"

"Those near here. There are dozens of caves in these miles of bluffs, and most of them branch off and go deep and interconnect with each other."

"Let's explore a couple of them today."

"You're up to it?"

"I'm up to it." She loved this man, and he was hurting. It was a quiet grief. She had found him on more than one occasion sitting on the back porch with Old Blue late at night. It was where he went to pray. When she'd asked what she could pray for him, Quinn had replied with one word: peace. He was searching so hard to find it. She understood. He was grieving his dad in a way he never had before. The killer had been found. Now he had to find a way to accept what had happened.

Quinn was preparing to resign from the marshal service and return here for good; she wanted to make it a clean transition for him. If she had to search these bluffs for months, she would try to find those final pieces of the puzzle. Walter had revealed enough in his words and actions that she knew it had to be possible to put the pieces together.

Walter had said Amy had been hidden. He'd used that word because it was his predominant impression twenty years later of what he'd done.

Lisa could easily imagine that day in Walter's life. Scared. Faced with the idea that Christopher had killed. Wanting to ensure that Amy was never found…

The key was the water. She was convinced of it. Every murder since then he had hidden his victims near water because water had helped him hide that first victim. She knew it from a lifetime of seeing the graves. Patterns…it was all about patterns.

He'd bound Amy's hands because he had to bring her out here, probably on a horse given the terrain. The way rigor mortis would have set in, he'd probably had to tie her body down, bind not only her hands but her legs to keep her resting across a saddle without spooking the horse. He'd buried her near water. She just had to prove it.

She shifted the reins. "Come on, Annie."

"Are the batteries in your flashlight still strong?"

"Yes." Lisa slid the flashlight strap around her wrist. Even though the reason for the exploration was grim, the cave spelunking presented just enough of a challenge behind every turn to be fun. They'd found arrowheads, places rock hounds had chipped out samples, several shed snakeskins. This would be the fourth cave.

Quinn tied the guide rope to a boulder near the entrance. "The inclines in this cave are not steep, you can walk them without a problem, but there are several dropoffs that will require a rope descent."

"I'll stay close," she reassured. He had much more experience doing this than she did.

The entrance was no more than a four-foot-high opening in the bluff. She slid inside after Quinn, had to walk half crouched for the first four feet until the cavern opened up into a six-by-seven-foot hollow. It was cool in the cave, a slight draft of air suggesting at least one of the passages led back to the surface elsewhere. The rock floor showed two small depressions still holding water. "Is that moss?"

Quinn straightened as best he could. "Yes. There must be standing water in here most of the time." His light illuminated the options. "Which way? Left or right?"

"Right."

The passage grew taller and more narrow. Quinn had to turn his shoulders to slip through the tightest places; she found it narrow but passable.

"Good choice." His voice echoed, and a few steps later she understood why. It was a massive cavern a good fifteen feet high, ten feet wide, and thirty feet long, with limestone stalactites and stalagmites from the ceiling and floor meeting each other. His light illuminated the dripping formations. "There's been water running through here."

"The colors are pretty."

"Metal deposits in the limestone."

"I wish I had my camera."

"We'll come back," he promised. "It keeps going. There's another passage ahead."

"Let's go for it."

His light cast back his shadow on the wall as he moved to the far end of the cavern and ducked to enter the next passage. "We've got our first drop."

"How far?"

"Only about seven feet, but there's water down below."

She joined him, adding her light to his. It was more of a very steep slope than a dropoff. "The water is still. It could be another shallow depression."

"Or it could be similar to a well shaft with no bottom."

"I don't think so. The passage takes a bend and keeps going." She studied it; she really wanted to go see what was around that bend. "Even if the water is deep, that ledge is wide enough for two. You can go first, check it out."

Quinn shrugged off his climbing rope and pulled on his gloves.

She knelt beside the dropoff and lit his way as he walked backward down the slope, controlling the rope to make a graceful descent.

"Okay, your turn."

Holding the rope between her hands, playing it out slowly through the metal clip and balancing her weight, she took her time, determined to move as smoothly as Quinn. An afternoon of practice had removed the rust from her skills—she enjoyed this. She landed lightly on the ledge beside him. He steadied her with a hand on her back while she secured the rope.

"Lisa."

Quinn's light reflected off something in the water. It was tucked back under a rock outcrop. "I'm going to swing over to that outcrop."

She stepped back, made sure her rope didn't cross his. "You're clear." She held her light to help him out.

Quinn swung to the other side of the standing pool, caught hold of the protruding rock. Gripping it, bracing his feet against the rock wall, he eased out more rope so he could turn, reach down into the water, and pick the object up.

He aimed his light at it, then turned his light to search the water.

"What is it?"

He slipped it into his shirt pocket, buttoned it, and looked up at the rope. With a push of his foot, he swung back across to join her. She caught his arm and steadied him.

When he had his footing, he looped the rope once to secure it. "What do you make of this?" He pulled the object from his pocket.

It was a small piece of broken glass. The one side that was not jagged was a very smooth curve of thick glass. "Not something from a pair of eyeglasses, the curve is too circular, and it's too thick."

"A camera lens," Quinn replied.

He was right. She turned the glass over in her hand, not able to determine a sense of age. The glass wiped clean under her finger.

She looked up at him and saw the change. The cop was back in front while he pushed his private emotions down. She knew him well enough to know those private emotions were going to overwhelm him.

"What's up ahead?" It was time to finish this.

Quinn squeezed her hand and turned.

He led the way around the bend, had to crouch with the lower ceiling. The passage was wide but a gash had the right side of the floor dropping away, falling into a trough, water trickling through the limestone rock slide.

Quinn shone his light along the water and rocks.

"Back up. There. Pinned between the rocks."

"I see it."

He was just able to reach it.

It was a lens cap, a piece of black plastic. Her light picked out the impression in the plastic. "Nikon." She rubbed the plastic with her thumb. "Quinn."

"I know." She heard the change in the words. He'd turned the corner, absorbed the emotion, and was taking charge. "Turn around, let's go back to the entrance. If we're going to systematically search this cavern and its passages, we need more people and a lot more equipment."

Lisa let a handful of dirt trickle through her fingers. She sat beside the small fire keeping the chill away as night came.

Kate walked over from the truck to join her, knelt to warm her hands.

Lisa appreciated her sister's silence.

They had found the truth.

It was depressing.

She was relieved it had not been Quinn who had found the remains, but rather one of the sheriff's deputies. Amy had died like the others had, strangled, buried face down, hands bound. Her dental records would confirm identity, but it was a formality. The locket she wore on the gold chain still glistened, engraved with her name.

"Grant killed Amy."

Lisa nodded and tossed a twig onto the fire to watch it be consumed. Grant had killed Amy. And Grant had blamed Christopher in order to manipulate Walter into helping bury her.

For twenty years Walter had fought the internal turmoil of trying to reconcile what he had done with his need to relive it. Lisa had seen too many murders not to understand that fatal attraction.

Walter had seen someone get away with murder, had seen Grant come back to Chicago and grow in power and money. And Lisa understood the impact of that. Grant had seemed invulnerable. While Walter's life had been anything but.

Walter—the older brother who tried to make the world work, who fought to keep his brother in line, who struggled to make the nursery business succeed—had to deal with the fact his brother gambled and drank, his uncle would sell the business out from under him. He had nothing in his life except 4 A.M. mornings and work to do.

The forensic psychologist who had the job of reconstructing Walter's motivation was puzzled by the complexity of his actions.

Lisa thought she understood the patterns. Walter had a lifelong pattern of trying to protect his brother, and in the end he had tried to frame him. It explained so much. Walter wanted out. But he had to eliminate what he was responsible for in order to get out. He couldn't just walk away.

Walter blamed Christopher—so he would frame Christopher.

Walter saw Grant as a man who had escaped justice—so he would kill Grant's girlfriend Rita and frame Grant.

Walter saw his uncle as betraying him—so he would murder him when there was no other way to stop him.

Walter saw her investigation as a threat—so he would burn down her house to force her away.

Walter acted to reexert control when he felt he had lost it. Walter murdered, hid the victims, and framed his brother for each one. For a moment in time Walter had had the control he wanted in life. He became the invincible one.

Kate reached over and stilled her hand. "It wasn't something you missed."

"Walter went to his grave taking the reasons he chose those particular women." And she'd nearly fallen for his lies. Until the end she had thought it was Christopher. She'd liked Walter. And she hadn't seen the other side of him.

"Let it go," Kate said quietly. "Even if he had explained, how much of it would be the truth, how much a lie?"

"I know. It just makes me tired."

"Walter took a lot, from Quinn in the past, from you in the present.

Had he lived, it would have been hard to find sufficient justice. At least now it's over."

"Yes."

The battery-powered floodlights illuminating the cave entrance were attracting swarms of flying bugs by the time the men finally emerged from the cave carrying the body bag.

The coroner's van was opened, the body bag carefully lifted inside.

Kate went to meet Dave.

Lisa watched the men talking but chose to stay where she was. She had been in on discussions such as they were having many times in the past.

Quinn walked over to join her. He had aged during the last hours. And he had also turned the corner. The blanket of stress pressing him down for years was lifting away. In a week she bet his laughter would finally be fully alive. He crouched beside her, held out his hands to warm them.

"Her parents will be relieved to have closure," Lisa said softly.

"Yes."

The fire snapped, sending sparks into the air.

Lisa understood the silence, didn't try to break it.

"It removes a ghost."

Lisa nodded, appreciating the word he had chosen. She carried her ghosts. Quinn had carried his. That was what had changed. This had buried his ghost.

Quinn reached over and brushed back her hair. "Years ago, did you get to go to Andy's funeral?"

She shook her head.

"Would you like to have a service for him?"

It was such a simple question, and yet the comfort expressed behind it was salve over deep scars. "Quinn, I would."

"We'll have a private memorial service for Andy and my father. Finally have closure."

She wrapped her hand around his forearm and leaned her head against his shoulder. "Thank you."

They sat in silence for several minutes, watching the fire.

Quinn rubbed his thumb against her chin. "You're good for me, Lizzy."

"I know."

He chuckled and wrapped his arm around her shoulders. "Humble too."

"Somebody's got to keep you young." She gestured to the open land. "I like Montana. It kind of grows on you."

"I'm glad."

"I like your house too. Of course, that could be because I like your art collection."

He laughed, leaned over, and kissed her. "I like a lady with good taste who also tastes good."

"Horrible pun."

"It got a smile." He pulled her to her feet. "Let's go home."

"Sure."

"Want to ride double?"

"On your horse?"

"I promise Thunder will be on his best behavior."

"Quinn, he has no manners. He tried to take a nip out of my hat yesterday."

He groaned. "He didn't."

She held it out. "Look at it. You can see the teeth marks."

"Lizzy, you promised not to make a pet out of my horse."

"What?"

"He's falling in love with you."

She burst out laughing at his grim pronouncement.

"I'm serious," Quinn insisted. "What have you been feeding him?"

"I wasn't supposed to?"

"Lizzy."

"Sugar cubes. He likes them."

"You're hopeless, you know that?"

"I didn't mean to."

He wrapped his arm around her shoulders. "Sure you didn't. Please remember the cattle are sold as beef. This is a working ranch."

"Quinn—" she couldn't resist—"even the pretty little ones?"

Dear Reader,

Thank you for reading this book. I deeply appreciate it. I fell in love with Lisa O'Malley while writing *The Guardian,* and I knew her future with Quinn would make a great story. Her questions about the Resurrection were a look into the future that awaits us with Jesus.

Kate O'Malley and God's justice and mercy, Marcus O'Malley and prayer, Lisa O'Malley and the Resurrection—the stories in this series have offered me wonderfully broad canvases. I find this family fascinating. I hope you will join me for Jack's story in *The Protector.*

As always, I love to hear from my readers. Feel free to write me at:

Dee Henderson
c/o Multnomah Publishers
P.O. Box 1720
Sisters, Oregon 97759
E-mail: dee@deehenderson.com
or on-line: http://www.deehenderson.com

First chapters of all my books are on-line, please stop by and check them out. Thanks again for letting me share Lisa and Quinn's story.

Sincerely,

Multnomah Publishers

The publisher and author would love to hear your
comments about this book. Please contact us at:
www.multnomah.net/truthseeker

THE O'MALLEY SERIES

The Negotiator—Book One
FBI agent Dave Richman from *Danger in the Shadows* is back. He's about to meet Kate O'Malley, and his life will never be the same. She's a hostage negotiator. He protects people. Dave's about to find out that falling in love with a hostage negotiator is one thing, but keeping her safe is another!

ISBN 1-57673-819-1

The Guardian—Book Two
A federal judge has been murdered. There is only one witness. And an assassin wants her dead. U.S. Marshal Marcus O'Malley thought he knew the risks of the assignment...
He was wrong.

ISBN 1-57673-642-3

The Truth Seeker—Book Three
Women are turning up dead. Lisa O'Malley is a forensic pathologist and mysteries are her domain. When she's investigating a crime it means trouble is soon to follow. U.S. Marshal Quinn Diamond has found loving her is easier than keeping her out of danger. Lisa's found the killer, and now she's missing too...

ISBN 1-57673-753-5

THE O'MALLEY SERIES

The Protector—Book Four

Jack O'Malley is a fireman. He's fearless when it comes to facing an inferno. But when an arsonist begins targeting his district, his shift, his friends, Jack faces the ultimate challenge: protecting the lady who saw the arsonist before she pays an even higher price...

ISBN 1-57673-846-9

The Healer—Book Five

Rachel O'Malley makes her living as a trauma psychologist, working disaster relief for the Red Cross. Her specialty is helping children. When a school shooting rips through her community, she finds herself dealing with more than just grief among the children she's trying to help. There's a secret. One of them witnessed the shooting. And the murder weapon is still missing...

ISBN 1-57673-925-2

"Dee Henderson is an extraordinary author whose writing connects with your heart and soul. The O'Malley series is a classic meant for your 'keeper' shelf."

—The Belles and Beaux of Romance

"I highly recommend this book to anyone who likes suspense."

—Terri Blackstock, bestselling author of *Trial by Fire*

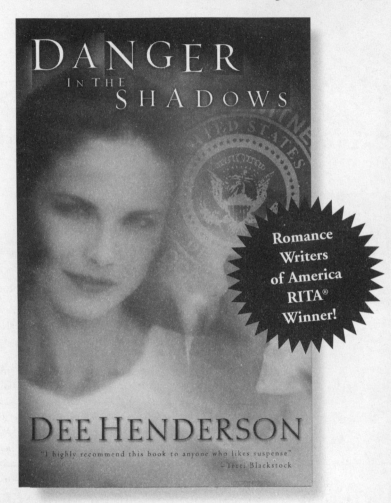

Don't miss the prequel to the O'Malley series!

Sara's terrified. She's doing the one thing she cannot afford to do: fall in love with former pro football player Adam Black, a man everyone knows. Sara's been hidden away in the witness protection program, her safety dependent on being invisible—and loving Adam could get her killed.

ISBN 1-57673-927-9

UNCOMMON HEROES SERIES

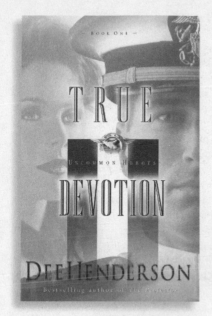

True Devotion, Book One

Kelly Jacobs has already paid the ultimate price of loving a warrior: She has the folded flag and the grateful thanks of a nation to prove it. Navy SEAL Joe "Bear" Baker can't ask her to accept that risk again—even though he loves her. But the man responsible for her husband's death is back, closer than either of them realize. Kelly's in danger, and Joe may not get there in time . . .

ISBN 1-57673-886-8

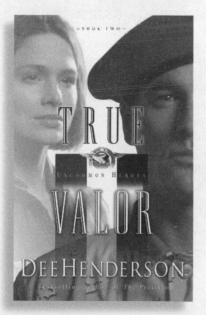

True Valor, Book Two

Air Force Pararescueman Bruce "Striker" Stanton spends his life rescuing pilots downed behind enemy lines. Grace "Gracie" Yates spends hers flying an F/A-18 Hornet for the Navy. With dangerous jobs, often away from home, they exchanged love letters. Now a fight between Turkey and its neighbors is spiraling into a confrontation. For the military deployed in the region, it's not just the occasional news headline—it's their daily problem. When Grace is shot down behind enemy lines, Bruce has got one mission: get Gracie out alive...

ISBN 1-57673-887-6

UNCOMMON HEROES SERIES

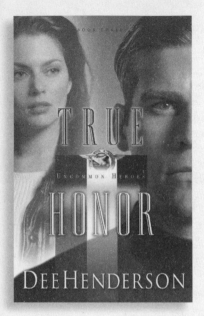

True Honor, Book Three

For CIA officer Darcy St. James, the terrorist attack on America is personal: Friends died at the Pentagon. She's after a man who knew September 11 would happen and who chose to profit from the knowledge. Navy SEAL Sam "Cougar" Houston is busy: The intelligence Darcy is generating has his team deploying around the world. Under the pressure of war, they discover the sweetness of love, and their romance flourishes. But it may be a short relationship—for the terrorists have chosen their next targets, and Darcy's name is high on the list...

ISBN 1-59052-043-2

True Courage, Book Four

Someone snatched his cousin's wife and son. FBI agent Luke Falcon is searching for a kidnapper and sorting out the crime. He's afraid they're already dead. And he'll do anything required to get them back alive...but he didn't plan on falling in love with the only witness.

ISBN 1-59052-082-3